Obscure Boundaries

Dr. Naomi Alexander, Book 2

S.F. Powell

Nib Karatasi Press, Upper Marlboro, MD

Copyright © 2011-2025, S.F. Powell.

All rights reserved. No part of this publication may be reproduced, distributed, or transmitted in any form or by any means, including photocopying, recording, or other electronic or mechanical methods, without the prior written permission of the publisher, except in the case of brief quotations embodied in critical reviews and certain other noncommercial uses permitted by copyright law. Unauthorized reproduction of any part of this work is illegal and punishable by law.

For permission requests, write to the publisher, addressed "Attention: Permissions Coordinator," at this address: ACT3 Enterprises, LLC–Nib Karatasi Press, PO Box 4726, Upper Marlboro, MD 20775

Online contact: visit www.sfpowell.com

Publisher's Note: This is a work of fiction. Names, characters, places, and incidents are a product of the author's imagination. Locales and public names are sometimes used for atmospheric purposes. Any resemblance to actual people, living or dead, or to businesses, companies, events, institutions, or locales is completely coincidental. The author is *not* a doctor. This work of fiction is for entertainment only and is not intended as a substitute for the medical advice of real physicians. The reader should regularly consult a licensed physician in matters relating to their mental/ physical health.

Obscure Boundaries / S.F. Powell

Library of Congress Control Number: 2023901549

ISBNs: 978-1-7327224-3-9 / 978-1-7327224-4-6 / 978-1-7327224-5-3

Book Cover Design by ebooklaunch.com

Also By S.F. Powell

Like Sweet Buttermilk
Broken Benevolence
Gracious Bitterness

Acknowledgments

Thanks and praise to God for many quiet blessings.

Thanks for your support:
Pam and Debbie
Kyana and Erinn
Vicki "Meis" Kelliebrew
Patsy Ramsey
Aletcia Skinner
Patricia Durham

And always: Momma

For my J-A-A.

"Well, every one can master a grief but he that has it."

—William Shakespeare, *Much Ado About Nothing*

Prologue

Months Ago...

"*L*imitations bind you," the Voice stated with soft, modulated sound, ringing with crystal-clear intonation.
"It's okay. Our love sustains him," she answered.
Silence.
"I don't want to scare him."
"You may, but your love secures him," the Voice answered.
"And my others?"
"As I know, so do you."
"...It's not much time."
"It will be enough."

Chapter 1

Rocks and Hard Places

He was hot and bothered, and it had nothing to do with the outdoor temperature.

In fact, it was cool for early September.

Jeff Winthrop sat back in his Adirondack chair of stained-ipe, running a palm over his bald head. He shifted his hips right and left, trying to contain a heated drive edging closer to an uncompromising desire entirely new to him. He wanted, in point-blank succinctness, to make love to his wife.

And therein lay the problem.

He wanted his wife. But she was dead. Had been for over three years. Besides that, he'd remarried, so his *wife* piddled around somewhere inside the house. But she was not whom he wanted.

He wanted *Julia*.

Jeff ran a palm over his head again; his body presented an obvious clue to his state of mind. Good thing he was alone.

"Jeffy?" Ruth's voice trailed through the window from the kitchen area, a sound both grating and lilting.

He cringed, rolling his eyes upward with an annoyed sigh he kept at whisper level. *Jeffy.* He hated being called that. *Hated it.* With a passion. He was 48 years old: damn-near 50. His mama never called him that; why did she insist on doing it?

Irritated, he didn't answer. Let her come searching for him (not that he looked forward to her finding him).

Ruth's interruption, however, didn't affect the hardness in his pants. He heard Ruth move to the kitchen bay window, felt her looking out at him. He didn't move. Instead, he focused on the treetops above the view of the alley and neighboring homes.

He loved living on Capitol Hill in Washington, DC. Loved the ethnic mix of its residents and the varying architectural styles of its homes. DC was a hub of diversity: lifestyle, socializing, art, politics, and culture. Ruth hinted many times about moving to the suburbs of Montgomery County, Maryland, but Jeff wasn't interested.

It was a mistake.

Maybe it was, perhaps it wasn't. Didn't matter now, anyway. He'd married her. What's done is done. Rome wasn't built in a day. No use crying over spilled milk. He was in it to win it. Apply other platitudes as needed.

Jeff concentrated on the trees (the leaves would change soon), willing his erection to subside while he was still alone. He didn't sense Ruth watching him anymore, so he figured she'd be joining him any minute.

A balmy breeze interrupted the cool, still Saturday morning. Strangely, the light wind somehow carried the timeless scent of Guerlain's Shalimar. An infusion of bergamot, iris, vanilla, jasmine, and roses filled Jeff's nostrils and dissipated in an instant, as if Julia sprinted past him.

His penis throbbed with newfound intensity. Jeff whispered, "Shit," and shifted his hips again. He needed to get it together.

Several houses down, the Stewart family's Rottweiler, Genesis, barked. Jeff turned his attention in the direction Genesis sounded his notification: toward the alley's entrance farthest away. His daughter, Mallory, slowed to a trot, finishing her morning run.

She waved as she approached their backyard.

He waved back.

A shuffling noise came through the bay window. The refrigerator door opened and then closed. It was too early for his son, Todd, to be out of bed, so it had to be Ruth continuing to make her presence known. But she stayed inside, and Jeff wondered if she'd changed her mind about joining him on the deck.

Mallory released the latch on the six-foot split-board fence and entered their yard with a wide smile. "Hi, Daddy."

"Mornin', M-Sweet." Jeff smiled back at his daughter, but knowing Ruth was nearby, his smile faltered with a mixture of pride...and mild irritation.

Since he'd married Ruth, Mallory hadn't been the least bit cooperative. She displayed abject tolerance—no more, no less. Since he never discussed Mallory's concerns with her in depth, some of the blame was his, but he didn't want to give the impression he needed his daughter's approval regarding decisions he made for his family.

Mallory's attitude toward Ruth aside, Jeff was proud of his daughter. At 16, she'd pursued and accomplished much academically, such that she could have skipped her junior year to be a senior at her private high school. He admired her decision to stay in her correct grade, and her work with underprivileged kids through the museum-sponsored art program also struck a chord with him. Mallory reminded him of Julia a lot—even though anyone could see he spit her out.

She crossed their concrete patio and started up the wooden steps leading to their deck.

Erection still hanging around, but at half-mast now, Jeff tugged his shirttail down as best he could, then slid the newspaper from the table, placing it in his lap for additional cover.

Mallory eyed the scenery while guzzling from the water bottle she left on the top step. Sweat beaded her brow and upper lip, lines of sweat trickled from her temples. Her plum-colored running gear (water-wicking tank and shorts) was only damp in spots. Finished drinking, she cocked her head and cut her eyes his way. "What's wrong, Daddy?"

"Nothing. Why?"

"Daddy..."

"Did you have a good run?"

She shrugged. "I guess. I always like it better when I head away from the Capitol." She used her forearm to clear the sweat from her face. "You didn't answer my question. What's wrong?"

"I did answer you. You going to see Todd play today?" His erection now subsided, Jeff put the newspaper back on the table.

Mallory sprung a half-smile. "These scrimmages don't even count, but yeah, Kelz and I will be there to cheer him on." She chugged more of her water.

Jeff tried to maintain a neutral expression but obviously failed.

"What now? Elliot?" With a shake of her head, Mallory twisted her lips and shifted her gaze away from him. "I've told you over and over. We're friends, Daddy. *Friends.* That's it."

"I know what you've told me. And I believe *you* see him as just a friend. But I have my doubts about that going both ways. Does Elliot have a girlfriend?"

"Not anymore, no."

"And he's not gay?" He didn't have a problem with Mallory having a boyfriend. And if the young man was gay, that was fine, too. He actually liked "Kelz." Elliot was clean-cut, respectful. But Jeff believed his role as her father was reinforcing the perception he was a hard sell for the males (or females if so ordered) in her life, regardless of whom M-Sweet brought into their home.

An odd expression crossed Mallory's face. "God, no."

"And you're so sure of this because...?"

She smirked at him. "Trust me, not for any of the reasons you're thinking. Look, Daddy, Kelz is cool people, and I get along better with him than with most of my so-called girlfriends." Her smirk shifted to a soft smile. "See, you're used to best friends being gender respective. These days, you're just friends with who you're friends with. It doesn't matter what sex they are—or what sexual orientation. But again, Elliot is not gay. And even if he was," Mallory shrugged, "I'd still be good friends with him."

"Listen to you, 'gender respective.' That private school has you ready to skip senior year next year and go right on to college."

"Uh, not quite, Daddy." She leaned against the railing behind her and folded her arms. "Are you going to tell me what's wrong?"

"I already did."

"C'mon; I know you."

And she did. He had a strong father-daughter bond with M-Sweet, laced with good friendship vibes, but Jeff couldn't let his daughter in on this one. His horniness for her mother wasn't father-daughter material. An image of Julia's electrocardiogram flatlining surfaced in his mind in tandem with the most profound urge to weep. "I'm fine, M-Sweet. You eatin' somethin'?" He wanted nothing more than to be alone.

"I don't know, I guess."

The sound of cookware being placed on the stove came through the window, accompanied by Ruth's humming. Jeff didn't know the tune—most likely something gospel. He and Mallory exchanged a look holding at least two years' worth of lost conversation, reminding him of one plain truth: he'd messed up. Jeff reached inward for another platitude, determined to make figurative lemonade from life's lemons.

Leaning back with interlocked fingers supporting his head, Jeff spoke first. "I think you should eat, but it's up to you."

Mallory shifted her gaze to the window but said nothing. After some seconds, she shook her head.

"What?" Jeff smiled, wanting to ease the tension brewing underneath such a tolerant atmosphere.

M-Sweet turned to him but didn't smile back. She held her water bottle poised at her mouth. "Nothing, Daddy." She drained the bottle.

As much as he loved his daughter, he didn't feel like probing to find out what was wrong with her (not this morning, anyway). He held his tongue.

The left panel of their french doors opened, and Ruth stepped onto the deck. Jeff read the slightest hint of irritation on her face before she smiled wide with merriment, her green eyes shining. "Morning meeting? What'd I miss?"

Ignoring Ruth's initial expression, he smiled back. "Not a thing. Just seeing if Mal was going to Todd's scrimmage, which she is."

Ruth turned her eyes to Mallory. "Oh, good. At least your dad will have some company." The smile she sent her stepdaughter wavered in its merriment.

"Uh-huh." Mallory offered a perfunctory upturn of her lips and then focused on the backs of the houses across the alley. His daughter was quite mature regarding her schoolwork and work-study activities, even her friends. But when it came to Ruth, Mallory acted every bit the 16-year-old teenager she was.

He caught Ruth's glance at him: a glance telling him she wanted him to say something in her defense about Mallory's response.

Jeff wanted to say something all right, but nothing his present audience would like to hear. He wanted to tell them both to get their shit together and leave him out of it. He'd married Ruth; no intention of divorcing her, so she wasn't going anywhere. Mallory needed to get over it. Mallory was his daughter, his blood; she sure as hell wasn't going anywhere. Ruth needed to swallow that pill and get over it.

Jeff sighed (a deep rumble in his throat). He shifted his gaze back and forth between the women. Ruth and Mallory looked at him expectantly, each wearing expressions of self-satisfaction as if they'd each won some unvoiced challenge, of which Jeff's siding was the prize.

Nothing out on this deck but rocks and hard places.

He shifted focus toward the alley. Genesis barked again as a Buick Century entered the alleyway. Jeff stretched his long legs out between them, the extension serving as an unintended line of division.

He studied the tops of his New Balance running shoes, thinking he should have run this morning himself. If he had, the likelihood of being on the deck in this situation would have been diminished. But he didn't run this morning, so here he was.

Without looking up (and resisting the impulse and desire to get up, go into the house, and leave them on the deck), Jeff again assumed the role of mediator. "Look, for a change, why don't we *all* try to be there?" He spoke to Ruth: "Todd's scrimmage isn't until three. Why don't you stop by the field during a break between one of your showings?"

Ruth's stiff smile signaled his response wasn't satisfactory. "I'll see."

His daughter mumbled something indistinct.

He turned his attention to her. "You were saying, Mallory?"

Mallory offered the same stiff smile. "Nothing."

Ruth sighed. "See, Jeff? I'm trying. But we will not get anywh—" She stopped short. "You need to talk to her, Jeff—with some firm direction this time. She needs to attend church more, too. A good sermon won't hurt her. It seems she's forgotten about honoring thy mother and father."

Jeff kept his eyes on his daughter, knowing what was coming.

Mallory, at first leaning against the deck railing, stood straight. She pointed her water bottle at Ruth before holding it down at her side. "First, I'm standing right here, so stop talking about me as if I weren't. Second, I honor my father—and my mother: my mother's *memory. You* are not my mother." Her brown eyes were wide, filled with anger, but also traces of what appeared to be wary trepidation.

Jeff stood. His suggestion that they all watch Todd play was middle-of-the-road, what seemed an ideal compromise. And still, neither was happy. He knew deeper issues swirled around them, unseen and unspoken, out there on the deck with them, but he didn't have whatever he needed to deal with it right now (or ever?). "Stop it, both of you."

The scent of Shalimar wafted past him again. Jeff narrowed his focus on Ruth and then Mallory, seeing if either detected it. Neither showed any sign of noticing a change in the aromatic atmosphere, but Mallory jerked her head around as if startled. Did she smell it, too, then? He leaned toward his daughter but froze, hesitant to ask her: the notion was just too crazy. Wasn't it?

Time stood still as Julia's scent faded. Damn, he wanted her.

"Jeffy?" Ruth prompted in a soft voice.

Jeff shifted his gaze to her, clenching his teeth against the awful sound of that nickname in his ears. It was still summer, but she stood before him in a lightweight fleece sweat suit of azure-blue, matching Adidas footwear, her freshly permed, ash-brown hair tied back in a ponytail. Earrings announcing her sorority affiliation dangled. And although she'd be changing into business attire in a few hours, she was dressed and ready to go at seven twenty-seven on a lazy Saturday morning. But that was Ruth; she preferred being ready to pick up and go. Unlike Julia, Ruth cared little for lounging in sweats and a T-shirt.

He could list a slew of *unlike-Julia* instances, but that was counter-productive to making the best of how he had to live his life now.

Ruth stepped closer, looking up at him. At five feet eight inches, she'd need another five inches to be as tall as he. She studied his face.

Jeff studied hers.

Her moisturized buttercream skin glowed. He liked her better without makeup, and she wore none now. Her hair pulled back from her face, however, accentuated her broad, slightly bulbous forehead, which gleamed like a beacon as he watched her. The size of her forehead didn't detract from her overall attractiveness. So, for those who liked her type, oh yeah, Ruth was as fine as she wanted to be (if you liked that type).

But when it came down to it, Jeff didn't prefer her type. He liked them shorter, browner, small-breasted, and round-assed. He liked the springy, textured feel of the naturally coiled roots of a Black woman's clean and unprocessed hair, twisted or locked and styled in so many alluring ways. Thus, his "type" nosedived in contrast to the physical features of his second wife—and dovetailed with the features of his first.

He did like Ruth, though.

Mallory leaned forward, peering up into his face. "Daddy?"

Jeff smiled at her. He wanted to get whatever was going on in this moment over with. They'd be into it again sometime later, anyway. "Come on, guys." He shook his head, maintaining the smile. "I'm not trying to do this right now. I want to see my boy play; that's it." He alternated gazes at both women before sitting again. He lost the smile.

Mallory leaned back against the railing. "That's all I want to do, too."

Jeff nodded at her. "Thanks, M-Sweet." He shifted attention to Ruth.

Her green eyes, a shade blending pear and olive (although his daughter deemed them "crocodile-green"), showed paler, but she didn't speak. With Ruth, her irises seeming to wash out wasn't a good thing.

Mallory slid between the railing and his chair. Standing behind him, she planted a kiss atop his head. "I've said all I wanted to say, and I think I'll pass on breakfast."

He tilted his head back, peering at Mallory upside down. "You sure?"

She grinned. "Yeah." She kissed his forehead and went into the house without looking Ruth's way.

One down, one to go.

Jeff sat upright, staring past Ruth and down the alley, bracing himself for her reaction. She rarely let anything go; there was always some...blowback.

Ruth moved between his legs and kneeled, resting her forearms on his thighs. She sighed yet again.

He forced his gaze in her general direction.

"It's been over two years, Jeff, and things aren't much better." Her voice shook but carried more attitude than wistful observation.

"She needs time." *We all do.*

"And Todd?"

"What about him?"

"Does he need time, too?"

"I don't know. But it's different with boys."

She crooked one corner of her mouth. "Yeah, okay."

Jeff now locked his eyes on hers, thinking (just maybe) Mallory's assessment of Ruth's eye color was truer than not—with a significance beyond their shade. Crocodiles. "What, Ruth?"

She sighed long and hard while looking skyward, then closed her eyes. "'Many are the afflictions of the righteous: but the Lord delivereth him out of them all.'" She returned her gaze to Jeff. "Psalms: chapter thirty-four, verse nineteen." She offered a small smile.

Now it was his turn to smirk. "Yeah, okay." He looked away, doing his best to keep his emotions in check. He knew she meant well, but...

They grew quiet. She squeezed his thigh. Any more pressure and her grip would have hurt. "And what about you, Jeffrey Adair Winthrop, the third? Do you need more time?"

Her grip, more than her words, captured his attention. He aligned his gaze with hers. "No, I don't, Ruth L. Cannon-Winthrop." Oh, but he did; he truly did. He needed all kinds of time.

Her grip on his thigh slackened as she held his gaze. Finally, she stood. "You know, Jeff, the kids take their cue from you. Think about that."

Jeff didn't respond. Even if her words were legit, he wasn't thinking about anything. He just wanted her to go.

"Why the fuck did you marry me, Jeff?"

Shaking his head, he let out a low breath. Bible quotes one minute, blue language the next. Nevertheless, she posed a valid question. He'd need even more time to ponder a valid answer.

"Never mind, Jeff." She stood with a huff, but after some seconds, drifted to stand behind him.

Never mind was right. He couldn't do the verbal give-and-take with her this morning—not with reminders of Julia swirling around him. But he couldn't allow his mood to mess with the rest of Ruth's Saturday, either. Jeff tilted his head back to her. "It'll be fine."

He could tell his response wasn't what she wanted or expected, but Ruth nodded anyway. She rested a palm on his forehead, then ran it back across his scalp. "You know what? I'm looking forward to seeing this doctor of yours next week. What's her name again?"

He stared past her, up at the slow-moving clouds. "Naomi. Doctor Naomi Alexander."

"Yeah, that's it. Maybe she can help. Todd being on the roof like that was concerning. You three may have cut your grief counseling with her too soon."

He contained a scoff. She didn't have the slightest idea what she was talking about. Or maybe she did. Jeff focused on the clouds, images of his son sitting on the roof in the rain two nights ago intruding. Even through that rain drenching his face, Todd's eyes had been so—

Ruth ran her hand over his head again, adding caresses to the back of his neck. She shifted some, leaning forward enough to block his line of vision with the clouds, in essence forcing him to look at her. To look away or avert his gaze would have sent a rudely unmistakable message or implied a victory of sorts for Ruth he had no intention of giving. He held her gaze.

A smile snaked her lips. "Winter's coming. It'll be getting cold out. Think you might let your hair grow this season? For me?"

Here she goes with this mess again. "Ruth..."

"I just want to see what you look like with hair."

"You've seen pictures."

"That's not the same thing, and you know it." She paused, her hand resting on his head. "Come on. At least some facial hair. Please?"

"We'll see," Jeff said, knowing full well they wouldn't see. Besides, he'd taken Julia's pictures down. Every single one. The kids had pictures of her in their rooms (he stood firm on that), but otherwise... So, as far as he was concerned, Ruth had reached her limit for "please me" concessions. He sat up, welcoming the disconnection from her caress. He checked his watch for no other reason than to give the semblance of caring about the time. "I think I'll skip breakfast, too. Make a run." Run where? He didn't know. But that wasn't the point. "See you at the scrimmage later?" He casually scanned the surrounding area—everywhere but back at her. Her response would tell him all he needed to know. Still, he didn't want her to touch him again.

"I won't be able to stay for the whole thing," she confided in a tone low but affable. She didn't touch him.

Jeff nodded, knowing as much already. "Going anywhere right now?"

"Not for a couple hours. Why?"

"No reason. Just make sure Todd puts something in his stomach." He had yet to look at her.

"Sure."

At last, he turned to his wife.

She smiled at him. "So, we're good?"

Jeff reached for the front of Ruth's sweat jacket. He drew her down and pecked her lips. "We're fine."

A hand on her hip, Ruth viewed the alleyway and blew a breath. "No one's eating but me. Guess I'll have a muffin and scrambled egg."

"Sounds good." What did she want him to say? What *could* he say?

"Okay, well...," she trailed off.

He hated awkward silences. "Go 'head, Ruth. I'll see you at the game. Maybe we'll talk more later. But give me a minute, okay?"

She patted his shoulder before retreating into the house. And, as light and fleeting as that pat was, it still annoyed him.

Jeff scanned the yards and backs of houses in the alley, seeing them but not really. He wanted that scent, Julia's scent, to waft past him again. He wanted that more than anything. Jeff waited a few minutes, hoping for it.

He drew a palm over his scalp. Ruth's request that he let his hair grow irked him.

He'd shaved his hair after losing a bet to Julia over college football. She loved him bald, so he never allowed his hair to grow back. On the first anniversary of Julia's death, he shaved his facial hair and didn't allow that to grow back, either. The act, for him, demonstrated symbolic homage to her. Jeff sometimes missed having hair, but he'd also grown used to not having it. He didn't know if he was going bald for real. Perhaps a derivative of his trace Native American ancestry negated any hair-loss genes in his African American gene pool; he'd never seen a balding Indigenous. His uncles had heads full of hair, and the youngest was 62. So, whatever the DNA case, there was hope. Ruth's request aside, every so often, even he was curious about how he'd look with hair now.

But Julia likes him bald, so...

Jeff cut his eyes to the hammock and other deck furniture stacked on the opposite side of the deck. He figured his chore for today would be to move it all to the storage shed on the patio below.

Six years ago, he and Julia brought the hammock back from a trip to Cancun, Mexico. He'd been in it once, maybe twice, since she died (always alone, never with Ruth). The hammock held a delightful assortment of happy, warm, and erotic memories, such that the idea of getting rid of it violated something sacrosanct. Yet the idea of getting back in it to reconnect with Julia seemed an inherent imperative. Jeff's thoughts shifted to a warm night four summers ago. His groin stirred again with memories of what they were up to in that hammock.

He shook his head, sending his gaze upward. "I'm fucked," he whispered to the clouds. If the bright, blue sky and pearly-white clouds were any indication, the day would be perfect for football—and they seemed to agree (wispily) with the whispered status of his predicament.

Wanting to wait, but knowing it was stupid to wait for Julia's scent to return, Jeff inspected the deck furniture. Admittedly, Julia warned against purchasing the cast-iron ensemble. *"That is going to bleed rust right onto the wood,"* she'd commented.

Jeff stooped for closer inspection of the meranti wood upon which the cast-iron chairs and table rested. He traced fingers across some of the rust stains, smiling to himself.

Before she died, Julia was head RN at Washington Hospital Center. But her medical knowledge contributed only a tiny part of her entire knowledge base. Julia knew a little or a lot about all kinds of stuff: the relationship between Mother Nature and home improvements being no exception. Jeff's small smile morphed into mild confusion as he tried to remember why he'd gotten the furniture anyway.

An infusion of iris, vanilla, and roses wafted across his nose again.

He shot to his feet, examining his surroundings with squinted focus.

Genesis barked fiercely, but no one and no thing appeared out of place. The serene atmosphere, however, prickled the nonexistent hair on his scalp.

Jeff took hesitant seconds lowering back into his Adirondack chair.

What is going on?

He slowly shook his head, his eyes searching the deck and alley for something deemed impossible to see—something his nose told him...was right before his eyes.

Their appointment with Dr. Alexander was scheduled for later in the coming week.

But if this shit keeps up...

Jeff realized he'd need an emergency private session with her much sooner.

Chapter 2

Doughnut Dreams

"I'm off to Dunkin' Donuts. Who wants what?" Tyson says. He fixes his walnut-brown eyes on Naomi and smiles.

Naomi feels a vestige of something not quite nameable inside but smiles back at her husband. "I want you to help me finish getting these begonias planted; that's what I want. But I'll take a half-dozen maple-iced, thanks, since my needs and wants are quite interchangeable at the moment."

"Uh-huh," Tyson replies. He turns to Leslie. "What do you have a taste for, Punkin?"

Naomi turns to Leslie, too.

Leslie removes her gardening gloves and swipes a wrist over her sweaty (and sparsely muddy) brow. "Uh, I don't know: two powdered raspberry jellies, two glazed apple-filled, and two powdered lemon-filled, I guess."

"You 'guess'?" Tyson's thin mustache twitches as his lips curl into a sardonic grin. His sardonic grin always gives Naomi a secret tingle.

Naomi gazes at her daughter, wondering when she put her forehead in the dirt.

Leslie grins back at her father. The childish expression contrasts sharply but approvingly with the young-adult maturity claiming her features. She is 16, looking more in her 20s. Or is she in her 20s, looking all of 16?

Watching the exchange between father and daughter, Naomi feels the unnamable tinge again. "Leslie, bring me another bag of soil from the garage, would you please?"

"Sure, Ma." Leslie shoots another smile at her father. "Bye, Daddy." There is something very final about how she says, *Bye, Daddy.* She retreats backward toward their opened garage, located several feet behind everyone.

"Well, is it like *that*? 'Bye, Daddy'? I'm just going to get doughnuts." Tyson faces Leslie as he speaks, so his back is to Naomi.

Leslie smiles again but doesn't look at her father. Instead, she locks eyes with her mother, and the unnamable inkling defines itself: foreboding. It seems hours pass before Naomi tears her gaze from Leslie's. "Tyson, don't go."

Tyson shifts his attention to her, keenly handsome in his Philadelphia Eagles cap. His mustache twitches again, but he doesn't smile this time. His expression is somber yet knowing. "You know I have to," he whispers.

The unsettling foreboding soon commingles with the ache of sorrow.

"Bye, Daddy." This time, the finality in Leslie's parting words rings clear.

"I love you, Punkin. Raspberry, apple-filled, and lemon-filled, right?"

Leslie nods, her face on the verge of teary crumple.

Tyson turns to Naomi. "Maple-iced for you." He paused, his brown eyes reflecting a gracious regret. "And you will love again."

Heartbroken, Naomi fights her tears. "I don't want to."

"Thank you. But I can't do anything with that." The cute sardonic grin returns. Tyson shrugs and heads for his Toyota Avalon.

...Don't go, Danny Boy. These words never cross her lips, remaining lodged in her sorrow-choked throat.

Nightfall.

From the sofa in her living room, Naomi stares at a Dunkin' Donuts box resting on the island counter in the kitchen. A reading lamp glows in the corner of the living room. No lights are on in the kitchen, but Naomi sees every detail of what she knows to be a half-empty Dunkin' Donuts box on the counter. Even the emerald-green granite countertop emits a soft glow, as if the box of doughnuts displayed in a jeweler's glass case and a spotlight shone down on it. Half-empty or filled beyond capacity, the box of sweet treats represents utter aberration given the context of...everything else. Music comes from the stereo, but Naomi doesn't hear it—she just knows it's on.

"Uh-hem," Tyson says, clearing his throat. He sits in a leather recliner in the same corner as the reading lamp. A hardback book rests in his lap. Naomi can't tell what holds his attention but is pretty sure it is a non-fiction work (a biography, most probable).

Tyson looks up from his book and smiles at Naomi. Something about how his glasses have come partway down his nose appeals to her.

"Why are you way over there looking all cute?" Naomi asks her husband. She can hear music playing now—but not quite.

"Well, where should I be?" The melodic timbre of Tyson's voice is arousing (and slightly out of place for him).

Naomi pats the space on the sofa next to her. No, it isn't the proper layout of her home, and the Dunkin' Donuts box shouldn't be there, and no, Tyson shouldn't be, either, but Naomi grabs for the happiness, nonetheless. She raises an eyebrow. "Right here would be a good place to start."

Tyson shakes his head slowly and thumbs toward the stairs. His nostrils flare the tiniest bit with the suggestion as he shifts his hips in his seat, and Naomi knows his erection is stiffening.

She shakes her head and pats the space next to her again, then rises and glides over to Tyson. Kneeling between his legs, she takes his book from him. "I didn't think you'd come back to me," she whispers.

"I know." Tyson pulls Naomi close and kisses her.

Closing her eyes in acceptance and delight, she returns his kiss, but the faint sensation of him equates to rendering him near nonexistent. Naomi opens her eyes: Tyson is still there.

There is a switch in location, or time, maybe both (doughnut dreams were unpredictable), and Naomi realizes she and Tyson are in bed, their bed, together. He feels good (nothing new), and there is music (but not, not quite). Another shift (different bedding, different bed). Naomi and Tyson lie on their sides, facing each other as mutual exploration ensues. Naomi's fingertips explore the contours of her husband's back while Tyson's lips explore the hollow spot above her collarbone. Tyson pulls her closer for a deep kiss, moving his hands soothingly down her back to squeeze and caress her backside.

Tyson isn't (wasn't?) a smoker, but a hint of menthol lingers on his tongue and at the back of his throat. The taste is strange and wonderful in the darkness of their bedroom, and Naomi wants more. As if sensing the change in her desire, Tyson's hands caress the sensitive spot between her shoulder blades. A sigh escapes her lips but breaks as her breath halts somewhere around her tonsils.

Something cold and unyielding slinks into Naomi's center.

The caress continues at her upper back, but Naomi realizes Tyson's hands are still at her backside. Fear and understanding of that implication move through her with icy-cruel certainty as she allows Tyson to take their kiss even deeper. She can't help shivering from a new sense of foreboding—there were too many hands.

Fingertips at Naomi's back glide to her shoulders, and she freezes. Strains of melody tease her ears. Not wanting to leave Tyson (this time with him was always special) but desperately wanting to resist responding to the knowing strokes at her shoulders and back, Naomi concentrates on the faint strains of music playing (but not, *not quite*).

Her husband shifts his left hand to the front of her thigh, sending it upward. An unmistakable rigidness jabs her there, too. She has missed him and wants this to go on forever. But the music is louder now, which is good, because Naomi can also feel herself responding to the other caress from behind her—and that is not good.

She concentrates harder on the music, wanting the escape into the familiar. The hand on her shoulder travels over and down toward the soft swell of her right breast. Naomi forces deeper concentration on the music because she can feel herself disengaging from Tyson's kiss to glimpse the owner of the other hands, and she doesn't want to do that.

Besides, she knows who it is.

This understanding mobilizes the fear. Concentration brings clarity to the music, but *Naomi's head is still turning away from Tyson to the other. Violins play as the familiarity of the music imparts the desired escape—but it comes seconds too late. Naomi sees the face: Leslie.*

Naomi bolted upright in her bed, simultaneously striking the snooze button on her alarm clock and instantly silencing Beethoven's Violin Sonata No. 5 in F major, Op. 24, *Spring*. She took several deep, calming breaths, sending unwelcomed remnants of her sleeping session away. As disturbing as the dream was, perspiration didn't dampen her body. She'd had one of the few variations of oft-recurring dreams about Tyson. This was the first to include Leslie in such a way, but Naomi hesitated to call this latest a nightmare.

Naomi swung her legs over the side of her bed. She struck the alarm clock a second time to allow Beethoven to float into the bedroom again, but *Spring* had ended. Chopin's The Prelude in E minor No. 4, Op. 28 filled the surrounding space instead.

She reached under her pillow and grasped her Glock-17 semi-automatic pistol. After checking the safety, she placed the gun back in its holster before tossing it onto the leather satchel resting in her reading chair.

Dr. Naomi Alexander padded to her bathroom to start her day. It was six forty-five a.m. A combined total of three and a half hours sleep (albeit broken): her most extended sleep session in months.

Not bad.

Chapter 3

Generation "Why?"

"**I** just know, I'm not sayin' jack." Mallory Èkerie Winthrop held the phone's receiver to her ear with her shoulder as she dug into her backpack for yet another piece of chewing gum.

She maintained a ten-to-fifteen-stick-a-day habit now that she was trying to quit biting her fingernails. Three years of biting her nails resulted in them having such a nasty, ugly look—never mind the tenderness and occasional trickles of blood from times her stress had her biting past the pain (or maybe even for the pain). Her nails were growing nicely with her switch to gum-chewing; that was encouraging. The switch from fingernails to gum originated from a passing suggestion from Dr. Alexander when they first started going to her (before her dad cut things short), a recommendation Mallory jotted down in her journal, forgot about, and then later came across and decided to try. She didn't know where that journal was now.

"How're you going to attend therapy with your family and say nothing?" Elliot "Kelz" Kelton sounded preoccupied at his end of the phone. More than a classmate, he was one of her best friends. Kelz was comical but a good listener, too.

Mallory reclined against her headboard. She gazed around her bedroom, deciding how to redecorate it. "I'm not going with my 'family,' as you put it."

"Mister Winthrop and Todd are your family, Mal."

"That's right. *My dad and brother.* Not her."

"I got what you were saying the first time. Still, it doesn't look like she's going anywhere, anytime soon, so..."

"Look, call me back on my cell. I don't want to talk about this on the house phone." She didn't want to talk about it at all.

"Oh, right. I forgot. Hold on."

A few seconds later, her cellphone emitted hip-hop music. She viewed her phone's LCD: Elliot. Mallory tapped her cellphone to accept his call and disconnected from the cordless house phone. "Uh-huh."

"Yeah. I was saying the lady isn't going anywhere, so you need to figure something out. How long has she been with you guys?"

"Around two years, give or take some months. Why?"

"And how long your mom's been gone?"

Mallory knew he meant no harm, but his question still hurt. "Three years ago, this past June. Your point?"

"Nothing. I'm just saying. As much as you talk about how your parents loved each other, it didn't take long for your dad to hook up again."

"Don't go there, Kelz." She wasn't going to let Elliot tarnish the memory of her parents' relationship—even if she did have questions about that herself. She stared at her copy of Sharon Draper's *Copper Sun* on her nightstand.

Elliot changed the subject. "You work tomorrow, don't you?"

Mallory changed it right back. "She constantly voices these subtle digs at my mother, trying to insult her memory and whatnot when my mother hasn't done a thing to her. And I don't like how she treats Todd."

"I thought you didn't want to go there. And Todd can handle himself; he's almost fifteen."

"I said leave my parents' relationship alone. I have plenty to say about Ruth; you know that. And Todd..." Kelz didn't know about Todd sitting on the roof in the rain (hugging his knees and rocking), and she hadn't been able to talk to her brother about that yet herself.

"'And Todd,' what?"

Mallory reached for another stick of gum. "Todd's not an assertive person. He's mostly shy, given his asthma, and still dealing with Mommy being gone. But I think Ruth started in on him from the beginning. She's had some time to break him down."

"Man, you've got a case of Wicked Stepmother Syndrome bad." He scoffed in friendship.

"Whatever, Kelz." She sucked her teeth. "I don't understand why he married her. I mean, *why?* Why did he do that?"

"It's a generational thing, I guess. Your dad's a Baby-Boomer, X-er?"

"Not sure. 'X-er,' I think. These titles for the different generations are too much: Boomers, Gen-X, Gen-Y, Millennials, Gen-Z, Centennials..." She sucked her teeth.

Kelz snickered. "Right now, you sound more like generation 'Why?'—the question, not the letter."

Mallory formed a halfhearted smile. "Anyway, I'm not feeling her. Never have. There's something about her. But Daddy..." Mallory trailed off with a wince, reflecting on the talk her father had with Todd and her about Ruth being in his life; this, after Mallory noticed him mentioning Ruth more and more. It wasn't much of a talk, not really an exchange of points of view. Daddy said Ruth was joining the family. And so, she did. "...Besides, he didn't have to get rid of the condo, anyway."

"You said Ruth ended up getting your family much money for that, even if you don't need it."

"True." Nobody said Ruth wasn't a good realtor; Mallory just didn't think Ruth was good for her dad—or their family, period.

"Your dad hold on to the property in Warfield, Virginia?"

"Yeah. He only got rid of the condo because it had too many memories tied to Mommy. The condo used to be their little getaway spot. I think he wanted to rent it out and leave it to us, but Ruth convinced him she could get him a nice piece of change for it because the market was right or whatever." And now that Mallory thought about it, maybe Ruth was on a mission to get rid of memories of Mommy as early as then. She made him take her pictures down. It was possible. Made sense.

"So, Ruth increased both your trust funds, then."

"Everything is not about the dollar. If he hadn't wanted to explore options for the property, he never would have met her."

"Yeah, but it woulda been some other realtor."

"Whatever. It wouldn't have been her."

"Damn!"

"What?" She shook her head, fighting tears. "Never mind; you don't understand."

"Your dad exhibiting some of his stuff this year? It's been a while."

"A piece or two, maybe, but on the real, I doubt it. Daddy's not into his art like he used to be." He wasn't into much of anything like he used to be, except—

"Since your mom's...?"

"Uh-huh." Mallory tried her best not to cry. She missed her mother. And (being honest) she missed her dad, too.

A peculiar knock sounded at her door—two slow knocks followed by two rapid ones: Todd.

"Hold on, Kelz." Mallory held her cellphone away from her mouth, directing her voice toward her bedroom door. "Come in, big head."

Todd Audric Winthrop opened Mallory's door a crack. She could only see one eye as he peered in at her. She missed her mother and wanted her dad back, but she had her brother. That bond made the rest bearable. With Ruth in their lives, though, Todd grew more and more withdrawn.

Mallory frowned at him. "What're you doing?"

"My head's so big; this is all I can fit through the door."

She held in a chuckle. "Oh, li'l brother's got jokes—the *unfunny* kind. What d'you want?"

Todd kept peering with one eye. "Nothin'. Trying to figure out what to eat. Want half a Dagwood?" The door and frame muffled his voice.

"Yeah, but don't make the super. Where's Daddy?"

Her brother opened the door wider, showing his entire face. His expression spoke volumes.

Mallory spoke into the phone: "Kelz, you want to hold a minute, or want me to call you back? ...Okay, 'bout half an hour? A'ight." Mallory disconnected with a phone tap and turned back to her brother. She sat forward, whispering, *"Again?"* She shook her head in disbelief, but a more significant part of her wasn't surprised. "He's in there again?"

Todd nodded and stepped into her room, partially closing the door.

"Music playin'?"

"Yep."

"Shit."

"You know he'll be out by the time *she* gets home." Her brother dropped his head for a minute, seeming in deep thought. When he lifted his head, he wore an inquiring smile. "Wanna watch *Medea's Family Reunion* wit' me? Or *Meet the Browns,* maybe?"

Todd did not want to watch a Tyler Perry production. Not really. He wanted to talk. Mallory knew that like she knew her name. It was an undercurrent of sibling understanding that only intensified after their mother died. "*Meet the Browns*—in *your* room this time." Mallory sent him an angled grin.

He smiled back. The tiny chip in his front tooth lent his smile a childlike appeal. He refused to get the thing fixed for some reason (some stupid "guy" reason, probably). He needed a haircut, though; Mallory thought his curls were getting unruly on the top. "I cleaned up the crumbs last time, girl."

"Yeah, but I had to remind you twice."

"Oh, but it's okay for you to keep wearing my Coppin State T-shirt, even though I've been asking for it for three weeks."

Mallory had to laugh; he had her on that one.

"Yeah, see? Uh-huh." With a smile, he left her room, closing the door behind him. She heard him laughing in the hallway.

Todd was gone and probably halfway down the stairs, but Mallory continued her guffaw. The joke had long ended, but she placed her hands over her aching belly (her stomach hurt, she laughed so hard) and howled even harder.

Hearing herself cackle, though, she paid closer attention to her laughter, wondering suddenly: what was so funny? She didn't have a concrete answer, but she had a general discussion point: something was wrong.

Wrong in an indefinable, scary way.

The joke had long ended, but the laughter coiled from the mild pain in her belly with a new purpose: she laughed to keep from crying. Not wanting to hear herself cackle again (and sound completely certifiable), Mallory forced her guffaws down.

When her laughter subsided, she sat back against her headboard and scanned her room again with a disapproving eye. The southwestern Aztec theme had to go. She thought about doing a more juvenile theme: maybe SpongeBob SquarePants, Rainbow Ryla, or Black Barbie. Something like that.

Her heart lightened with an even better decorating idea: a 60s-70s Hippie theme. It was inspired; her mother would've loved it, so it would be partial tribute to her.

Mallory tilted her head back with a sigh and watched the ceiling for several long minutes before closing her eyes. Moments ago, she laughed to keep from crying, but now, she wasn't laughing anymore; the urge to cry wanted its turn.

Something indefinable (and scary) was wrong, and Mallory worried. Worried for her father. Worried for her brother. Even for herself on some level.

But not for Ruth. Mallory wasn't worried for her.

If anything, she worried warily *about* her.

Todd used a tad too much Dijon mustard, but the sandwich tasted fine. He had the hang of their father's Dagwood recipe down pat. Mallory popped her last spicy-nacho Doritos chip into her mouth with her last bite of sandwich. The nacho spices provided an unusual yet tasty flavor combination. She savored that last bite before handing her plate full of crumbs to her brother.

She draped prone across the foot of her brother's bed while Todd sat on the floor beside his bed with his back resting against his nightstand. Taking the plate from her, he stacked their plates and placed them behind him on the nightstand.

Meet the Browns was on, but Mallory knew Todd wasn't watching it. Several of his favorite parts passed without him rolling on the floor in a giggling fit. She noticed he barely cracked a smile. When the part came when Mr. Brown was "Slayin' in the Spirit," hitting folk in the head, and Todd didn't even grin, Mallory had had it. She knew he wanted to talk anyway, so enough with the preamble. She grabbed the remote and paused the video.

On the TV, L.B.'s and Sarah's frozen video expressions were hilarious.

Mallory cracked up, surprising Todd. Her laughter must have gotten to him because he started laughing with her. She rolled onto her back, clutching her stomach, trying to catch her breath.

This laughter was better than that episode alone in her room. That laughter battled some underlying fear and misery; this laughter was genuine humor. The two hooted for a good minute or two, with Todd's chortles dying out first.

Attempting to quell the giggles swirling in her throat, Mallory kept her eyes on her brother, using his serious expression to get the job done. She sensed maybe now he was ready to talk.

They were silent awhile. She spotted a copy of *Sky Man* by Stacie Johnson poking from under his pillow.

Todd stared at her. "...Why does he go into the room like that, Mal?"

Mallory thought she might know but shrugged, thinking about Kelz's 'Generation Why?' comment. There were certainly many *whys* in their home that needed answers.

"He'd stopped for a while," he added. His perplexity knotted the furrows of his neat but thick brows. He shook his head. "It creeps me out." He turned his attention back to the television.

Mallory did, too: L.B. and Sarah remained frozen in mid-crazy expression. She turned back to her brother.

A hint of a smile creased his jaw, and she then noticed the amount of hair on his face. Her little brother needed to shave. Mallory's eyes widened. She couldn't believe she'd missed this before. "Todd!"

"What?!" He jerked his head her way, eyes wide. "What's the matter?"

"Your face."

"What about it?" The timbre of his voice dropped late last year.

Deeper voice, hair on his face, another two inches in height since June—her little brother was becoming a man at the speed of days (not years). Mallory wondered if any other aspects of manhood claimed him.

Todd stared at her with a look of part concentration, part apprehension, as if trying to read her thoughts, doing their sibling-communication thing. After a moment, he put on a shrewd grin before rising and sitting next to her on his bed. "And no, I'm not anymore."

She turned back to L.B. and Sarah. "Not what? And you'd better be." Mallory focused on the paused figures on Todd's television.

"Yeah, okay." He added a scoffing chuckle.

"...When?"

"This past summer: end of July."

She turned to him. "You don't have the date?"

He frowned. "Guys don't do that shit. Memorializin' dates is for girls."

"Whatever." Mallory sucked her teeth with a lip curl and looked away. Her little brother had one-upped her. She now doubted she could teach or tell him anything; her level of authority may have just dropped a notch in his eyes. She didn't want to be jealous, but... "Why didn't you say anything?" She was his sister, not his brother, but they were close: talking about sex wasn't new ground for them.

He bounced his shoulders, displaying uncertainty.

"So, you big man now, or what?"

"Am I acting the big man? You wouldn't have known if it wasn't for this conversation." He nudged her. "But I would've told you...eventually."

"So, who was it? Do I know her?" She wouldn't look him in the eye.

"...Divinia Watson."

"Oh, she's cute— Wait!" She whipped her attention to Todd and sat up more. "*Divinia Watson?* She's what, eighteen?"

"Not until November."

"Daaamn." Mallory gave her brother the once-over again, trying to step outside of being his sister to view him in a neutral light. She could only go so far with it. Todd was cute, becoming more handsome as he grew older (the facial hair helped), but he was still just 14. He could pass for 16, maybe 18, Mallory guessed, but Divinia *knew* Todd, so... *Ugh!* "So how did— Has it been just the once? You wore a condom, right?"

"Nosy, ain't we? And, of course, I did."

"Oh, so now that you've popped your collar, we can't talk like before?"

He reached for his almost-empty glass of ginger ale. "I didn't say that."

"Okay then." Mallory waited.

Todd finished his soda and glanced at her sideways. He settled the glass back down with a sigh. "So,...you want the nitty-gritty or just the high-level?"

"Somewhere in between."

He sighed again and stuck his tongue in the space created by his chipped tooth; something he did when he wanted to concentrate or was lost in thought.

Curious as she was, Mallory changed her mind about wanting the details—at least for now. "You know what? Save it for another time."

"Huh?"

"You heard me. Tell me about it some other time. I still wanna know your business; don't worry." She smiled teasingly at her brother.

Todd shook his head. "Women."

"Don't even try it."

He didn't seem to know how to respond to that, and Mallory took semi-selfish pride in shutting her brother up. Maybe she retained some level of authority after all. They sat silent until the pause button released and the cast whirled back into action.

This time, Todd grabbed the remote. He stopped the video, turned the television off, and then stared at the dark screen with pondering concentration.

"Done with the Browns?"

Todd didn't look at her. "You never answered my question."

"To reconnect with Mommy."

He nodded with deliberation and grew quiet again. When he spoke again, Mallory had to lean closer to hear him. "Daddy's got big money: from the inheritance, his art, his properties. He's got us. What'd he marry her for?"

They were talking about Ruth now. "I don't know, Todd."

"She doesn't even look like Mommy." He mumbled his words with frustrated anger. Todd finally turned to her. His eyes were wet, but he didn't cry. "And she's mean to me, Mal." He probably didn't want his voice to waver, but it did. She listened for wheezing, just in case.

"She...did something? Is... Is that why you were on the roof the other night, in the rain like that?" Mallory stiffened with the memory, seeing her drenched dad inching toward her brother to avoid spooking him. Todd wasn't crying now, but he'd been crying then; the rain didn't camouflage it.

Her brother nodded, but his head barely moved.

That fear and misery knotted in her stomach again, and the air grew thick, making it harder to breathe. With no laughter to fight it off this time (nothing was even remotely funny at this moment), the fear and misery now coiled around the disgust, sympathy, and anger in her center, too. She wasn't cold, but she gripped her upper arms to pause her tremors of disquiet.

Ignoring the helplessness threatening to send her into a round of crying or laughing hysterics, Mallory stared at the dichotomy that was her brother.

Mr. Hairy Face (now two inches taller than she) had cashed in his V-Card.

But when it came to their stepmother, the unsettledness in Todd's eyes revealed how much of a little boy the almost-man really was.

Chapter 4

Signifying Nothing

The Winthrops' first session progressed poorly on several levels for one main reason.

And, despite her love of the color and design of the oversized leather sofas and her linen-fabric tufted barrel chair, Dr. Naomi Alexander entertained the idea of changing her office décor and getting rid of the mustard-yellow seating group.

The Winthrops' first session.

Changing her office décor.

Those two notions were unrelated, but Naomi's attention to both was equal, and yet, (she knew) somehow tied to one another. A part of her couldn't wait for revelation of the connection.

Five people sat in varying postures on the yellow furniture, like poppy seeds on a lemon muffin. Five people sitting, one person talking. And talking. On and on for the last eleven minutes.

When Julia Winthrop died three years ago, Naomi knew then, after counseling Jeffrey, Mallory, and Todd, that her sessions with them accomplished little. She'd worked to get them through the initial shock of losing their wife and mother unexpectedly, but Jeffrey Winthrop stopped the sessions once Mallory and Todd started back to school. He stopped attending sessions when he began presenting symptoms of complicated grief.

Mr. Winthrop didn't mention any hallucinatory experiences back then, but his mourning for his wife persisted and intensified beyond simple depression. Her mysterious yet innate ability to see flickers of auric fields continuously informed her of Jeff's depression states. Those rare times his aura flickered for her back then: nothing but this dark, muddy, heavy blue, thick with woe. In those previous sessions, his yearning for Julia was poignantly lucid. He'd since remarried, but she expected more of the same with these sessions.

Her tolerance for her patients' varying afflictions waned as of late, but she did her job and did it well when treating people. Still, she reserved particular empathy and tolerance for patients struggling with losing a loved one. But, while Naomi very much wanted to redirect Mr. Winthrop away from his detour into a grief pathological three years ago, he'd ended the sessions, and thus her hands were tied. And now, a second chance presented itself.

Unbeknownst to anyone, along with auric sight, she also experienced what she'd termed *flashes of truth*: these acute hunches (at times with imagery) somehow, someway, grounded in truth. But she'd had no occurrence of a "flash" while counseling the Winthrops years back.

Naomi sat in her sizable mustard-yellow chair, facing her patients sitting on the leather sofa and loveseat, positioned in an inverted "L" across from her chair and in front of her office window. She entertained the idea of moving the sofa to the opposite side so that it faced away from the window but thought better of it. Often, that window served as an assistant of sorts, giving patients the distraction needed to gather their thoughts and open up when Naomi's professional approach reached a roadblock. So, she guessed, the office layout would stay the same, which left the décor—meaning the big-ass yellow furniture...

Jeff Winthrop sat on the sofa with his hands folded in his lap. He shifted attention between his children and the view outside, his baldpate gleaming in the late morning light. For a big guy with a tall, muscular stature, Mr. Winthrop's posture appeared prim. The folded hands indicated to Naomi: the man exercised control—doing what he could to keep it together.

Mrs. Winthrop (Naomi believed her name was "Ruth") continued talking.

Naomi shifted her attention from prim-looking Mr. Winthrop to his daughter, Mallory. Mallory sat beside her father in repose, looking very much like him, with copper-brown skin and deep-set eyes. She was a pretty girl, but her facial expression was not. Whereas her father did all he could to contain his emotion, Mallory sulked and did not disguise her displeasure. Whether that displeasure stemmed from being in therapy or from disdain for her stepmother, Naomi didn't know.

Mrs. Winthrop shifted in her seat, mentioning something about being on the deaconess board at her church.

Mallory rolled her eyes upward with what Naomi knew to be an internal sigh, thus solving the mystery.

Suppressing the urge to smile at her discovery, Naomi moved on to the youngest Winthrop. Mrs. Winthrop (*"Ruth," right?*) completed the trio on the sofa, sitting next to Mallory and rambling on about something or other, which left Todd with the loveseat all to himself.

Unlike his sister, Todd took cue from his father and appeared to be exercising restraint with a posture stiff but not prim. He sat across from Naomi, but his attention focused somewhere overhead and behind her. She looked over her shoulder to determine what held his attention: her wall showcasing framed prints of jazz artists and classical music composers.

The wall once held her credentials, along with a plethora of awards and plaques of recognition. She'd since removed the filler and fluff and cut to the chase by taking down the awards and plaques and leaving only her credentials, which now adorned the wall behind the sofa opposite her office window. A proud alumnus, she took particular pleasure having her medical degree from Johns Hopkins University, centering her license and board certs.

That was all her patients needed to know anyway: that she was qualified, certified, and doctor-fied to treat them. If they needed proof of her success as a psychiatrist, evidence rested in the bottom left-hand drawer of her desk and on the bottom shelf of her corner bookcase.

Naomi turned back to Todd, who continued studying the pictures. Obvious tension stiffened the muscles along his jawline, and on further observation, his focus on the images wasn't as intense as Naomi first imagined. He didn't fidget or show outward signs of disinterest, so she wasn't sure if the boy exercised restraint or had mentally checked out of the session altogether.

Given his age, Naomi figured it to be the latter, but she had no way of knowing what was going on with any of them unless she got this session started officially. That meant *she* needed to be the one doing some talking—not Miss Talkity-Talk Winthrop (*"Ruth," right?*).

Naomi clapped once, creating a resounding pop. "All righty, then!"

All four Winthrops startled at the suddenness and volume of her interruption, but they each looked her way. Very good.

"Why are you here, Missus Winthrop?" Naomi asked.

"Call me 'Ruth,' please." Mrs. Winthrop offered a smile.

"'Ruth,' then. Why are you here, Ruth?" Naomi didn't smile back.

It was instinctual and instantaneous: she didn't much care for this woman. Sometimes you *could* judge a book by its cover. There was something pretentious, underhanded, and unsympathetic about her, coming through something as ordinary as her smile and tone of voice. Liking Ruth, however, had nothing to do with treating this family, so Naomi would have to exercise some restraint herself (well, she'd manage an effort, anyway). At least she had the woman's name right.

With eyes holding a tentative expectancy, Ruth gazed at Naomi's unsmiling face. Yes, there was a touch of darkness about her.

After some reluctant milliseconds, Naomi offered a scant upward turn at the corners of her mouth.

Ruth seemed encouraged. "I'm here because several problems at home need to be worked out." She sat taller but didn't look at Jeff.

Mallory turned to Ruth with eyes narrowed.

With only a flit of eye movement in Mallory's direction, Ruth continued looking at Naomi.

Naomi dispersed her attention among the group.

During therapy with them three years ago, the Winthrop kids' auras didn't flicker for her, only Jeff's. And although they were young, the non-occurrence had little to do with their ages; she'd received aura-flickers from young children before and since. But it happened that way sometimes. Naomi didn't rely on her flashes of truth nor her aura-flickers—especially for treatment; it was a pointless pursuit at best.

The unpredictable nature of her flashes and the oft-changing nature of auras (and thus, her flickers) made the occurrences quite a loosey-goosey capricious experience. Her flashes were serious events (and not always dire), and her flickers were informative, but this was the thing: oftentimes, she experienced them when she didn't want to—and didn't experience them when she did want to.

She was a young college student when these talents awakened, and back then, she initially responded to the occurrences with the naiveté and awe her young age dictated. But youthful she was not anymore; she now responded to the events of her flashes or flickers with a casual indifference and acceptance as she would...walking, showering, or cooking.

But that was neither here nor there.

Discounting any supernatural or paranormal notions about her abilities (she didn't require use of a special camera to see auras), Naomi saw people as people, not their aura colors, so regardless of her flashes and flickers, what she relied on was her training and skill, her people-knowledge repository, her keen intuition. Today's session would be no different.

Todd watched his sister. Intense focus (absent earlier) seeped in.

Her eyes landed on Jeff Winthrop, and it surprised Naomi to find him looking back at her. His expression suggested he wanted her approval of Ruth's response.

The smile Naomi gave Jeff was genuine. Whether he surmised approval from her response was immaterial, but for the record, she sided neutral on the woman's response.

Naomi shifted her gaze back to Todd. "Why are you here, Todd?"

Todd's big, round eyes now focused on Naomi. She thought his soft curly hair, smooth pecan-colored skin, and big, caramel-brown eyes were enough to have plenty of 14- and 15-year-old girls blowing up the cellphone clipped to his hip. His facial hair likely drew the interest of a few older teenage girls as well, but rather than being cocky and full of adolescent hubris, the boy appeared reserved and vulnerable: traits more appealing than his aesthetic appearance. He shrugged and mumbled something suggesting the equivalent of "I don't know."

Completely satisfied with Todd's answer, Naomi turned to his sister. "And where are you with all of this? Why are you here, Mallory?"

Mallory kept her eyes on Ruth. "There are issues, yes, but I'm mainly concerned about my brother—and my dad." Mallory now turned toward her father, and 16 melted into nine.

Jeff Winthrop put a hand on his daughter's thigh and patted it with a light touch. He smiled at Mallory, but Naomi recognized authentic emotion bottled in the cords of his neck muscles. "Daddy's fine, baby." His voice offered feigned reassurance.

Mallory shook her head; she detected the pretense. "No, you're not, Daddy."

"Mister Winthrop, why are you here?"

"Call me 'Jeff,' Naomi; you know that."

"Okay, okay. But there have been some changes..." Naomi looked pointedly at Ruth, then back at Jeff, "...since you were here last, Mister Winthrop, so I wasn't sure."

"It's *Jeff*, Naomi." He smirked with kind eyes and a wan smile.

"Okay, well, *Jeff*, why're you here?"

Naomi's light sarcasm reached Jeff's funny bone. He chuckled briefly. However, the pain in those deep-set eyes revealed that maybe he'd rather be crying. Jeff put a knuckle up to one eye, and Naomi knew she wasn't too far off. "Yeah, there're some things needing attention, I guess. The incident with Todd tops the list..." Jeff nodded slowly as he studied the floor. He lifted his eyes to Naomi. "Yeah," he concluded, blowing a thin breath of resignation.

Naomi sat forward some. "We'll get into the roof incident in time. But okay. So: we have 'problems.' Right?" She ticked the index finger of her left hand and looked at Ruth.

Ruth nodded.

Naomi eyed Jeff and ticked her middle finger. "We have 'things,' no?"

Jeff nodded.

Naomi identified number three by ticking her ring finger. "There are 'issues' with concern. Yes?" Naomi focused on Mallory.

Mallory nodded.

Naomi turned to Todd. "And then there's simply 'I don't know.' Right?" Naomi ticked her pinkie finger to represent number four.

Todd nodded with a sarcastic smirk full of charm.

Naomi glanced at the clock. She'd allowed Ruth to go on too long. In any event, she needed to ask her customary question and keep things moving.

"Well, it seems Todd and Mallory are closer to their truths than their parents are. Now—"

"Parent," Mallory corrected. She didn't look Ruth's way, having made her point.

Naomi fully expected the correction—that it came from Mallory didn't surprise, either.

Ruth gave no facial clue Mallory's correction affected her, but her backboard posture lost some rigidness.

Todd gazed at his sister with pride—as if she'd voiced something he wanted to say. Naomi also picked up additional cues in his expression (something translating much less enthusiastic than unvoiced pride), and she felt sorry for him. Todd still grieved his mother's passing, but her sympathy sourced differently, beyond sadness for his loss.

She didn't bother checking for Jeff's reaction to Mallory's statement. "Well, before we explore the reason or reasons you all are here again, I'd like first to get a feel for everyone's—"

"Spiritual compass," Mallory finished.

Naomi grinned at her. "Remember from the previous sessions, huh?"

Mallory nodded, but Todd answered (with his own nod): "Yeah, I remember that, too."

Ruth shook her head. "I don't remember any religious questions on the questionnaire we filled out."

"Because there weren't any. I reserve those discussions for in-person sessions. It's a 'Doctor Alexander' thing. I can gain only so much from what's on those forms." Verily, she'd discerned quite a bit from her pre-therapy questionnaires, but no one need know that but her.

"I see," Ruth responded.

Naomi wondered if she did. "Okay. Well, who'd like to start?"

Ruth opened her mouth to speak, but Naomi had heard enough from her for the time being. She'd tuned out most of what the woman said, but she'd gotten the gist: God-fearing, church-going woman, realtor and property manager, deaconess board, etcetera, etcetera.

All of it, sound and fury...

Naomi wanted to hear from the others (those actually needing treatment), so she spoke before Ruth could get a word out. "Todd?"

If Todd's eyes could have widened any further, his eyeballs would have spilled from their sockets. "Me?"

Naomi plunged her chin in confirmation. Shades of gray and cranberry could work for her décor. She preferred the jolting brightness of her yellow, but the new colors offered a version of mood, too.

"Um, I believe in God, I guess."

"Your faith is your armor, Todd. You can't be guessing," Ruth stated.

Todd's posture sunk deeper into the back of the loveseat.

"If you're referring to Ephesians, chapter six, Todd's faith is his *shield*, which is only a part of God's armor. But thank you, Ruth. I got this."

There was nothing Christian about the scowl Ruth sent her at being corrected, but a wan smile immediately replaced it.

"Go ahead, Todd," Naomi prompted.

"I wasn't saying I guess there is a God. All I meant, was that if Doctor Alexander wanted to know how we felt about religious stuff and whatever, well, I believe in God. I said, 'I guess,' because I don't know how specific she wants me to be or whatever. I—"

"Todd," Naomi interrupted. "It's cool; your response was fine."

The gratitude in his eyes made Naomi that much more irritated with Ruth. Something needed to be explored between these two.

"You go to church, Todd?"

After a confirming glance toward Mallory, he nodded.

"Do you like church?"

"Sometimes."

"So, where you feel you are spiritually—is that working for you?"

He furrowed his brow with a hesitant smile. "Huh?"

"Never mind, sweetie. That's more of a question for your dad and Ruth...and maybe your sister." Naomi swiveled her eyes to Mallory.

"I'm non-denominational like my mother was. That's working for me just fine." She snapped, stopping short of sucking her teeth.

"Well, good for you. But have I done something to you? What's with all the attitude?"

"Sorry, Doctor Alexander," Mallory's voice rose and shook, "It's not you. I'm just—"

"Wait. Wait, Mallory. It's okay. It's my fault. Let me back up and initiate the session by letting Ruth know how things go. Okay?"

Mallory dipped her chin in hesitant concession.

Naomi turned to Ruth. "Ruth, as the rest of the family knows, with me, the conversation should flow. While I use my medical background in therapy, I don't use it to the exclusion of all else because I believe that regular, correlated time in the prudencesphere, using *common sense*, is invaluable in resolving some or even most basic forms of mental and emotional stress. To that end, conversation drives the sessions. Starting next week, I may take notes during the sessions or record portions of them. As you know, confidentiality rules the roost; my advice is to say what you want. Neither my approval nor opinion of what you say is of concern here. Okay?"

Still seeming bothered by their earlier exchange, Ruth nodded.

"Jeff? Mallory? Todd?" Naomi observed each of them in turn.

Each gestured their understanding and assent.

"Good. Now, let's get back to our spiritual compasses."

"Why do you ask about this, Doctor Alexander?" Ruth drew her burgundy Bottega Veneta hobo bag closer to her body.

Naomi refrained from giving her permission to call her by her first name. "Well, it will give me a better understanding of how each of you approaches death, grief, or mourning, as well as family conflict." She sensed family conflict at the heart of the *issues*, *problems*, and *things* referred to earlier.

"Oh, I see."

Naomi still didn't think she did. "Good. So now, how about you?"

"Well, as I said earlier, I'm a deaconess at my church, I'm on the youth ministry team, and I sing with the Praise and Glory Voices choir with my church on second Sundays."

"Okay, that's nice, but where are you spiritually?"

Ruth gawked as if to convey she'd already answered that. In other words, like Naomi was crazy. She frowned. "I just—"

"No, you recited a list of your church roles and activities."

"Oh." Ruth directed a scanning gaze at the other members of her family. "Well, my church is non-denominational with Baptist influence. I guess..." She tried not to look at Mallory but failed, sending a glance her stepdaughter's way. "I believe we are born with original sin and that the way to the Lord and Salvation is through Jesus Christ."

"Mmm..." Naomi nodded noncommittally.

Mallory sucked her teeth.

"Is that working for you, Ruth?" Jeff asked.

Ruth's lips parted with a slight startle, as if surprised Jeff spoke.

Naomi wasn't shocked at all.

Ruth fixed her eyes on her husband. "Yes, Jeffy, it is."

Now Jeff sucked his teeth, his brow bent with annoyance.

"What, Jeff?" Ruth appeared hurt, but a tad annoyed herself.

Naomi didn't want to hear Jeff's answer to Ruth—not yet, anyway. And she didn't know about Jeff, but Naomi thought that nickname, "Jeffy," blew chunks. Blew huge, saccharine, trying-too-hard chunks. The moniker sounded forced, sappy, unfitting, and false. But maybe he liked it. "So, Jeff: your turn. Let's hear from you and round this thing out in a tidy knot."

Jeff offered a small smile. "You're something else, Doctor Alexander."

"So I keep hearing. And stick with 'Naomi,' Jeff. Okay?"

"Okay. Yeah, um..." He sat taller and cleared his throat. "I, uh, I don't know, Naomi. Like my son, I believe in God, but here lately..." He paused, shaking his head, and then let out a sigh. "I don't know where I am on a spiritual level. Believin's all I got for you right now. And to be honest, no, it's not working for me, before you even ask." A knuckle came up to that eye again.

"I hear you, Daddy," Mallory uttered.

"Yeah," Todd added in a volume equating a whisper.

Ruth looked as if wanting to add her own supportive comment; her lips worked, but no words came out. An initial expression of sympathy on her face transformed into irritation again. Naomi then noticed Ruth's green eyes: a shade the color of Cerignola olives. How that physical feature escaped her notice before, Naomi didn't know. Maybe it was distraction derived from all Ruth's other sound and fury...

"Do you believe in an afterlife, Jeff?" Naomi asked quietly.

"No," he responded just as quietly.

"So, you don't believe in spirits and such?"

"My wife is dead, Naomi." His tone was stiff, final. But his eyes held what Naomi best guessed to be hope—that just maybe he was wrong.

"No, your *wife* is right here, Jeff." Ruth's expression was almost stern. The woman could have offered her statement more gently, but clear defiance came across instead.

Mallory sucked her teeth. "Oh, whatever!"

It was all Naomi could do not to laugh. Sometimes professionalism proved a pain in the ass. Jeff's response, though, killed the giggle rising in Naomi's throat.

"And *why* are you my wife, Ruth?" Jeff's voice cracked, but his eyes burned with an anger overtaking the torment in them seconds before.

Naomi's desire to laugh shifted into intense curiosity. *What did that question mean?* She held her tongue and tensed, waiting for Ruth's response. In the edges of her vision, Naomi noticed Mallory and Todd waited likewise; their father's question surely stirred a level of apprehension.

Ruth glanced at the others in the room before fixing a glare on Jeff. "No, you didn't." She didn't do a neck-roll or a finger-wave, but the inflection in her tone exposed her urban upbringing. Bible quotes would not fit in at this particular juncture.

Jeff held her gaze, unmoved by her change in tone and disposition. "Why are we married, Ruth?"

"Because we love each other," Ruth answered. Again, the gentleness of the words did not match her tone.

"Bullshit," Mallory muttered.

Jeff snapped his focus to Mallory. "Unh-uh, M-Sweet."

"But, Daddy—"

"No."

Mallory checked the resoluteness in her father's posture; his demeanor ended further debate. She mouthed, "Sorry," and sat back.

Jeff turned back to Ruth. "There is love, yes."

He means there is love now, but that doesn't mean there was love in the beginning, Naomi determined. And whatever love there was now, she doubted it was the good, Black love he shared with Julia. She saw nothing between Jeff and Ruth even approaching it. "Okay, beautiful people, this is obviously a topic for a later session. I'd like to get everyone back on track with the focus of today's session: spiritual compasses." Listening to herself, Naomi almost wanted to howl again. *Spiritual compasses? What the hell?*

Jeff sat up, sniffed, and drew a hand down and over his face, stretching his jaw muscles. "You're right, Naomi." He stared out the window. He was clean-shaven now. Jeff was handsome, but it was an odd look for him. Three years ago, he sported a mustache and beard stubble.

Todd lifted his posture, too, as did Ruth. Mallory seemed to slink deeper into the cushions; sitting between her dad and stepmother was not the best choice.

"Good. Now,..." Naomi watched Jeff, seeing the pain creep back into his eyes, witnessing the grief settling over him once again.

Except for the faint ticking of the wall clock, the room hushed. Periods of silence were normal and frequent, even beyond the first session.

"I miss my— Julia, Doctor Alexander." Jeff's furtive glance at Ruth appeared to suggest apology for his admission, but Naomi believed he started to say *my wife* again (instead of *Julia*). Jeff cleared his throat.

"And believing in God or an afterlife is not helping me deal with what's here, what's *now*. I—" He let out a heavy sigh and tilted his head back, watching the ceiling for several seconds before closing his eyes and letting out another sigh. He shook his head against the sofa cushions. His movements sounded a wispy crunch against the sofa's leather upholstery. "I... I— I can't," Jeff started, "I— I can't..." No longer shaking his head, he stared at the ceiling. A tear trailed into his right ear.

"Then don't," Naomi replied. Professionalism aside, she wanted to hug the poor man. "Then don't," she repeated. "At least not today." It would come soon enough.

"'The grass withereth, the flower fadeth: but the Word of our God shall stand forever,'" Ruth recited softly.

For Naomi, the tone was right this time, but the words sounded out of place. Isaiah, chapter forty, was ideal biblical reference for the discouraged, but Naomi thought the first verse, *'Comfort ye, comfort ye...'* may have been better to recite. "Thanks, Ruth."

Ruth nodded, eyes somber and mouth glum.

Naomi thought the gesture a bit too theatrical. *Maybe I'll use grays and blues for the wall and have linear black furniture—something sleek and contemporary.*

"Doctor Alexander?"

"Yes, Todd?" Naomi didn't forget the boy was in the room. She paid close attention to his reactions to the discussion. She'd expected, however, for him to remain silent for the remainder of the session.

"Do you pray?"

"Yes, I do."

Todd nodded—it was answer enough for him.

Naomi didn't pursue it further; it was answer enough for her, too.

"See, Todd: even Doctor Alexander lives by the Scripture. She's a God-fearing woman. See?" Ruth regarded her stepson with a direct, pertinacious gaze.

Naomi watched Ruth nod her approval but resisted clarifying anything for the woman, at most glad Ruth didn't use her first name. "In light of what your stepmother said, I want to say this to you, Todd: when people determine they're going to follow scripture or live the life they preach or teach about, it should be a happy decision, and they should be happy doing it. We refer to biblical scripture as 'the food of life,' right?

But when it's done with angst or regret, or done halfheartedly, or for sake of appearance, what's the point? Get what I'm saying?"

"I think so," Mallory replied.

Todd nodded his understanding as well.

Naomi hoped Ruth wouldn't come back with anything. She returned her attention to Jeff. "You okay, Jeff?"

"Yeah, I'm good." Jeff lifted his head, looking around at the others. "Sorry about that."

"It's cool, Dad."

"Yeah, Daddy. We understand." Mallory patted her father's thigh. "We miss her, too."

Ruth leaned forward, reaching across Mallory for Jeff's hand.

Jeff waved her off. "I'm good, Ruth. Seriously."

The glower Mallory shot Ruth should have vaporized her.

Jeff's semi-rejection appeared to bother Ruth, but she recovered with a not-quite-there smile as she turned to Naomi. "So, you have a problem with people trying to live spiritual lives, Doctor Alexander?" Her tone was neither defensive nor challenging.

There were times, though, when Naomi thought she engaged in dialogue with her patients a tad too much. "Well, these days, being 'spiritual' is more like a trend or club thing, with people using the term with more rigid connotations. And it's more alienating than welcoming. It's not everyone, mind you, but lately, with those I've run into, that's been my experience." Naomi paused. "But to answer your question, I have no problem with people trying to live spiritual lives. We should all do that—to the best of our ability."

Not that Naomi cared, but Ruth seemed satisfied. Her olive-green eyes scanned Naomi before taking in her office, pausing now and again on the furniture. She returned her attention to Naomi: "You know, Naomi, for a therapist, you seem to have chosen the wrong colors for your office, don't you think?"

"Meaning?" Naomi wished Ruth had stuck with addressing her as "Doctor Alexander." She could tell Ruth she preferred she didn't use her first name, but it could cause problems that might hinder helping the other (younger) Winthrops.

Mallory swept her gaze around the office while Jeff ran a hand over his head, trying not to look embarrassed.

Todd glanced at Mallory and shrugged. He then took interest in the loveseat, giving it a level of observation it didn't deserve.

"Well," Ruth continued, "I've had basic psychology, so I know enough to know that yellow represents cowardice."

"Yeah, and...?" Naomi had suspicions about Ruth's inquiry, but she wanted her to say it. Ruth's semester or two of introductory psychology apparently ranked high for opinion-giving and psychological analysis and interpretation. In her mission over the years, Naomi leaned more toward her inner psychologist than toward the psychiatric aspects of her calling. But Naomi wondered what she suffered through ten-plus years of medical training for then, when a semester or two of Psychology 101 would have sufficed.

Mallory dropped her head with a snicker.

Jeff and Todd channeled their concentration out the window, Todd chewing his bottom lip.

"Yellow also represents happiness, positivity, energy, optimism, enlightenment, remembrance, honor, and joy, Ruth. So, what's up? What's this got to do with anything?" Jeff kept his attention on the view outside.

She wants to get a dig in, Jeff. Bring me down a peg or two.

"Nothing, Jeffy. Just saying. As a realtor, I see many model ho—"

Mallory blew a breath with her eyeroll. "And *nothing* is yellow?"

Ruth cut her eyes at her stepdaughter. "Don't be smart, Mallory."

Todd's attention zipped to his sister, checking warily for her response.

Mallory postured as if she wanted to come back with something, but after a glimpse toward her brother, she altered course with a suck of her teeth and shake of her head.

"Let it go, Ruth," Jeff advised with succinct weariness.

Naomi watched and listened to this exchange with mild indifference. The exchange helped some, however. How interesting that Ruth would comment on her office décor when Naomi was thinking about changing it. "Well, beautiful people, we need to wrap this up. This was par for the course for a first session. Aside from the grief and mourning needing to be worked through, other dynamics at play here also require exploration." Naomi eyed everyone but Ruth as she spoke.

Indeed, not very professional. She'll try to do better.

Ruth and Mallory stood, ready to leave. This dull but deep magenta shading emanated around Mallory for quick seconds before disappearing. It suggested Mallory experienced the negative vibes of red or blue energies. Perhaps the anger or impatience of red, but Naomi believed Mallory harnessed more of the burdens and depressive thoughts tied to bluer hues. Understandable.

Naomi stood as well.

The menfolk appeared hesitant to leave, as both remained seated a few seconds longer. Jeff chuffed a light chuckle as he looked over at his son. "Well, man, I guess we'd best prepare for departure, too. The ladies seem eager to call it a day."

Todd smiled at his father. "Yeah, I guess we'd better."

Father and son shared another look before rising from their seats.

Naomi wished she knew what that look meant.

"Okay then." Naomi looked up at Jeff, extending a hand to him. "Same time next week?"

His curt shake possessed a solid grip. "Next week."

Eyes on Ruth, Naomi invited confirmation for the next session.

Ruth nodded with an I-guess-so shrug.

"Next week, Doctor Alexander." Mallory's smile spread too wide.

"Todd?" Naomi asked.

Todd gestured toward the others. "Well, I'll be in the car with them..."

Varying degrees of titters followed (Todd included).

Naomi preferred ending her sessions on a positive note, but somehow this rendered a hollow victory. She let it pass. "That'll work." She headed back to her desk. "You all take care. Be safe."

The Winthrops echoed assorted goodbyes and were gone.

Naomi sat at her desk in her still-considered-strange ergonomic chair (the thing *was* ugly, but it helped with her posture). She wanted to reach for the flask in the back of her desk drawer, but dismissed the thought. Although the session with the Winthrops (well, *one* Winthrop in particular) gave her enough cause, she was on a new tip nowadays.

Or trying to be, anyway.

In response to a comment by former patient Rick Phillips, Naomi was doing her best to limit how often and how much she drank. So instead of going for her flask, she opened a cabinet door of the credenza behind her and retrieved a bottle of raspberry-flavored tea. She was a regular hot tea drinker (varied herbals a delight), either during session or while reviewing a case, so this tea indulgence was simply a new take. Naomi guzzled thirstily, wondering how Rick was doing. She kept regular contact with him, and since she planned to visit him in the coming weeks, she guessed she'd find out then. Her visits with him, although still exploratory, were also becoming these relaxed exchanges, more caring and friendship based.

The raspberry and tea flavors mingled and danced in her mouth with a refreshing jolt. It wasn't necessary beverages be cold; Naomi preferred bottled waters and juices at room temperature. Her thirst slated, Naomi focused on summarizing the Winthrops' session for their file.

Someone knocked on the door.

"Yes?"

The door opened. Dr. Imani Greene, Naomi's resident physician in training, poked her head in. She smiled as she held her spring twists back from her face with one hand. "Willette Hargrove's file is ready, Doctor Alexander. And Vivian Phillips left a message for you to call."

Speaking of Rick... "Thanks, Imani. I know you'll be glad when you can email me or leave a voicemail, huh?"

Imani stepped into the office further. "No. I like that you require us to interact with you. Digital communication has its place, but for our line of work, interpersonal skills need to be worked on at every opportunity."

Imani reminded Naomi of her daughter, Leslie. "I at times think so."

"I'm on the Masterson case study, but if there's something else..."

Naomi imparted a full smile. "Are you campaigning for the Best Resident Assistant of the Year award, Doctor Greene?"

Imani smiled back. "Nah, Doctor Alexander. I just—" She shrugged.

Naomi snickered in fun. "I may have another task or three for you, but I have another resident to help share the load, so I can't ignore him, now can I?" She patted a folder on her desk. "But I'll tell you what. Let me wrap up the session summary for the Winthrops, and you can draft a preliminary profile for me to review. How's that?"

Imani shook her head at a considering pace. "Doctor Alexander, we're not supposed to..." she trailed off, eyes on Naomi with eager anticipation despite the cautionary reminder.

Naomi gazed back, her expression calm.

Imani returned a big smile. "Thanks, Doctor Alexander!"

"Not a problem." She wished Imani could address her by her first name, but protocol dictated otherwise (for now, anyway). "Now, go. Masterson awaits." Naomi shooed her out of her office.

She returned to the Winthrop file before the door closed.

Naomi relied on her medical training for therapeutic approaches, but psychiatrists also utilized select manuals to support or guide their process. Three sources were always in her reference rotation: the *Diagnostic & Statistical Manual of Mental Disorders* (DSM); the *Applied Behavior Analysis Advanced Guidebook: A Manual for Professional Practice* (ABA); and handbooks or volumes published by the American Psychological Association (APA). She kept copies in both offices. Naomi considered some of that reference reading now.

Grief. An emotion with such elusive properties, the boundaries defining its manifestation were so obscure as to be nonexistent. Unlike depression or post-traumatic stress disorder (PTSD), the clinical arena for grief had its starting point and then just kind of...dissolved. Grief, however, was a valid emotion, and Naomi used her firsthand knowledge of it when trying to help patients. Not that she no longer grieved herself, but she'd come a ways—it depended on the day. Some days she'd come further than others, but there were still days grief held her in its crippling grip as much as it did moments after those policemen arrived at her house five years ago. As it did bedside in a little boy's nautical-themed bedroom eight years before that.

Naomi stared at the Winthrop file data for some seconds, lost in thought, before straightening her shoulders and allowing the words on the page to make sense again.

Contained grief reflected aspects of depression and PTSD in that the symptoms lingered. The symptoms, if left unresolved, could become protracted then traumatic, leading to complicated grief. Complicated grief could result from normal bereavement, in which case the sufferer needed more than the usual comfort and support.

Naomi was reasonably sure Jeff Winthrop was experiencing some form of complicated grief, but only more sessions would bring this to light. If indeed complicated grief was the case for Jeff, it would be atypical. Jeff's records didn't indicate any history of depression or anxiety disorders.

Unlike the APA and the recent-edition DSM, the ABA manual didn't officially establish a standard diagnosis of complicated grief. Still, Naomi entertained the idea of utilizing traumatic grief therapy for the Winthrops, using cognitive-behavioral and interpersonal techniques. This approach should mitigate Jeff's (and thus the family's) trauma and relieve stress, but Naomi remained somewhat iffy on the whole imaginal exposure part of the therapy with this case.

If Jeff was having hallucinatory experiences, Naomi needed to find out. This particular PTSD symptom would most likely stem from Julia's death being premature.

Naomi continued writing notes on her legal pad for another twenty minutes. She rarely used her digital recorder (go figure). When she finished, she reviewed what she'd written and shook her head.

It all sounded good on paper. And maybe she'd rely primarily on her interpersonal techniques. Because when all was said and done, Naomi still had her common-sense diagnosis: Jeff had some issues, yes, but basically, Ruth had to go. No in-depth analysis needed. Naomi, however, needed to treat this family for their grief as well as move them along to that realization.

"...And why are you my wife, Ruth?"

Naomi finished the file prep work; she could give it to doctor's-pet Imani. She stood and surveyed her office, taking in the décor.

Cranberry? Grays and blues? Something old-fashioned? Something sleeker and more contemporary?

She put her hands on her hips, trying to decide. She'd conducted her session with the Winthrops while considering a change to her décor, suspecting the two were related.

"I've had basic psychology... yellow represents cowardice."

Naomi scoffed and took her hands off her hips. She picked up the Winthrop file and headed out the door.

The yellow furniture and everything else stays.

Forget her.

Chapter 5

Perchance to Dream

He existed in that weird state of being where you know you're dreaming, but reality remains a remote possibility. Julia's essence enveloped him, and he welcomed it with his heart and soul.

Jeff's eyes fluttered restlessly behind their lids.

This was more memory than dream. Being a memory somehow lent itself to being more real than anything. He'd experienced these moments to some extent. Was he experiencing them yet again?

This wasn't déjà vu (he didn't speak French, anyway). No, his senses were alive and responding to the fleeting tactile presence of his wife. On some level, Jeff knew Julia was not there with him, couldn't be there with him—but she was.

It is some years ago (sixteen, seventeen years), but it is now.

Jeff sits across from Julia in their favorite lunch café. He has his vinaigrette salad with feta cheese before him. She has her single slice of pepperoni pizza and a bottled water for them to share. Iris, vanilla, and rose elements tickle his nostrils. Despite the multiple aromas present, Jeff smells nothing else; even the vinegar in his salad can't compete with her scent. A tight black knot of grief threatens to rise from the pit of his stomach as the part of him that knows his wife is gone tries to claim itself, but Jeff won't have it.

What he will have, though, is this time with her. He remembers this particular day, having lunch in the café downtown. He remembers and moves toward reliving it.

Jeff's eyelids constantly fluttered in his memory-dream state. He shifted his body, now lying prone on the bed, and subconsciously reached down between himself and the mattress for the part of him that ached (and stiffened) with remembering Julia...

She plucks a slice of pepperoni from the melted cheese of her pizza and puts it in his mouth, allowing the pressure of her index finger to rest momentarily on his tongue. Her eyes lock with his as she finally allows him to chew the meat sample. Love and desire sparkle through the caramel-brown of her irises. This daring and open side of her negated the need for porn in their home (although they indulged in viewing some from time to time). In their bedroom, he knew how to lay it down; she knew how to as well. His response to her, as always, is instant. However, they were in a public place, so her intentions intrigue him, adding to his excitement. With his eyes, Jeff asks: "Where? How?"

Julia smiles. Years ago, Jeff remembered her laughing instead, but it is now, not then (right?).

Jeff's eyelids ceased their continuous flutter long enough for him to sigh heavily with a grin. His breathing quickened as his eyelids began their dream dance once again.

Jeff surveys the other patrons. Their animated conversations are in-audible. When he returns his attention to their table, Julia no longer sits across from him. He searches to find her at the rear of the café, directly across from the restrooms in the alcove leading to a back stairway. Jeff remembers only stealing a kiss with her in that alcove in another memory. This time, there will be much more.

He doesn't remember getting up, but Jeff now stands before Julia, doing his best to keep his face from cracking from the pull of his broad smile. The smile hurts some, but he can't help himself; he's so happy to see her. He's missed her so. Julia takes his left hand. When her fingers graze his ring finger, she looks down at it and raises his hand between them, examining the ring. Jeff looks, too, fully expecting to see his old wedding band but not surprised to find the new one in its place.

He returns his gaze to Julia, offering apology without words. She shakes her head and places his old wedding band (*her* wedding band) on his finger. His new band fades into nothingness as she slides her ring into place, and a tiny tingle of rightness travels through him in tandem with the sound of the faintest click. *"Come with me,"* Jeff hears Julia say in his head. She squeezes his hand and begins pulling him toward the exit doors at the rear of the alcove.

The cooler air in the stairwell chills his sweat-dampened skin, and he wonders if it's even possible to feel either hot or cold when you're dreaming (*if* he's dreaming). He follows his wife up, up, up to the top of the concrete stairwell, pausing before doors leading to the roof. The fans in the air duct blow forcefully (the fan blades' circular spin is almost hypnotic), but all is eerily quiet despite that. He looks back at the spiral of stairs. He is surprised by how wide the steps are, even more surprised they're now carpeted.

Julia moves behind him and encircles his waist from behind. She kisses his back as she hugs him, and all thoughts of the stairs evaporate. Julia trails a hand up his back before palming his bare scalp (a move all too familiar to him), and Jeff loses it. Turning around in her embrace, he lifts his wife and holds her to him. It is like holding the mist of heavy fog. She is there, but not there—and Jeff doesn't care. He desires responding to and enjoying the "there" that Julia is. His mouth finds hers, and her kiss leaves him breathless. Her lips are icy cold, yet her tongue *melts on his like cotton candy. Jeff holds Julia to him, content to kiss her in the stairwell forever.*

Still holding himself, Jeff shifted to lie on his left side. Tears streamed from his right eye, across the bridge of his nose, onto the pillow supporting his head.

Julia begins breaking their kiss, and Jeff resists, but Julia is stronger than him now (much stronger), and their lips part. As Jeff catches his breath, his wife grips the front of his shirt and pulls him to her as she backs toward the wall. Leaning against the wall, she unbuttons her blouse. Julia is braless, and he takes his visual fill. The nipples of her small but shapely breasts seem to wink at him, and his erection strains against his clothing. Jeff lowers to indulge in his wife's titties, tasting each bud before nipping her neck and shoulders, then moving back to her nipples again, all the while breathing in her familiar fragrance.

He hears Julia's moans of pleasure in his head and reaches down to undo the jeans she'd been wearing—to find her nude below the waist. Jeff looks down between their bodies, gazing lazily at her purple-polished toes. Julia uses a hand under his chin to lift his head and return his gaze to hers. "Now, Jeff," she whispers in his head. She lifts *a leg and wraps it around his hip. Wasting no time, Jeff releases his hardness and enters her.*

Jeff turned onto his back, his face calm, his body still. Only the rhythmic rise and fall of his chest meant life—now accompanied by the newly forming but faint smile creasing his lips.

The pleasure of her kiss pales compared to being inside her. She feels so good, too good—and it is over before they get going good (a rarity for him). Julia, however, is not at all surprised. She strokes his back as Jeff leans in, holding her, once again trying to catch his breath. "I miss you, baby," she says in Jeff's head. He misses her too, but he can't speak. *Grief is reclaiming him, and his heart hurts. His heart hurts...*

Jeff's eyes popped open. His breathing flowed in quick spurts, as if awakening from a nightmare, but his dream (memory?) was quite the opposite.

He checked the digital clock on his nightstand: 3:39 p.m. Not a nightmare, but the most vivid and exquisite of daydreams. Jeff rubbed a hand across his chest, trying to soothe the abstract, symbolic pain there: not a literal, physical pain, but pain, nonetheless.

His breathing steadied, Jeff swung his legs over and sat on the side of the bed. He smiled, realizing the wetness in his pants didn't come from his bladder. "Dammit, Julia," he whispered. Then (at a near whisper, feeling more alone than he'd ever felt in his life): "I love you." Jeff leaned forward with his elbows on his thighs and held his head in his hands. He wanted to pray, but words failed him. So, he sat there, determined not to weep, trying to get himself together.

He'd told himself he would not lie down again. Told himself he would stop revisiting these memories. The first time he lay down for a nap and dreamed of Julia so vividly, he thought it was a fluke. That was ten months ago, with several "flukes" since, such that the memory lane dreams were addictive. The dreams (or whatever they were) didn't feel like dreams or flukes, anyway. God help him; they felt...*real.* It was like traveling back in time—no time machine necessary.

With a sigh, Jeff stood. He needed to change his pants, at least. He didn't feel like showering (or much of anything else). More than anything, he wanted to lie back down and drift off again. He didn't experience Julia every time, but he always hoped. And the times that he did? More than worth it.

Jeff went to his chest of drawers and retrieved a pair of carpenter shorts from the bottom drawer. The security system signaled door entry as he gathered the rust-orange shorts in his fist. Given the time of day, it had to be Ruth. Jeff opened his top drawer, pulled out a pair of boxer-briefs, and hurried to their en suite.

He took his time in the bathroom, hoping Ruth was only home for a quick minute. However, hearing sounds from the TV in their bedroom, his heart sank. Resigned to having to interact with his present wife, Jeff exited the bathroom.

She was sitting on her side of their bed with her back against the headboard, clad only in her stockings and full slip. Her fuchsia St. John knit dress draped the arm of the reading chair in the corner. Her matching Via Spiga pumps were on the floor, halfway under the bed.

He didn't want to, but Jeff went over to Ruth and placed a hello peck on her lips. "Early day?"

Ruth, her eyes on the screen, languidly bobbed her head. "Something like that."

"Okay." He headed toward the bedroom door (and freedom).

"Jeffy?"

Cringing, Jeff paused in his step but kept moving. "Uh-huh?"

"Wait a minute, please." She silenced the television by shutting it off instead of muting the sound. "I want to talk to you for a second. Short and sweet, honest."

Jeff paused, tension coiling in his lower back. "About?" He waited reluctantly, his back to her. He didn't want to talk right now. Regardless of how *short*. Irrespective of how *sweet*.

"Well, *you*, for starters." She probably wasn't even aware of it, but the "sweetness" was gone already.

"Ruth—"

"Come on, Jeff. Just hear me out, dammit!"

He snapped his body around to face her. The afternoon light coming through the bow window made the pear-olive tints in her eyes sparkle. In terms of her looks, yeah, in a conventional sense, Ruth would be considered "fine."

"That got your attention, huh? Well, now that I have it, I want to know what's up with all the sleeping. I know you just woke up; it's all over your face. Been sleeping hard, too. Why're you sleeping so much again?"

"How do you know how much I sleep or whatever? You're hardly here. And what difference does it make, anyway?"

"It's an insult to me, Jeff."

"What?"

"An insult."

Jeff frowned. Women drew the strangest conclusions to shit sometimes. "How is my sleeping, napping, whatever, an 'insult' to you?"

Ruth stared at the blank TV screen before responding. She rested her gaze on him. "Because it means you're not moving on."

Jeff waited. He knew where she was going (she went there often enough), but since he didn't want to have this discussion as it was anyway, he waited for her to continue. The more she talked, the less he'd have to.

Seeing he would not be immediately forthcoming with dialogue, Ruth went on: "You're still depressed over your first wife, Jeff."

"How come you avoid saying her name?" He worked to keep his rising anger down.

She frowned defensively, but he also recognized angry awareness. "I don't avo—"

"Yes, you do. You rarely, if ever, say, 'Julia.' It's: 'your first wife' or 'their mother.' Why do you do that?"

"I..." She looked away, gazing at the dark screen of their television as if wanting to escape right through it.

Fine with him. "Say her name," Jeff challenged. He wanted to turn the tables on this discussion to shut it down.

She turned to him, the green in her eyes dulling and fading, declaring the anger behind them. "The *lovely* Julia Èkerie Simms Winthrop." Her statement dripped with the scorn and jealousy he'd been listening to regularly from her since... Well, since they married.

Jeff came right back at her. "You're damn right." He turned away. If he hadn't, he'd have stepped to her with physical harm in mind—something altogether *not* his character. The woman, this situation he'd found himself in with her, sometimes stimulated the darker side in him (and it bothered him terribly).

"I'm not finished, Jeff."

He turned back to her with a chuckle. "Oh, but I am."

"Will you put your guard down about her and just listen to me for one fu- flippin' minute?"

"Shoulda went with that first one—it's closer to the real you."

If possible, the faded pear-olive (crocodile?) ice of her eyes hardened (and, if not crocodile, certainly some other green-eyed monster).

He couldn't have cared less.

"Jeff..." Ruth shook her head slowly with somberness.

The sudden change in her demeanor was almost comical, but Jeff remained stone-faced. As usual, and so, as expected, this discussion wasn't getting them anywhere.

She continued: "All I'm saying is that maybe you should return to your art. Sculpt again. Paint again. Something, anything to help you—"

"Help me what?"

She blew her cheeks out with an airy but curt breath. "Jeff..."

"No. Help me *what*, Ruth?" The knot of grief in his stomach tightened. "Help me what? Get over Julia?"

Ruth stood. "Yes!"

Although not toe-to-toe, they stared at each other across the ten to fifteen feet separating them.

A tinge of Guerlain's Shalimar wafted into the room.

Ruth spoke first. "Yes, Jeff. Yes. I've been a good mother to your children. I care for them as if I'd birthed them myself. I try to be a good wife to you. You need to do your part."

Jeff studied Ruth's face for any reaction to the scent. There was none. *Am I losing it?* He released the tension in his neck and shoulders with a sigh. "You're right, Ruth. You've been good to my kids. I thank you for that—seriously."

She appeared to be waiting for him to continue. She raised a hand to the back of her neck and massaged it.

"Listen, I'll get back into something. I don't know what, but something. I don't know when, but soon." Jeff paused, willing his anger down as he stepped in her direction. "But I offer this piece of advice to you, Ruth..." Rage and pain coursed his insides as she glared back at him with this rude indifference that only made him angrier. "Don't you *ever* try to force me to put Julia out of my mind or out of my heart." He paused again, this time willing his grief back along with the anger. It was never a good time for him after the memory-dreams. He gazed out their bedroom window, taking calming breaths. Calmer (but not by much), he shifted focus back to his current wife, a forever truth rolling from his lips. "...The first is improbable...because the second—is *impossible*."

Pain at his words registered on Ruth's face as her mouth slackened and her gaze softened. It didn't last, however. Defiance claimed her buttercream features, moving from the lines in her wide forehead to the jut of her chin. She showed a smile, clearly forced. "Okay, thanks."

"I do love you, Ruth," he felt compelled to add.

Ruth returned a clipped nod. "Okay." She glanced over at the clock on his night table. "I'm supposed to show the Campbell home in an hour."

"Ruth…"

"It's fine, Jeff."

"Maybe sculpting."

She scoffed, "Okay," while reaching for the fuchsia dress on the chair, slipping it over her head.

Jeff watched with little interest as the dress slid fittingly over her form.

The aroma of Shalimar lingered.

"Well, you do still play piano from time to time; that's something."

It was Jeff's turn to scoff. "Yeah, I guess." He left it alone. If Thom, his *agent*, understood enough to back off, give him the space and time he needed, why couldn't she (as his wife)?

Ruth slid her foot into one shoe. "In the book of Isaiah, it says: 'He giveth power to the faint; and to them that have no might he increaseth strength.'" She slipped her foot into the other pump.

Jeff recoiled internally but turned the edges of his mouth upward, teeth showing. "Thanks."

She approached him, planting a kiss on his cheek as she passed him. "You're welcome. See you later."

Jeff watched her exit the room. "Okay. Good luck."

She called over her head from the stairs: "Thank you."

He soon heard the alarm reset, the front door close. He didn't realize he was holding his breath until releasing it upon hearing her car start.

Jeff listened to the silence. He closed his eyes. "Julia?" He half-waited for some noise or draft of air or, he didn't know, *something*…

The concentration of Shalimar didn't increase, but it didn't diminish, either. Jeff sat on the bed, knowing he wasn't crazy (yet) but afraid to think too much about what was going on. He rubbed his eyes and reclined onto the mattress, his face toward the ceiling and his feet on the floor. He remained that way for several minutes, thinking about the exchange with Ruth.

She thinks he's depressed, and maybe he is, but that's not why he sleeps so much. Sleeping grants him an escape of sorts, yes, but sleeping also provided an even better benefit. His daytime naps usually result in him having those memory-dreams with Julia. They seem so real to him; it's scary—but in a *good* way. He's with her, and it's as if the last three years never happened.

The erotic experiences with Julia were potent, palpable.

Even if he is depressed... Well, depression is *not* why he sleeps.

Jeff rolled onto his side, propping his head on his hand. He gazed at the thin streams of light coming through the closed wood blinds, thinking of the pictures he kept in an envelope taped under the bottom of the third drawer of his chest: nine of his favorite shots of Julia. All of them merely natural photos of Julia, but whenever he pored over those pics, he became just as aroused as if they were the raciest, most explicit pictures of her he'd ever seen.

Jeff grinned bashfully to himself.

Until the regular occurrences of the erotic memory-dreams, he used to steal away and masturbate like a schoolboy while viewing the pictures. He'd listen to different renditions of "Your Precious Love" while he did it—transcending into his own version of memory-dreams of being with Julia. What he wouldn't give to just...

The urge to weep settled in his throat, and Jeff swallowed the urge down. He rolled onto his back again and viewed the ceiling, wanting very much to go back to sleep (perchance to dream).

The scent of vanilla and iris and roses still called to him. He whispered, "What are you doing to me, Jules?" into the room, then ran a hand across his scalp, feeling the prickly beginnings of stubble there. Ruth wanted him to grow it out, but he didn't want to do it. He figured he wouldn't look too bad since he had good hair and— "Sorry, Jules, I mean, *'softer roots.'*" He smiled at correcting himself (and missed his wife that much more).

Julia would always admonish him, Mallory, or Todd, if they used the term *good hair*. She'd say: *"What exactly does that mean? Okay, some people have hair with straighter or softer roots, but if it's dirty and damaged, so what? I'd rather run my fingers over the healthy kinks of tightly coiled roots than have my hand caught up and grossed out by a soft mess of unhealthy, nasty hair. You get me? We all have so-called 'good' hair when we take care of it."* Use of the term *good hair* soon faded around their household.

Jeff sat up. He could lie around and think about Julia all day. Many days, that was all he did. But Ruth was right; he needed to start somewhere. He considered taking one quick peek at Julia's pictures hidden in his chest of drawers but pushed the thought out of his mind (somewhat annoyed he had to hide the pictures, to begin with). He needed to get his creative juices flowing, needed to get his body moving and his mind moving forward.

He needed to try, anyway.

Jeff trudged to the bathroom (the scent of Shalimar didn't follow him) and splashed cold water on his face. The cold splash helped sharpen his senses. When he returned to the bedroom, Julia's scent remained, tantalizing him. He left the bedroom, marching decisively toward the stairs leading up to the fourth level of the house.

Jeff first noticed the heat when he reached the top floor. He hurried back down to the third level, turned on the air for the upper zones, and then returned to level four.

There were only two rooms on this floor. To Jeff's right: storage. To his left, the artist studio: his art room, music room—his leave-me-alone room, where his creativity flowed freely with keystroke or brushstroke or rasp-chisel.

At least, it used to flow freely.

Jeff paused in front of its entrance, gazing at the vintage concert poster of the legendary Sam Cooke on the door. In his mind, Sam was the only true King of Soul. The poster was from one of Sam Cooke's shows in 1961. It was Julia's idea to place the poster on the door leading to his art-slash-music studio. An excellent (and inspiring) idea.

Lately, he'd only come to this room to play music (and think about Julia). He'd been playing more reggae than anything recently; stuff by Jimmy Cliff or Freddie Notes often in the rotation—especially Cliff's "Many Rivers to Cross." Today, though, he intended a fresh approach.

Jeff closed the door behind him. Having left the blinds open, he concentrated his gaze on the scenic view of trees and rooftops outside, tiny wafts of linseed oil offering its atmospheric contribution. It depended on his mood, the mood of the piece, but linseed oil remained a staple as either binder or vehicle for his oil paintings. He most times used linseed as a binder. Linseed oil was combustible, though, so he had lots of ventilation outlets installed on this side. Jules always appreciated the natural and pure nuttiness of the scent. He did, too.

No one else was allowed in his artist studio—except Julia.

He didn't know where to start. Paint? Sculpt? Play piano?

Jeff stared toward the opposite end of his art-music room (and the art that wasn't much happening anymore), in the direction of the covered blank canvases of various sizes stacked and leaning against the wall, at easels devoid of their purpose. One of those canvases captured his initial experimentation with encaustic panting; a foray abruptly halted in the wake of—

Play. That would be a good start. Ruth seemed to think he played more than he did, but today he would play. He'd play piano. Play what? Jeff didn't know. He moved to his stacks of CDs and searched through them (searching for what; he didn't know). Todd and Mallory used apps on their cellphones for music, but he was old-school, preferring albums and CDs here in the studio, at least. And the return of albums and record players indicated old-school remained legit.

Finally, he came across something he wanted to play.

Julia loved music by Brenda Russell. Jeff closed the blinds and drew the room-darkening curtains (another of Julia's good ideas), casting the room in shadowy hues of blackish gray. He sat on his piano bench, poised his hands above the keys, and closed his eyes.

He began with "If Only for One Night." Twenty minutes later, he finished with "Piano in the Dark," tears streaming.

He didn't hear the phone ringing.

It was a start.

Chapter 6

Two for Two

Mallory hung up the phone with a huff and reached for a piece of gum, stuffing the stick in her mouth and chewing with irritation. She knew her father was home; he was always home since Mommy died. She hoped he wasn't sleeping again, but knew it was likely: seems he slept all the time now.

Worry furrowed the lines of her brow. Their sessions with Dr. Alexander were fine, but she wanted immediate help for her father. Todd, too, seemed as if he needed a direct intervention of some sort. Most times, he was his old self, but Mallory knew her brother, so she knew when he was pretending to be okay—and he seemed to do that more and more.

"Here, Mallory."

Mallory startled before turning around to face Valeda Gaskins. Valeda was a senior at their high school and doing her second work-study term. Mallory liked her, but the girl could be stuck-up sometimes.

As if hearing her thoughts, Valeda handed a blue folder toward her and flung her long black weave in true California-girl style. "And Ms. Loebel said to cc Mister Wilkes on the last form letter."

Mallory accepted the folder from her coworker. "First, she said *not* to cc 'im." She enjoyed being a work-study, but some days...

"You know how she does." Valeda started away but turned back. "You going to the game tonight?"

"I doubt it. I have to revise my research paper and finish my bibliography for Ms. Connelly's class."

"Bibliography." Valeda sucked her teeth, curling her lip with confused disgust. "Why do they need all of that?"

Mallory twitched her shoulder with indifference. She wasn't trying to go to the game, anyway. It was too early for the games to matter.

Valeda shrugged, too. This time, she did walk away.

Mallory turned back to her desk. She plugged her earphones back in her ears and turned up the volume on her cellphone. "Aqua Boogie" by Parliament Funkadelic filled her ears. Along with her music app, she'd loaded several tracks from her parents' music collection: stuff her parents had them listening to since she and Todd were little. What was interesting for her now, though: how much of today's music sampled so much of the old stuff. Her father could go on and on about that point—long after she and Todd conceded—and long after their mother told him to let it go. Grinning and shaking her head, she giggled warmly to herself with the fond memory.

She brought her most recent form letter up on her computer and started applying Ms. Loebel's edits. She'd just finished adding Mr. Wilkes as a cc when she noticed the line blinking on her desk phone. She removed one earphone and picked up the receiver. "Bureau of Ways and Means. How may I direct your call?"

"Mallory, this is Ruth."

Just the sound of her voice made Mallory uncomfortable, obliterating all that warm fuzziness of moments ago. "Uh-huh."

"A 'hello' would be nicer, Mallory."

"Is my dad okay?"

"As far as his physical well-being, yes."

Mallory didn't respond. She was not discussing her father without Dr. Alexander around.

"I wanted to talk to you about some of the activity in your savings account. I noticed two withdrawals this mon—"

"Why are you all in my money?" Mallory did her best to keep her voice down, but she looked behind her, checking if anyone was within earshot. Seeing no one, she turned back around and lowered her voice. "How do you even know—?"

"I've been added to the account."

"What? Why?"

"Your father thought it was best."

"That's a lie. Why didn't he say anything to me? Don't I have to agree or something?"

"You're not of age, so technically, no."

"Is he still on it?" Nausea curdled her stomach.

"Yes."

"So, why *you*? You know what? Never mind. I'll ask him later."

"That's fine. Now, about those withdraw—"

Mallory disconnected her.

She sat there, not knowing what to do, waiting with bated breath for the line to ring again. This could not be happening. Ruth having access to her accounts, sucked royally. She rested her head in her hands, shaking her head in disbelief. Why would her father do that?

As expected, the line rang again. Mallory didn't want to answer, but she bit her bottom lip and lifted the receiver anyway; it might not be her stepmother. Mallory eyed the number: it was. "Bureau of Ways and Means," she huffed.

"For someone wanting to be grown, that was very childish, Mallory. I expected as much if I'd called your cell. But calling you at work yielded nothing different."

You also figured I'd see it was you on my cell—and probably wouldn't have answered.

Tears welled in Mallory's eyes. She started to disconnect her again. Instead: "What do you want, Ruth?"

"An answer to my question."

"You never asked one."

"What were those two withdrawals for? You have an allotted spending allowance, so explain yourself."

Mallory stared at the form letter she was working on. "It's my money, Ruth. My father didn't place any restrictions on how I use it." Maybe she'd go to Todd's game after all.

"That was a mistake," Ruth replied in a tone suggesting she was conversing with a mentally challenged child of eight or nine.

"Leave me alone, Ruth." It was a simple request spoken calmly. She didn't whine or sound bratty.

"Oh, I can't do that..." Her stepmother's reply held that same teacher-to-idiot tone. Mallory could almost see Ruth shaking her head with a mocking tsk. "I can't because, well, because you all need structure. 'Children, obey your parents in everything, for this pleases the Lord.' Colossians three, verse twenty."

Mallory wished she could give her a comeback à la Dr. Alexander. The *last thing* this woman provided was structure.

"I'm waiting, Mallory."

You can keep on waiting. The urge to cry welled in her chest again. She regularly used her money to purchase flowers for her mother's headstone. But that wasn't anybody's business but hers. Neither her dad nor Todd knew about it. It was her thing. And she knew any mention of her mother...could make things worse.

Mallory didn't want to answer Ruth—not even to offer a simple appeasement, so she didn't. "I'm at work, Ruth. I gotta go." She hung up before hearing Ruth's reply.

She sat at her desk, breathing hard and fast. The form letter on her monitor displayed at 150 percent, but Mallory still couldn't read it well: tears blurred her vision.

She reached blindly for her cellphone and turned it off.

The effects of Hurricane Liam moving through the Southeast chilled the September air as dusk descended farther up the Atlantic, but Mallory didn't hurry to arrive home. She casually strolled the two blocks from the bus stop, gazing every so often through the windows of houses in her neighborhood as she passed them. She got a weird kick out of seeing how people decorated their homes, how they lived their lives.

Any other time, she would have been home much sooner. Today, she did all her homework at work. She had every intention of going home and straight to bed. She didn't want to talk—not even to Todd (so it was good he had a game).

From the corner of their block (on Wells Brown Place), Mallory made out her father's black Audi Q7 parked in front of their corner-lot home. It was often in the same spot (he rarely left the house these days). His metallic-white Mercedes Benz S550 was covered and parked closer to the middle of their block. Ruth's champagne-brown Lexus (personal tag: RELRTH9) sat parked across the street.

She didn't want to talk to anyone, but Mallory recognized the lone figure sitting on their front steps.

The figure (wearing an A-shirt and jeans) stood and then yanked very low-hanging jeans up over his butt before leaning against the porch railing: Todd.

He shouldn't have been home yet. Todd stared at their mother's memorial tree. His posture alone told her something was wrong.

Putting her issues aside for the moment, she quickened her pace.

When she reached the house, she paused on the sidewalk at the bottom of the steps, staring up at her brother. She slung her backpack off her shoulder, letting one strap slide down her arm to her hand. From the way Todd rhythmically drummed a clenched fist against the railing beside him, his anger practically shrouded him. He was barefoot, too: pissed for sure. "Why you out here?"

Todd looked down at her. He shook his head, frowning his annoyance. "What, you brought your ghetto-card home from school?"

"Don't take it out on me." She started up the steps. "Isn't that how most of your friends talk?"

"Whatever, Mal." He directed his attention down the street.

Mallory tried again. "Aren't you cold?" She dropped her bag to the porch and rubbed Todd's arm; goose bumps dotted his flesh.

Todd shook his head slowly. They stayed on the porch that way for several seconds.

"Where's Daddy?"

He scoffed, keeping his gaze on the activity in the next block. "Sleep."

Mallory huffed her aggravation. "Again? Damn." She shouldn't have been surprised, but she always hoped.

"It's all he does, man. Shit! I'm *tired* o' this!" He blew out a breath of embittered, angry air.

Mallory watched her brother closely. She gradually stopped rubbing his arm. The muscles there tensed. "What happened, Todd? Why are you out here like this? Shouldn't you be at the game?"

Shaking his head, he grunted low with frustration. With each labored breath, the air he held in his cheeks meant he was trying not to cry.

"Where's Ruth?"

Todd continued surveying the activity happening down the street.

Mallory figured it didn't matter.

"Somethin' happening with Divinia?"

Todd shook his head and sat on the steps again.

"Did Ruth h—?"

He shook his head again, vehemently, before she could finish.

She sat next to him. "Anything I can do?"

He shrugged. "Doubt it."

Probably why he didn't call her when it went down. Mallory waited. Todd didn't talk much as it was. Now that he was upset, he would be even less communicative.

"Whatever it is, maybe Daddy—"

Todd turned to her, wide-eyed. "You're joking, right?"

Saddened, she lowered her eyes. At least Ruth wasn't *at* him this time.

Their neighbors, Mr. and Mrs. Aislich, drove up in their maroon Toyota minivan and parked behind her dad's Audi. Mallory enjoyed living in a neighborhood of diverse races. She smiled and waved at Mrs. Aislich, who never failed with having her blonde hair pushed back with a wide headband. Mallory couldn't remember her hair being in any other style. Mrs. Aislich waved back and pointed at her husband. She made a funny gesture with her hand and covered her mouth with a giggle.

"Hi there, Mallory, Todd." Mr. Aislich looked over at his wife. "What're you doing, Suzanne?"

"Nothing, Jim. Come on."

"Hi, Mister Aislich," Mallory greeted. She thought Mr. Aislich had the sexiest blue eyes.

Todd waved his hello but otherwise remained silent.

The couple made their way up the steps and into their house.

More silence.

Mallory didn't know what to do or say.

Eyes still on the next block, Todd exhaled a single heavy breath. "Why're you so late?"

Mallory didn't hesitate. She didn't feel like talking at first, but now... "Because Ruth pissed me off, I did my school stuff at work instead."

Todd nodded his understanding and then shook his head. "Two for two," he uttered quietly.

Mallory waited.

"...She's pulling me off football, Mal."

"Who?" It was a dumb question; she knew that.

"Who you think?"

"But why?"

"Some bull about my asthma and grades."

"But—" Mallory paused to contain her own frustration, then started again. "But the coach, or school, will drop you from the team if your grades fall."

"Yeah, but only if below a 'C.'"

"So? You maintain a high 'B.' Besides, this is September; the school year's just starting."

"No shit."

Mallory ignored him. "And as far as your asthma, you've managed that fine, too." She gripped into her hair, tugging with both hands. "What is wrong with her?!" She wanted to hit something, or, better yet, *someone*—someone who sure did *their* fair share of hitting (but she'd been figuratively sworn to secrecy about that).

Todd seized her forearms. "Hold up, Sis. Chill-ax. I can't have both you and Dad on mental vacations." He held her forearms, his eyes searching hers.

She allowed him to lower her hands from her hair. "I'm fine. It's just—"

"Yeah, I know." He released her.

"What're we gonna do, Todd? How—?"

"*That*, I don't know."

"Are you going to talk to Daddy at all?"

"For what, Mal? He's just going to give in to her. He always does."

Mallory nodded, thinking about her situation regarding her bank account. "So, you think Daddy already knows about it?"

"If he doesn't, I'm sure she'll let him know his position on it."

"Daddy's not that bad, Todd."

"He didn't use to be. Now..." He shook his head.

"Yeah, *now*..." Mallory echoed. She didn't have any gum in her backpack (several new packs were in her room), but she stubbornly refused to bring a fingernail anywhere near her teeth.

"If she's not getting me one way, she's getting me another, I guess." Todd reached behind him, giving his lower back this quick, faint rub. He turned away, again checking out the activity one block over. "Oo-hoo! *Sweet:*...a sixty-seven."

Mallory turned in the direction of his gaze: a 1967 Pontiac Firebird (a pretty, silvery-bluish color) turned the corner. She nodded her agreement as sirens wailed somewhere in the distance.

Her thoughts turned mean but honest. "Wish they were coming for her." Mean, but honest.

Her brother grumbled a barbed laugh. "Yeah."

"Yeah."

They were silent again for a while. The sound of police sirens faded altogether, and she was weirdly disappointed the police *didn't* stop in front of their home.

The distinct redolence of leaves, wet from the previous night's rain, suffused the approaching darkness.

"...Her birthday would've been in a couple weeks." Todd's voice was low, but he wasn't angry anymore. "...Think Mommy's watching all this?"

"What?" She glanced at the potted Japanese Maple memorial.

"I really miss her, Mal." He paused, shaking his head with weighty thought. "Why did God take her so soon?" He kept his head turned away.

"I miss her, too, Todd." She didn't know how to answer his questions, though. She wasn't sure if their mother watched it all (although she believed she did), didn't know why God...had been so cruel.

Mallory tensed, waiting for her mother's scent to waft around her, which it sometimes did during times of stress.

Only the fitting aroma of wet autumn leaves greeted her.

Todd's brown eyes widened her way. "You smell 'at?"

Mallory startled. She sniffed the air. No jasmine. No vanilla. "Smell what?"

"Ronnie's frying chicken!"

"Ronnie B." lived on the next block. He traveled a lot for his job, but whenever he was home with his family, the delicious aroma of his fried chicken wings brought many in the neighborhood to his door. The recipe for his breaded seasoning remained a well-kept secret.

Todd stood, peering down at her. "Wanna piece?" He offered the weakest of smiles.

A taste of those wings might lift her spirits. "Sure. Why not?"

Todd hiked up his jeans and started inside the house. "Thanks for listenin'," he added over his shoulder and disappeared. Mallory heard his ascent on the hardwood stairs.

He brought back two golden-fried wings for her. She'd finished them over forty-five minutes ago, yet she remained on the porch steps. She took over Todd's job of watching the neighborhood in pensive silence.

Her father came to the door and said hello, but little else. Ruth never came to the door (that Mallory was aware of, anyway).

Dusk settled into night.

Mallory sat on her porch steps, thinking and praying, praying and thinking. She talked to her mother. She even talked to her father (in her mind). The period of solitude on the porch reinforced how much she sorely missed both her parents. She wasn't a baby, but at 16, she knew she wasn't quite woman enough to deal with Ruth head-on, either.

Tired of thinking, Mallory went in and up to bed.

Chapter 7

An Awful Untruth

As far as Naomi was concerned, amusement parks would be better off extending their daily operating period into late fall. With global warming, summer-like weather reached further into October and even November as the years went by. This October was no exception: a warm day without the humidity of summer. That alone made the entire visit to this local amusement park worthwhile.

Although she paid for her season passes to local amusement parks (like Kings Dominion) in the spring, she usually didn't use them until the September-October limited run period (carrying the whole "pays for itself in two visits" selling point to the extreme). She may have been wasting her money, but well, there it was. She liked to go at the end of the season, period. This trip to the park served as a date belatedly celebrating two September birthdays: hers and Dr. Kevin Oheneba's.

"You want funnel cake now?" Kevin's Ghanaian accent was faint but detectable.

Naomi got a furtive charge out of hearing him speak. "Not yet, but definitely, before we leave." She considered funnel cake an integral part of any amusement park experience.

He took her hand as they headed for the Kid-Town area. She got a kick out of watching the kids ride and the parents negotiate (for time away from the kiddie section). Naomi allowed Kevin's hand to swallow her own and smiled to herself. She'd been dating him for some time; even so, displays like holding hands felt new to her.

Naomi inhaled, taking in the theme-park bouquet of oil and grease, syrups and batters, fried somethings, and frozen other things. A gentle breeze brought with it the fragrance of mums and goldenrod; she breathed that in, too.

In that instant, losing Tyson hit her. Her breathing slowed with memories of him (of them), a faint soreness lined her throat, and Kevin's hand became a paperweight.

She released Kevin's hand.

Kevin stopped. "Everything all right?" His eyes conveyed a love and concern for her he had yet to express verbally.

"Uh-huh," Naomi lied. She offered a smile of reassurance.

He held her gaze. "You're sure?"

She nodded and clutched his elbow, turning him so that they continued their stroll.

They dawdled toward the kiddie-ride section in silence. Naomi observed the sights around her: from the changing colors of fall foliage (yellows, browns, reds, and oranges) to the changing props of the park's different themes. Despite the atmosphere of fun, her headspace edged toward an unsettled melancholy, a moody blue. Naomi didn't want that. She needed conversation, but introverts weren't natural conversation starters—not even psychiatrist ones (in non-medical settings).

Thankfully, Kevin broke the silence. "Are we still meeting Les for dinner tomorrow?"

She wasn't quite used to him using her nickname for her daughter. "Yeah. She said around five, so she'll have enough time to prepare for the showing." She couldn't help grinning.

"Aren't you the proud mama?"

"Indeed, I am."

"It's well deserved, Ms. Alexander."

"I think so." Naomi reclaimed Kevin's hand. She reflected fleetingly on the troubles she and her daughter battled through over the last few years, but pushed the thoughts aside, determined to enjoy her date.

"I look forward to seeing Missus Phillips's pictures."

"Yeah, me, too. It was Leslie's idea to combine the two art forms. Viv initially resisted, but once I got her in front of Leslie's sculptures, Viv had all kinds of photography ideas. It was therapeutic, I think."

"Still?"

Naomi nodded. "Still."

"But Mister Phillips is just—"

"Grief and mourning are not exclusively tied to the death of a person, Kevin." Naomi considered Viv and Rick Phillips's situation. She reflected on the Winthrop family's grief. She thought about her own grief—over the loss of many things; Jassiel's and Tyson's deaths were only starting points.

The two found a prime spot to watch families: a bench near a frozen-treat stand. Naomi watched as children begged parents for "blue," "red," or "green" cold treats of shaved ice and flavored syrup (always colors, never flavors).

Kevin nudged her arm, drawing her attention to a family of Asian descent, the little boy (about three or four) making it clear he was unhappy with a recent authoritative decision. Little fellow edged toward an on-the-ground tantrum, when the woman snatched the little boy's arm and sat him on the raised wall of the fountain with force, making the child's dark hair flop once as he landed hard. The man with them (his aura flickering a strong-willed, manipulative maroon) watched the exchange intently but otherwise didn't speak. The little boy exclaimed in pain once, looked at the man, and then instantly quieted.

Sitting and people-watching, scanning and profiling others during interaction (and non) in the park, reminded her much of attending flea markets and forming psychological portraits of the people selling—especially those selling their used, "like new" household effects. Neighborhood flea markets were the best in that regard. She couldn't remember her last time going to a flea market, though, and somewhere inside, she missed it.

Naomi observed Kevin as he watched the family. The initial concern in his expression softened as a smirk drew across the sharp features of his narrow but attractive carob-brown face.

"Oh, there will be some kickoff later, won't it?" he posed.

Amusement hooked her mouth. "You mean, 'there will be something kicking off' with that family later. And yes, I believe there will be. The father, if that's who he is, seems more the 'wait till we get home' type."

"Well, maybe if the little fella gets his act together—"

"For the father, it's already TLTB," Naomi mused.

Kevin's brows arched with puzzlement and amused inquiry. "T-L-T-B?"

"Uh-huh."

"Which is…?"

"Too Late and Too Bad."

"I see." He turned back to the couple, his eyes analyzing and speculating. "Well, the mother should be able to smooth things a bit."

She chuckled with amused cynicism. "He doesn't give a hey-non-ny-nonny about the woman."

Kevin looked at her. "Naomi!"

Naomi kept a straight face. "I'm telling you, he doesn't."

"How do you know these things? From being a therapist?" His gaze turned curious.

Naomi wasn't sure how to answer. Primarily, it did come from observing and analyzing behaviors. Occasionally, it came from her cursed flashes of truth (as in this case) or her cursed aura-flickers. "I guess you could say that."

"'Hey-nonny-nonny,'" Kevin quoted with a temperate chortle.

"Like it?"

"I'm getting used to it. Do you even know what it means?"

Naomi smirked at him, incredulous. "Please! Do you?"

"I've heard."

"Uh-huh."

"So that's your version of an expletive?"

"I like to use it here and there, but you know I access the real, or shall I say, *blue* ones when needed."

He squeezed her hand tighter, wearing a sloped grin. "Yes, you do."

Another child began crying on the opposite side of the fountain. "I think I've had my fill of the six-and-under section." Naomi stood. "I'm ready for my funnel cake now." She wasn't ready for it, but the melancholy was insistent—the funnel cake served as counter maneuver.

Several minutes later, Naomi strolled alongside Kevin, enjoying warm and sugary funnel cake: her favorite amusement park activity (well, that and the roller coasters). And it had to be amusement park funnel cake. She didn't want funnel cake made at home, the mall, or anywhere other than an amusement park. Simple. There existed an atmospheric element associated with the treat (related to big rides and huge theme props), making any other funnel cake experience unsavory, unenjoyable. Good funnel cake experience. Amusement parks. For Naomi, the two were interdependent.

Kevin scarfed his strawberry-topped curls within something close to seconds and now eyed her plate as they walked. "Can I have a bite?"

She shook her head. "I don't think so."

"Come on; all of mine is gone."

"Well, that's just TDB. One should always savor the fine culinary experience of funnel cake. It's a phenomenon, really."

"Funnel cake?"

"Funnel cake—and Baltimore coddies." She'd been craving the codfish-and-potato-cake delicacy, missing B-more (its sights and sounds, its...*feel*) a little. For her coddies, she liked a dollop of mustard but preferred rectangular butter crackers rather than saltines.

Kevin bent a brow with consideration. "Coddies, huh? Well, we can take a trip to your Charm City...or make some for dinner."

That wasn't a bad plan. "We'll see."

"Okay. And uh, 'T-D-B'?"

"Too Damn Bad!" Naomi laughed, suppressing the melancholy.

Kevin laughed, too: a gruff, pleasant sound. He reached for her upper arm, drawing her into a hug such that Naomi almost dropped her caky twists. "Hey! Watch the funnel cake, my brutha." She forced herself to relax into him and not tense up (as was her habit).

He guided her a step back, gazing down into her eyes. "I love you." His saddle-brown eyes conveyed sincerity.

It took milliseconds, but Naomi's heart skipped, and her breath caught at his words. "I love you, too."

And that...was a mistake.

Because she didn't love him. Not how he meant it. She liked Kevin well enough (his aura-flickers still consistently presented a steady, warm turquoise the rare times his aura appeared), but romantic love? Right now, that still belonged to Tyson. But what do you say when someone says that to you? Naomi considered *I love you, too,* as automatic a response to *I love you,* as *Fine, thanks* was to *How are you?* And, as easy as it would have been to pull the words back, to correct and clarify, she wasn't the Tinman; being no-nonsense still required discernment.

Kevin pulled her to him again and held her tighter. She tried to balance the funnel cake on her plate with her arms around him. When they parted, he pecked her lips.

Sealed with a kiss.

Annoyed with herself, Naomi disengaged from his embrace and took a bite of cake. The sweet coils were cold now; she offered the plate to Kevin, which he accepted. Naomi walked slightly ahead of him toward the Old-West themed area; it was roller coaster time.

"Hey, what's the rush?"

She didn't reply, just strode on.

"Naomi?" Kevin caught up, placing a palm of pause and concern on her shoulder closest to him. "You okay?"

She didn't stop to answer; rather, she slowed her pace. "Yes. Just suffering from a little CSD."

"Another acronym?"

"I'm sure plenty are floating around among you forensics experts in the medical examiner's office."

"You have a point there." His hand dropped to curl her waist. They walked together that way, with his arm around her.

This time, Naomi did tense; she couldn't help it.

Kevin didn't notice or ignored it (as Naomi knew he sometimes did). "So, what's C-S-D?"

"Common Sense Deficiency." She failed to disguise her tone's edge.

Kevin chuckled. "Cute. Just a sec, sweetie..." He stepped away from her to put the plate in the trash.

She admired his lanky form as he headed back to her, but attraction did not true love make. But watching his lean form moving easily and invitingly in that navy and cobalt-blue striped golf shirt (paired with the blue chinos) was a good place to start.

He stopped before her. Up close, his five feet eleven inches seemed much taller. "So, you're suffering with some CSD, huh? Didn't spend enough time in—"

"In the prudencesphere. Yeah, something like that." Her response was snippy; she heard her clipped enunciation.

"Why is that?"

Naomi lifted a sullen shoulder in answer. She took Kevin's hand to get him walking again. *Walking*, not talking. "Let's enjoy the atmosphere on the way to the flight coaster, shall we?"

"Again?"

She rested her index finger across her lips. "Shhh."

With a sigh, he resumed their stroll in silence.

Naomi needed silence. She was annoyed with herself for telling Kevin such an awful untruth and needed to collect her thoughts to avoid putting a damper on the evening. A semi-quiet meander among the dissipating crowd, plus two or three trips on the flight coaster, would help get the ball rolling—a few rounds on the Velocity-X roller coaster would top things off. She always kept her options open regarding the kaleidoscopic facets of therapy in all its forms.

Curtains of violet streaked the horizon as day drew to a close. Even in twilight, Naomi recognized the figure standing in a line for popcorn a few yards away.

Todd Winthrop laughed with the young lady in front of him as he pulled up on the waist of denim shorts needing a tighter notch on the belt he wore. Even in the fading light, the young man proved an attractive teen. She thought he needed a haircut, but other than that, he was indeed a young hunk.

Naomi decided the roller coaster could wait. "C'mon, Kev." She nudged him in the direction of the popcorn stand.

"You want popcorn now?"

"No. Just come on." She headed toward the young man and his date.

The girl giggling with Todd touched his chest with one hand in a flirting gesture as old as the sexes. If the young lady was 14, she was 17. Watching her, Naomi knew it to be the latter.

Go 'head Todd.

The girl tried to take Todd's vintage Redskins cap off, but Todd was too quick for her to be successful.

Naomi stood behind Todd, purposely crowding his space.

Both the girl and Todd stopped playing, the girl sending Naomi a nasty look as Todd turned around.

"Uh, Naomi..." Kevin started.

Seeing who it was, Todd took his cap off. "Hi, Doctor Alexander." He leaned in to hug her.

"Hi." Chuckling, Naomi hugged him back. She didn't jibe too well with public displays of affection (and there shouldn't be any displays with her patients, public or otherwise). But Todd was a child, and this canceled many of the associated protocols as far as she was concerned. The young lady's expression relaxed as Naomi hugged him (not that Naomi cared).

"How's everything, Todd?" Naomi took a small step back as they separated. "Gettin' in some last-minute thrills?"

"Yeah." Todd's grin widened into a smile. The chip in his tooth made him darling. Naomi hoped he carried the flattering flaw into adulthood.

"Mallory here, too?"

The young lady turned her attention to the stand attendant and ordered her popcorn.

Kevin cleared his throat.

Todd looked kindly at Kevin, but Naomi intended no introductions.

"Hey, Todd. I'm Kevin Oheneba." He shook Todd's hand.

Nodding, Todd smiled and pumped Kevin's hand. "Hello, Sir."

"Your mom and dad taught you well, Todd. You can put your cap back on." Naomi grinned, gesturing at the hat in his hand.

"Oh, a'ight." Todd placed his cap back on his head, setting it just so. "My *real* mother," he muttered.

Having gotten her popcorn, the young lady nudged the box against Todd's arm to offer him some.

Todd accepted the box absentmindedly but with a mumbled, "Thanks." He turned back to Naomi without eating any popcorn, and the young lady folded her arms across her chest—attitude back intact.

"Mallory?" Naomi prompted.

"Oh, yeah. She and Kelz went to ride the Drop one more time."

Naomi didn't know who "Kelz" was, but she was glad the kids were out having a good time. Inwardly, she lamented the times spent similarly with her late younger brother, CJ. Naomi sensed Todd didn't want her to ask about anyone else. "Your Dad? Ruth?" The doctor in her couldn't help it. She also sensed something else, but ignored it for now.

The doors behind Todd's eyes began to close as the young man shut down. He shrugged and partly turned away.

Kevin jangled the change in his pocket. "What's your last ride going to be, Todd?"

The switch in topic helped. Todd turned more toward them. "Sky Wing, probably." The young lady took the popcorn back from him, clearly ready to get on with their date.

"I like the flight coaster," Naomi offered, "and the Velocity-X."

Todd's wide grin returned. "Yeah, that's my sh—" Catching himself, his eyes filled with embarrassment.

"That's my shit, too, sweetie." Naomi smiled with warmth and fondness. Todd was a good kid. But there was something...

"Well, I guess I'll see you on Tuesday, Doctor Alex. I'll tell Mal I saw you." He turned with a smile, but then covered his mouth to stifle a cough.

"You take your pill today, Todd?" Based on their counseling three years ago and the information in the profile Jeff completed, she knew Todd took prescribed asthma medicine.

Todd wore an expression she couldn't quite read. "Yeah, Doctor Alex. It was just a cough."

"Just checking," she responded maternally, thoroughly enjoying the whole "Doctor Alex" thing.

"I'm fine," Todd stressed.

Having been ignored completely, Little Miss Date started en route to the Sky Wing with her popcorn.

Naomi noticed that Kevin, too, no longer stood with them. She searched the immediate area in time to spot him heading into the men's room. She returned her gaze to Todd.

"I'm fine," he stressed again. "I gotta go, okay?"

"Yeah, you do, or you won't get any play later."

He smirked, giving a hedging nod. "Kinda sorta."

"I understand perfectly." She gripped the upper part of his left arm, pressing her thumb against his biceps. It was her turn to stress a point. "You be *careful*, all right?"

Todd seemed perplexed. Then, as realization dawned, he nodded at the ground before easing his arm from her grasp. "I will." He glanced at her before catching up with the girl. He looked back once, raised his cap to Naomi, and then put the hat back in place. The two soon blended into the thinning crowd.

Naomi didn't move, staring in Todd's wake, wishing his aura would flicker for her. Todd was 11 when he first came to her with his father and sister, grieving over Julia Winthrop, and Naomi often thought of Jassiel during sessions with them back then. Todd and Jassiel didn't look alike (of course), but it wasn't about that. Watching Todd now, thoughts of her son surfaced again, but she pushed them aside. Todd was 14, turning 15 in short months, while Jassiel...

The stand attendant cleared her throat. "Scuse me. Can I help you?"

"Uh, no, sorry." Naomi resisted the veil of moody-blue threatening to descend. She headed for the restrooms, seeing Kevin heading her way.

He came up to her and smiled, then shifted to stand next to her. "Ready to have your mind take flight on the flight coaster?"

Among other things, Naomi wanted to say.

When she gripped Todd's arm, she had a disturbing flash of truth involving Ruth and the Winthrop kids. And while her flashes didn't play like a scene from a movie, she discerned enough to know that Ruth meant harm to Todd, Mallory, or both. Intuitively, Naomi felt it most likely to be Todd.

"Hey, you okay?" Kevin placed a hand on the small of her back, his fingers pressing with mild concern.

His calming touch released Naomi from her thoughts. "Yeah, I'm okay. Just thinking." Kevin lowered his hand to her waist, which, admittedly, she liked. Still, she remained irritated with herself for telling him she loved him.

"You're sure?"

"I'm sure. Let's go." She wanted to get on with ending the evening on a high note.

The thinning crowd made it easy to ride the coaster three times. A good thing because the first ride didn't provide the therapeutic benefits expected. By ride three, though, Naomi and Kevin were in good spirits.

After their minds took flight, they then soared high and zoomed fast a few times on the Velocity-X, the exhilarating G-forces working its magic. She and Kevin poked their tongues at the popping on-ride camera.

That evening, instead of trekking to Baltimore for coddies, they together prepared a dinner centering steak (for him) and shrimp (for her); Kevin both joking and curiously fascinated regarding her failure to cry as she chopped raw onion—while he stood back a non-tear-zone distance. Oddly, with the reflections on her dead husband and son (and brother) during the day, a part of her wanted to prepare a grilled olive and cream cheese sandwich; an indulgence tied to her grieving bouts.

After dinner, the two spent a quiet period on the balcony of Kevin's condominium in Crystal City.

The October air on the balcony was perfect: a little nippy but not biting cold. Naomi and Kevin talked, played Scrabble, and played two rounds of Mancala. Later, they sipped glasses of pinot grigio and enjoyed the view, Naomi popping Niçoise olives into her mouth one after another. She was partial to Niçoise or Cerignola olives, and varieties of Dalmatia olive tapenade.

Their birthday date ranked as one of the loveliest celebrations she'd had in a long time.

After sex (an encounter both soothing and intense), she indulged in several chapters of a Connie Briscoe novel. Kevin was sleeping when Naomi left his bed at two fifty-one in the morning. She dressed quietly and left his condo (as she always did), enjoying the classical music and solitude during the ride home. Handel's "Arrival of the Queen of Sheba" closed as Naomi pulled into her garage. She turned the radio off and sat in silence.

Naomi didn't sleep much as it was. Given her concern for the Winthrop children's welfare, tonight would be no exception. She didn't know when or where, or how. Her flashes didn't work that way. All she had was a who, a semi-what, and an obvious why. The lack of details she could act upon made the whole thing that much more frustrating.

Her cellphone rang: Kevin.

"Mister Oheneba," she answered.

"Making sure you arrived home safely." Sleepiness filled his voice.

"I did. Thanks, Kev."

A long pause ensued.

"Tonight was very nice, Naomi. The whole day with you, in fact. Which isn't unusual, but...quite a pleasant birthday celebration."

"I agree, Kevin. All of it: very enjoyable. And no, not unusual for us."

"...Are you ever going to stay the night, Naomi?"

"In time."

"I won't press you. But it's odd that you allow me to stay the night when I'm there with you. Why is that?"

"I don't know," Naomi answered honestly.

Kevin dispelled a sleepy sigh. "Okay. Goodnight, Naomi. Get some sleep. I love you."

"Goodnight, Kevin. I'll call you around two, okay?"

"Yes."

"Bye."

"Bye."

Naomi disconnected.

Naomi entered the house with her Glock-17 comfortably tucked (and ready) at the small of her back. She poured herself a glass of orange juice (entertaining the option of fixing herself a screwdriver cocktail). She carried the containing-orange-juice-only glass upstairs, checking in on Leslie before going to her bedroom.

When the alarm sounded four hours later, there was no need for it: Naomi wasn't asleep.

Chapter 8

The Camel's Back

Big, fat, comfy, *yellow* furniture. Naomi settled deeper into the mustard-yellow loveseat cushions, relishing the leather's plush softness.

Willette Hargrove just finished her session, and as Naomi waited for the Winthrops, she deliberated if, at this point, she was taking Willette's money without rhyme or reason. The woman had exhibited no progressive signs of healing. If anything, she'd reached a plateau. And although Ms. Hargrove remained savagely jealous of her sister, Alicia, Willette hadn't regressed any, so maybe Naomi was being paid a "mental maintenance" or non-regression fee, if you will.

Naomi didn't care for it either way, but decided today she'd be okay with it. Hear the woman's stories, send her on her way, take her money, and be done with it. Today? Yep. That attitude would serve fine. She couldn't save the world, anyway.

She ran her hands along one arm of the loveseat, taking comfort from the chilled smoothness. Her mood fused melancholy, discontent, and indifference.

She wanted a shot of Belvedere vodka, but she was on a new tip now (wasn't she?), so she put thoughts of alcohol out of her mind—at least until she finished with the Winthrop family's session. She hoped the coming session would be one to break some ground.

It was always a little slower with grief counseling, but Naomi didn't think she'd made much progress with the Winthrops beyond the initial session. It was as if she rented the space in her office to them, with herself serving as chaperone. And "chaperone" aptly described her role.

She certainly wasn't referee because Ruth still did most of the talking. Rounds of talking, which Naomi entertained somewhat at length in the beginning, if for no other reason than to procure a better feel for who the woman was—if she could decipher anything through the incessant Bible references, that is. Spiritual viewpoint differences aside, she couldn't take much more of Ruth's Bible-thumping. So far, she'd let Ruth have her say and didn't debate with her. But today, well, Naomi didn't know.

Naomi went to her credenza and retrieved a bottle of green tea with citrus flavoring. She drank slowly, listening to a muffled exchange of voices outside her door. When the door opened, she rested the now half-empty bottle on her desk (and realized she might need a pee-pee break midsession).

Jeff Winthrop entered first, holding the door open for his family. He wore a suit rather than the usual casual attire of jeans or khakis with a button-down shirt. The byzantium-colored stripes in Jeff's dress shirt contrasted favorably against his copper-brown skin and offset the damson and dark lavender striping in his tie. He looked thinner. As Mallory entered, Jeff handed her his slate-gray suit jacket and smiled at Naomi. "Mornin', Doc."

Naomi offered him a wry smile. "Mister Winthrop."

"Hi, Naomi." Mallory advanced into the room, smiling brightly, as if pleased with testing the idea of being on a first-name basis with an adult. She draped her father's jacket across the back of the settee.

Naomi maintained her wry smile. "Mallory," she greeted with a nod. Mildly buoyed by these initial cheerful greetings, she held her enthusiasm in check as Ruth and then Todd entered her office. Closing the door after them, Jeff brought up the rear.

"Good morning, Doctor Alexander," Ruth said in a voice ringing with cheer. The loden-green pantsuit she wore (paired with a jam-colored shell top blouse) brought out the green in her eyes.

Naomi tensed. "Top o' the mornin' to you, Ruth."

Ruth proffered a perfunctory smile.

"Hi, Todd."

"Hey, Doctor Alex." Todd's greeting lacked the counterfeit gaiety of the others. He covered his mouth to contain four short coughs.

Everyone aligned themselves with the spots where they sat in recent sessions but didn't sit. They paused their gazes on Naomi and waited.

Naomi gestured with her hand for everyone to sit as she took her place at her tufted barrel chair (her *yellow* chair) and sat. Approaching five feet three inches, she was petite, so the sizable chair surrounded her in the roundness of the mustard-yellow linen-fabric seat. Something about that appealed to her.

The Winthrops followed suit and took their seats. In the first session, Jeff, Mallory, and Ruth sat on the sofa, and Todd sat on the loveseat. As of late, the configuration changed: an implied line had been drawn in the sand. Ruth now occupied the loveseat while Jeff, Mallory, and Todd stationed themselves on the sofa. *The Brady Bunch* they were not.

"Now, in the future, simply take your seats after the fake greetings. You don't have to wait for me, okay? Oh, except you, Todd; your greeting was sincere." Naomi didn't smile, pleased she kept her enthusiasm at bay.

"Are you angry, Doctor Alexander?" Mallory looked worried.

Naomi sighed, "No." She paused, then rested her gaze on each as she spoke: "Look, this therapy thing is hard; I know that. I appreciate you all trying to put a 'best foot forward,' so to speak, but it's unnecessary. I must work with your authentic emotions to help you—not pretense."

Todd coughed again. It sounded bronchial.

"I'm fine," Todd stated before Naomi could say anything.

She held his gaze for several seconds, wanting to be sure.

Todd tilted his head in silent confirmation.

Naomi nodded back. "Okay then, let's do this." She scanned Ruth. "That's a nice Marc Jacobs suit, Ruth."

Ruth's eyes widened, seemingly surprised at Naomi's couture knowledge. "Oh, why thank you. I didn't think— I mean, I'm surprised—"

"It's okay, Ruth," Naomi interrupted. "Just accept the compliment."

Mallory snickered.

Ruth nodded her appreciation.

Naomi turned to Jeff with a raised eyebrow. "And how are you?"

"Pretty good, Naomi." He crossed an ankle over his knee and rested an arm behind Mallory. "You?"

"Partly sunny, with a chance of thunderstorms later in the day."

"Oh,..." Todd smiled with an exaggerated nod, gesturing toward her. "I like that."

"Yeah," Mallory agreed. She plucked a piece of gum from her bag, unwrapped it, and plopped it on her tongue. Naomi remembered suggesting Mallory chew gum as a stress-outlet redirect alternative to biting her fingernails. Mallory's fingernails weren't the nubs they were three years ago; seems the gum-chewing suggestion proved beneficial.

"Well, thank you. Now, let's recap where we are with these sessions."

"In layman's terms?" Mallory grinned with a questioning smirk.

Jeff and Todd rendered muted snickers.

Naomi smiled, giving a solitary head dip. "In layman's terms." She scooted forward, sitting on the edge of the chair cushion. "Now, from our discussions and exercises so far, this is where you are individually and as a group or—" Naomi glanced at Ruth. "Or family."

"Group," Mallory muttered.

"Mal...," Jeff warned.

Mallory folded her arms, chewing in a slow, spiritless manner.

The folded arms could signal Mallory's withdrawal from the session, so Naomi started with her to keep Mallory engaged.

So much for their pretense moments ago.

"Mallory," Naomi began, "on a progress scale of one to six, with six being ready to solo and one being little to no progress: Mallory, I'd give you a three, three and a half."

The corners of Mallory's mouth turned up a pleased millimeter. She sent a distinct gaze to her brother and father before turning to Naomi. "That's better than I was expecting. I thought you were going to give me something like a two."

"No, three and a half. But you still have some work to do." Naomi blinked over to Jeff.

He vented this long breath (of dejection). "Let me have it."

Naomi hesitated. His assessment score was low. She decided to skip him for now. "Let's save the best for last, shall we?"

"Best?" Jeff's raised eyebrows suggested hope.

She returned two quick shakes of her head. "Uh— No."

Jeff's eyes offered what Naomi could describe as nothing but desperation. "Thanks." The dejection in his voice broke Naomi's heart. Resigned to help him, she turned her attention to Todd.

Todd concentrated on the view outside, so he didn't notice her looking at him, but he turned to Mallory when she nudged him. "What?" Lines of irritation appeared fleetingly between his brows. He coughed and rubbed his chest as he awaited reason for his sister's nudge.

Mallory jerked her head twice in Naomi's direction.

Todd turned to Naomi, his hand still on his chest.

Naomi raised an eyebrow, looked into Todd's eyes, then at the hand on his chest.

"I'm *fine*, Doctor Alex." Perspiration dotted Todd's face.

Naomi rose from her chair. "That seems to be your standard response, Todd." She went behind her desk and paused, facing her credenza. Clouds passed over the sun, casting rays of flint-gray off the walls as shadows filled the spaces. Naomi sighed and opened the left panel.

Jeff and Mallory both called for her: Jeff with "Naomi?" and Mallory with a low but audible, "Doctor Alex?"

Naomi didn't turn to them. "Sit tight, folks." She bent down and retrieved her doctor's bag from the credenza. She took pleasure in the bag's familiar heftiness as she turned and placed it on her desk. "Got a little doctoring to do."

She paused, admiring the antique, brown leather satchel with its flat bottom and rounded sides. The soft crunch of the leather echoed in the silence of her office as Naomi separated the two large handles, exposing the cavernous interior. The classic bag was a Christmas gift from Tyson twelve years ago. She glanced up to find the Winthrops staring at her dumbfounded (Jeff and Mallory also with concern). Naomi's fingers fumbled over her otoscope and blood pressure cuff before finding the stethoscope. She watched Todd as she pulled it from her bag. "Come here, Todd," she directed in a tone calm, encouraging.

Todd hesitated, appearing as if going to reiterate being fine.

"Is he okay, Naomi?" Jeff sat forward. "He gets a little worked up sometimes, but he hasn't had anything major happen for some time."

Naomi nodded. "Just a precaution, Jeff. He seems fine, but while he has a doctor here to check him, why not do that?"

Todd still didn't move. "I'm okay, Doctor Alexander." He glanced over at his stepmother.

"Then let Doctor Alexander confirm it, stupid," Mallory suggested with sisterly annoyance.

"Mal...," Jeff warned again.

Mallory sucked her teeth. "Whatever."

Naomi focused on Todd. She didn't want to exacerbate any problems he might already have—problems not necessarily related to physical distress. "Why don't I come to you? Either way, I'm going to check you out." She started toward him, stethoscope in hand.

"Okay, okay, okay," Todd sighed. He got up and stepped past Ruth with a mumbled, "Scuse me."

Having met Naomi halfway, Todd stood before her but kept his eyes focused on everything other than her face.

Naomi didn't mind. His proximity allowed her to hear him breathe. He wheezed, but not very much. She inserted the tips of the stethoscope into her ears.

"Naomi?" The concern in Jeff's voice was more substantial.

"He has a bit of a prolonged expiration, Jeff. A little wheezy."

"Yeah, I hear it now," Ruth offered.

"I just wanna check for any signs of tachycardia or rhonchus lung sounds," Naomi explained. "Do I have your permission to continue?"

Jeff nodded with an affirmative gesture of his hand. "Of course."

Naomi took Todd's wrist and placed her fingers on his pulse there; it wasn't paradoxical—good. "Open your jacket and lift your shirt, Todd." He wore a Coppin State University T-shirt: his mother's alma mater.

Todd rolled his eyes but did as he was told, showing the muscles of his slight frame.

Naomi smiled at him (she couldn't help it).

Todd tried not to smile at her but ultimately couldn't help it, either. His winsome smile was self-deprecating. "Come on, Doctor Alex."

Naomi gripped the bell of the chestpiece, placing the diaphragm against the left side of Todd's torso, then against his right side and abdomen. She then motioned for him to turn around.

Todd gave her the funniest look.

Naomi read it and understood perfectly. Instead of him turning around (and facing his family), she walked around and behind Todd. A fading bruise showed on the lower right side of his back. Naomi ran a hand over it. "Todd...?"

"D-Nine got me good when I was going up for the ball." He chuckled (somewhat nervously, Naomi thought).

"Hmmm... Okay." The bruise was below where protection padding likely ended, so that was plausible, but... She'd spent years learning and deciphering authenticity in words, in people. His response came across as readymade to her, practiced even.

Jeff offered light strains of laughter. "Yeah, they play for keeps on that field—even in practice."

Naomi turned to Jeff, but Mallory's expression gave her pause: fixed and unblinking with either worry or fear as she stared at the area of Todd's bruise. Football practice?

Maybe, maybe not...

That explanation didn't completely satisfy her (and Mallory's reaction supported her misgiving), but she'd have to circle back. Naomi placed the stethoscope against his back. "Three deep breaths with a hold."

Todd coughed once during the second breath.

If he didn't have it with him, Naomi thought it best if he brought his metered dose inhaler (MDI) to future sessions (to be on the safe side). "Okay, I'm done. You can put your shirt down."

"Thank you!" Todd jerked his clothing back into place and turned around.

Naomi looked up at him. "Have your MDI handy?"

Again, Todd glanced at Ruth.

Naomi wanted to know what rooted those repeated reference glances at his stepmother. His glances her way carried a disconcerting wariness and fear. She could ask what the deal was outright, but protecting Todd came first; she didn't want to put Todd on the spot.

Todd hesitated before shaking his head.

"Why not?"

Todd glanced in Ruth's direction again before focusing on Naomi. His lips parted and eyebrows lifted as if to speak, but his sister cut him off.

"I have it, Doctor Alex." Mallory reached into her bag and pulled out an inhaler and a small plastic cylinder. She held both out to Todd and beamed his way.

Todd glanced at Ruth yet again before going over and accepting the items from his sister.

Naomi turned to Ruth.

Ruth's expression was hard to read: an unusual balance of irritation and neutrality.

What the hell? Naomi smiled at Todd. "Still using a spacer?"

Todd paused before Naomi and shrugged with a weak smile, attempting to downplay his discomfiture. "Yeah, I guess. It works better for me, as far as I'm concerned."

"Hey, it's cool. Your concern is the one that matters. We gotta go with what works, right?" Naomi patted his shoulder, then gestured for him to take his medicine.

Todd rubbed his chest. "I'm okay, Doctor Alexander."

"I believe you. As a favor to me, then."

Todd returned a wry, uneven smile. He regarded his father, sister, and stepmother. His attention stayed on Ruth a second or three longer than with the others before he attached the inhaler and spacer with some reluctance and took his medicine.

Naomi watched him. "Are you using your bronchodilator properly whenever needed?"

With the spacer still against his nose and mouth, Todd nodded with a vigorous head bob. The response was a little too exaggerated for Naomi, but she let it go—for now. Timing was everything.

"Yeah, he uses it, Doctor Alexander." Mouth pinched, Ruth crossed her arms. Her tone blared cynicism and disdain.

Naomi observed Jeff and Mallory for reaction to Ruth's response.

Foot shaking, Mallory fumed as if ready to kill Ruth. And Jeff? Well, Jeff seemed to have checked out of the session. Upon first glance, it appeared Jeff was actively in tune with the discussion, but Naomi knew better. She didn't know when, but at some point, during the last three minutes, Jeff Winthrop "left" the session. She couldn't pinpoint precisely when, but she had a good handle on why: for the same reason Todd's asthma likely presented—psychological stress.

The two males were possibly caught in a vicious cycle. With Jeff's adult anxiety, depression, and grief, and then Todd's instances of grief and stress (an interwoven extension of his father's affliction): those emotions triggered Jeff's detachment phases and Todd's mild attacks. Naomi sensed Ruth's relationship with Todd key to his circumstance.

Todd lowered the inhaler from his face and closed his eyes. He stood still, taking deep, calm breaths. When he opened his eyes, he looked directly at Naomi and grinned, his eyes offering a million thank-yous.

Naomi mouthed, "You're welcome," and signaled he take his seat.

He delivered Mallory a shy thumbs-up as he stepped across Ruth. "Thanks, Mal."

Ruth performed such exaggerated movements to allow him to pass; Mallory surveyed her almost angrily. As Todd took his seat, she smiled at her brother and offered him an admonishing "Stupid," filled with sibling love as she nudged him.

Todd set his eyes on his father. "Dad?"

"Yeah, man. I'm good. I was worried about you for a sec there."

Todd's expression told Naomi he realized his father's words rang true and false simultaneously. Jeff was worried "for a sec there"—until something lured him into some other place in his mind, where the worry about his son took a backseat to...something it was Naomi's job to determine what. Gazing at his father, Todd's face registered disappointment before melding into sad resignation.

It upset Naomi to see it. Jeff Winthrop, however, was back with them—at least for the time being. Naomi needed to take advantage of that. She began. "Okay, after that brief but necessary interruption, let's continue. But first: Todd?"

He looked at her, wide-eyed and wary. "Yes?"

"Keep your inhaler and spacer with you at all times. Got it?" When Todd glanced at Ruth, Naomi concentrated her gaze on her, still speaking to Todd. "You need both the pill and the inhaler, okay? Right now, especially. No excuses. Are we clear?" She turned her attention back to Todd for his answer.

Ruth sat forward with a twist and a huff. "Now, wait a minute, Doctor Alexan—"

"Are we clear, Todd?"

"Yes, ma'am."

"Thank you. Now, Ruth, you were going to say?" Naomi turned to her.

"Oh, that's okay, Doctor Alexander. I'll speak with Todd when we get home." Ruth eyed Naomi coolly before sitting back and plucking imaginary lint from her pant leg.

"That's fine. But my directive doesn't change." Naomi once again conferred with the youngest Winthrop. "Is that understood, Todd?"

Todd dropped his head.

"Understood." Mallory nudged her father. "Daddy?"

"Understood," Jeff answered.

"Doctor Alexander, I know you're a physician, but how dare you? I mean, who do you think you are?"

"You just said who I was: his physician." Naomi checked her watch. "Can we get back to the session, please?"

Ruth maintained her cool green stare on Naomi for several seconds (the olive color fading some) before finally nodding.

"Wonderful." Naomi turned to Todd. "So, we were talking about hypothetical scores on a progress-of-healing scale, and we left off with you, Todd."

Todd nodded with grave eyes, anticipating negative news.

"It's not that bad, Todd. I'd give you a four."

"Huh?" Mallory interjected. "That's higher than mine."

"I know," Naomi replied.

Todd looked just as perplexed.

"But—" Mallory frowned, shaking her head with confusion.

"You think, just because you're older, because you're the 'big sis,' that that somehow means you're supposed to be further along with this than your brother?"

Mallory's surprised expression slid into uncertainty. "I don't know. I guess. I mean..." Apparently unable to say what she meant, she shrugged.

"It's okay, Ms. Winthrop." Naomi broke into a slanted smile. "Everyone's different and handles things differently. It sounds cliché, but it's true nonetheless."

Mallory smiled a little, and Naomi could tell it was partly because she'd addressed her as "Ms. Winthrop."

"So, a 'four,' huh?" Todd mused aloud.

As far as grieving for your mother, yes. But only because you're dealing with additional issues now, and scores on that scale are lower.

Naomi nodded. "Uh-huh."

Todd poked his tongue at his sister.

"You're still stupid." Mallory rolled her eyes with a playful scoff.

Naomi chuckled, shifting her attention to Mrs. Winthrop. "Now, Ruth—"

"*Me?*"

"Sure. You don't have grieving complications associated with Julia Winthrop's death in the traditional sense, but Julia's death is affecting your familial relationships. So, in that light, I'd also give you a hypothetical score of four at this point."

It was a lie, yes.

But there were times, although not many, when trips to fibnation were necessary. Realistically, Ruth was somewhere around a two,

two-and-a-half regarding any progress and being able to help this family heal. It was wrong, but on many levels, Naomi didn't care. Her primary concern remained: Jeff, Todd, and Mallory.

And Ruth? Naomi considered her parsley on a plate: a figurative piece of garnish—whose potential benefits Naomi fully intended to ignore—because Ruth's detriments far outweighed anything else (especially within the sensitive context of the Winthrop family). Again, liking Ruth had nothing to do with helping this family—or maybe it did.

Ruth sat back against the loveseat cushions, looking as if she, too, wanted to poke her tongue at Mallory. The smug expression on her face said so. "Scripture says: 'Be merciful to me, O Lord, for I am weak.'"

Todd and Mallory exchanged glances and rolled their eyes up in their heads, Mallory echoing a long, dry sigh. And Jeff? Well, Naomi recognized him disengaging again.

Ruth shot a reprimanding glance Mallory's way. "It's what you need to hear, girl." She almost sounded puritanical—almost.

Mallory looked for help from her father and recognized none would be forthcoming. Her brow furrowed. Her full lips formed a thin line. The clouds moved away from the sun, and Naomi's office brightened. The sun's reappearance drew Mallory's attention, and she focused on scenes outside the window.

With a small pat to her thigh, Todd offered his sister what he probably thought was an inconspicuous sign of support. Mallory's face stiffened at his touch—as if trying not to cry.

Naomi responded to Ruth: "Maybe."

"Excuse me?" Ruth replied.

From the corner of her eye, Naomi saw she had Mallory's attention. "I said, 'maybe.' Maybe it's what she needs to hear, maybe not. You've made it quite clear you're a church-going woman, and you quote Bible scripture a lot. That's cool. But, and this is just my opinion, I never got the impression, in my years of spiritual growth and church atten-dance, and non-attendance for that matter, that Jesus walked around scripture-feeding people. The New Testament was finished after they crucified him, but you get what I'm saying. To me, Jesus always came across as a quiet, peaceful soul."

"Your point?" Ruth tried to contort her indignant expression into one of smiling curiosity.

"Well, that's just it. I'm not trying to make one per se. A few minutes ago, you offered Psalm six, verse two, as if you were trying to make a point rather than comfort or help. And maybe that wasn't your intention, but you saw how they reacted…"

Ruth glanced in the general direction of those sitting on the sofa.

Naomi continued: "All I'm saying is, if you feel the family needs more spiritual guidance, that's fine. But maybe your approach isn't working. Jesus never went on and on. On balance, seems he was rather a reserved and unassuming fellow. Now, being 'human,' we know he sometimes got angry. But other than those times, he wasn't big-mouthed and boisterous with his message and didn't harass or badger. Well, the Gospels don't portray him that way." She tried to make sure her tone held no challenge.

Ruth stared at her for several seconds. Her eyes narrowed with suspicion before returning to normal. "What're you up to?"

The question caught Naomi off guard, left her confused. "Huh?"

"Are you on the level, Doctor Alexander?" Ruth smiled, but only with her mouth.

Mallory's hand went to her mouth.

Todd sank lower on the cushions.

Jeff cleared his throat. "Ruth—"

Naomi held up a hand to quiet him. "At all times, to the best of my ability, Ruth. Why?" She wondered how she kept getting herself into these discussions, wondered how she could avoid them in the future.

Ruth plucked more imaginary lint from her suit and shook her head. Her face held less defiance and suspicion, more uncertainty. "I'm not sure. You don't seem…"

"Forget it, Ruth." Naomi tried to smile. "It was just an observation and suggestion. If you felt I was out of line, I apologize."

Ruth's eyes narrowed again.

Does this woman think I'm trying to chouse her or something?

"Okay, Doctor Alexander. And there's always time to discuss the Lord, right? Jesus said—"

"Ruth, stop. Okay?" Naomi interrupted.

Camel's back broken and straws everywhere!

She now realized Ruth's scripture-quoting was a crutch and an avoidance response. She didn't much care for Ruth, but this realization shed some light on things. Naomi sympathized with Ruth (but it was minimal).

Naomi continued: "You seem a little old-school with this. We're in my office, my 'home,' so to speak, so I'll say where I'm coming from. Jesus taught his lessons in a calm, cool, collected manner, Ruth. Because, well, in my opinion, he was calm, cool, and collected. His sermons don't come across as longwinded preaching sessions. I don't believe he berated, and he didn't judge. Don't preach to me, Ruth. I'm not interested." Her tone was not as placating this time, but she'd had her fill. In Naomi's book, the whole psychiatrists-are-neutral concept was 85 percent myth. Naomi didn't find it helpful to hold everything in pertaining to personal commentary with patients—she had her own sanity to consider.

As expected, silence followed. Naomi watched her patients find interest in something other than Naomi's face, other than each other's faces, as the silence extended.

Todd broke it. "Will we be doing exercises or seeing a film today, Doctor Alex?"

Naomi offered him a warm smile. She liked Todd. "You like those, do ya, son?"

"Sumthin' like that."

"I kinda like 'em too, especially the bubble-wrap exercise." Mallory chimed in. "And the one where you have us blow bubbles, too. Doing those makes it more like research or a school project and less like...like..." She frowned, trying to come up with what to say.

"Less like mental therapy?" Naomi suggested.

Mallory shrugged with a hint of chagrin. She smiled, apology in her brown eyes. "Sorry, but yeah."

"Don't apologize to me. My feelings aren't hurt. *Y'all* the crazy ones."

Mallory and Todd cracked up.

Jeff's faint laughter sprinkled the air.

Even Ruth offered a tiny grin.

Naomi checked her watch, trying to determine whether there was enough time for a quick jaunt to the liquor store for a bottle of Belvedere. She knew she shouldn't (being on a new tip and all), but...

"To answer your question, Todd: no. We won't work through any exercises or worksheets or view a presentation today."

"Besides, I haven't gotten my score yet..." Jeff gazed at her anxiously but (again) with hope.

Naomi watched him for a moment. She recognized hints of classic Native American influence in his cheekbones and eyes. Jeff smiled a hopeful smile at her, and she smiled back.

Not for the first time, she wondered why she chose this profession, why she didn't ignore her flash of truth decades ago. Astronomy looked pretty good from where she stood now. In-depth exploration and analysis of celestial objects, space, and the physical universe offered a particular mystery, too—compared to the same mystery involved with the exploration and analysis of a patient's mind. But with planets, galaxies, and asteroids, the findings were much more concrete.

"Two," she answered. "A hypothetical 'two,' that is."

Ruth sounded an odd noise down in her throat. "Excuse me."

Mallory patted her father's knee. "It's okay, Daddy. We'll get you better. I miss her, too."

Todd studied his New Balance shoes with intense concentration, poking the tip of his tongue in the space created by his chipped tooth.

The hopeful light faded from Jeff's eyes, leaving only the anxiety in them as he gaped at Naomi. "Just 'two'? No two-and-a-half, or two-and-a-quarter, maybe? I'm thinking I'm handling things okay here." He looked to Mallory for confirmation. "Right, M-Sweet?"

Mallory didn't maintain eye contact with him. Staring out the window again, she shook her head at a considering pace. "I guess so, Daddy."

Jeff stared at his daughter for another second or two before returning his attention to Naomi. "So, what am I doing wrong, Naomi?"

"That's the first thing." Naomi shifted forward, sitting on the edge of her yellow chair cushion again. "Inasmuch as it's not solely a matter of missing Julia, it's not a matter of you 'doing anything wrong' either, okay? Let's do away with that line of thinking on this. We're talking about emotions as much as we are talking about actions. Because while you cannot reverse losing Julia—"

Jeff made the strangest expression at that statement.

Naomi filed it and continued: "You can adopt behaviors that will help you realize and better manage how you respond emotionally to situations." She looked around at everyone. "That was layman's terms, wasn't it?"

Mallory smiled, a wry tilt to her lips. "For the most part, yeah, Doctor Alexander. We're not idiots. Go 'head, finish."

Jeff frowned. "So, I'm not managing my emotions correctly?"

"That still holds connotations of right and wrong. But since we're just trying to grasp this on a basic level, I'm saying yes, but with reservations. But you know what? I have an even better answer for you, Jeff, and then we can wrap the session." Naomi paused, alternating looks between Jeff and Mallory before she continued. "To answer how well you've been managing your emotions, I want you to reflect for the next couple of days on Mallory's response to you a few moments ago when you proposed how you were handling things." When he parted his lips to respond, Naomi cut him off. "Say nothing, Jeff. Just think about your daughter's response. She replied, 'I guess,' while shaking her head. Right?"

Jeff's chin dipped in acknowledgment.

"Think about that."

"Okay, so my husband is still having some problems, but as individuals, we have two fours, a three plus, and a two. How are we doing as a family, then?"

Mallory sucked her teeth.

"I'm sure that attitude doesn't help," Ruth responded.

Ruth had a point, but Naomi didn't comment. Something about the woman bothered her in the worst way. "I guess that averages out to be about a three, give or take."

"So, we're halfway...," Todd mused.

Naomi smirked at him with partial humor. "Yes, and no."

Todd rolled his eyes upward and tilted his head back with a smile. "Here we go," he said sweetly, bringing his head back down and looking at her. "Is anything cut-and-dry with you?"

Naomi smiled back, adding a wink. "Most things. Not this." She stood. "And so, Winthrops, on that note, I regret this session must draw to a close somewhat prematurely."

Ruth retrieved her Hermès bag from the floor next to the loveseat and stood. She sighed, ready to go.

Mallory stood, followed by Todd.

Jeff remained seated.

While Mallory, Todd, and Ruth stared at Jeff, waiting for him to (again) prepare for departure, Naomi spoke to them. "I want to remind you about some things you can do to help yourselves between sessions.

Coping with grief is a mother. You're open to a wide variety of emotions that can exhaust you."

"But it's been years," Ruth stated. She sounded borderline whiny and put-out about it, as if the idea of grieving for a period longer than a week (maybe a month) disturbed her psyche.

"Doesn't matter. Have you lost a loved one, Ruth? I can't remember from the questionnaire."

"My father, grandparents."

"Were you close to any of them? You know what I mean."

Ruth shook her head. "Not really." She gave a little shoulder hop.

"Okay." Naomi left it at that and addressed everyone once again. "So, between sessions, make sure you eat right and exercise. Take your meds, Todd." Naomi looked pointedly at Todd on this.

He smiled and nodded.

"Thank you. And get plenty of sleep, everyone. Like I said, bereavement can be exhausting, okay?"

Todd lifted his cellphone from his pocket. "Oh, Dad's got *that one* covered for all of us. Right, Dad?" He began texting.

"Tell me about it," Ruth added.

With that, Jeff scoffed at his family and stood. He adjusted his tie, a frown of either annoyance or confusion (or both) deepening his brow.

Naomi took note and filed that bit of info, too. It sounded more like his sleeping was avoidance response (which wasn't good) or possibly detachment, which was similar to avoidance, but not quite the same thing. Either way, Jeff's excessive sleeping needed further exploration.

Ruth extended her hand. "Next week then, Doctor Alexander."

Naomi accepted her hand. Ruth's palm was sweaty, her handshake weak. Naomi gripped a little tighter. "The Lord be with you," she said without equivocation.

Ruth hesitated before returning Naomi's grip and shake. "With you, too." She headed to the door.

Todd offered the peace sign with his left hand. "Peace, Doctor Alex." He headed to the door as well.

"You stay outta trouble, young man. Till next week, anyway."

"You got it, Doc."

Mallory stepped forward. "See ya next week, Doctor Alex." She appeared at a loss for something to say next.

Naomi knew the young lady wanted to hug her; she put a hand on the girl's shoulder and assured in a quiet tone: "We'll get there, Mallory. Hold tight, okay?"

"I'm trying, Doctor Alex."

"I know you are. There's another thing you can do to help cope. And that's doing something for *you*, whether that's allowing yourself to cry or buying an ice cream cone. Do something that's going to help you get through. Nothing harmful, mind you, but you know what I'm saying. Can you do that?"

Mallory rolled a shoulder with ambivalence. "I guess." Her eyes scanned Naomi's office. "But I don't know what I—"

"You'll know, sweetie. It's a daily thing, and... Well, you'll know."

"Thanks, Doctor Alexander."

Naomi sensed another opening for a hug approaching. "Not a prob. Now, get out of here." She guided Mallory's shoulder in a turn toward the door.

With a wave, Mallory picked up her bag from the sofa and went to stand next to her brother. There was some exchange between Ruth and the Winthrop kids. Naomi couldn't make it out, but the faces and body cues suggested neutrality.

Ruth rested her hand on the doorknob and waited.

Jeff extended his hand with a hitched breath. "Well, Naomi, I can't say it's been a pleasure."

Looking up at him, Naomi accepted his hand. "Oh, you can say it; you just don't want to."

Jeff chuckled with their handshake. "I'll go with that."

"Well, let's say it's been *my* pleasure. How 'bout that? Until next week? Or do you feel you need something sooner?"

Jeff's smile faded; his expression turned somber. "I... I still..." He swallowed. "Julia. She's still..." Confusion mixed with emotional pain leapt from his eyes. He started again. "I still see— I feel like she's—" He closed his eyes with a long sigh. "Never mind. I'm having a hard time knowing how I feel. You said so yourself."

"That's not what I said exactly, but I hear you. Well, let me know. If I find more is needed, I'll take care of it."

"Fine with me."

"Good. See you next week."

"Yeah." Jeff sighed and headed toward the others. The Winthrops offered another round of sundry parting words and were gone.

Naomi stared at her closed door for a bit before leaning back against her desk, thinking.

The Winthrop family's healing progress rested with the parent and stepparent. And that was as it should be.

Unfortunately, Naomi sensed Jeff, Todd, and even Ruth (to some extent) were all counting on Mallory. And in all likelihood, Mallory believed the family's recovery rested on her shoulders, too. Jeff Winthrop subsisted in the throes of complicated grief. Mallory couldn't attenuate the volatility of the situation; she was only 16 and grieving herself.

That Julia's birthday would have been only days ago, surely contributed to the extra weightiness of their joint grief.

Navigating the obscure boundaries of grief (its stages, its treatment) required a delicate approach on all fronts. When examining the case, Naomi considered many factors. Central to all of it, of course, was Jeff.

Jeff may have been conditioned as a boy to limit his emotional responses. Although the tide is changing, most young males are conditioned as such. It contributed to the whole Mars-Venus dichotomy and was a factor many women lost sight of when trying to understand why the males in their lives refrained from dealing with their feelings openly or directly. That their hormones, testosterone particularly, dampened feelings of anxiety or depression under stressful situations, didn't help. Still, preconditioning and male hormones aside, Jeff Winthrop was losing parts of the emotional battle. And it went beyond simply missing his dead wife.

"I still see..."

Naomi presumed Jeff started to say he still saw Julia. On the one hand, Julia still making her presence known, delved into an arena of treatment of which Naomi's experience hovered around nil; she was nobody's ghost-whisperer (flashes of truth and aura-flickers notwithstanding). On the other hand, his comment confirmed her suspicions he was having hallucinatory experiences, although he likely wouldn't admit as much during their sessions.

Rather than a rush to resolution (and some doctors did), Naomi preferred her patients get well in their own time. Grief counseling lent itself to exactly that by its very nature. But Jeff Winthrop required more direct prodding in the healing direction because his children needed him—his son especially.

She didn't want to prescribe antidepressant or anti-anxiety meds for Jeff. Not yet. Although a few selective serotonin reuptake inhibitors (SSRIs) came to mind, Naomi most times considered meds a last resort. But given Mallory's response to her father, his excessive sleeping, and Jeff's almost-confession at seeing Julia, meds might have to enter the picture.

The Physicians' Desk Reference (PDR) would be her first stop. She'd go through her PDR to determine the best therapeutic method and recipe. And she still wanted to get to the bottom of why Jeff and Ruth married. Her role as sleuth of a patient's mind and emotions almost mandated it.

There were some psychological reasons Jeff may have attached himself to Ruth (including a glaring one Naomi hoped to divulge in a session soon), but Jeff implied something more specific.

Whatever that more specific thing was, it rooted the discord Naomi sensed in Jeff and Ruth's marriage. A degree of malice underscored that romance-free union on both sides. And while she had her theories about Ruth's closeted enmity and Jeff's suppressed regret, she'd need another session or two to bring that "marriage of malice" to its necessary crossroad.

Naomi checked her wall clock. She had time, but she abandoned the idea of a jaunt to the liquor store and instead went to her credenza and turned on her digital music player to calm her nerves.

"Tchaikovsky Pas de Deux" floated into the room. She turned the volume up to allow the music to fill the space around her and wrap her in its soothing melody.

It was inevitable and enjoyable, thinking of her father whenever she listened to this piece.

Her father attended the ballet premiere at the City Center of Music and Drama in New York in the spring of 1960. He told her about it often, always recalling something new and different with each retelling, keeping the memory fresh and exciting.

Naomi closed her eyes and took several deep breaths, pushing away thoughts of the late (great) Elijah Leonard Matthews. She focused on her breathing and listened to Tchaikovsky, feeling better shortly thereafter.

Some herbal tea in her Cambridge mug would do to continue the soothing and nerve-settling.

She lowered the volume and then prepared a mug of lemon balm tea, classical music serving as background. Naomi sipped from her Cambridge as she sat at her desk, particularly enjoying the contributions of bass clarinet, timpani, and tuba in Tchaikovsky's piece. She ruminated necessary notes on the Winthrop case before seeing her next patient.

Chapter 9

Hit the Showers

H e wanted to tell Naomi he still saw Julia, still *felt* Julia. That Julia was still *here*. But in the end, he couldn't do it.

Jeff Winthrop sat in a most uncomfortable high school desk and chair, one of those polyethylene shell chair-desk combo jobs that didn't give a damn the size of the student because nothing was adjustable. He shifted his torso to the left, trying to relieve the pressure under his rib cage.

They weren't seven weeks into the school year, yet this was the third impromptu parent-teacher conference concerning Todd that Jeff and Ruth attended. The previous two meetings were with Todd's science and English-Lit teachers, respectively, with Todd in attendance as well. Those conferences were close to identical in their execution and resolution: Todd is not a problem child per se, but he'd become quieter and more introverted. They wanted to confer before anything started affecting his schoolwork, blah, blah, blah...

Now, only Ruth and he sat before Mr. Belair: Todd's history teacher and (as luck would have it) his guidance counselor.

Mr. Belair faced them, leaning his rear against the edge of his desk. He was a short, stocky man in his 40s with dark, acajou-brown skin and small wide-set eyes. He folded his arms and offered the classic teacher-smile. His well-honed triceps strained against the sleeves of his sky-blue dress shirt. His smile and laidback demeanor canceled any notions Jeff had of the man having a Napoleon complex to compensate for being vertically challenged.

He grinned to himself, thinking some of Dr. Alexander had rubbed off on him.

Jeff looked over at Ruth, who appeared just as uncomfortable as he felt, although she fit into her desk much better than he in his. He wondered, though, if her discomfort was physical—or derived from concern over getting her pantsuit wrinkled.

Mr. Belair's smile grew into a chuckle. "We can move this discussion to the reading table at the back if you'd like."

"Oh, that's okay," Ruth replied with a half-smile, half-grimace. "It's not that bad. I'm fine."

Holding his amused expression, Mr. Belair turned to Jeff.

Jeff gave a single head jerk toward the rear of the classroom.

Mr. Belair chuckled again. "I thought so." He held a manila folder in one hand and gestured to Ruth with a ladies-first wave of his other hand. "Shall we, Missus Winthrop?"

Jeff almost guffawed as Ruth smiled at Todd's history teacher, offering a demure bat of her eyelashes. He held it in, though—and his side hurt that much more for it.

Ruth slid from the desk with ease and then practically sashayed to the back of the room. Jeff watched the teacher roam his gaze over Ruth's advancing form, his focus on Ruth's semi-twitching rump. He observed Mr. Belair checking out Ruth's butt and experienced the slightest inkling of...nothing—neither jealousy nor pride.

It took more effort for Jeff to remove himself from the confines of his desk, but he did so with little fanfare. He sighed into the room with the release of pressure on his rib cage. "Aren't these high school kids as big as adults these days? These desks sure seem small."

"Jeffy, you're over six feet tall...and used to be close to two hundred pounds." Ruth sat prim and proper in her seat at the table, her chastising words just as prim (but maybe not as proper).

He hated when she called him "Jeffy." Just plain hated it. He hated himself more for not saying anything to her about it. Her comment about his weight wasn't necessary, either—and that annoyed the hell out of him, too. Yeah, he'd lost some weight (a loss of appetite did that) but not that damn much. Jeff bit his tongue and ambled over to the table.

The opened windows allowed the early October air to counter any stuffiness in the classroom. An oscillating fan (situated behind a row of computers in the far corner of the room) also contributed to the anti-stuffiness campaign. Across the top of the back wall, a huge banner decorated by students fluttered with the fan's air on it. It read: *History Happens...Every day!*

Sounds of whistles and the impact sound of padded bodies against padded bodies or some padded apparatus (and the naturally occurring yell or grunt) drifted from the school's adjacent football field. Jeff wished Todd was in this meeting with them rather than at football practice.

Ruth got the discussion going. "So, Mister Belair, we've already met with Ms. Hopkins and Mister Coulucci about Todd. Wouldn't it have been simpler to do a panel meeting or something? I thought he was improving in those other classes."

Mr. Belair cleared his throat and ran a hand over his close-shaven haircut. "Call me 'Palmer,' please. Now, I can't say Todd's a problem child per se..."

Jeff leaned back in his seat, containing a smirk. *There it is, same as the others. Do they rehearse this shit?*

Palmer Belair scanned pages in the manila folder. "No, he's not a 'getting into trouble' kind of student, and his grades are quite decent."

"But he's quieter than usual, more introverted...," Jeff led, trying his best not to sound mocking.

Mr. Belair didn't seem offended, but under the table, Ruth nudged his thigh with her knee in private admonishment.

"Well, yes and no," Palmer answered. "We're not here because of Todd's grades. They're pretty good, actually—"

"Humph, they'd better be. Is it the football? Because I told—"

"Ruth...," Jeff warned.

She fixed her unhappy gaze on him, defiance in her taut neck and shoulders. In recent months, seemed she reached for defiance before any other emotion.

Jeff shook his head. "It's not the football. It isn't. Besides, he needs that outlet."

"He can find other 'outlets,' Jeff."

Jeff stared at her for solid seconds and then dropped his gaze. He wasn't going to do this in front of this man. He'd already bargained with her to allow the boy to play when she tried to ban him from football weeks ago. That should have been the end of it. He knew where she was headed, though; it was where she always headed. "He's on the youth ministry, Ruth."

The jut of her jaw said she was not appeased. "He can do more."

Jeff let it go and didn't respond. He glanced at Mr. Belair, who looked quite interested in their exchange. Jeff figured his interest came more from being nosy about their personal lives than from any concern for Todd's well-being at home. His eyes held a greedy concentration, giving some credence to the notion.

Jeff eked a lengthy breath. "So, why're we here, Mister Belair?" He was tired. He wanted to get this over with and go home. Go home and get some sleep. So much less was required when he was sleeping. So much more...was offered.

Palmer rifled through several papers in the folder. "As you may know, here at Holden-Wells, we have random locker searches as both precautionary and security measures." He looked up as he relayed this, seeking their reaction.

Jeff kept his face still but glanced at Ruth: she seemed pleased.

He wasn't pleased, but he wasn't surprised, either. School personnel discussed random locker searches at both the back-to-school PTA meeting and in the academy student manual. It was a sign of the times—private school or not.

"We understand, Mister Belair." Ruth's placating tone sounded odd coming from her. "What did you find?" She sounded concerned, but her eyes reflected that same greedy, prying look Mr. Belair's eyes held moments ago.

Damn, did she want the boy to be in serious trouble?

Jeff wanted to say something to her but took the path of least resistance—it was just better that way: fewer words meant faster escape.

Mr. Belair selected a few sheets from the folder. He handed some to Ruth and some to him. Jeff noticed the teacher wore no wedding band.

Palmer began: "Nothing in Todd's locker violated the codes, but—"

Jeff accepted the papers from the teacher-slash-counselor but didn't look at them. "You check papers, too? I thought you concentrated on drugs, weapons: that type of thing."

"Those are the more obvious items, yes, but we also check for evidence of bullying, sexual misconduct, and the like, which can be found in nasty letters, pictures, etcetera."

Ruth nodded, her head-bob full of energy. "I see." She leaned forward in her seat the tiniest bit, seeming to forget the papers in her hand.

"So, while we found nothing in violation, we held on to these, primarily because, as we've mentioned, his teachers, including myself, noticed a change in him." He nodded toward the papers. "Take a look."

Jeff reviewed what he guessed were Todd's handwritten poems and musings, noting his neat and rather prissy-looking handwriting.

"Oh my," Ruth murmured, her brow wrinkled with concern.

Jeff looked down at his sample of papers again. He'd been looking without reading. This time, he read a few lines of the poems and a paragraph or two from the musings. He read enough to appreciate the idea that his son had literary talent. His style and themes echoed Edgar Allan Poe. Being an artist himself, Jeff relished seeing his son's creative side. That was Jules's influence; she had dabbled in poetry.

"Oh my," Ruth repeated as she flipped a page.

Jeff leaned toward Ruth to get an idea of what she was reading. He looked at Mr. Belair. "Are we reading the same thing?"

"Essentially, yes."

Jeff scanned Ruth again. Her brow furrowed deeper as she read.

Jeff read more of Todd's work. He didn't get it. "What's the problem?" He flipped through a few more pages and then paused, scanning a particular page with renewed interest. Todd had written a tribute to his mother. The words carried such eloquent emotion; Jeff's chest tightened. Still, he didn't see the problem (but he hoped like hell Ruth didn't have something similar in her sample of papers).

"What?" Jeff repeated and shrugged, looking from Ruth to Mr. Belair.

"Jeff, this stuff is morbid and ghoulish."

"I wouldn't say that—" Jeff started.

"I wouldn't either, Missus Winthrop. Todd's writings are akin to Edgar Allan Poe. 'The Fall of the House of Usher' comes to mi—"

"Thank you!" Jeff interjected, fighting images of tombs...and death.

"But...," Mr. Belair cautioned, "But, because of his recent changes in behavior, we want to bring it to your attention to be sure his 'inspiration,' if you will, is purely artistic and not expressing some darker emotional turmoil."

Jeff took pause. He hadn't considered it that way. He still didn't think it to be any more than Todd showing his writing talent, but maybe...

Ruth shuffled through the papers. "Should we show them to Doctor Alexander?"

"What? Oh, I don't think so," Jeff said, dismissing the idea.

"You may want to, Mister Winthrop," Mr. Belair advised. "Just in case."

Jeff watched Palmer's face for a few seconds. "Just in case what?" He didn't want to deal with this right now. He pushed his chair back from the table and stood. "Look, Todd's fine. Okay? His so-called 'behavior changes' are probably tied to several things: new school, being a teen, still mourning his mother... All reasonable. Take your pick."

Ruth looked up at him, frowning with dissatisfaction. "So, 'boys will be boys.' Is that it?"

Jeff ignored her sarcastic tone, but tendrils of anxiety crept upward from his belly. "Call it what you want. My son is not crazy." He sat again and leaned forward, propped onto his thighs, and studied the flooring pattern. He'd feel much better if he could get some sleep.

"Please understand, Mister Winthrop, neither the school nor I feel Todd is unstable. We wanted you to be aware of what we notice here, just in case..." Mr. Belair trailed off, obviously unsure of how to finish.

Jeff locked eyes with the teacher. "You said that a moment ago. 'Just in case,' *what?* In case...he's not getting the attention he needs at home? Is that what you're getting at, Mister Belair? Are you accusing me of neglecting my son?!" Protective anger over his child surfaced, intertwined with sobering tinges of self-doubt. Weeks ago, he'd found his son on the roof of their home, rocking in an upright fetal position and soaked from the driving rain, his eyes reflecting much of the same desperation Jeff himself suffered. Finding him that way, Todd's reluctance to say any more about it: resulted in a revisit to Naomi—so maybe more than a tinge of self-doubt. He knew he'd lost a bit of touch with Todd and M-Sweet, but...

Mr. Belair shook his head, hands raised and waving to protect and defend against a further parental attack. "This is getting a little out of hand. No one's saying— The school just wanted you to be aware—"

"That my son is talented," Jeff interrupted. "Thank you, we're aware." He studied more of the floor.

Mr. Belair sighed.

"It's the devil's work," Ruth mumbled to herself.

Jeff heard her. He was pretty sure Mr. Belair heard her. You couldn't help it in the quiet classroom.

So, he's not crazy; he's just possessed?

Jeff didn't even look up. Whatever fight he had in him drained away. He just wanted to get his son and go home. Go home, shower,...and maybe turn in early.

"He's my son, too, Jeff."

Jeff scoffed and shook his head. Sometimes it was as if she were two different people. "Okay, Ruth." It was all he could manage. He continued staring at the flooring, doing his best not to think about Julia—and failing miserably. After swallowing a sigh, he lifted his head and eyed the teacher. "Are we finished here?"

Mr. Belair nodded, his expression solemn. "I'd say so. Again, I apologize for upsetting you. It wasn't my intent at all."

"I know that, Palmer. No need to apologize. I should've kept my cool. You're just doing your job." Jeff stood. He extended a hand across the table to Mr. Belair. "Thanks for the heads up."

The teacher smiled and stood, appearing relieved. He accepted his hand with a firm shake. "You're welcome. We'll continue to keep an eye out, but let us know if there's something we can do specifically."

"Sure thing." Jeff turned to Ruth with raised eyebrows, waiting for her to rise. He didn't want to speak to her. Not yet. The words wouldn't be good ones.

Ruth stood with a heavy sigh. She, too, extended her hand and shook Mr. Belair's. Jeff noticed Mr. Belair using both his hands to shake hers. "I don't know what to say, Palmer. His mother's been dead for over three years, and yet here we are still with this kind of thing."

"Not a problem, Missus Winthrop," Mr. Belair replied, sounding uncomfortable. He glanced at Jeff.

Jeff kept a straight face. Her comment hurt, but he didn't have it in him to argue about it. He nodded to Mr. Belair and headed for the door. He heard movement and the click-clack of Ruth's heels behind him and assumed she followed suit.

They zipped through the halls of Holden-Wells Academy in silence, arriving outside within minutes. Scents of cut grass mingled with the earthy whiff of wet leaves in the early evening air. The air was still but chilly. Jeff turned the collar up on his jacket and pulled his trilby hat further down around his bald head (he had yet to let his hair grow as Ruth wanted). The time for heavier coats fast approached. Jeff strode toward the football field, not caring if Ruth kept pace.

She managed to keep up.

Someone blew a whistle, and a male voice shouted: "All in!"

As he approached the field, Jeff watched the players come together for a semi-huddle, trying to make out which of them was his son. From the top of the hill, he could hear rumblings of the coach's speech.

She stood next to him, arms folded, her body posture rigid with attitude.

Watching the men and boys, the practice equipment littering a field growing shadowy with the lowering sun, Jeff imagined a painting capturing the moment. Visualized a work influenced by the Expressionism movement and embodying his emotional turmoil with lots of exaggerated distortion of those tackle and blocking dummies (felt like he was being tackled and blocked twenty-four-seven), with colors jarring and vivid. Oh, yeah. He hadn't imagined painting anything in so long; it distinguished the moment. But it was gone like a shot, so Jeff didn't put much faith in it. It would come. And if it didn't, well, that was fine, too. He painted and sculpted his ass off in his dreams, though. Everything was better...in slumber.

The coach didn't talk long. After maybe two minutes, he yelled, "Hit the showers!" The players dispersed across the field in the general direction of the locker room. Jeff picked out his son's #39 jersey as he trotted away with his teammates, helmet held down at his side; he looked happy.

Jeff figured he had another twenty minutes before Todd was ready.

With a huff, Ruth turned and headed for the car.

Jeff didn't move; he watched the field empty of men and young men, listening to his second wife's retreat.

He hadn't spoken a word to her that entire time.

The stinging pellets of hot water against his skin were just what he needed. Jeff bent his head forward and rolled his neck back and forth, allowing the water to pepper his neck and back. The hot water draped his neck and around his face before pouring off his nose. He grabbed the soap and turned away from the water, allowing the wet assault across his shoulders and down his back. He braced his hands against the shower stall and closed his eyes, vanquishing thoughts of Julia's birthday passed, enjoying the pounding to his flesh by the driving water.

When they arrived home, everyone disappeared into their respective corners of the house. Mallory prepared a light dinner while they were out, but so far (as of him stepping in the shower), it'd gone uneaten. She came out of her room to say hello, then retreated.

Jeff felt no need to discuss the parent-teacher conference with Todd on the way home, so when Todd came in, he popped his head into his sister's room for a few minutes before retreating to his room. When Jeff checked in on him later, he was fast asleep. It was barely seven o'clock.

Like father, like son?

Ruth came in, changed her clothes, and left for her exercise class. The two still hadn't spoken since leaving Mr. Belair's classroom.

With his household disbursed, Jeff elected to hit the showers. He rounded his spine for a better water massage.

He wasn't proud of himself for it, but Jeff welcomed the isolation and solitude. He breathed in, allowing the steam to open his nasal passages. The escape and restorative influence of sleep called, but the shower contributed its salutary effects. Tension from the day sluiced off him down the shower drain. If he could, he'd sleep standing in the shower.

Jeff held the soft mushy bar of soap in his left hand braced against the stall. The mountain-air scent permeated his now wide-open sinuses. He didn't want to soap himself yet, content to let the water soothe him.

Soothe...him.

He inhaled more of the soap's mountain-air scent and detected the underlying but distinct aroma of iris, vanilla, and roses.

The water, too, now felt more like tiny fingers and less like pellets. Thumb-like pressure pressed into his shoulder blades.

Jeff jerked around wide-eyed, almost slipping. He pressed his back against the stall. His heart raced. Sweat popped across his brow, washed away by the showering water. He stared intently through the glass of the booth, into the rest of the bathroom: nothing, no one.

Shalimar's iris, roses, and vanilla strengthened, weaving a delicious course through the steam.

Finger and palm pressure moved across his torso, squeezing and relaxing, steadily moving downward.

Jeff pressed a fist to his mouth, suppressing the sob rising from his throat. An outcry, not from any fear or revulsion over possible lunacy overtaking him—but a sob of relief, embracing whatever the hell was happening in this shower.

The massage continued, working his thighs and calves before traveling upward to his shoulders, chest, and abdomen again. Jeff looked down at his body: his skin moved with the feel of her caress. He tilted his head back against the stall, and the sob escaped him this time. He shook his head. "Julia, this can't be. I mean ... I— I can't...," he moaned.

Nevertheless, the parts of him that were male showed he could.

Jeff released the soap, allowing his hands to secure whatever purchase they could against the slippery panel of the stall. He ignored the resounding muffled clang of the soap hitting the stall floor as he received a hand-job from his dead wife.

He trembled with the pleasure yet bared his teeth against the odd sensations moving over him. How could something be so cold and deliciously hot at the same time?

He wasn't sleeping, and he wasn't crazy (was he?). But God help him; it felt like Julia's touch. No, dammit, it *was* her touch. He looked down at himself again. For the tiniest moment, he thought he saw an outline of a small hand working his erection.

Shit, it was good.

And as he climaxed, with Julia's name on his lips, Jeff decided, if he was crazy, if he was truly crazy...

It wasn't such a bad thing after all.

Chapter 10

Options Analysis

S o far, hanging out with her brother turned out better than she expected, but Mallory still reserved judgment until the end of the outing. Their venture to the amusement park a few weeks ago wasn't quite the same thing because they'd gone their separate ways, only hooking up for a ride or two. She sensed something different about their time together this go-round.

For better or worse, something different.

She should have known something was up this morning when Todd asked to join her on her morning run. He usually slept until noon on (non-football) Saturdays, so seeing him in running garb and ready to go at five forty-three a.m. raised Mallory's antennae.

She preferred running solo but didn't mind the company this morning. They didn't talk much; both tuned in to their music players as blocks of Capitol Hill whisked past. But something about him being out there with her made a difference.

When they returned, their stepmother's car wasn't parked outside (a plus). Todd downed a peanut butter protein smoothie (he'd obviously prepared earlier) and then went upstairs. Mallory heard the shower start soon afterward.

She took her sweet time with her morning. Alone at the kitchen table, she browsed a fashion magazine while enjoying a small bowl of Honey Nut Cheerios in peace. She finished all her homework the night before, so a free weekend lay ahead.

After her cereal, she arrived in her room to find the movie section lying across the pillows on her bed. Someone (Todd) circled two afternoon theater showings: one for a horror flick at one-fifteen and a second for the sci-fi blockbuster showing at two o'clock. He texted her, too:

"No game today. Let's bail. Can't do another wknd n this hse!"

Mallory smiled to herself. She didn't know what her brother was up to (if anything), but Kelz was out of town, and she didn't much feel like hanging out with a bunch of girls, so why not? It was something to do.

She had just enough time after her shower to put on her underwear and jeans when Todd knocked on her door to see if she was ready. She didn't know why he was so pressed and didn't care—he wasn't stressing her out on her lazy Saturday. In her own time, Mallory finished dressing and said goodbye to her father. Ruth left earlier without a word to anyone. It was close to ten-fifteen before she and Todd left the house and headed for the Capitol South Metro station.

They killed time window-shopping after deciding on the sci-fi movie and purchasing their tickets early. Mallory thought Todd wanted this time to talk like they did in his room weeks ago or on the porch the other day, but Todd never ventured to discuss anything more profound than the latest gossip in Black entertainment.

After two hours and eleven minutes in the world of science fiction (a good movie, actually, with an ending killing any hopes for a sequel; Mallory liked that), they now sat in the mall's busy food court.

Mallory watched her brother enjoy his second deluxe cheeseburger with his large order of curly fries while she sipped her passion fruit smoothie and dabbled with the few sweet potato fries remaining on her plate. She couldn't finish her too-big chicken sandwich. She noticed Todd eyeing what was left of her sandwich as he chomped his.

Todd paused just enough to wash down what he'd eaten with a sip of his super-large ginger ale. He belched and tapped his chest with a fist. "Scuse me."

"Pig. Slow down." Shaking her head, she rolled her eyes with a sigh.

"It's good!"

"So."

He eyed her plate again. "You gonna eat that?"

Mallory sucked her teeth as she shifted her plate closer to her brother.

"Thanks." Todd smiled the brightest smile at her.

He looked so much like their mother; it was a shame. Mallory turned away, memories of her mother zipping through with almost thirteen years of mother-daughter stuff. Before things turned morose, however, she turned back to Todd.

He garbled, "What?" around a bite of sandwich. Dabs of sauce speck-led the corners of his mouth.

"Will you hurry up?"

Todd swallowed his bite. "But you just told me to slow down."

She scoffed, eyeing him hard. "Right. Slow down and hurry up." She extended a napkin his way. "Wipe your mouth. Here's a left-handed napkin for you."

He playfully snatched the napkin. "Ha-ha. At least I'm in my *right* mind." He wiped his mouth. "But seriously. What?" Todd smiled again, one bright and curious—bringing Julia Winthrop front and center.

Mallory looked away again. "Nothing." She divided her attention be-tween Todd and the mall patrons before settling focus on her brother.

"Oh." Todd put his sandwich down and reached for his drink, poising the straw at his lips. "I know what it is." He sipped.

Mallory sat back, arms folded. "You don't know anything because I said, 'nothing.'"

His gaze transitioned to something more serious, knowing. "...It's how much I look like Mommy."

Neither said a word for several seconds, allowing Todd's summation to vibrate between them.

Finally, Mallory returned a faint nod.

Todd nodded back. He leaned back in his chair, crossing his ankles while folding his hands behind his head.

The two retreated into their private thoughts as the cacophony of people shopping, eating, and socializing filled the comfortable silence.

Mallory spoke first: "How'd you—?"

"Dad reacts to me the same way. Ruth, too, sometimes. Dad says I look so much like her, it hurts."

"Yeah, something like that." Mallory sat forward with a sigh. "And Ruth does it, too? She's never met Mommy."

Todd glanced around self-consciously, as he did in Dr. Alexander's office. It seemed subconscious, like he was checking around for Ruth or something.

Mallory hated it.

"She knows what Mommy looked like, Mal. The portrait Dad used to have in his studio, remember? The pictures now in that bottom drawer in the dining room, the ones in our rooms. But yeah, she'll say: 'Well, she just spit you right out, didn't she?' or 'Mallory is definitely daddy's baby, but you might be a papa's maybe,' or saying Dad might want to get a paternity test on me. Shit like that."

"What?! Are you serious?"

Todd raised an eyebrow and twisted his lips sideways. "Nah, I'm making it up. Whatchu think?"

"I know. I'm sorry. It's just—"

"How it comes out depends on her mood, but yeah, Miss God-fearing, church-going woman says that shit to me."

"Her eyes doing—"

"That weird 'wash out' thing, where the green fades and shit?" He gave an abrupt nod. "You know it."

Mallory envisioned it, hated it. But it was important Todd understand something above all else. "Todd, we have the same parents. Mother *and* father."

Todd waved a dismissive hand at her. At that moment, Mallory saw their dad in him. "I know that, Mal." He sucked his teeth. "I mean, that shit used to bother me in the beginning, but I ain't worryin' 'bout that now." He sat forward, forearms across his thighs, and interlocked his fingers. "It's all good. Fuck 'er, man." He looked away, but Mallory saw his eyes were wet. She noticed a tiny wet spot dotted a denim-clad thigh.

He sniffed and drew a hand down his face. "You ready?"

"She still doing stuff to you since we started back with Doctor Alex?" She knew the answer but needed to know, hear it from his lips.

Todd wiped his hand on his jeans. He reached for another napkin, wiped his face again, and cleared his throat. "She— She doesn't pinch me, punch my arms, or pop the back of my head *as much* anymore, but...she...she still says and does stuff to hurt me, yeah. My back...has been her recent favorite target when she does anything now." He scanned the food court in that "checking for Ruth" way again.

Even though Todd said Ruth didn't do it as much anymore, Mallory seethed at hearing how their stepmother treated her brother. And he'd described all of it with this casual acceptance both perverse and sad. That nasty bruise she saw on his back in Dr. Alex's office came to mind, and she breathed deeply to calm herself. That was Ruth ("D-Nine," her rear-end). "But, Todd, if you know she's trying to get to you, why do you let her? Do you want me to say something?"

Todd just looked at her.

"Well, tell Daddy then!"

His expression remained static.

"What about Doctor Alexander?"

Todd's eyes softened. He shrugged and leaned back in his chair again. "I 'on't know. I mean, for what?"

"What other options do we have? We don't have much family, and that which we do, well... Uncle Bruce is in jail—"

Todd perked up. "Hey, with his connections, we can—"

"Quit it. Anyway, like I was saying: Uncle Bruce: locked up; Pa-Pa Tilden: in a nursing home and way too sick, anyway; and Auntie Lila won't be home from her tour of duty for another year."

"So, options limited, huh?" Todd sipped his soda.

"That's the conclusion of my analysis, yeah: very limited," Mallory answered. And the options analysis was bleak. Her throat tightened, and she fought getting tearful. She reached for her smoothie and slurped slowly until it was gone.

"...Well, I still don't know about saying anything to Doctor Alex. I mean, she seems cool and all. I just..." Todd trailed off, shrugging and shaking his head.

Someone shouted Todd's name.

Looking somewhere over Mallory's head and behind her, he issued an upward jerk of his head, adding a hand-gesture wave in greeting.

Mallory turned around in time to see Walter Lyons bringing his hand down from his wave. He walked on with two other fellows, laughing and exchanging dap with them. Walter Lyons was cute, clever, and on total lockdown with Kendra Allred. Still, Mallory sometimes talked to him in biology or English-Lit class. She watched the guys head away, figuring

Walter didn't recognize her. Didn't matter much, anyway. She turned back to her brother.

"They broke up, you know." Todd nibbled a fry and then pushed his plate away with a frown. "Guess I won't be eatin' any more of this: everything's cold now."

"Who?" Mallory did her best to feign ignorance and disguise her pleasure at the news.

Todd shook his head with a knowing mirth. "Why do girls do that?" His demeanor with the question made him appear more as if in his 20s rather than 14.

"What? What'd I do?"

"Nothing. Forget it. D-Nine and Kendra broke up, that's who?" He ate another fry anyway.

"Oh,...okay. Why're you telling me?"

"Just thought you might want to know. Came up in the locker room after Thursday's game."

"Whatever."

He smirked. "Yeah, right. Just lettin' you know. ...And he asked me about you—with message and meaning."

Mallory gazed at him intently to imply serious nonchalance, doing her best to counter the flutters of hope in her belly. Maybe their talks in class could go further (since he's asking Todd about her and all). "Thanks for the update, but I'm not pressed."

"Didn't say you were." Todd shrugged, shaking his head with a chuckle (once again seeming older than his years).

Mallory brought them back to topic. She had her brother talking and didn't want to ruin it (she'll follow up about Walter later). "Doctor Alex'll probably figure it out in our sessions anyway..."

"You really like her, don't you?"

"You don't?"

"I said she seemed cool, didn't I?"

"You did." She shrugged and then nodded. "I don't know... Yeah, I like her. It's the way she holds our sessions. She's not patronizing, you know? I think Mommy would've liked her."

He sipped his soda, holding the straw between his teeth as he spoke. "I like how she deals with Ruth."

"Ha!" Mallory laughed, giving her brother a high-five. "No cut cards!"

The amusement on Todd's face faded into something more neutral. "Yeah, but we pay for that shit after. Or at least,...*I do.*" His expression grew somber.

"I guess," Mallory uttered regrettably, wincing inside over her brother's predicament with their stepmother. She paused, wondering something. "Todd, have you..." She didn't quite know how to ask the question.

"Have I...?" he prompted.

She shook her head. "Nothing. Never mind. If you had, you would have said something. ...I think," Mallory hedged.

He frowned. "If I had what?"

She stared at her brother, trying to decide whether she should ask him something that may make her seem crazy, but was something she needed to know.

Todd's eyes steadied on her with concern while his brows curved in curiosity.

She had him in a talking mood; she'd best take advantage of it. She plunged ahead. "Have you seen, heard, smelled, or felt Mommy lately?"

Todd's concerned curiosity melded into confusion; his frown deepened. "Huh? What, you mean like...a ghost or something?"

"Or something. Have you? I mean, recently. Around the house, or—"

"No." He scoffed, shaking his head with displeasure. "That shit ain't funny, Mal."

Mallory turned grave. "I am *not* joking."

He stared at her for some seconds, his eyes trying to gauge her sincerity. His gaze turned serious upon seeing she was sincere—very much so. "...So, you're saying you're seeing our mother's ghost?"

"No. I...don't *see* her. I just... It's just that...that there have been times when I *feel* her around me. And sometimes I can smell her."

"Seriously?"

"Seriously."

Todd let out a heavy sigh, puffing his cheeks out. He looked around, observing the activity of the food court, before returning his attention to her. "I don't know, Mal. Maybe you just really miss her—like Daddy or something."

"So, you're saying I should tell Doctor Alexander?"

"Yeah. Maybe she can help before you *really* get like Daddy. Know what I'm saying?"

Mallory freed a puff of air. Todd had a point, but she also knew she wasn't imagining things (was she?). "Yeah, okay. I can't do it in a session, though. That would be too much."

"No shit."

Mallory locked eyes with her brother. "I'm not crazy, Todd."

Todd leaned toward her with mock seriousness. "I know you're not crazy, Sis." And although he mocked her, he was sincere; Mallory appreciated hearing it.

"Thank you."

Todd's expression morphed into genuine seriousness. "What do you smell, you know,...when you 'smell' her?"

"Shalimar."

Her brother's eyes softened with memory. "Oh yeah. I liked when she wore that. Smelled kinda sweet without being too strong."

"You probably picked up on the vanilla highlights in the fragrance."

"Well, la-di-da. Whatever. It smelled good on her." Todd sipped his soda. "You ever smell anything else? She wore stuff besides Shalimar. Like her freesia oil, or—"

"No. No, just the Shalimar. She wore that more than anything."

"Yeah, she did." He fiddled with his straw. "So,...is it scary?"

Mallory reflected on the sensation whenever she smelled or felt her mother nearby. "Not at all. It was scary at first, yeah, because I didn't know what the heck was happening. But now..." She shook her head to punctuate her response.

The siblings observed the mall activity. "...Mal?"

"Mm-hmm?" Mallory continued eyeing a desert-brown leather purse in the shop window across the way, contemplating its purchase. She cringed inside over thoughts of Ruth asking about the purchase later.

"What was the name of that song Mommy would play, and then have all of us dancing around the dining room and—"

"'Respect Yourself' by the Staple Singers."

"Yeah, that's it."

Deciding to purchase the cute bag despite possible negative repercussions with her stepmother, Mallory turned to her brother. "Why?"

Todd offered the saddest shrug. "I 'on't know. Just thinking about some of the goofy, fun stuff Mommy came up with. Remember how Daddy always kissed her at the end of that song?"

Mallory gradually nodded with agreement, with memory. Images of the four of them dancing around the first floor of the house, singing along with the Staple Singers (their parents making sure she and her brother understood the importance of the lyrics as they sang them), made Mallory wistful for the old days. The simple but tender peck her dad would place on their mother's lips when that song ended remained a treasured memory (and grounded her faith in Black love). "Yeah, I remember."

They were silent again until Valeda and a friend came up to them and spoke. Valeda engaged Mallory in some small talk about office gossip at their work-study jobs while her friend stood patiently to the side. Mallory noticed Todd and the friend checking each other out.

When they left, Mallory wasted no time. "She's got to be at least seventeen, Todd."

"Wasn't scoping Valeda. I was checking out... What was her name?"

"She said, 'Genette.' With a 'G,' not a 'J,' no 'A,'" Mallory recited, holding in a titter.

"Yeah, her."

"And that's whom I'm talking about!"

"So. I'll be fifteen in four months."

"So, what, you like a slightly older woman?"

"Maybe. That mermaid tattoo on her neck, though: *nice*."

Mallory thought so, too. "Anyway, back to our family situa—"

"Come on, man! We don't have to keep talking about it."

"Why? Ruth doesn't care about us, Todd. Not really. And how do I know? Because she allows you to dress with your pants hanging off you and whatnot, whereas Mommy would have been all over you to get your act together and present yourself in a more welcoming manner—at least to some extent."

Todd focused on her for several seconds before responding. "'Welcoming manner'? Mommy wasn't a conformist, Mal."

Mallory drew her head back, appraising her brother. "Listen to you: 'conformist.' And no, she wasn't. Mommy was a free spirit and all, but I don't think she cared too much for this form of self-expression."

"Maybe, maybe not." He watched the people, his expression changing to something mixing anger and hurt. "...You know, I thought you were going to say the lady didn't care because of what she does to me, not—"

"Parents discipline their children, Todd. But really caring about someone goes beyond that—or it should, anyway."

He turned back to her, his big brown eyes (the color much like their mother's) angrier than she'd ever seen them. "First of all, I'm *not* her child. Second of all, what she does to me is *not* discipline. Don't tell me that shit again. Okay?" Hurt and anger drew his posture inward as if to protect himself—or pounce. He looked away again.

Todd was right. Whenever the subject came up, the *first* thing she stressed was Ruth not being her mother. And that second thing... Well, Todd was absolutely right. She should have known better (had his back). "I'm sorry," Mallory expressed with all sincerity.

Todd didn't look at her. "It's a'ight."

"For real, Todd."

He continued looking elsewhere. "I know. It's a'ight. Let it go, okay?"

"Why?"

Todd settled his gaze on her. "Look, you're gonna be gone in two years. I'ma be out in less than four. Let the shit play out." He started gathering the trash on their table and piling it on his tray.

"Daddy cannot stay married to her!"

"Well, it doesn't look like Dad either gives a care or is in any condition to think for himself, let alone think about us in all this. He wanted us to have a mother, Mal."

Her eyes stung. "You think that's all this is?"

He shrugged.

Mallory wiped away a tear. "Well, we have to let him know we don't have to have a mother—at least not *her.*"

Todd maintained a neutral expression.

"I know. Dad's having a real hard time..."

He shrugged again. He stood with the tray of trash in hand, obviously done talking about it. "Dessert?"

Mallory peered up at her brother. His eyes told her to let it go for now. Defeat curling her insides, she rose with a sigh. "Yeah, I guess..." She wondered what her father might be doing but then knew instantly: *sleeping.* "Yeah, let's go to the bakery."

"I'll buy."

"No, I got it. You've paid for everything today. Besides, where are you getting all this money from, anyway?"

"I don't go through my money like you do. And no, I got it. We don't need Ruth all in your pockets any more than she already is. Not for this one. So, *I* got it." He started toward the trashcan.

Mallory followed. "Thanks. I guess we both get it from her in different ways, huh?" Although, the way she "got it" didn't compare, in any way, to how her brother did. She had to do something to help him. The analysis of available recourse inside their small family wasn't good. Still, telling their dad was an option. But getting up the nerve for it...was another matter entirely.

"I guess. If I had access to my bank account, I'm sure she'd be all up in my money, too." He dropped the tray contents in the receptacle and placed the tray on top. "Your problem is, you do stuff requiring more than your monthly allotment, sending 'alarm' bells resulting in Ruth's motherly concern..." He chuckled, not with humor, but with a wisdom and irony that, again, aged him.

"Yeah, but you should still track your balance, Todd. Dad'll let you do that. Ask him about it. You can download the app or something and monitor your account."

Todd shrugged, giving Mallory a sideways smirk. "You don't trust what Ruth might do with my cut, huh? If her name's been added to yours, she's most likely on mine. She might get some ideas..." he posed with calculating curiosity. He walked a few steps ahead of her. "Enough on that crap. Come on. Let's hit the bookstore, too."

Mallory smiled to herself when her brother pulled his jeans over his butt. Stepping up beside him, she almost hugged Todd when he fastened his belt tighter at the waist as they walked, making his belt functional rather than just a decorative accessory. She ruffled her brother's hair. "You need a haircut!"

Todd ducked out of her reach and frowned. "Quit it." He stood erect. "I know I do. We can stop by the barbershop on the way home. See if Preston is there."

"If not, I can at least trim it for you."

"Uh, I don't think so."

"What? Why? I've done it before."

They moseyed in the direction of Fogusto's Bakery. Mallory had a taste for one of their red velvet cupcakes.

"My point exactly. I'll pass."

"It wasn't that bad. Seriously though, the curls are getting too curly." Mallory reached for his head again.

And again, Todd ducked away from her. "Quit it, I said."

Both of them cracked up, momentarily distracted from the sorrow over their dead mother, worry over their mourning father, and distress over their (wicked) stepmother.

In the end (after enjoying a cupcake from Fogusto's), she bought the cute leather purse, both bought book one in a new YA Fantasy series, and Preston cut Todd's hair.

Chapter 11

Trying to Love Two

If only he could stay here. Here, on this side. Here, there was love and fun, laughter and peace,...and Julia. That, above all else, remained the best part of these...these...these memory-dreams—or whatever they were. A name, a title for the experiences, wasn't necessary or important. Jeff twirls a finger around one of Julia's twists as they sit on their family room floor, leaning back against the sofa. Julia's Coppin State throw blanket wraps mostly around her legs but partly around his, too. They watch a television show that, on some level, Jeff knows didn't exist until after Julia's death, but that *doesn't matter. Little does, here.*

Jeff smiled in his sleep. His breathing deepened as his finger twirled against his pillow. It is four thirty-nine in the afternoon.

Nothing burns in the fireplace, but the room glows with hues of amber, anyway. It is a golden, lazy time for them. Golden, lazy times have been the order of the day these last few weeks. Their wedding anniversary approached. They hadn't made love during his latest visits with her, but sitting here on the floor with her (smelling her, touching her), Jeff didn't know if he could allow another visit to go by without having her again. Thoughts of it stirred his groin with desire.

Julia looks up at him with a knowing smile. Without losing her smile, she speaks as she always does here (only in his head). "I love you. I must go soon." She maintains her knowing smile and trails a hand down his thigh and back up again. Her fingers inch over and around him, where it matters most, and Jeff's breath catches in his throat.

Seemingly satisfied with his response, Julia returns her attention to the show and snuggles in closer, giving him those now familiar, tiny, chilly-yet-hot tingles as her body pressed against his. "Our babies need you," she says. But Jeff *knows her lips never move. Jeff pulls his wife tighter to him, content to play in her hair.*

Jeff shook his head against his pillow and whimpered in sleepy protest. His hand clenched and released as his eyelids fluttered.

They watch television (a live comedy act by an up-and-coming co-median). The monologue and audience participation are inaudible, yet Jeff and Julia watch and laugh together at all the appropriate moments. Laughing with Jules supplemented all the good rest of it.

Golden, lazy times.

Although the comedian is of present-day popularity, Jeff enjoys the show with his wife in the family room as it was nine, ten years ago. He knows the family room has since changed: past and present *are commingling. It doesn't matter. Not here. The comedian segues into act three of his shtick. Jeff and Julia laugh.*

Jeff chuckled low in his throat and changed position on the bed, moving from his side to a prone position. He smiled before the muscles in his face slackened. His relaxed jaw drew his mouth open as he "slept."

The scene shifts without warning (as it sometimes does in these memory-dreams). Jeff sits at the piano in the art-slash-music room and plays a bridge to Maxwell's "Whenever, Wherever, Whatever." No sound emanates, but as Jeff strikes the keys, he and Julia hear the notes of the melody anyway. Julia moves about the studio at her leisure, pausing when she comes near him to caress his head, shoulders, or back.

In tandem with the change in scene, the hues of amber have changed, too, leaving the golden, lazy times behind. Cool beams of blues and grays emit the room. In the artist room, he plays, she listens.

These are cool blue, easy times. Jeff watches Julia saunter about the room. She wears ianthine leggings with a form-fitting shirt of olive.

She pauses in front of the Bose Acoustic Wave and searches through a stack of CDs lined against its side. He watches as her finger stops at a CD. She turns to give him another knowing smile before selecting the CD and putting it in the system.

"Love So True" resounds (but doesn't) with the eloquence of Maysa Leak. Jeff nods with an acknowledging smile. Julia loves Maysa (and so does he), so he maintained the collection of her work. He tinkles on the piano, offering occasional pieces of accompaniment.

Iris, vanilla, and rose fragrances ebb and flow with the song's cadence and his wife's saunter and sway through the art-music room: Guerlain Shalimar. Julia moves toward him, but time skips, and she is beside him on the piano bench much sooner than she should have been. Jeff plays on, quite used to how things worked in these memory-dreams. Julia leans on him, and he is wonderfully affected. Her heady scent envelopes him, and he stops playing, Maysa continuing her performance from the player and all around them.

Julia kisses his outer ear, one hand placed at his back. Jeff needs her hand there. Emotion moves through him, and he falters backward with the weight of it, but Julia is strong and holds him upright. "I'm always here, Jeffrey," she says in his head. He is rocking now, and Julia places her other hand at his chest—to steady him, calm him. But the calming is only temporary; he is anxious without knowing why. Jeff shakes his head; something isn't right. It feels as if time isn't moving at all but quickly. "Our babies need you," she says, and Jeff shakes his head, fiercely resisting the meaning behind those words. *He* needs her.

His Julia is already gone, but she cannot leave him again. He knows she will not always be here, yet these memory-dreams make it so. He looks at her, and she at him. "Love So True" is *unending (in these dream states, at least), and they hold each other's gaze for some time. Julia's eyes reflect a blend of caramel hues; Jeff is lost in them.*

A door slammed in the house, making Jeff startle in his sleep.

Julia pecks his lips, and Jeff tilts his head back with a sob. Memory-dream or not, the kiss feels as real as any he'd ever received from her. "What is this?" he asks no one in particular, wondering if his words are only in Julia's head.

Jeff lowers his head. They no longer sit on the piano bench but on the window seat on the opposite side of the artist room. He and Julia built the window seat together about a year before she died. He remembers sex with her doggy-style, some reggae by Bob Marley on low in the background as they both took in the cityscape of Capitol Hill. But they sit side-by-side now, holding hands with the window view at their backs, the nutty essence of linseed oil only mildly pervasive with the ample ventilation.

They gaze into the room's interior, but Jeff senses Julia's unease. The cool blue, easy times are shifting to something grayer and less easy.

He squeezes her hand. She returns the pressure, and Jeff gets hard instantly, almost painfully. Julia straddles him, kissing him with loving voracity. That indefinable yet familiar coldness seeps into him, but her mouth is deliciously warm and inviting, too. She unbuttons her shirt, and the front clasp of her bra seems to unhook itself for him. Jeff fills his hands with the curves of her behind as his mouth and tongue *caress her small but firm breasts and taut nipples. She tastes of chocolate amaretto with hints of vanilla.*

Jeff shifted in his sleep as his erection pressed into the mattress. He reached beneath and shifted himself against his inner thigh, giving himself a gentle squeeze and stroke before returning his hands to his pillow, oblivious to the dampness from his tears. Another door slammed somewhere in the house, but Jeff didn't startle this time. He slept.

Maysa continues her serenade while Julia places kiss upon kiss on his head, occasionally licking his scalp (he didn't understand why either of them got off on that shit, but they did). While she kneads his shoulders, Jeff feasts on her neck, her breasts. She grinds against him with fantastic technique, driving them both crazy. Mouths rejoin, and Jeff mingles Julia's tongue and excited breathing with his until he must have her.

Rising from her lap dance, she puts a hand on her hip and a sexy smile on her lips as she waits for him to free himself. Jeff watches her and can't move, transfixed at seeing her leggings fade away from her body, revealing her sex. He likes the magic in his memory-dreams—*if* he's dreaming (because they're more memory than dream).

Impatience moves her to reach for his zipper to do the freeing herself. She strokes him with a tantalizing mix of timidity and aggression. Her touch sends him to the brink of letting go, but neither wants that.

Julia reads the familiar signals of his body and straddles him, holding onto his shoulders. She hovers above him at the frustrating point of entry. Jeff moans and thrusts upward to complete the connection. Julia smiles and adjusts out of reach. She then lowers *herself just enough to resume their kiss and nothing more. Jeff laughs into her mouth. The simple pleasure of her comforts him.*

Someone knocked on the door.

Jeff's eyelids fluttered as his breathing grew shallow. He turned his head to the other side and back again, a frown of annoyance creasing his brow. He wanted to sleep.

They kiss, but Julia is noticeably lighter now. Jeff strains upward to enter her. Julia laughs (a soft, lilting sound in his head) and settles down onto him. She is cold and warm and wet and tight (and so *cold*). They move together as they've done so many times before, but Jeff feels himself straining to move toward her warmth. It is so good. But she's becoming lighter and more nebulous with each thrust. She is leaving him. "No, wait!" he whines. Even Maysa deserts him as "Love So True" fades. Jeff thrusts harder, faster, wanting nothing more than to finish what they started.

He tries his best to hold her to him because she can't leave him. Not like this. She can't. She can't... She...can't. *Jeff whispers "Julia" into the nothingness that is his fading memory-dream.*

Another knock on the door bolted Jeff from his nap. He lifted his head, checking his surroundings: his bedroom, his bed. Jeff dropped his head back onto the pillow. He hated this part: the being-awake-after-be-ing-with-Julia part. If he could get a few more minutes...

Another knock. "Daddy?" It was Mallory.

"What!?" He answered, maybe a little too harshly; it was never good for him right after the memory-dreams (but only he knew that). Jeff released a tension-loosening exhale and altered course. "Whassup, M-Sweet?" he called this time, wanting to soften any impact of his initial response. He took a deep breath and allowed his heartbeat to slow from fourth to second gear.

"You okay? Can I come in?"

"Just getting some shuteye." And no, he didn't want her to come in, but what could he say? Jeff closed his eyes, envisioning the art-music room upstairs. The space was unoccupied at present, but he thought he heard...

"Daddy?"

Shit.

Jeff sighed. His erection was stubborn; it hadn't subsided even the teeniest bit yet. Still lying prone, he mumbled, "It's not locked, Mal," halfway into his pillow, keeping one eye on the door.

"Huh?"

"Open!"

Mallory opened the door and stepped inside. "Sorry." She closed the door, leaning back against it with her hands behind her. His daughter looked pretty in her multicolored empire-waist top and black skinny-jeans. But the lines around her mouth meant she was not in a pretty mood. "Sorry, Daddy."

Jeff remained prone on the bed, quite averse to changing his position. This was the second time in as many months that his daughter happened upon him at a most inopportune time. "It's all right, Mal." He twisted his upper torso enough to prop his elbow and support his head with his hand. "What's up, sweetheart?" He did his best to think of all things conducive to flaccidity. The desired results weren't immediately forthcoming; Julia had that effect on him (and he'd been right on the verge of an intense orgasm).

He shifted with the discomfort, trying to be as inconspicuous as he could. He glanced for a split second toward his night table. "Time izzit?"

Mallory didn't speak for a second or two before responding. "After five." She gestured toward the windows. Sunset filtered through the wood blinds.

Jeff stared at his daughter.

She now added a smile, but it was too late: he'd already discerned the admonishment in her tone.

At last, his erection subsided (if only a little). "Ruth home?" *Thoughts of her should get the mission accomplished.* He didn't like feeling that way, but hey.

"Downstairs, watching the news." Mallory stared straight ahead, speaking in renewed monotone. And Jeff knew instantly the source of her discontent (big surprise).

"What'd she do?" he sighed over the sound of his stomach growling. He'd eaten today, hadn't he? "I've already talked to her about your bank account. Now—"

She turned to him, shaking her head with an expression he couldn't read. "No, Daddy. It's not the account situation. I mean, it is, but... Well, that's only a part of it."

"So, what'd she do?" He asked again. It was never a good time for him after the memory-dreams; it just wasn't. *Our babies need you...* Jeff used the hand supporting his head to massage his temples and forehead. No headache, just...weary.

"She didn't 'do' anything, Daddy. I mean, not *today* specifically. It's... It's ...her in general."

Jeff shook his head. Flaccidity accomplished, he shifted his legs around to sit on the side of the bed and turned on his lamp. "Generalities won't do it, Mal. No one's perfect."

Mallory rolled her eyes upward and sucked her teeth. She folded her arms and leaned back against the door with a huff. "I know that."

Jeff lowered his head and shook it. This was why sleeping was better. "Ruth's not all bad, Mal," he looked up at her, "but if you have something specific, I'm all ears."

"If I have something specific, you'll divorce her?"

Such a drastic proposition revealed the extent of Mallory's distress over whatever was going on—as well as her state of mind regarding the changes in their household. Jeff gazed at his daughter, determining how best to answer her. "...Depends on what it is, and even then, it's not as simple as that—you know that, too."

"It should be," she muttered.

"Well, it isn't." He adjusted the covers around him. "So, what's happened? What's wrong?" He wasn't sure he wanted to know.

She studied him. "...You're losing weight."

Jeff administered a cursory self-inspection. "You think so? Nah, I'm about the same."

"No, you're not."

"Did you want to talk about me or Ruth?"

"The whole thing?"

"Stick with the original plan; stick with Ruth. What'd she do?"

Mallory hesitated for seconds too annoyingly long (it wasn't a good time for him after being with Jules in the memory-dreams). "Well, besides the money thing, you know how we don't get along..."

"The teen years are usually difficult for mothers and daught—"

"She's *not* my mother."

"Within the context of our family as it is now, she's in that role." Jeff paused, words in his head refusing to pass over his tongue. "And I'd be willing to bet that if— that if... that...if nothing had changed for us, you and your mother would be battling these years out, too."

"It'd be different."

"Maybe, maybe not." But M-Sweet was right: it would be. Jeff ran a hand over his head. Stubble dotted his scalp: time to take his razor to it soon. Ruth would be pissed—but those were the breaks.

"October twenty-second's right around the corner." The edge in her tone carried a snippet of plea, too.

That dagger was well-placed. His chest did a brisk hiccup of movement upon hearing the date of his and Jules' wedding anniversary. Jeff appreciated the poignant meaning, but it wasn't necessary; that date lived in his thoughts since October began. "So it is," Jeff said, swirling in post-memory-dream despair and so, refusing to give his daughter a drop of emotional blood. "Look, Mal, 'not getting along' doesn't cut it."

"Well..."

"Well...? Yes?" He used a hand in a prompting gesture for her to finish whatever it was he didn't really want to hear in the first place.

"Well..." Mallory looked down. "What about Todd?"

"What about 'im? There was the whole thing about him playing ball, but that's squashed now."

She returned her gaze to him. "There're other things..."

Jeff clutched the bedding to keep from rising. Nothing against his baby girl, but irritability lingered from being interrupted from his time with Julia. None of this hedging and mystery about Ruth helped matters. "You know what? Let Todd tell me these 'things.' Okay?!"

Mallory's eyes widened with hurt feelings. He rarely, if ever, spoke to her that way. Her mouth worked, but no sound came out. She didn't cry, but her voice wavered when she next spoke. "I'm just trying to get you to see no one is happy with her, Daddy. ...Including you."

Jeff didn't answer right away.

Mallory wasn't a baby, but she wasn't adult enough to understand or appreciate that, what he'd done, the decisions he'd made, were in his children's best interest. Besides, aside from the football fiasco, Todd hadn't shown or expressed having any problems with Ruth. Yeah, boys were different, but Jeff believed he knew his son.

You didn't know about his writing.

Jeff ignored the intruding thought. If something were going on, Todd would say something (wouldn't he?). This was probably Mallory just going through a teen thing with her stepmother.

Our babies need you...

Jeff cleared his throat. He thought all those things, but he couldn't lie, either (not entirely). "Ruth and I have our differences. Married people usually do. Your mother and I did, too."

"It's nowhere near the same, Daddy, and you know it. Never mind." She turned and left the room, closing the door behind her.

Jeff plopped back onto the bed and watched the ceiling. No, it wasn't anywhere near the same. Nothing was. He needed to get back on track with Ruth. *Back on track? Were you ever...on track?* Find a way to make the marriage work because his children needed a mother. No, having a mother in the home wasn't the sole reason he married Ruth, but it was his primary one. And, well, he loved Ruth (in a manner of speaking).

Oh, but he loved Julia Èkerie Simms Winthrop so...*differently*.

The urge to crawl back under the covers and shut the world out surfaced, but Jeff resisted it, albeit under mental and emotional protest. After another minute or two of debate, he forced himself up and went to the bathroom to freshen up before going downstairs to join Ruth.

On a scale of one to ten (one being murder-in-mind, and ten being murder-can-wait), the evening thus far ranked a solid seven-point-five.

Overall, it'd been just the two of them. The Rhodes family held ward over Todd for the night, and Mallory elected to skip dinner and study in her room. He and Ruth spent the better part of the evening in the family room watching television, with him listening somewhat attentively to Ruth's recap of her day and related real estate prospects. He was determined to put a brighter spin on things.

Ruth, too, seemed pleased with the evening's progress. As they watched some crime drama during the ten o'clock hour, she leaned against him for a little while before snuggling into him altogether.

He couldn't help making mental comparison to his time spent snuggling with Julia on the floor of their family room in his memory-dream, but he didn't dwell on the differences—or at least he tried not to.

She tilted her head back and looked up at him, her verdant irises curious. "You ever do the water paints?"

He frowned. "You mean, painting in watercolor?"

She nodded.

"No. Why?"

She shrugged, returning her attention to the television. "Your other stuff's so bold, deep. I don't know; just thought maybe something easy and light would help you get back in artist mode."

Jeff closed his eyes, breathing lightly, trying to keep the seven-point-five from sliding. After another soft breath, he opened his eyes. "Watercolor, whether transparent or opaque, is a very sensitive media—nothing 'easy' about it, Ruth. Even the slightest mis-stroke can ruin a work and make it an uninterpretable mess after over corrections."

"I see."

He doubted she did. But this constant pressing him about resuming his art—left him even more disinclined to be creative. Kind and subtle hints from M-Sweet or Todd were okay. He didn't appreciate it as much coming from Ruth, though, possibly because he suspected some *crocodile* purpose behind it all. "Anyway, my stuff's on a larger scale; watercolor tends to roll a smaller format. I'd be more inclined to dry-brush rather than do wash styles, I guess—" He shook his head. "I appreciate the suggestion, but watercolor isn't a direction for me."

It occurred to him: Ruth even posing the question, said so much about how little she knew him, about how little she'd invested in learning about something so integral to his...*existence*, really. If Ruth cared to *know* him these last years—the matter of him painting in watercolor wouldn't have come up.

She shrugged again, her shoulder digging into his side. "Oh. Didn't realize it was all so... Anyway, sorry." But there was *bite* to that apology.

Jeff rubbed her upper arm. "No worries. Let's finish the show."

She sighed, "Fine."

It would have to be.

The show ended (the criminal got off on a surprise technicality) and rolled on to the eleven o'clock news.

Ruth sat up. She looked at him and squeezed his thigh. "The first fifteen minutes have the bad news. You ready to go up...?"

Please don't add "Jeffy," or I'll kill somebody.

She didn't.

Jeff stretched. "Yeah, yeah. Sure, if you are. We can call it a night."

She squeezed his thigh again, letting the pressure linger for an extra second. Her viridescent eyes carried every meaning of her intentions. "Well, it's just a change in venue. The night's not over."

Jeff swallowed, nodding his understanding. "I hear you." Absolutely nothing stirred in his groin. "You go ahead up." He pecked her lips. "Let me check the doors first."

Ruth took her hair out of its ponytail and combed through it with her fingers, loosening it and letting it out. "Okay. Oh, and I found something, Jeff, that I want to show you, talk to you about."

Her face and tone were neutral, so Jeff didn't know how to respond. "Oh, okay." Unease wormed its way into his belly.

"I just need five minutes." She pecked his lips before heading upstairs.

He took his time moving about the lower level, giving her thirteen minutes instead. He entered their bedroom with footsteps hesitant but not timid, curious and wary about what she wanted to talk about.

Ruth lounged in her chair in what served as their sitting area. She wore a pale-yellow tank-top with lady boxer shorts to match. A human-interest story played low from the high-definition flat-panel TV.

Seeing him, her face livened with a genuine smile. Lately, it wasn't often he interacted with this side of Ruth. He was glad to see it, but remained wary. You never knew with her, these days. And Ruth was textbook fine: the hair, the body, the face. But Jeff doubted it would be enough. The persistent softness of his penis suggested it wasn't.

Ruth patted the arm of her chair, suggesting he sit there. She wore no bra, so her full breasts jiggled with her movement, the nipples pressing against the fabric of her tank. Her boxers rode up high, revealing her buttercream thighs. The pale-yellow ensemble (however "sexy" and revealing) bothered his artist's eye. Ruth's light complexion, the yellow-tinged buttercream shading of her skin, coupled with the pale-yellow tank and boxers, gave her a sallow look. Pale-yellow was especially bothersome because it was so close to her skin color. A pale blue or even pale pink would've worked better—but still wouldn't have mattered.

An envelope sat perched between the cushion and the frame of the chair she sat in.

"I'ma shower first." He needed time to make himself hard, because he had yet to grow even a little excited. He closed the door to their bedroom.

"You don't need it." Ruth patted the arm of her chair again. "Come, sit with me. I want to say something to you, and I want you close." She reached for the remote and turned the volume down more.

Plot derailed, Jeff held in a sigh and trudged toward her, eyeing the envelope as he did so. That envelope seemed strangely famil—

Recognition hit him, tightening the knot already in his stomach.

Are you shittin' me?

He did his best to keep a straight face. Now that he knew what she'd "found," he was curious (angry, but curious) to hear what she had to say. He sat on the arm of the chair. He glanced at her cleavage and then looked into her face. "What's up?" The knot in his stomach tightened.

Gazing up at him, Ruth smiled with warmth and innuendo. She smelled of camellia and citrus. Not bad, but not iris, vanilla, jasmine, and roses. She rested a hand on his knee closest to her, stroking with more innuendo.

What the hell?

"I came across something, Jeff."

Came across or searched for? "Uh-huh...?"

She turned behind and seized the envelope from its spot between the cushion, holding it forward like an attorney presenting Exhibit A. Jeff noticed her hand tremble. "These, Jeff." Her voice wavered. She straightened her posture and cleared her throat. "They're—"

"Pictures of Julia. I know what they are." He tried to remember the last time he'd gotten the photos out and if he'd taped them back or just tossed them in the drawer, intending to tape them back later, and later just never came. Pictures of Jules were now stuffed in bottom drawers and stacked behind concealing drop cloths upstairs, so he also grew a bit irritated over having to hide photos of his wife (dead or not, in his heart of hearts, Julia would always be his wife), to begin with. Julia *died*. They weren't divorced. Julia didn't do him wrong or leave him—not of her own accord, anyway. Why should he feel like he was doing something wrong for having pictures of her? The shit wasn't right.

This discussion was turning as combustible...as linseed oil.

Ruth rubbed his knee. "It's okay. I understand, I think. None of them are especially risqué or anything."

She didn't get it, but that was the whole goddamn point. He got off on seeing Julia in natural, chill modes, without even a hint of explicit view of what made her female—it wasn't necessary. Those pictures weren't of Ruth, had nothing to do with her, yet...she had them in her hand. He imagined Ruth staring at the photos, her green (crocodile) eyes roaming over his first wife with jealous disdain.

His anger wanting to surface full-fledged (murder-in-mind), Jeff maintained his neutral expression.

Ruth looked down at her hand on his knee and then back up at him. She shrugged and sighed. "Well, what do we do?"

Nothing.

He understood she was trying to be understanding, taking the high road. He got that. And he wanted to sympathize. But feelings of betrayal, of his privacy being compromised, won out. He took the envelope. "What were you doing in my chest of drawers?"

She'd anticipated the question; she answered readily enough: "I wanted to wear a pair of your sweatpants to finish going through that stuff in the basement. I knew they'd be big on me, but I figured the drawstring would be enough to keep 'em on."

And it was because she answered so readily (too readily) that he knew it was a lie. Adding the drawstring detail did her in, too. When you're bullshitting, sometimes less is more.

"It's okay, Jeffy," she repeated. She moved her hand from his knee to rub his back in a gesture of compassion, then placed her other hand on his upper thigh and rubbed there, too. "I found the pictures, but I'm not going to give you a hard time about them. You can let go of those now. I'm here." Her caress on his thigh turned distinctly sensual.

Jeff tensed. *Are you fucking kidding me?!*

He couldn't get it up before the whole pictures-thing, *and now?* Jeff scoffed and shook his head. This was going nowhere fast. He stood, moving out of her reach, away from her touch, and placed the envelope of pics on his side of the bed. He turned back to her.

Ruth glared up at him. Shards of pear-olive pigment faded with the anger in her eyes, allowing a bit of the Ruth-of-late to push forward.

The glare vanished, and she stood, moving closer to him. "I said I wasn't mad, Jeffy." His hands were down by his side. She reached for his left hand and held it.

She also said he could let go of Julia's pictures, suggesting he *let go* of Julia period probably—because *she* was here. In that, there was little comfort (maybe even a bit of *dis*comfort). He disengaged his hand from hers and stepped back, preferring she not touch him right now. Seems recently he'd been averse to her coming in contact with him in any form. "It has nothing to do with you being mad or not."

"Should I have just ignored them?"

Yes. "Maybe."

"Like you do me and everything else around here?"

Jeff didn't respond, fighting all kinds of impulses (she sometimes stimulated his darker side). Their evening started fine. And now...

She moved closer, stepping in front of him again. "Jeffy, we need to connect, and I... I think *physically* is the best way to start. It's been a while, you know..." She drew her arms around his neck and hugged him.

He hugged her but then pushed her back, using a gentle touch. "I know. And we will, Ruth. Just...not tonight." And he had no idea what night, either (if any?)—especially if he didn't shut that "Jeffy" crap down.

Ruth blew her cheeks out in a way bordering theatrical. "I can't win, can I?"

Jeff had no answer. Trying to love two, wasn't easy to do. And maybe that was because...

Confusion worsened the knot of tension in his stomach. Knowing he needed to get back on track with Ruth, he should have welcomed the opportunity to begin mending fences with her. Sex was always a good start (if he could *rise* to the occasion).

But what held him back, what put a damper on things, had nothing to do with Ruth presenting the photos. It didn't help matters, but in her defense, she had the backward idea the photos would be a catalyst for intimacy.

No, Ruth finding the pictures wasn't what held him back.

Jeff held back out of guilt.

He'd be cheating on Julia.

Chapter 12

A Tuesday Chronicle

Sunlight twinkled through the stained-glass windows as Naomi regarded the biblical scenes depicted on the glass panels behind the pulpit. In particular, she studied the depiction of Christ's baptism (a scene awash in primary colors) as she sang the closing hymn. This was her third visit to an Assembly of God (AG) church this year. She enjoyed attending church services of all denominations of which she was welcomed: Protestant, Catholic, Pentecostal, Methodist, Lutheran, or whatever; it didn't matter. She researched and explored various spiritual traditions and sects (Yoruba, Kabbalah, Muslim, Taoism, Christianity, Buddhism, Sikhism, Judaism, Bahá'í Faith, Confucianism, and Jainism, for example). Her goal was to fellowship with all spirituality.

She gained an added something by taking in the similarities and differences in the religious approaches. In her desire to experience varying spiritual perspectives, curiosity piqued, she looked up a local Hindu temple. Granted, she'd have to do her homework on customs and etiquette, but that was fine. She gave herself until next summer to learn the basics before attending. She looked forward to it. For her, it all boiled down to One Absolute—regardless of worship method.

Crisp October air—warmed only in spots by the sun—greeted her when she stepped outside. She exchanged pleasantries with a few members of the congregation as she headed for her silver BMW. As of late, she seriously considered upgrading her X5 to a newer model (she didn't much care for the new body style but wanted to stay with the crossover vehicle). Naomi shut the October air out as she got in and turned on her radio. Tye Tribbett's "Bless the Lord (Son of Man)" blared at her.

She switched to her MP3 player hooked up through an adapter (yeah; she needed to upgrade). Dvořák's Humoresque No. 7 in G-Flat major, Op. 101 floated around her. Splendid stuff. Buoyed spiritually and intellectually, Naomi headed to the grocery store.

If only the pleasantness of Sunday continued through Tuesday.

After church, she enjoyed a football doubleheader with Leslie, Kevin, and Kevin's niece, Faustina, who was visiting from Ghana. Faustina and Kevin prepared delicious dishes of jollof rice with shrimp, palm nut soup, and fufu, and Leslie contributed a punch bowl cake for dessert.

Good food, good people, and their teams won their respective games—an all-around good day.

Some of that joy rolled into Monday as well.

She finished and submitted her work for the psychology journal, and her sessions with two patients went well: she'd even documented progression for one of them. So, she could chalk Monday up in the pro column, too. Sunday, Monday: she was on a roll of good days.

Tuesday, however, did its best to balance the scales.

Concerning the deaths of her husband and son, Tuesdays already had a bad rap.

Her morning started at four twenty-three (well, the *active* part of her morning, anyway; she'd been awake since two-nineteen a.m.) It began with performing her humanitarian work. She'd said goodbye to the good people of Hardluck Rebound during the previous summer and had embarked on a new volunteer effort with Abiding Ways Outreach.

Naomi missed the Hardluck Rebound crew almost immediately. The cast of characters she now worked with wasn't a friendly group of people, despite their mission (maybe one or two were okay). Because of the continued sense of community, camaraderie, and fun, she'd stayed longer than usual with Hardluck Rebound. She didn't expect the same for Abiding Ways. She figured six months, and she was out of there.

So, she started Tuesday working alongside people she didn't much care for. But this wasn't her first Tuesday with them, so the negative vibes associated with the volunteer effort didn't count.

But, sitting in session with the two before her, Tuesday still made its least-favorite-weekday case. If she ever needed (wanted) a drink...

Naomi checked the clock. The Winthrops were her next session and weren't scheduled for another hour. That meant she still had another twenty minutes or so in this session. Naomi didn't know if she could do it. She doubted she could help these people at all.

Porter Ralston and Dawsyn Haynes were referred to her through an employer-employee counseling program. Naomi primarily worked with family members in her group therapy sessions, but a colleague thought she'd get a "new perspective" (read, a kick) from working with these two.

She was in month three with Porter and Dawsyn, and so far, the only "kick" she got was the desire to kick these people out of her office. And this work was pro bono: she had little qualms about letting these people go. As with Willette Hargrove, the whole fee-for-mental-maintenance thing wore thin after a while.

Porter and Dawsyn began therapy with Naomi with the (now misguided) belief she could help them manage their coworker relationship better. The two worked for the same company and in the same office, and neither had any desire to find new jobs. So essentially, they resigned themselves to working together despite their (now revealed to be imagined) points of contention. Today's big topic: the non-sharing of information and how it impacts the team.

Naomi checked her watch: eighteen minutes left.

She couldn't understand why they insisted on stressing the coworker aspect of their relationship when clearly, to anyone listening to them interact (which Naomi had the great (mis)fortune of doing every other Tuesday for the past three months), the two were friends more than anything. In fact, when Naomi dissected her notes, she discovered how little they discussed professional issues and how much more of the sessions leaned toward personal stuff. This employee counseling was more akin to her regular-type gig than anything. Which made sense: people were people, doing people "crazy" things—in all walks of daily life. Still, Naomi expected something different.

And so here she was, listening to quite a list of personal, non-coworker-related matters, under the guise of employee counseling. Truth be told, she thought the two were better suited for marriage counseling (but that was another story).

Fourteen minutes left.

"You said that two weeks ago, Dawsyn." Porter Ralston smiled and stretched his long gangly legs out from their bent position. At six feet three, his feet almost reached Naomi.

"And I'll say it again in another two weeks, cuz you don't listen. And with those ears, I'm surprised." Dawsyn issued a quick snort at her joke. She then lifted her purse from the floor and began searching through it. The gaping maw of her Gucci knockoff appeared to swallow her small, plump hands. Dawsyn smiled as she searched (for what, Naomi didn't know). Her thin lips (in stark contrast to the rest of her) stretched almost evilly across her teeth. The smile didn't suit such an attractive lady.

"What are you looking for?" Irritation tinged the weighty bass of Porter's voice and etched more lines in the creases of his Nubian features. Porter did have big ears, but not that big; his haircut just brought direct attention to them.

"Don't worry about it. Never mind me. I'm done." Dawsyn continued shifting around items only she could see. Her spiced-cognac spiral curls bounced with her search.

"But you..." Porter sighed. He turned to Naomi, shaking his head apologetically.

Naomi didn't understand why he did that; no apologies were necessary. This was par for the course for them. She glimpsed the clock on the wall. Ten minutes left.

Dawsyn continued her digging. "I'm trying to find my... I thought I put it in—" Her cellphone sounded, and she silenced it with a huff of annoyance.

Porter watched his coworker (friend). His almond-brown eyes sparkled with hauteur. "You need one of those organizer bags with the slots and pockets instead of that one large area that holds everything."

"Those bags are ugly." Dawsyn glanced up at him. "And everybody can't be as organized as you." She went back to her search.

Porter and Naomi watched Dawsyn in silence.

"...Not everyone can." Porter barely contained a smirk.

"What?" Dawsyn asked into her bag. Exasperated, she looked up at Porter again. "What're you saying?"

"You said, 'everybody can't.'" Porter paused. "'Not everyone *can*' is better."

His comment conjured thoughts of Viv, and Naomi smiled to herself.

Dawsyn, even more exasperated, gawked at Naomi. "See? This is what I'm talking about. He—"

"Okay, Porter and Dawsyn, this is what we have for today," Naomi interrupted. She didn't want to hear anymore—not today...or maybe ever. Time was almost up for the session. Naomi observed the pseudo-couple for a moment. No, not just this session. Time was up for their time with her, period. Naomi ran a hand over her close-cropped hair (she needed a haircut). She checked the clock: seven minutes to go.

Dawsyn and Porter held expressions blending anticipation and trepidation, but Porter's eyes soon narrowed with suspicion. "You're kicking us out, aren't you?"

Dawsyn's mouth dropped open as she looked first at Porter and then at Naomi. Suddenly she took on an insightful grin (as though she half-expected as much). She abandoned her search for whatever was in her purse.

Finally, Naomi nodded. "I'm afraid so, folks. When you cut it to the quick, you're not here for any employee relations problems." She addressed Porter: "Porter, you're a Christian-focused man who's trustworthy and smart but can be distant despite your desire to connect on a more personal level with Dawsyn. You're particular, neat, organized. You prefer plans and structure—all of which help you maintain a barrier around your emotions. It's cliché, but clichés are born out of truth."

Naomi didn't wait for Porter's response. She turned to Dawsyn. "Dawsyn, you, on the other hand, prefer non-structure and are slow to anger. Although you sometimes present yourself as less than brainy, you're an extremely smart woman who works better off the cuff. I find that you're generous, but not to a fault, and you like a regular drink of something stronger than fruit juice more than twice a week." Discerning that last was relatively easy—especially since she could relate.

With a shake of her head, Dawsyn closed her mouth. The insightful grin crept back.

Their auras hadn't flickered for her over the three months of counseling them, but she'd pegged Porter as a Logical Tan with hints of contrasting orange influence, while Dawsyn gave her strong orange aura vibes. She could be wrong, but she doubted it. Naomi continued: "Ms. Haynes, you're more closed-mouthed than Mister Ralston, but similar to Mister Ralston with his structure and organization, you make a joke of everything as a barrier to your emotions." She watched the two of them for a second or two before continuing. "Honestly, for these last three months, I have not seen where you two have any concrete problems working together—quite the contrary. Your diverse approaches to your work complement each other nicely in getting your work done. You two are fashion-conscious and try to be health-conscious, which is a nice bonus, I guess, but my work with you was supposed to be an exploration and study of new avenues of my profession I hadn't delved into too heavily. Turns out, you guys are better suited for what I already specialize in. I'm not discovering new ground here. You're supposed to be here for employee relations counseling, not family therapy. That being said, yes, Porter, I'm kicking you guys out." She offered this last a bit warmly because she did like them well enough.

Porter looked at Dawsyn.

Dawsyn jerked her shoulders in absolute "whatever."

Silence ensued for a bit as she allowed them to absorb her summary. The two surveyed her office with thoughtful expressions before finally looking at each other.

They brought to mind an African American male-female version of Laurel and Hardy. Naomi smirked inwardly and checked the session timer: 00:02:37 (and counting). Time was up (more or less). She stood.

Porter and Dawsyn were slow to stand. Porter said, "Well, do we at least get an exit session or something?" That bass in his voice had Naomi wondering if he sang with an informal group or something. She didn't know if a bass speaking voice translated well to a singing one, but she believed a correlation existed. Someone else she knew spoke with a warm (and rather sexy) mellow baritone that, from her understanding, translated into song very well.

Naomi looked up at him. "Do you really think you need one? I just gave you something to chew on, didn't I?"

Porter jerked his chin downward. "That you did. But that goes to show that we do have some issues to be worked on, doesn't it?" His eyes were wide, pleading.

Naomi almost caved. Almost. "Maybe you should see someone else your employer recommends." It was her turn to smile apologetically. She extended her hand to Porter.

"But..." Porter accepted Naomi's palm. Understandably, his shake didn't hold the power of previous ones.

Dawsyn shook Naomi's hand as she always did, but Naomi couldn't read her expression. She suspected Dawsyn could take it or leave it. "You've got quite a grip for a small woman," Dawsyn commented with a smile. "I've been wanting to say that to you for some time." Perspiration dotted her upper lip and around the dimple in her chin.

Naomi chuckled. "You're not the first to say something like that, but no, you can't take small stature for granted." She looked from Dawsyn to Porter and back again. "For what it's worth, you guys will be fine. It's... Well, it's been interesting. Take care now."

Dawsyn nodded with a smile, situated the handles to her bag on her forearm, and headed around the sofa to the door. "You take care, too, Doctor Alexander." Her pantsuit, close to ill-fitting with its snugness, showed off her high rear as she walked.

Porter looked as if he needed a little more convincing. The muscles in his narrow face twitched, but he didn't say anything. Without pause, he reached down and around Naomi, gathering her in a hug.

Naomi stiffened and resisted the embrace. All of which went unnoticed (or without care) by Porter. He ended the hug and started away without another word. She didn't know what to make of it.

Naomi watched them leave. As Dawsyn proceeded through the door, she turned her head to Porter, whispering: "What'd you do that for?"

"I just wanted t—" The door closed on the rest of Porter's response. They were gone.

Naomi checked her watch, realizing she'd have to find another pro bono case. She'd gone a little overtime with Porter and Dawsyn, but she still had some time to prep for the Winthrops.

Instead of going over to her desk, retrieving their case file, and sitting down and getting started, Naomi plopped down in her mustard-yellow chair. She wanted something more potent than fruit juice herself right about now.

A bottle of Hennessy X.O. rested at the back of her bottom desk drawer, untouched for ten days. Not that she hadn't had anything to drink in ten days: she had—just not from that bottle. Mr. Hennessy called to her from inside her desk, whispering cajoling words of encouragement—as any good friend would.

Naomi sat and thought of everything other than the X.O. as her fingers gripped the seat cushion. She resisted going to her desk. Winthrop file or not, if she went to her desk, she'd partake. Not that she hadn't done so before or wouldn't in the future (the bottle was there, wasn't it?). She wanted to resist the increasingly strong desire, especially now.

Naomi fixed the pliable fabric arms of her chair in her grip and rocked rhythmically, her back lightly buffeting against the tufted chair cushion. Her stomach cramped and released, cramped and then released. She paused, breathed in through clenched teeth, held it, and then let her breath out slowly in a backward count from five. She repeated the deep breathing until she felt better, stronger.

She would not have a drink before the Winthrops' session. She'd make it until late this evening to have one—*if* she had one then. All things considered, she'd last without something for the next day or two: piece of cake.

Feeling better, she went purposefully to her desk. She lifted the Winthrop file from the top of the pile of papers and folders on her desk and returned to her chair. Feeling better or not, she could not sit at her desk right now—that 80-proof "piece of cake" would be eaten if she did. She checked her watch: plenty of time. She started reading.

Twenty minutes later, Naomi closed the file with a sigh.

The Winthrops.

Naomi had some excellent theory on how to treat them, but obstacles abounded. Primordial to their treatment: Naomi had to address Jeff's impuissance in the context of Ruth's hermetic approach to parenting Mallory and Todd. Ruth's version of mothering was an underlying source of tension and disharmony Jeff has either ignored or avoided for too long. He'd relinquished his power of "No" to Ruth, allowing her to take over.

He showed signs of strength from time to time during their sessions, but not enough to positively influence their healing as a family. And honestly, if the Winthrops were to get better and heal from Julia's death as a family, it rested with Jeff.

For most patients, without detailed medical histories and records, it was difficult for therapists to isolate any predisposing factors affecting a patient's clinical presentation. Psychological or emotional disorders usually follow a general model of having past or preexisting influences, a catalytic event, and some sustaining elements. Jeff's records didn't point readily to any predisposing factors, but the precipitating or catalytic event was easily Julia's sudden death. The sustaining elements? Jeff perpetuated his complicated grief by sleeping an inordinate amount of time and indulging in fantasy behavior. From the looks of him over the last few sessions, he wasn't eating much, either. These maladaptive behavior patterns could easily keep Jeff permanently isolated from his children and lead to a complete mental breakdown, thus creating an entirely new set of predisposing (and possibly precipitating) factors for his children's mental health.

Naomi reflected on the expression of confusion mixed with emotional pain on Jeff's face as he tried to tell her, perhaps, that he could still see his wife. Grief was a mighty beast (she still battled with it herself), but Naomi needed to alter Jeff's cognitive triad to fight it. Fight it and win. If she didn't help him change (for the better) how he viewed himself, the world, and the future, all would be lost. Losing was not an option; Mallory and Todd needed their father healthy and thriving.

Naomi stood and stretched with a yawn. She had a little time before the session to pee and freshen up. The evaluating hand she ran over her hair again confirmed a trip to the barber was in order.

She placed the Winthrop file back on her desk pile and retrieved her notepad, setting it on the end table next to her yellow chair. Plucking rogue pieces of lint from the sleeves of her navy-blue blazer, Naomi entered her private bathroom to freshen up, considering filling her Cambridge mug with some soothing chamomile.

Her thoughts touched on the bottle of X.O. in her drawer.

She dismissed them.

They were well into the session and all staring at Mallory.

Naomi didn't know what she said exactly, but whatever it was gave Mallory a severe case of the giggles. Mallory leaned on her father's arm and turned her face into it. Her giggles, now muffled, continued.

She thought it was a sweet moment as Jeff's tense expression softened into the beginnings of a smile. He needed to smile.

They were at a point in the session where the Winthrops (except Ruth) were recalling their experiences the day Julia died: a difficult but necessary part of Naomi's grief counseling. Sometimes the recollections proved cathartic, and other times... Well, it could have the opposite effect. Naomi couldn't yet tell which way the Winthrops listed.

Mallory's giggles subsided, and she lifted away from her dad. "I'm sorry, Doctor Alexand—"

"Care to share, Mallory?" Ruth interrupted. She leaned back against the loveseat cushions, crossed her arms, then one burgundy Prada pump over the other, and waited.

Mallory cut her eyes to Ruth dismissively before looking at Naomi. "Anyway, I'm sorry, Doctor Alex, for real. But that 'hey nonny nonny' thing got to me!" She covered her mouth to contain another onset.

"Yeah, that was kinda funny," Todd agreed. He raised both eyebrows at Naomi. "You don't curse?"

Naomi fixed him with a sardonic grin. "Course I do—when the moment calls. It all depends. But, if I can catch myself, I pick an alternative something that still gets the point across. Hey non—" Naomi pointed at Mallory with a smile. "Don't start. Anyway, that phrase does it for me."

"See? You both can take a page from Doctor Alexander's book. That language isn't necessary—and this isn't coming from me." Ruth's eyes gleamed with triumph.

Mallory and Todd shared a look riddled with sibling meaning, then returned their gazes to Naomi. It was rude without being, well, rude. Naomi, however, had the strongest sense the siblings expressed more bravado here in these sessions than they did at home. It was understandable but also unfortunate because the two might need to show some strength at home to help their father. Fair or not, children sometimes have to assist parents in ways unassociated with old age and post-retirement finances.

"Well, that's not exactly how I put it," Naomi said to Ruth. "But it's not important." She looked at everyone. "Can we resume topic now?"

Ruth uncrossed her Pradas and sat forward on the settee.

Todd stuck his tongue through the space created by his chipped tooth, concentrating on the drawstring in his black hoodie. He held one end in each hand and jerked it back and forth, glancing from one disappearing end to the other. Naomi held in a smile; such a CJ move.

Mallory put a hand on her father's knee and turned to him, waiting. "Go ahead, Daddy. You heard Todd and me. Finish yours. You were saying Mommy had clutched your tie to pull you down to her. This was just before you came to get us, but she—"

Jeff reached for the hand resting on his knee, squeezing it. His gaze didn't appear to focus on anything specific.

Mallory startled and winced at what had to be fresh pain in the fingers Jeff held. "Daddy, *ow!*"

Ruth and Todd started as well.

Naomi rose and moved to Mallory and Jeff's position on the couch, where she gripped Jeff's shoulder, digging her thumb into the pressure point there.

Jeff barely flinched, but he released his daughter's hand. He gazed up at Naomi, blinking vacantly.

Naomi held his gaze, watching the focus seep back in. He seemed to startle himself now at realizing what had taken place and then turned to his daughter. "I'm so sorry, M-Sweet." He rubbed his daughter's fingers.

Mallory's bottom lip quivered, but there were no tears.

Jeff stood. He excused himself past Naomi and went to the window, taking it upon himself to shift the vertical blinds to one side. They all bathed in the light of the October sunshine pouring into Naomi's office.

With her eyes, Naomi asked Mallory if she was okay.

Holding her fingers, Mallory nodded.

Naomi returned to her seat. She picked up her notepad and started writing. She wanted to hold off on prescribing antidepressants for Jeff, and a couple SSRIs made the consideration list, but a norepinephrine and dopamine reuptake inhibitor (NDRI) may prove necessary. She liked (and had success with) Bupropion, so maybe she could start him at 200mgs...

"You're left-handed, Doctor Alex?" Todd asked.

Naomi didn't look up. "Mm-hmm: just like you." Other than casual observation of him, Naomi knew Todd was left-handed, that Jeff, Mallory, and Ruth were right-handed, based on the pre-therapy questionnaire and the new question on handedness added in response to events with Rick and Viv Phillips some eighteen months ago. She continued writing.

Silence.

Naomi glanced at Mallory, Todd, and Ruth as she made notes.

Mallory rubbed her fingers and watched her father, who remained at the window.

Drawstring momentarily forgotten, Todd watched Mallory.

Ruth concerned herself with the embroidery on her Carolina Herrera ruched silk sweater. Naomi easily recognized designer wear because she had an extensive range of clientele as patients, many of whom were relatively shallow and often felt compelled to mention whom they were wearing. Not all of them did that, but enough of them did. She wondered if Ruth ever bothered with the likes of a Target store or T.J. Maxx. Not that it mattered; she just wondered (and doubted it).

Naomi spoke without looking at the grieving man at the window. "We're ready whenever you are, Jeff." She checked her watch: still good on time.

Another bout of silence followed before Jeff finally spoke. "I... I can't do it out loud, Naomi. ...Hurts too much." He put his hands in his pockets and kept his back to them. He continued, directing his words toward the activity outside her fifth-floor office window. "I... I recollect, remember, or whatever you want to ca—" He shook his head. "No. No, I *relive* that experience in some form or another, damn near every day still, Naomi. But... But saying these things aloud is a whole new ballgame. I can't do it." Anger and hurt emanated from his words. "...And it doesn't help; the fact that Julia's still..." Jeff dropped his head.

Everyone waited for him to finish.

Naomi had a good idea of what he started to say.

"Mommy's still what, Daddy?" The eagerness in Mallory's eyes concerned Naomi. It was as if she, too, had the same idea of what her father was going to say, believed it herself, and wanted him to confirm it.

"Nothing, M-Sweet. Never mind." Jeff kept his back to them. Naomi thought she heard him sniff.

Naomi's cellphone vibrated against her hip. She removed the phone from its clip and read a text message from Viv Phillips. Naomi forgot Viv planned to come by her office for a late lunch. A pleasant surprise. Tuesday may not turn out to be so bad after all. Viv Phillips was fast becoming one of her favorite people in the grand scheme of the rest of it. Naomi placed her phone back on her hip.

"Come sit down, Dad. It's all good." Todd's breathing was rhythmic, steady. Naomi frequently listened for any changes in it.

Jeff vented a heavy but serrated breath. He ran a hand back and forth over his scalp for several contemplating seconds before returning to his seat. He sat next to Mallory, landing semi-hard with another sigh. Jeff took his daughter's hand (the one he squeezed), placed a quick kiss to her fingers, and then held her gaze with an intense look of his own. This time, an unspoken father-daughter exchange went on for a few seconds before Mallory finally nodded and lowered her head onto her father's chest (yet another sweet moment). Jeff hugged his daughter to him, kissing the top of her head. When they parted, Jeff turned his attention to somewhere away and behind Naomi in the area of her desk and credenza. Brows furrowed, his eyes sometimes lifted to take in the object of Todd's frequent resource for mental refuge: the prints of jazz musicians and classical music composers.

Ruth reached across the distance separating Jeff's legs and hers (from her place on the loveseat to his on the sofa) and placed a hand on Jeff's thigh. "Take your time, Jeffy."

Naomi watched Jeff's brow furrow even more. His jaw clenched. He semi-rolled his eyes up in his head with potent distaste. Ruth couldn't fully observe his response from her angle. If she had...

"Ruth, I don't think he cares for that too much."

Ruth looked perplexed (and a little indignant). "For...?"

"For 'Jeffy,'" Naomi answered.

"I know I don't," Mallory mumbled.

"Mallory." Naomi shook her head at Mallory for her to understand this was not the time.

Chastened, Mallory nodded contritely and sunk into the cushions.

In tune with his sister, Todd nodded contritely, too.

Ruth looked from Mallory to Naomi to Jeff and back to Naomi. It was her turn to sigh heavily. She shook her head and sat deeper into the cushions, too, dropping her gaze to her lap. When she looked up again, her eyes glistened. "So, is this what these therapy sessions are going to be about? Setting me up as the bad guy? I'm the new wife and stepmother, so I'm the villain just on GP? Is that it?" Ruth shook her head again. "I... I can't win here."

Mallory and Todd both stared at her with angry incredulity.

Naomi wished she could bring Jeff's attention to his children's faces. Their expressions alone would help shed light on a few things for him;

Naomi was sure of it. But she couldn't call his attention to it, so she chalked it up to a missed opportunity. She believed Jeff was aware (subconsciously) of his children's unhappiness, but that awareness was distanced through a disabling lens of grief and loss and a compromised power of *No*. She addressed Ruth: "No one is 'setting you up,' and I don't yet know about the rest. I'm just letting you know that 'Jeffy' doesn't sit well with him. I'd venture to say he hates it."

Ruth peered Jeff's way. "Well, he's never said anything before. If he hates it so much, he can tell me himself."

Jeff continued to focus away and behind Naomi.

"Jeff?" Naomi prompted. This "Jeffy" thing was a nugget for him to take a stand on. The rest could come later. Right now, they needed this little piece...

"It's fine," Jeff responded. He caught Naomi's gaze out of the corner of his eye. He gave her an almost-imperceptible shake of his head and closed his eyes briefly, running a hand over his scalp while clearing his throat. He sat back and returned his attention to the group.

"See? *Thank* you, honey."

Jeff offered a barely-there smile.

Mallory shook her head, a mixture of disappointment and annoyance marking her expression.

Todd renewed his interest in his drawstrings.

Disappointed, Naomi chuckled to herself. Another missed opportunity. She was zero for two. She'd do her best not to miss another one.

"Which anniversary would this have been?" Naomi didn't have to specify anything; everyone in that room knew what she referred to.

"Our twentieth."

"Yeah. Between Mommy's birthday, their anniversary, and Halloween...," Mallory said with a nodding half-grin, "October's covered in our house." Her warm titter traveled to Todd and partway to Jeff.

Jeff's small smile faded as he ran a hand back and forth across his scalp again.

Naomi recognized the motion for what it was. "Need a haircut, Jeff?"

He smiled a little brighter this time. "Know the move, huh? Feels like it, so I guess I do."

"I didn't mention it before, but I see the facial hair's gone, too..." He was a handsome man, but it was not a good look for him—especially with the recent (and unfortunately, continuing) weight loss—but he wasn't here for a beauty contest.

Jeff drew a hand across his clean-shaven face. "Yeah, completed the eggshell look on the first anniversary of her d—" His eyes filled with pain before he closed them. He took a deep breath and then looked at Naomi. "Anyway, I meant to shave it this morning, but..." He shrugged.

"Don't worry. He'll have everything shaved by tomorrow," Ruth offered. "It's the only thing he stays on top of these days. I want him to let it grow out. I've never seen him with hair. You can look at the kids to know he has good hair." Ruth beamed, her eyes imbued with pride and appreciation.

"Mm-hmm, I see. Well, what kind of hair do I have, Ruth?"

"Huh? I mean, well, your hair is natural, Doctor Alexander." A hint of olive-tinged irritation sparked in Ruth's eyes.

Naomi raised an eyebrow at her. "What kind of answer is that? Any hair that grows out of a person's scalp is their 'natural' hair."

"Here we go," Ruth discharged a grunted breath of either defensiveness or hostility (or both).

"No, no. It's not like that. I'm just saying. Whether it's processed or weaved-up or whatever, if the hair growing out of the scalp is clean and healthy, it's good hair. At least, I think so."

She noticed Jeff, Mallory, and Todd gawking at her—Jeff, mainly.

Naomi continued: "Look, we all know what it means when someone says another person has 'good hair,' especially Black folk. I'm suggesting finding another way to—"

"Softer roots," Mallory, Jeff, and Todd voiced in near unison (Todd finished a millisecond after his dad). The three looked at each other with a proud familial bond before returning their attention to Naomi.

Ruth and Naomi interchanged gazes at them, too, before Naomi addressed Ruth: "Look, I'm not getting on your case. Not like that. But when you say someone has 'good hair' or 'that White people's stuff' or the like, it translates into meaning that those of us who don't have..." Naomi glanced at Mallory, Todd, and Jeff, "'softer roots,'" she resumed focus on Ruth, "have 'bad' hair. The negative connotations can be offensive and divisive. That's all."

A wrinkle cut across Ruth's broad forehead. "That's not the first time I've heard that, Doctor Alexander. Old habits die hard, I guess. I never gave it a second thought when someone described my hair that way, so I didn't think it was a big deal." She shrugged.

"It is, and it isn't," Naomi replied. She focused on the other Winthrops. "So, 'softer roots,' huh?"

Todd spoke up. "Yeah. Came from my mom's philosophy. She didn't care for people saying, 'good hair,' either. All that stuff you said about hair being clean and healthy and whatever?" Todd nodded with pride. "My mother used to give those same speeches."

"I see. And your mother's hair...?" Naomi was curious.

"Not as straight as Daddy's or Todd's; more like mine." Mallory curved a palm around the ponytail twisting over her shoulder. "Her roots were a little tighter; that's all." She, too, spoke with a level of pride.

"And you share your mother's middle name, too, I believe..." Since they were in it (she'd started it with the anniversary prompt), Naomi wanted to emphasize additional non-obvious but pleasant ties to Julia.

"'Èkerie,' yes," Mallory said through the display of almost every tooth in her head. "Her name, her hair..."

"Little things...but big," Naomi said, remembering Viv also passed her middle name to her daughter, Alna; that Leslie's middle name was handed down from her grandmother.

Mallory nodded, her smile softer and her eyes moist in a way not sad.

"She never processed her hair, though," Jeff added. "Jules kept her twists clean and healthy, natural without chemicals—*good hair*," he voiced somewhat strongly, although he smiled when he said it. He smiled with only his mouth, though: he was on the verge of tears.

This time, Naomi sent Jeff an almost imperceptible shake of her head.

Jeff nodded, redirecting his attention toward the window.

"Well, okay... We've spent a tad too much time on this. You all are not here for hair counseling. ...Any closing concerns before we wrap up?"

Everyone grew quiet, having retreated into their thoughts.

To Naomi's surprise, Jeff spoke. "Do you think Julia's in heaven, Naomi?" He kept focus outside the window.

Shit.

Naomi sighed, her eyes on Jeff. "Spiritual compass?"

"Spiritual compass," Jeff confirmed out the window. He turned to her.

"Jeff, I don't know how my answer to that will—"

"Course, she's in heaven," Todd broke in. "Where else would she be?"

"Hell," Ruth said to Todd in a tone weighted with pompous emphasis. She paused and continued in a softer tone, but her squint at Todd was something Naomi could only interpret as contempt. Ruth's aura then flickered a hunter-green in what Naomi viewed as jealousy-infused confirmation. That aura (as brief as it was) signaled *green with envy* virtually personified. "Even your mother is subject to the Lord's judgment."

Here we go.

Not for the first time, Naomi considered abandoning the spiritual compass component of her therapy. It just got to be too much sometimes. But with grief counseling, avoiding spiritual discussions was difficult. And Naomi believed spiritual explorations vital to one's overall mental well-being, let alone an integral part of her therapy approach. But sometimes... damn!

Todd looked hurt, defeated even.

Mallory's face registered shock, and she appeared hugely offended.

Naomi figured Ruth's statement regarding Julia being in hell would surely be the straw for Jeff. Insulting a loved one's memory was an explosive trigger, so she awaited his outburst or comeback, whatever it was. But Jeff kept his eyes on her, waiting for her answer to his question; it was as if Ruth's comment (even Ruth herself, for that matter) didn't register with him at all.

Todd spoke: "What did my mother do to you? You've never even met her." He gazed at Ruth with genuine perplexity—and traces of anger.

Ruth seemed as if going to ignore him. "I know I never met her; that's not the point."

Keeping his eyes on his stepmother, Todd shook his head. "Well, no, that's... that's the *whole* point." His brow now furrowed with his headshake. He glanced toward his father before looking at his sister.

Mallory nodded. Her expression grew somber, however, with her shift in attention to Ruth. Her lips parted and then closed.

"We'll discuss it later, Todd." Ruth glowered in Jeff's direction. "I believe it's time to wrap up."

Throughout the exchange, Jeff stayed focused on Naomi. He waited.

"Do I believe she's in heaven?" Naomi reiterated.

He nodded slowly.

"Well, Jeff. I'd have to desist on that and redirect. First, do you believe in heaven and hell?"

"Didn't we cover that already?" he replied with a smirk. "Do you, Naomi?"

Appearing irritated with her husband's lack of response to her and ready to wrap up today's session, Ruth shifted in her seat.

Mallory and Todd leaned forward in theirs.

"Oh, you're good, Jeff. But why does what I think matter on something so personal?"

Jeff scrunched his bony shoulders upward. "It just does."

"Yeah, it just does," Todd voiced.

"Yeah," Mallory chimed in. That eagerness returned to her eyes.

Ruth shifted in her seat again. "Go ahead, Doctor Alexander."

Naomi sighed with a breathy snicker and shook her head. The aim of most therapy sessions during any psychoanalysis is to have the patient open up, dialogue, and expound on their innermost thoughts and feelings. It was why therapists were often characterized with quotes of overused variations of *How do you feel about that?*

But sometimes, *sometimes*, helping the patient open up meant allowing said patient some exposure to the thoughts and feelings of the therapist. That was Naomi's view, anyway. It wasn't standard practice, and there were guidelines governing the interpersonal boundaries of the therapist-patient relationship. Still, Naomi had no problem deviating from standard procedures and policies if she thought it would help her patient.

Naomi cleared her throat. "Well, for me, one of the most curious dichotomies about Christianity-based religions is the underlying doctrine of obedience or holy behavior rooted in fear of punishment rather than doing so simply because it's the right thing to do. People seem to be 'preaching' or 'living' the taught Gospels primarily because of the fear of hell. So, one can say, people aren't being their true selves or who they want to be, which is how God made them. And isn't that 'denial of self,' if you will, blasphemy against our Creator? Anyway, I believe there is something after this earthly existence. But while I believe in an afterlife of sorts, I'm neither sold on the many-roomed mansions and gold-paved streets nor its fire-and-brimstone alternative." She waited, watching her patients for reaction to her words.

Jeff nodded with careful deliberation.

Mallory did as well.

Ruth's expression was ambiguous, but held no animus.

And Todd? Well, Todd smiled. And it was all Naomi could do not to smile back.

Naomi addressed Jeff: "That help any?" She doubted it did.

"Not sure. I wanted to know if you thought Jules was in heaven. But since you don't really believe in heaven, I guess I didn't get what I was looking for."

"And that was?" Naomi prompted.

Jeff shrugged. "I'm just trying to put some things in better perspective. Next session, I guess." He frowned with the heaviest (and saddest) of sighs.

"Next session is fine, Jeff." Naomi raised an eyebrow at him in inquiry. "Think I might see some stubble on that face of yours by then?"

Her attempt at levity got through. "Here we go." The corners of Jeff's mouth turned upward the tiniest bit. "Maybe."

"Well, I think a man should at least have hair on his face. I like a bald head on a man, but a bald face?" Naomi shook her head. "Not so much. But that's just me. I'm taking nothing away from your symbolic gesture two years ago, mind you..."

"I like hair on a man's face, too, Naomi." Ruth sent a tentative glance in Jeff's direction before turning a more assured gaze on Naomi. "Whatever type of hair he has, he's a good-looking man. I think it'd be nice to see." She gestured toward her stepson. "Even Todd has hair on his face."

If the floor directly under Todd could open and swallow him, Naomi believed Todd would have welcomed it. His wide-eyed, open-mouthed expression asked why Ruth was bringing him into the conversation.

Todd started to speak, but Naomi spoke first: "It's okay, Todd." She zeroed in on Ruth. From Ruth's tone and expression, Naomi realized the bald-head-and-face thing was a point of contention. "It was my attempt to lighten the mood, Ruth. There are bigger things to worry about besides Jeff's decision to grow a mustache, don't you think?" Naomi observed Jeff, checking for detachment cues: still with them.

Jeff gazed back calmly but then closed his eyes; the almost-smile vanished. And Naomi knew: for as long as he was with Ruth, Ruth would not see Jeff with any hair on his face or head. That event was a pure case of TLTB. Naomi didn't know why that was, but it was a stand detrimental to sustaining a healthy marriage, because his resistance carried personal tribute (Julia)—but more so... spite (Ruth). Jeff opened his eyes and fixed his gaze on the view outside.

Naomi glimpsed everyone in turn, preparing to close the session before her absolute end-of-session timer went off. Upon viewing Ruth, she discerned a question resting behind Ruth's eyes.

"You want to say something, Ruth?"

Challenge set in her jaw. "I just wanted to know if we can stop making me the heavy in these sessions."

"Well, to be honest, Ruth, you are only the 'heavy' if you are purposely, either directly or indirectly, impeding the emotional health of this family as they cope with their loss—however long ago the loss was."

Ruth's eyes glinted with anger and then softened. Her lips remained stiff, however. "I'm considered the wicked stepmother."

Although she detected reaction to Ruth's statement from others in the room, Naomi made it a point to maintain eye contact with Ruth and not look at the other Winthrops. "Undeservedly so?"

The green in Ruth's eyes blanched. The muscles in her face twitched as she tried to adopt the appropriate facial expression as response. Naomi found it interesting (and revealing) to watch. "Undeservedly so," Ruth agreed at last.

Naomi perceived Mallory having some sort of retort, but she was pleased the girl practiced restraint.

Naomi focused on Jeff. Instead of countering or supporting Ruth's summation, he stared out of the window, stone-faced, as if blocking out Ruth's presence.

Damn the timer; Naomi had one more question. "How did you two end up together?" *End up together* may not have been the best way to put it, but then again, maybe it was. She turned to Ruth.

Ruth's expression brightened. "Jeff had some property to move. I was his agent..." Ruth trailed off with a shrug and a smile. When her eyes landed on Jeff, however, the smile faltered.

Naomi looked at Jeff, too, surprised to find his attention with them. "So, is that it, Jeff? Business ended up being pleasure?"

Jeff offered Naomi a patronizing smile. "I'm not yet fifty, but I'm an old-fashioned guy, Naomi, despite my age. And apparently, I'm a sucker, too." He turned back to the window without so much as a glimpse Ruth's way. "...Spent negligible time in the prudencesphere with that one."

Ruth drew in a breath.

The Winthrop children exchanged a curious glance, and then heads lowered, gazes now directed toward their laps.

After that: silence.

Naomi hated closing on such a note. "Okay, well—"

"Sorry, everyone," Jeff said, but his focus was on Naomi. "I was out of line. I didn't mean it the way it sounded."

But Naomi had every reason to believe he meant it exactly the way it sounded. She offered a reassuring smile to him and nodded. She turned to Ruth and did the same.

Ruth glanced toward Jeff before looking at Naomi. Mollified, she lowered her gaze to her lap and nodded, but the tension in her neck and jaw muscles remained; she was definitely saving something for her husband at home.

Naomi, however, doubted Jeff would give Ruth what she was needing from him then, either. A fight with Ruth, an argument, at bare minimum, would suggest to Ruth that he cared—but Jeff already showed he didn't have much fight in him (which also translated into him not having much care—for Ruth).

"Well, people, this is an awful time to end the session, but unfortunately, we are out of time." Naomi stood.

The Winthrops stood in staggered order, Jeff standing last. "I'm sorry," he repeated.

"Accepted. Just be prepared to explore that further." Naomi raised an eyebrow at him. "I'm sure you're familiar with the term *Freudian Slip*..."

Jeff scoffed and then shook his head with a semi-smile.

"I'm quite familiar with it, Doctor Alexander." The edge in Ruth's tone broadcast her displeasure (and embarrassment).

Todd and Mallory moved closer together, but Naomi thought the act more subliminal than anything. Mallory popped a stick of gum into her mouth and offered a stick to Todd. Watching them, a flash came. It was fleeting but a flash nonetheless: Todd at risk and soon. That was all.

Naomi returned her attention to Jeff and Ruth. "Well, you two will likely get into this more later; I don't see any way around that." She envisioned Ruth getting into it more so than Jeff; he'd be just as dispassionate then, too. "But I mean it. Save some for next session. It's important." Naomi regarded everyone. "Okay?"

The Winthrops each offered their individual form of assent.

"Thank you. Even with this last bit, you all did good work in here today. Remember, you're scheduled for this coming Thursday afternoon in addition to next Tuesday. In two days, not a week."

Mallory tipped her head forward. "We remembered." She resumed chewing, and Naomi detected some nervousness in it; the ride home should prove interesting.

"Good. Now, get outta here." Naomi shooed them toward the door. She made it a point to smile at Todd—just because.

The Winthrops left without further fanfare.

It was none too soon. Naomi had just enough time to make some closing notes before Viv Phillips arrived.

Viv and her husband, Rick, were former patients. Rick was away in prison, serving time for manslaughter, but since his bench trial, Naomi stayed in regular contact with Rick (and the therapist assigned to him). Over the past year, Viv and Rick, each at their respective paces, were making their way into her friend zone (as small as it was).

Naomi had few (if any) real friends; it cost too much. Then, too, smaller circles were more manageable, more...meaningful.

Viv whisked in, threw her Dior purse and a huge, heavy-duty envelope on the settee, and gave Naomi a big hug. She would do this even though Naomi sometimes stiffened against her in protest.

Viv grew her chestnut hair out from the bob she used to wear. Her high ponytail bounced with her movement. As usual, she wore Rick's wedding ring on a floating illusion necklace. His ring dangled like a levitating charm, suspended in the hollow of her throat. "Got some new photos for the spring exhibit. I want you to take a look at 'em during lunch." She smiled warmly, shaking her head in humor. "Leslie doesn't want to wait for spring, though; she wants to have them for the upcoming showcase, so she submitted for that one, too."

"That sounds like Leslie." Naomi's thoughts were still with the Winthrops—especially Todd. But Viv had her own set of mental stresses Naomi wanted to acknowledge. "How's everything?"

Viv waved a hand. "Alna's good; enjoying her violin lessons. RJ's still getting over his cold. It's awful when they're sick. ...With his little self." Viv made a pity face before replacing it with a smile.

Naomi held her gaze. "...How's everything?"

Viv's smile faded, recapturing some of the pity—for herself this time. She wore a hurt expression before those black eyes of hers softened with intense emotion. "I miss him."

Naomi surmised a wealth of meanings from Viv's simple statement: no words in the unabridged described how much she missed him; raising their children without him was lonely and painful; her ache and longing for his company, for the feel of his body on hers, was beyond anything anybody could ever understand. That each day was consumed with thoughts of him—of one day being with him again.

Viv's imposing love and patent longing for her husband lined the atmosphere.

Although nowhere near Viv's arena, Naomi missed Rick, too, or rather, she missed seeing them together. In her short time counseling them, the couple, despite needing therapy, demonstrated a unique and unparagoned level of marital connection and intimacy (not purely sexual) Naomi hadn't seen before (or since). Together or apart (current circumstances aside), they were quality people. Rick was the reason she was on a new tip with drinking bottled teas instead of, well...

"I know, Viv."

Viv made her way over to Naomi's desk, where she picked up Naomi's Einstein bobblehead, studying it. Viv considered her body pear-shaped, but, with the stress of Rick being away, after birthing RJ, Viv lost more weight than she gained during her pregnancy—especially in her waist and hip areas. Viv was more hourglass than "pear"; very much so.

Viv paused Einstein's bobble. She lifted a hand, touching Rick's floating wedding band. "...Do you know Phyllis Hyman's 'No One Can Love You More' or 'Meet Me on the Moon'?"

"I do." Naomi speculated the vibrancy of Viv's normal, natural, yellow-based aura carried more depressive gray tones now, creating elements of olive green in her aura that likely wouldn't go away until—

"Yeah. Phyllis is my girl." Viv nodded at Einstein, looking solemn. "...Yesterday was pretty bad. Lately, I've really been missing kicking back with him at Takoma Station Tavern—one of our haunts." Viv tilted an eyebrow her way in humor. "Girl, I'd even go for sampling his PB-and-J with sardines, to be with him again."

"Now, that's saying something."

"I know, right? Believe it or not, something as ordinary as working a jigsaw puzzle with him would be near perfection right now."

Naomi believed it.

Shaking her head with a momentary forlorn expression, Viv took a breath and briefly closed her eyes. "Our anniversary's approaching, so, there's that. And something about the fall foliage makes me sadder, more wistful for him; we fancy autumn. The colors of fall, though, the reds and golds... are a constant reminder of his eyes." She paused, gazing at Einstein. Her brows dented with this mild anguish before she continued. "...But today's a little better, I guess." The smile she offered was just sad. "Things are flowing like sweet buttermilk, Naomi. ...Rick and I just can't fully enjoy it yet."

Naomi grinned her understanding, believing her grin was just as sad.

Viv sighed. "Focusing on the kids usually helps. The art exhibit is helpful distraction, too." She rested her eyes on Naomi. "I'm glad you brought Leslie and me together for this. She's fantastic, Naomi."

In the artistic arenas of photography and woodworking, local reviews deemed Mrs. Phillips quite good herself. "Thanks. Maybe Leslie is right. Why wait for spring?"

Viv put Einstein down, giving her a probing look. "How're you two?"

"Improving. Any rough spots stem from me."

"Are you ever going to tell me what happened? I mean, *specifically*. Bump the dumb stuff: I know it's more than normal mother-daughter shit." Viv spoke with caring concern, and Naomi realized she wasn't making her way into the friend zone; Viv Phillips had taken residence.

Naomi returned a friendly smirk. "So, where're we eating?"

Viv was her friend, yes, and Naomi knew she could tell Viv anything without fear of judgment or even a sideways glance. But what happened with Leslie would always remain a topic dead for discussion. Topic dead. Casket closed and buried. Ashes to ashes, dust to dust. Forever and ever. Amen.

Viv gave Naomi another considering look before showing her pearly whites. "Well, you've been mentioning your B-more coddies, I'm leaning cheeseburger." Wafts of lemongrass from her body oil drifted.

Naomi repaid Viv's smile with her own. Viv was right; she had been talking coddies up a lot lately. "Well, Ganky Paul's it is then." Ganky Paul's wasn't in her beloved Charm City, but it would do: their coddie recipe came close to the right combo of flavors, and their cheeseburgers were very good.

Lunch with Viv did indeed brighten Tuesday considerably. There was laughter and varying discussion, with tasty, greasy comfort food topped by a dessert of pineapple sherbet with caramel drizzle (she loved pineapple sherbet in the fall).

It was October, and the season for flea markets was ending, but on the return from lunch, Viv spotted one and suggested stopping past it. Naomi declined (reason known but unexplained) but secretly checked off another mark in Viv's "cool people" column. Naomi even found herself on the verge of revealing the shameful secret she shared with Leslie. She stopped herself several times. If ever she dug that casket up, though—only she and Viv Phillips would be there to view the contents.

Unfortunately, despite the friendly fun with Viv, the day ended with a bookend to how Tuesday began, imparting an infusion of moody blue.

She was snacking on Cerignola olives and working on a sudoku puzzle ("There Must Be a God Somewhere" by Inez Andrews and the Andrewettes playing in the background) when Jeff Winthrop called. Thursday's session would be missed: Todd had an asthma attack and was hospitalized.

Tuesdays.

Naomi had every intention of making it through to late evening before having a drink, maybe even going an entire day or two without one.

She prepared herself a Henney Brandy Alexander, adding an extra dash of nutmeg.

It's been said the road to hell was paved with good intentions, so maybe it was for the best.

Chapter 13

False Starts

The facial hair threw everything off. He wondered why such a little boy would have such serious showings of a mustache and beard. Such a little boy.

His little boy.

Jeff Winthrop watched his sleeping son, a montage of scenes from Todd's boyhood scrolling through his mind. He didn't care that Todd was going on 15. He was still his little boy. "I'm sorry, little man. Daddy's sorry." He swallowed hard, but the lump of distress remained. "I'll make it right." But *making it right* meant so many messed-up things. He lowered his head, allowing quiet sobs to take him.

"Mister Winthrop?" a voice inquired from behind him. It was Gloria, the duty nurse. "Everything satisfactory?"

Jeff sniffed and lifted his head.

Todd stirred.

Jeff cleared his throat. "Uh, yeah." The hand he swiped downward across his face served as a makeshift handkerchief. "Come on in." He rubbed his wet palm on his jeans but didn't turn around.

A gameshow broadcast on the television above and behind him.

Gloria proceeded in. She checked Todd's IV bag and removed his lunch tray. Jeff watched her work. She sent him a sympathetic parting smile and paused at the door. "I'm not the doctor, but he's *fine*, Mister Winthrop. Or at least he's going to be soon. You know that, don't you?"

Looking back at her, Jeff nodded. "Yeah, I know."

Gloria nodded her head toward Todd. "He'll be up soon." She pulled the door but didn't close it.

Jeff turned back to his sleeping son and then shifted his gaze to the rain-splattered window and the moderate drizzle pattering outside it.

Memories of a life-no-longer, surfaced. Surfaced and tortured. He forced down the new sobs rising. Slouched in his chair, Jeff watched his son sleeping. "This is going to sound crazy, but as crazy as it sounds, it's true, man. Julia's *here*, Todd. I smell her. I *feel* her," he whispered. He closed his eyes, speaking a little louder. "You and your sister: you need a mother…" Jeff sighed, he sniffed. "…But I'm not over your mother."

He grew silent, eyes closed, listening to the gameshow emanating from the speaker on Todd's bed. Admitting out loud that he wasn't over Julia should have made him feel better. So why didn't it? It just made him miss Jules that much more. And their wedding anniversary was upon him. Loomed like the dripping, bleeding, broken heart it was.

He had to do something. He had to—

"Dad?" Todd's croak sounded watery but not weak.

Jeff sat straighter. "Yeah, man. I'm here."

"Man, what time is it?" Todd pushed himself up into a sitting position.

"A little after two. How're you feeling?"

His son shrugged.

Jeff nodded his understanding. "Look, uh, I know you're probably ready to go home, but they wanna keep you in here another day or two."

Todd gazed at him with serious eyes (eyes so like his mother's). "I'm in no hurry to get home."

Jeff didn't know why (or maybe he did), but he couldn't hold his son's gaze. His laughter stammered from his throat as he shifted his focus to Todd's IV drip. "Yeah, I'm sure you're not pressed to get back to school…" He swept his eyes across Todd's and over to the window, simply unable to look his son in the eye.

"Yeah, Dad, okay: a break from school," Todd deadpanned.

Jeff didn't have to look at his son to appreciate the ringing sarcasm.

He stood and grabbed the arms of his chair to turn it around to face the television. He held the chair mid-turn. "Your sister's bringing a few chocolate-covered PayDays for y—" Jeff dropped the chair.

The blended scent of roses, iris, and vanilla was so strong, it bordered pungent.

Jeff coughed and checked Todd, expecting to see an overt response to Julia's scent permeating the room.

Todd's brows folded and his mouth slanted, but his response appeared centered on concern over him dropping the chair—and nothing more. "You okay, Dad?"

Jeff used a few seconds to read his son's expression, determining whether his son masked a secondary response (and hoping he was). Todd glanced at the chair again before meeting his father's eyes, so it turned out Todd's concerned expression was genuine and finite; he hadn't noticed any aromatic change. Still, Jeff asked: "You smell 'at?"

Todd sniffed. His eyes widened. "Smell what?"

"I don't know—some fast-food or something. Smelled good," Jeff lied. "Guess I'm hungry or something. Imagining things." But he wasn't imagining Jules's presence. He just needed her to step out from behind the window curtain already and drop the charade. They wouldn't be mad at her—quite the opposite.

"Nah, I don't smell anything, but now that you mention it..." Todd reached over to his side table and opened the drawer. "Mal can sneak me a double-fish with extra sauce to go with my candy." He collected his cellphone and started texting, then raised eyebrows at his father. "You want one?"

Jeff was nowhere near hungry (the trend these days). "Yeah. Yeah, that'll work."

Todd grinned and nodded, going back to business on his phone.

Jeff sat in the chair. He gazed in the general area of the television above him, but paid little attention to it. A knot formed in his stomach, sending tendrils of anxiety and excitement toward his groin. He kept checking the room with sideways glances.

Julia was here.

Not just her scent. Julia. *Here.*

And he didn't give a damn how crazy it sounded.

Todd plopped his phone onto the bed. "Mal's on her way. She didn't feel like stopping, but I guilted her." His son chuckled, then smiled a bit mischievously at that before reaching for the remote to channel-surf.

Jeff loved his children so much. "Elliot coming with her?"

"Yeah, he—"

"Hello? Hi, guys!" Ruth peeped around the door as she pushed it open. "Can a lady join in, or is it men-only time?" She sounded playful, but the cheeriness carried Ruth's usual notes of defiance underneath it.

Jeff forced a smile. Julia's scent didn't wane; it strengthened, intensified (as did the ever-present knot in his stomach). If he didn't know any better, he believed Julia's fragrance sharpened with...anger?

He was a scintilla annoyed himself. Yeah, it was "men-only time"—and a lady had already joined them (so, it was men-only...and Julia).

He kept the smile. "Sure." He rose to greet his second wife as she entered Todd's room, carrying two Get Well Soon balloons and a bag. "How was your day?" He planted a kiss on Ruth's cheek. *They need a mother.*

They had a mother—and she lurked unseen somewhere in this hospital room.

"Pretty good. My DC properties are moving well." Ruth placed her purse on the floor of the small wardrobe before going over to Todd. "I couldn't concentrate, though, worrying about this one..." She leaned over and kissed Todd's forehead. "How're you doing? Better?" She situated his balloons in the corner beside his bed.

Jeff watched his son watch Ruth.

Todd's eyes held a wariness Jeff wanted to believe was tied to his present health situation. However, it didn't escape his notice that Todd hadn't spoken since Ruth arrived—not even a perfunctory greeting. He didn't review his cellphone, didn't comment on whatever was happening on the television. Todd just eyed Ruth, watching her with that guarded expression.

Todd finally spoke: "I'm a'ight, I guess." He went back to changing channels. "Thanks for the balloons," he added without looking at her.

Ruth glanced Jeff's way.

Jeff didn't know whether to say something to Todd. Then again, he didn't know what to say to his son. Not just because Todd was in the hospital and he didn't want to give him grief, but because—

Jeff contained a sigh. He was tired. Tired in so many ways.

Ruth held up the bag she carried, shaking it with a grin. "Brought you something..." She reached into the bag and brought out two PayDay candy bars. "You can snack on these later." She placed the bars on Todd's side table.

"Thanks, Ruth," Todd chuckled, but it had an edge to it. Jeff heard it.

"What?" Ruth looked from Todd to Jeff. "What now?" Her inquiring smile wavered, but Jeff also caught a hint of irritation flutter through her features. Seemed she was tired, too; tired of being *set up*, of being "the heavy," as she'd called herself in session.

But Jeff agreed with Naomi's response to that.

Jeff grinned, ignoring the now overpowering aroma of Shalimar and Ruth's hint of irritation. "Nothing, Ruth. You did fine. Todd prefers the chocolate-covered ones, that's all. They aren't sold widely in stores as much. Gotta come across 'em in certain shops."

"Ohh..." Ruth mused.

"I'ma still eat 'em, Ruth," Todd assured with an enthusiasm that bothered Jeff. His son looked...fearful.

What the fuck...?

Maybe it was carryover from his asthma attack. He realized the step-parenting thing carried its own unique dynamics to deal with, but men had intuition, too: something wasn't right. He had the feeling...

Jeff let it go for now. He was probably making something out of nothing. His son was in the hospital. He wanted to focus on getting him home.

The three watched television in relative silence for a little while, with Ruth (weirdly) doting on Todd whenever the opportunity presented itself. As with the drawstring-to-his-sweatpants lie, the doting on Todd seemed *extra* (again, when you're bullshitting, sometimes less is more).

To quit while he was ahead and avoid the added element of the Ruth-Mallory issue, he left with Ruth almost immediately after Mallory and Elliot arrived (double-fish with extra sauce in hand).

Jeff, however, noticed two constants before leaving his son for the night: the guarded apprehension in Todd's eyes...and the unwavering scent of a fragrance once worn by his dead wife.

He could do it this way.

If it had to be done (and it did), he could do it this way...

When they came home from visiting Todd, Jeff extended every gesture he could toward Ruth to compensate for Todd's attitude earlier. He joked with her, prepared a light supper, joked some more. Only a tiny portion of his efforts was genuine. But he hoped the pretense would become reality if he tried long and hard enough. His kids needed a mother; he'd married Ruth; he had to make this work. And so began the charade (on his part) Jeff hoped would lead to just that: making it work.

Jeff figured he and Ruth would be fine (murder can wait) if they stayed on neutral ground. No old wounds (Ruth's "miscarriage"; anything Julia); no current events (anything related to Mallory and Todd); and no future events (discussions about moving, about growing his hair back, or about his getting back into art). All other topics were fair game. Limited discussions regarding the past, present, or future didn't leave room for much else, but they managed.

As the evening progressed, Jeff got the feeling Ruth picked up on the same keep-it-neutral vibe. A series of false starts was better than no start at all. The idea of doing better at being a family looked promising, such that Jeff even suggested something he never thought he would.

"Want to take some time and pray together?" He wasn't sure he wanted to (it was something he and Julia did many nights before bed), but he was prepared to go through with it if Ruth agreed.

She glanced at him, then turned back to the commercial for auto insurance. Jeff waited. The insurance commercial rolled into one for a bladder medication with so many side effects, Jeff didn't think it worth it. The medication advertisement rolled on to one for yogurt.

"Not this time, Jeffy— I mean, *Jeff.*" Ruth didn't take her eyes off the television, but from his angle, Jeff watched the muscles in her face and neck tense and relax in such a rhythmical way, it registered as a practiced effort, as something she'd done many times before. He didn't know what to make of it. The commercials ended. She turned her green eyes to him. "Ready to go up? Make this renewed effort official?" Her tone lowered with innuendo.

So, she didn't want to pray; the woman wanted something...altogether *different*.

He understood Ruth's desire for intimacy with him; women had horny needs just like men. Yet the uncertainty in her eyes told him she wasn't sure he'd go for it. Her doubt was warranted. Their last attempt at sex didn't go well. Jeff had doubts about the outcome of this attempt.

Ruth's eyes searched his, waiting.

Jeff, not knowing what else to do, pecked a kiss on her nose to fill the awkward silence (he hated awkward silences).

She scrunched her face quizzically. "What was that?"

"I don't know. Nothing. C'mon." He stood and offered a hand to help Ruth up. He was ready to head upstairs (he was tired and wanted sleep), but he could not make any promises about what would happen once they got there.

Ruth accepted his hand, gripping with subtle nervousness. "Thanks." She rose and pecked his lips, using the remote to turn the television off.

Jeff wished against the palpable awkwardness the situation presented as of late, but he could do nothing about it. The knot of anxiety growing in his center attested to that. He wanted to reconnect with Ruth and reestablish their marriage and their status as a family. He did. His children needed a mother. He liked, and well, loved Ruth. But he didn't want sex with her (not right now, anyway). His loins didn't even stir. The now-familiar knot in his stomach tightened.

Ruth moved toward the staircase.

Jeff watched her walk, paying close attention to her ass and willing his nether region to respond. She hadn't changed out of her business suit; the brown mid-thigh skirt hugged her appreciatively, hinting at the inverted heart-shaped flesh beneath the fabric. Jeff watched Ruth approach the stairs and...

Nothing. White noise. Nullity.

Until...

Julia's scent wafted to him from somewhere to his right. The knot in his center diminished in a rush, taking the tension in his shoulders and back with it.

Ruth paused at the bottom of the stairs and looked at him.

Jeff drew a long inhale (roses and iris and vanilla—*oh, my!*), and smiled back at her. Good sensation stirred below his waist.

She headed up the stairs.

Jeff soon followed.

He dips his tongue into her mouth with teasing enticement while pressing his fingertips into the small of her back. The scents of vanilla and roses and iris flowers envelope him.

Yes, he could do it this way. With her help.

Jeff closes his eyes tighter and drives his tongue further, and she responds in kind with an enthusiasm he knew Julia would.

He understands he is with Ruth, yet he fully embraces the fantasy of being with Julia (for their anniversary). Embracing the fantasy was key. He could do it this way. This way made it easier.

If it had to be done (and it did), he could do it this way.

Jeff trails his hands up and down her back, pausing at her waist or ass to fondle and squeeze with a sensual pressure designed to drive them both crazy. Julia's and Ruth's proportions are different. Jeff concentrates on melding his form with those proportions most dear to him. He lightens his kiss and nibbles at her lips, tasting hints of fading lipstick.

A hand trails down his torso and stops at his belt before continuing and resting on his hardness. Jeff sighs but resists opening his eyes—for God help him, the touch is distinctly Julia's. Distinctly. Julia's. He couldn't say whether fantasy had become reality. He didn't care.

In sweet emphasis, fingers squeeze with erotic purpose along the length of his erection. That and that alone is Julia. Ruth tended to be more hesitant with his erection; she has never, ever *touched him like this. Not ever. Jeff's heart and throat swell with emotion. His erection intensifies almost painfully.*

"Very nice, Jeff," Ruth murmured.

He opened his eyes and put the first three fingers of one hand to her lips. He shook his head. "No words, okay? Not this time." Gazing into Ruth's green eyes, Jeff (for a moment) thought he saw that pear-olive coloring transform into the caramel hues of—

She lowered his fingers. "But this is strange, Jeff, *different*. It's nice; it truly is. But something's weird. I—"

He shook his head again. "Shhh. No words. Just be."

Ruth nodded. Her demeanor reflected quite the opposite of her usual self, and the reason for that was supernaturally clear—in his view, at least.

"Close your eyes, Ruth." That would make the rest of it even easier. She did.

With Julia's scent around him, Jeff took the time to remove Ruth's clothing, hearing warm sighs signaling her pleasure at the technique he used getting her undressed.

He closed his eyes and pressed his body against Ruth (Julia). "No words. Just be," he uttered. Eyes closed, Jeff resumed the fantasy. He didn't know if or when Ruth opened her eyes again. He didn't care.

He swayed with her in a smooth movement, guiding her back, back, closer to their bed. His eyes remained closed as he lay down with her in one swift motion. He didn't need to see. Not for this. His mind's eye held perfect vision...

Jeff runs his hands over her body's contours, reimagining them as they should be. He plants butterfly kisses on each nipple the way she likes before moving up to tease her tongue with his own. Her mouth tastes of watermelon and the kiss he remembers from the day he proposed.

And he could do it this way.

The scent of Shalimar intensifies, and Jeff smiles into her mouth as he kisses her, squeezing her plump orbs and gently tugging her hard nipples. The change in her kiss tells him he has her hot. He trails a hand down from the playground of her chest to more enticing territory. The ache in his pants (coupled with the longing in his heart) needs relief. Slippery moisture greets his fingers, and he plays there, moving his fingers over and around, in and out of her, until her contractions and moans signal her climax.

How he loves her so!

They were on the bed, but Jeff re-imagines a time when they were on the floor of the studio upstairs (the night before she left him) when it seemed they couldn't get enough of each other—and their Black love knew no bounds. Oh yes. Mouths and hands were everywhere then, and Jeff encourages the same from her this time.

Iris. Roses. Vanilla.

Each blended to create a fragrance emblazoned across his memories for life, yet he could identify the individual elements and the beauty of each contribution singularly.

A moan of pleasure. His? Hers? Didn't matter. What mattered was being with her. She was here, and he was with her (and God help him, she felt good). His erection strains with a renewed sense of urgency, which moves him to action. Jeff frees himself while he kisses her, then shifts between her spread legs, positioning himself above her for intimacy missionary style. He braces himself above her with one hand and holds his hardness against her with the other, gliding the head along her wetness and eliciting another deep moan from her. He pauses despite the urgency, *remembering how sexy she looked lying beneath him on the floor of the art-music room. Jeff slows his breathing, relishing the memory...*

"Look at me, Jeff. Open your eyes," Ruth urged with a whisper.

Jeff shook his head without opening his eyes. "Shhh." It was important she *didn't talk*.

He could do it (this way) if she didn't talk.

Jeff slides into her warmth and pauses again, enjoying the initial sensation of being inside her. He thrusts into her, handling his business. Nibbling her neck, he varies the rhythm of his thrusts, sometimes giving it to her slowly for long seconds, making sure she enjoys the friction of his length, and then sometimes faster, harder—making sure he enjoys the friction, period.

She tells him how good he feels, encouraging him with grips to his body, suggesting he never stop.

His eyes remain closed, but as he loves her, his mind's eye gazes into the depths of her caramel-brown ones. His breathing changes with hers as they move closer to the conclusion they both want.

But, as good as it is, he doesn't want to climax because it would mean the end (albeit temporarily) of *this time with her. She moans softly but emphatically ("Yes, Jeff! Ohhh!") before he feels her climax.*

His release, when it comes, is bittersweet.

Not wanting to let go, Jeff took his time opening his eyes and reconnecting to the here and now. He pulled out and rolled off Ruth, lying supine beside her on the bed and gazing at the ceiling.

He did it.

He made love to his wife while giving Ruth the sex she wanted, too.

"Jeff, that was... Oh, yes," Ruth sighed with a breathy moan. It sounded loud in the stillness of their bedroom.

The scent of *Shalimar*, though faint, remained. Penis softening, Jeff saddened as the redolence faded, and he made up his mind: he would make this work with Ruth, if for no other reason than to experience Julia that way again.

Ruth left the bed for the bathroom but said nothing more.

Jeff was thankful.

Chapter 14

Visiting Hours

Naomi sat in her rounded wood-carved chair on the mini-balustrade adjoining her bedroom, holding a Rubik's Cube while enjoying the mild October sunshine and a tall glass of sweetened iced tea.

Yeah, she'd had a shot of Belvedere first, but so what?

She sipped with leisure, surveying the multitude of fall foliage colors presenting before her, while inside, Florence Price's Violin Concerto No. 2 in D minor traveled to her at mid-volume from the player in her bedroom, infusing the atmosphere with some Black girl magic. She could still smell the leaves, richly earthy from being wet with yesterday's rain. Kevin's city view was pleasant, but Naomi much preferred the solitude and natural wonder of her view of the woods.

The foliage made her think of Rick and Viv and Viv's mention of their wedding anniversary approaching next month, of how much the couple favored autumn. The foliage, too, made her think about the striking color of Rick's irises.

"I'm gone!" Leslie hollered up the stairs to her.

"Okay, thanks!" Naomi hollered back.

Moments later, she heard Leslie's Honda CR-V start and her driving away. Leslie spent less and less time at home. Over the last few weeks, Leslie tried broaching getting her own place; she'd be graduating soon and thought it was time, now that she was working, too.

Naomi didn't squash the subject when Leslie brought it up, but she didn't present a welcoming arena for its discussion either. She had reasons for not wanting her daughter to move out.

Maybe not the *best* of reasons, but reasons, nonetheless.

Naomi took a long swig of tea. Enough thinking about Leslie. Actually, she could use another shot of vodka, but that would not mesh with her plans for the day. She had only two sessions scheduled, and she'd rescheduled the first so she could visit Todd Winthrop in the hospital. They were releasing him tomorrow. Visiting hours stretched far into early evening. Hopefully, no one else would be there, and she could have time alone with the young man—maybe get him to open up a little, explore more of his relationship with his stepmother. She doubted she'd get much; teenagers could be contrary when they wanted, but it was worth a shot.

Todd's asthma attack ranked borderline life-threatening and was likely stress-induced. Naomi knew it. Hunch or not, flash or not, Naomi was more than sure Ruth was behind it (even if remotely). Whatever her personal theories, none of it mattered without speaking with Todd first.

A breeze swirled around her before moving on to rustle the reds, golds, and browns adorning the branches of the trees across from her. Enough icy chill in the breeze reminded Naomi that, resurgent summer weather or not, it was indeed fall—with winter soon to follow. Maybe a cup of hot hibiscus tea would've been better. She took a deep breath and sighed, turning the bill of her Baltimore Ravens cap to the back. Naomi carried the Rubik's Cube inside and prepared for a trip to the hospital.

The butterflies in her stomach signaled she was oddly nervous about visiting the young man.

Despite the myriad of antiseptic aromas permeating the halls and rooms of hospitals, Naomi always thought it did little to mask the underlying pall of sickness hospitals housed. Rather, the medicinal odors of disinfectants and germicides only emphasized the point: you're here because something somewhere, somehow, didn't go quite right with your body or with the body of someone you loved.

Apart from the maternity ward and the delivery of healthy babies, that about sized it up.

When she arrived on Todd's floor, Naomi stopped by the nurses' station (bedecked in a Halloween theme featuring cobwebs, jack-o-lanterns, and ghosts) to request access to review Todd's medical chart. Fortunately, Jeff listed Naomi as one of his doctors. Even after Naomi presented her ID, the duty nurse (her nametag read: "Gabriella") still wasn't forthcoming with the data tablet. Naomi wasn't mad at her. She considered that a good thing: you can't be too careful these days.

Gabriella showed genuine surprise at Naomi's ability to navigate the screens. She was worn-looking, probably 30-ish but looking 50-ish.

Naomi engaged her in small talk, encouraging the nurse to show her medical knowledge. Gabriella soon let her guard down enough to smile and discuss Todd Audric Winthrop as one of her favorite patients.

Naomi performed a cursory review of the data in Todd's charts. The mucous secretion levels in his lungs were down, approaching normal. Good. After her review, Naomi smiled at Gabriella and shook her hand, a gesture the nurse appreciated.

Heartfelt courtesy smoothed many roads.

Naomi entered Todd's room just as he stepped out of the bathroom. He didn't appear at all surprised to see her.

"Hey, Doctor Alex." He gathered his hospital gown around him and climbed back into bed. "I get outta here tomorrow." He offered a perfunctory smile that didn't quite mesh with the suggested enthusiasm of his words. At a low volume, the speaker on his bed broadcast sports updates from the sports channel on the TV above them.

"Well, I guess that's good and bad," Naomi responded as she eased the door partway closed. She resisted the urge to go over and give the boy a hello hug. Instead, she smiled and walked around to the other side of his bed, sitting in the chair closest to him. "It's good you'll be out of the hospital soon; in time for Halloween."

Todd shook his head. "Not hyped about ghouling. Pro'ly won't do much again this year. But it'll be good getting out of here tomorrow..."

"Hmm. But all after that, well, not so good."

Todd glanced at the television and then stared at Naomi for several seconds without speaking.

Naomi stared right back for those same seconds. "I mean, your minor break from school is ending, and who wants that, right?" She added the comment primarily for Todd's reaction to it.

Todd scoffed and turned away from her, then opened and reached into his side table drawer, feel-searching. He spoke with his back to her: "Why e'rybody harpin' on the 'break from school'?" He continued his search in the drawer. "I know I put— Oh yeah, thought so." Todd turned back around, pulling the top half of the wrapper off a chocolate-covered PayDay candy bar. "Some of us don't mind school, ya know." He tilted the candy in her direction with an inquiring grin. "Wanna piece?"

Naomi shook her head with a smile of appreciation. She hadn't seen a chocolate-covered PayDay in... She didn't know. She didn't realize you could still get them. "Chocolate doesn't aggravate your asthma?"

He jounced one shoulder. "Nah, I don't eat it a lot, anyway. But hey, I'm already in the hospital now, so..." He tilted the candy toward her again. "Sure? Mal found a store carrying 'em."

Naomi hit him with a smiling headshake. So that solved the Choco-PayDay mystery. "Thanks, anyway. I'm more of a Peanut Chew kind of girl. Original dark—not the milk chocolate." She was also a York Peppermint Pattie girl.

"I hear you. Never had those, though."

"It's an old-school candy. Forty-and-over crowd. I'll let you sample a piece next session. I think you'll like them."

He bit his candy. "I 'on't know," he remarked, pointing at the bar with a gleeful smirk. "This my joint right here," he finished around a mouthful.

Naomi uttered a hushed laugh. "I'm not trying to convert you, just exposing you to what else is out there..."

Todd's smile faltered as he stared toward the door to his room. "...Yeah, I guess we all need to know what else is out there. Don't we, Doctor Alex?"

They weren't talking about candy anymore.

"It's always good to know what your options are in life, Todd."

He glimpsed her way before returning his attention to the television. He then located the remote on the bed and lowered the volume even more. Sitting back against his pillows, he now gazed up at the screen. Naomi could tell he was looking without seeing. After a moment: "Yeah, but kids don't have many options, Doctor Alex. We gotta go with what the adults have us go with. Even if we don't like it, we gotta deal." Todd kept his eyes on the television. He took another bite of his candy and chewed slowly.

"How'd you end up in here, sweetie?" Naomi wanted info beyond the medical charts. But she wasn't sure Todd would answer.

Keeping his eyes on the television, it seemed Todd wouldn't answer. He ran a hand over his comb-needing curls. Viewing his other features, Naomi realized how much he resembled Julia Winthrop. He scratched at sideburns lengthening down and around his jawline—and belonged on someone older. "You won't tell my dad?" He glanced at her sideways. He was 14, looking all of 18, looking all of 9 years old.

"Not if you don't want me to." Truth was, it all depended on what he told her, but for now, the half-truth would have to suffice.

Todd grew silent again. His candy rested at his side.

Naomi watched the lines of his face fluctuate with his internal struggle: to tell or not to tell. "Take your time, Todd."

The sportscaster on the television updated the status of an injury of one of the Baltimore Orioles' pitchers. While waiting for Todd, Naomi lent some of her attention to this bit of sports news. She was interested in most, if not all, things B-more. She may have been born in Sioux City, Iowa, but Charm City had been her home since she was a toddler. Even after moving more central to the DC-Maryland-Virginia (DMV) area for her internship, Baltimore remained special, remained home.

"I shouldn't have said anything to her about my mom's..."

"You mean during the session?" Naomi had a surefire inkling what he was talking about; she just wanted to be sure. She didn't have to ask whom "her" referred to.

Todd's eyes darted in her direction again and then back to the television. He gave a rapid head nod.

"She said she'd discuss it with you later. Did she?"

A nurse poked her head in. "Need anything, Todd?" Her hair held shades of red, brown, and orange—like the leaves of the trees.

Naomi smiled at her, then checked Todd's monitor to see if that prompted the inquiry: his blood pressure was slightly elevated.

"Nah, I'm good. Thanks, Cherise."

Cherise un-poked her head, leaving the door inches ajar once again.

Naomi turned back to Todd. He re-wrapped what remained of his candy bar and placed it on his side table on top of his downtime entertainment: *Chameleon* by Charles R. Smith. He sat back against his pillows but turned his body such that he faced her more. The young man then offered a wan smile and cleared his throat, looking at her with eyes holding this restrained apprehension she hoped to quell soon.

Naomi folded her hands and leaned forward. "Like I said, take your time. Don't sweat the details if you don't want to. I'm pretty good at filling in the blanks. Highlights will do if that makes the telling better."

"It's not all 'at though, Doctor Alex. I'm a'ight now."

"Let me decide that for myself, okay?" As far as Naomi was concerned, it *was* all that.

Psychiatrist or not, it still baffled her how victims of abuse, or any mistreatment, still tried to protect the offender, downplay the actions of the aggressor. Todd was a child, point taken, but Naomi didn't think self-preservation had an age restriction. Psychoanalytical theories be damned; Naomi didn't get it.

Todd opened his mouth to speak, but Naomi interrupted him. "Before you begin, I need to know something. Have you been taking your medication or—?"

"Well, they're taking care of that while I'm in here. But at home, yeah. Been much better about it anyway, so..." He shook his head steadily, telling her silently but nicely to back off.

"Okay, okay, just checking. Go ahead, then. What happened?"

The boy let go of a pent-up breath. He looked up at the sports news for a second or ten. His tongue traced the edge of his chipped tooth before he started. "After the session, Mal and I decided we didn't want to go back to school, but Mallory still wanted to go to work, and I still had practice, but I needed to finish my social studies paper..."

"Uh-huh." Naomi checked Todd's blood pressure: back to normal.

"So, after we got home, Dad dropped Mal off at work, which, to be honest, was cool because you know, it was like a real family situation and everything with him taking her. Dad's been M-I-A in many ways lately, so...yeah. Anyway, that meant only Ruth and I were at the house."

"How was everyone's mood after the session?"

"Pretty good, I guess. Even though there were some tense moments with you before we left, wasn't anybody sulking or anything—not that I could tell, anyway. Until later."

"I got you. Go ahead."

"So, I'm prepping to go upstairs and finish my social studies paper for Ms. Bundy's class, but Ruth asks me to get the leaves in the yard first."

"But it's early autumn; the leaves aren't falling like that yet."

Todd tilted his head to the side with a jerk and just stared at her. The look said: *No shit.*

Naomi swallowed her chuckle. "Okay. Gotcha. Continue."

His courage apparently buoyed, Todd sat up a little to tell the tale. "I didn't wanna mess with the leaves cuz I had practice later, but since it wasn't that much out there, I said fu—" He glanced her way.

"Said, hey-nonny-nonny it. Uh-huh, continue."

Todd smiled. It was big, and it was genuine.

Naomi smiled back.

"So, I rake the front and whatever really quick and head on to the backyard, which is less work than the front and side because of the patio. I could feel my chest tightening, but I was still mostly all right. I'm back there, raking and bagging up,…and Ruth is standing on the porch watching me. Creeped me out a li'l bit, but I let it go." He waved his hand dismissively. "When I finish, I stand in the backyard looking up at her, checking to see if she was satisfied or whatever."

"And?"

"She just nodded and waved me in."

"No words?"

"Nope. Should've figured she was salty then, but, well, whatever." Todd shrugged. "Now, I'm in the kitchen washing my hands, and she comes in and starts in on me about what I said in the session."

"Just like that?"

"I mean, she didn't come in and start goin' off, but she built up to it."

"I see." And she did. She saw Ruth leaning a hip against a counter, sneakily wheedling the discussion toward the source of her irritation: Todd standing up for his mother against her in session.

"So, I'm trippin' cuz I need to get my paper done because Ms. Bundy doesn't play. I also need to chill my chest down before practice, but here she is giving me grief 'bout her hang-ups over my mom's—"

"What'd she say?" Naomi reflected on Ruth's hunter-green aura flickering during discussion about Julia Winthrop.

"Just stuff about never forgetting our mother, but don't keep her on a pedestal; how we don't appreciate Ruth and what she's trying to do; that my mother musta died early for a reason."

"What?!"

"Yeah, stuff like that."

"What'd you say?"

"I stood by what I said in the session. She never knew my mother, so she needs to quit with some of the stuff she says."

"Okay."

"Anyway, we're going back and forth with it, not really arguing, but almost. The more we talk, the tighter my chest is getting. So, I know I have an inhaler in the kitchen drawer, right? So, I go to get it, but it's not in there. I check a couple more drawers—nothing. Meanwhile, Ruth's still going on—"

"While you're having an attack?"

"Yup. She don't halfway believe I have it no way." Todd paused and frowned at the television for a moment.

Naomi watched him calm himself. She took a second to calm down, too, but intruding images of the scenario made it difficult.

The way Todd told the tale, however, tickled her. His narration was infused with urban colloquialisms and vernacular in direct opposition to how he presented and expressed himself to her in other settings. Todd straddled the line well: because she was sure he was selective in his speaking, depending on the audience. Todd could intellectualize it up or go to the gutter with his word choices: a precious asset in life—especially a young Black man's life. He would need to access that superpower often in the years ahead. Since Naomi experienced both versions of his communication style, she guessed she was in a unique category.

"You okay?" Naomi checked the monitor: pressure elevated again.

"I'm fine. It's just..." He focused on the television.

"I know. You don't have to finish, Todd—"

"I'm almost done, anyway." He returned his gaze to her and swallowed. "So, at this point, I can't really talk, so I lean against the counter to try and get it together. It lightens up enough for me to hurry upstairs to my room to get the one by my bed. I get up there—and that one's gone, too. I look around my bed, on the floor, in the drawer: nothing. So, I'm like, in panic mode now." Todd moved his arms and body about, acting out what Naomi guessed to be close to what he was doing at the time things happened. He shook his head. "By this time, I'm breathin', but it's real hard work."

"Where's Ruth?" Naomi leaned forward, gripping her knee to curtail her rising anger.

A frown accompanied Todd's scoff. "Following me around while I searched. Standin' in my doorway, she tells me to calm down, that we should follow the five-to-ten-minute rule to see if things get better, but I can tell it's getting too late for that—especially since I don't have any rescue inhalers." Todd paused thoughtfully. "Not being able to breathe... It's scary as shit, Doctor Alex."

"I believe you," was all Naomi could manage. She hoped Ruth didn't show up to visit while she was there. It was just best.

"Well, I wasn't gonna wait. I pushed past her and practically ran down the hall to my dad's room. I pressed the ambulance button on the alarm panel and slid to the floor to wait. And, Doctor Alex, I swear." Todd raised his right hand. "I swear I ain't making this up. But I saw her smile. She was down the hall and all, but..." He shook his head and lowered his hand.

"Lack of oxygen might've been messing with you," Naomi offered.

"Whatever you say. I know what I saw."

Naomi knew what he saw, too: his stepmother smile at his distress.

"Anyway, my dad comes in and finds us; Ruth shifts into concerned-parent mode, apologizing to my dad and me, saying she thought the inhalers were empty."

"Thought they were empty?!"

Anger flared in those caramel-brown eyes. "Yeah. And that's why she threw them out. She thought I had extras." He turned back to the television. Football news transmitted softly from the speaker.

"I'm sorry, sweetie."

Todd rolled his shoulders with (what she knew to be) a feigned apathy.

They listened to news about the upcoming Washington-Dallas game in pensive silence.

Naomi wanted to probe deeper, learn more about the dynamics between Todd and his stepmother, but she thought better of it. Deeper exploration (if the boy didn't shut down entirely) could aggravate his health issues—even while hospitalized. But she had one question, of which Todd's answer would encapsulate confirmation of several hunches: "You went to the roof in response to interaction with her." She posed it as a statement to make it easier for him to agree with her summation rather than experience internal distress over answering such a sensitive question—even if only in one word.

Todd stared at her, his lips bending toward another suggestion of *no shit* as answer. "...Nowhere else to go."

Asked and answered.

Naomi nodded and checked her watch. "I'm going to get out of here; let you rest. But I appreciate you sharing what happened." She stood, gazing at Todd more seriously. "I'm not going to tell your dad, but I am going to tell your dad. You understand?"

Todd's gaze at her held a mixture of bravado and gratitude. With a nod, he turned back to the television.

Naomi patted his knee and headed to the door.

"Thanks, Doctor Alex."

She smiled at him. "We roller-coaster lovers gotta stick together."

He grinned, but there was still worry and sadness in his eyes.

Naomi nodded and resumed heading for the door.

"I'm as tall as she is." His words were low, under his breath.

Naomi acted like she didn't hear him and left his room.

Todd's closing comment meant nothing more than the boy fantasized about violence or something against the woman. Maybe be able to stand up to her. And, well, Naomi knew she had to step in before anything else happened. She couldn't allow Todd to fixate on any violent fantasies if he had them—even those against Ruth.

Back in her car, Naomi bowed her head with closed eyes, bringing her heart and mind together in prayer.

Once finished, she found the short version of "God is Love" by Marvin Gaye on her MP3 and set it to repeat. After discussing with Todd about what happened and hearing Ruth's part in his resulting hospital stay, she needed a little spiritual uplift. The song was one of her favorites because its succinct yet melodic message summed it up for her perfectly.

She reflected on her visit with Todd.

A stress-induced asthma attack. Or rather, an asthma attack magnified by stress.

Todd's attack was likely brought on by the petty yard work Ruth insisted he do, along with the minor argument over Todd's comments regarding his mother during their session. Although it could be argued there was a significant level of stress in the boy's life to begin with, Naomi had every reason to believe the woman knew what she was doing. But why, though? The Winthrops seemed a nice enough family to marry into, and even Ruth (though Naomi didn't like her much) appeared to have a redeeming quality or two.

Naomi turned the volume up.

Although there were concerns for Todd's health with this case, Naomi still believed it all rested with Jeff. Todd probably told her the details about what happened because, on some level, he was ashamed to tell his father. With Jeff not being the most dependable of people for his children right now, telling Naomi was possibly Todd's hope someone would do something—be an unwavering flicker of light in his darkness.

She did not intend to let him down. She'd endeavor to open Jeff's eyes to the truth of Ruth.

Naomi pulled into the office park and parked in front of her building, but she didn't exit. She let "God Is Love" play twice more before killing the engine. Another forty minutes remained before her session with Willette Hargrove (thankfully, she rescheduled the Basheims altogether). Naomi sighed, thinking maybe this would be the time to just—

Her cellphone rang, startling her. She viewed the display panel: it was Leslie. Naomi answered through her Bluetooth headset. "Yes, ma'am?"

"So, how'd it go?" Leslie asked. Although Naomi couldn't give details on her cases, Leslie knew enough general information to inquire about Naomi's change in plans this morning.

"I'd say better than expected."

"Very good. Don't forget, I'm staying with Brendan and Joy instead of coming home after the exhibit."

"I didn't forget." Naomi sighed. "Cut to the chase, Les. All of this sounds like a bunch of small talk to me."

She listened to the traffic in Leslie's background.

"...I went to see Boppa today. He seems better."

"Mmm... I wish you'd have waited for me, Les." Naomi watched people enter and exit the office building. Disappointment melded into irritation. Leslie knew better. "I'm glad your grandfather's doing better."

"And your father-in-law."

"Just wish you would have waited."

"I know."

"I see. Well, thanks for the update—"

"Why do you avoid visiting Boppa by yourself? What's up with that?"

Naomi voiced a biting, one-note chuckle. "And so, what? Your going without me was supposed to force my hand into going alone or something?"

"I'm not saying that. I just don't underst—"

"No, you don't. Don't worry about it, though, okay? I have to go, Leslie. My session will start shortly. Talk to you later tonight." Naomi disconnected without waiting for Leslie's response. She didn't expect her daughter to call back.

Naomi watched the traffic, both pedestrian and vehicular, wasting some of her precious pre-session prep time. The only prep she needed at this moment was a shot of something at least 60-proof. But, alas, that was out of the question.

She turned the ignition to the accessories (or ACC) position, allowing Marvin Gaye's melodic singing to fill the interior of her X5. Naomi sang along, feeling much better by song's end. She turned off the ignition with a grin swooped to one side. "Music hath charms..."

Naomi felt better but still wanted (needed) a drink. She could take a solid sip from the bottle of Hennessy in the storage compartment behind her seat, but a new tip was a new tip; she intended to stay the course (pressing "restart" as needed). Taking several deep breaths, she watched the people. She even watched Willette Hargrove arrive and enter the building. Naomi checked the time. Willette was twenty minutes early.

"It'll have to wait." Naomi exited her car and headed inside.

Chapter 15

JJMT

"This is *so cool*, Mallory." Daphne Murray playfully punched Mallory's shoulder. She and Daphne had been buddies since middle school. Not BFFs, but buddies. "I'm glad we came. I feel all sophisticated and everything. This art show is nice."

"She only invited you because you have the three-point play, Daphne." Elliot stood beside them, holding a glass of ice water. "Ain't nothin' like friends with a three-point play: a driver's license *and* their own car. The car, of course, is worth two points alone." Elliot nodded, wearing this friendly smirk. "Yeah, Mallory knows what she's doing."

Mallory nudged back at him. "Shut up, Kelz." She sent kind eyes to Daphne. "Ignore him, Daph. You're here because we thought it would be fun. We could have taken the subway for all that. I'm glad you're having a good time."

"Oh, I ain't thinking about Kelz." Daphne sent an appraising eye-roam over Elliot, full of sarcastic attitude. "So, why you here? Last I checked, you didn't even have your license, let alone a car. Humph." Her braids swished around her as she turned away and stepped forward for a gander at a sculpture display before them.

"Oooh, shots fired!" Elliot came back.

Daphne looked back at him over her shoulder. "I know, right!" She laughed, louder than necessary (given the heads turning their way).

Elliot and Daphne snickered together, modulating their volume.

"Anybody going to Calista's Halloween party?" Daphne asked.

"No," Elliot said. "Sounds like it's gonna be bougie, not spooky."

Daphne scoffed. "Anyway. I'm going as a Munchkin. Get it? Mal?"

"I doubt it, Daph. Haven't thought about it, really. No costume..." Mallory shrugged, considering Daphne's Wizard-of-Oz-themed costume idea. They didn't have a Dorothy in her family, but Todd could be the Tinman, having lost his heart to deal with their family drama. Her dad? Well, the Scarecrow; his grief and stress have weakened his mental (his brain). Which left her as the Cowardly Lion. Yeah, that was her: no courage. And the Wicked Witch couldn't be more obvious.

Kelz frowned. "I can already hear you over-explaining your Munchkin costume, Three-Point. You need something like a flying monkey."

Daphne bent her head his way. "So, you're joining me without a costume, then?"

Kelz stared at Daph as if forming an unfriendly comeback, then lowered his head with a tiny laugh. "Yeah, okay."

It was funny, but Mallory barely smiled. She stood in the main hall of the Jamison-Ajai Art Gallery, taking in the unique angles and expressive contours of several sculptures—and wondered if coming to the showcase was such a good idea. Her father instilled in her an appreciation for most, if not all, art forms, but viewing the exhibits made her miss the old days before her mother died. Before her father sorta died.

An article in the weekend newspaper magazine prompted her to come. It featured profiles of up-and-coming local artists scheduled for exhibit at fall festivals and art shows. Mallory liked the pictures by photographer Vivian Phillips and wanted to see more. The sculptures by Mabel C. Turner and Leslie Alexander appealed to her, too.

Unbeknownst to her dad, months ago, she submitted his name for an artist revival initiative, so she also thought she'd see something of her father's on display: a pleasant surprise for him, perhaps a motivation, too. She didn't know; it was a hope and a prayer, something she tried on a whim after coming across a few of his "castoff" paintings in the basement. She then contacted her dad's agent Mr. Clude for his advice and guidance...

This morning, she'd left the article on her father's chest of drawers, hoping he would at least comment if he didn't join her. But he did neither, and Mallory didn't press the issue. She started to ask Todd to come with her; he was fine now and probably would have come, but she decided not to. And now a part of her wished she'd stayed home, too (or found something else to do).

"You okay, Mal?" At five feet eleven, Daphne was one of the tallest girls in Mallory's class, yet she had no interest in playing basketball, despite the many hints and suggestions.

"Uh-huh." She was suddenly close to tears.

"Thinkin' 'bout your fam?" Elliot asked. Mallory appreciated his astuteness. Plus, he was a good kisser. Kelz wasn't her boyfriend, far from it, but as friends, they'd had their minor boy-girl moments.

Mallory shrugged. "Something like that, I guess."

"You wanna leave?" Daphne and Elliot voiced simultaneously. They looked at each other, sharing more snickers.

"Knock on wood," Mallory commented.

Elliot and Daphne peered at her with quizzical smiles.

Mallory chuckled at their expressions. "Never mind; it's something I got from my parents." Taking in her surroundings, her smile faded. She observed the myriad of people perusing the artwork, holding toothpicks now devoid of the cheeses and meats once adorning them. Strains of New Age music accompanied the many pockets of conversation floating throughout the gallery.

She'd never felt so alone.

"So, do you?" Daphne's eyes held a hint of concern Mallory wasn't comfortable with. "...Want to leave, that is?"

Mallory hesitated, thinking, if she were going to go, now would be as good a time as any, but a part of her wanted to stay. "No, no. I want to meet some artists if I get a chance—especially Missus Phillips."

Elliot whistled low and approvingly. "Yeah, I wouldn't mind meeting *her*, either: she is *hella* fine. Pretty as shit. Body right out the comic books, bruh. She can take my picture all night *long*. Unh!" He shook his head in that guy-way as additional emphasis.

Daphne sucked her teeth, adding a dismissing hand flip. "Whatever, Kelz. We're not here for your perverted interests."

"I'm just saying. She's *hot*." Elliot adopted an expression hard to interpret but was teasing and funny.

Daphne pushed his arm flirtingly, which should have told Kelz she liked him, but boys were stupid like that—he had no clue.

Chuckling, Mallory headed toward the rear of the gallery. "C'mon."

Elliot stepped up, walking beside her.

"Your dad's an artist, right?" Daphne asked from behind them.

Mallory nodded, wandering semi-purposely toward the combo-expression exhibit featuring Phillips and Alexander (the reason she was here to begin with). She didn't want to talk—least of all about her father.

"Yeah, he is," Elliot confirmed. "It's been a while, though. Have you seen anything of his?" He looked back at Daphne.

Mallory did, too.

Daphne nodded. "Yeah."

"He's pretty good—and I'm not into the whole art scene at all." Elliot took a swallow of his water and crunched a piece of ice.

Daphne maneuvered to stroll alongside Elliot and Mallory. "My uncle has two J. Adair Winthrops: a painting by him and a statue."

Sculpture, not statue, Mallory thought.

"Sculpture," Elliot said.

Daphne frowned her confusion. "Huh?"

"You mean he has one of his *sculptures*, not statues," Elliot corrected. "I'm not into it, but Mal talks about it enough, so..." He shrugged.

"Okay, well yeah. My uncle has two pieces." Daphne leaned forward to catch Mallory's eye. "To hear my uncle tell it, he's paid for at least two semesters' worth of college for you or your little brother."

Mallory offered a wan smile. "Thanks, I guess." Daphne was one of the few to provide friendly support and distraction when her mother died, but this discussion wasn't helping in that vein.

"That could mean a lot or a little—depends on the college. I mean, what're we talking: tuition for Bates or Li'l Shack Community College?" Elliot teased. His baby locs gleamed from the sheen of oils in his freshly twisted hair. He was cute (muscular with sandy-brown skin and a friendly smile), but Mallory didn't see him in that boyfriend-material way—not like she did Walter "D-Nine" Lyons.

Daphne snickered daintily. "Boy, you stupid. Anyway, you know what I'm saying." She leaned to peer at Mallory again. "Your father having anything coming out soon?"

Mallory hunched her shoulders. She didn't want to talk about her father. He was on her mind enough as it was, just being here.

Elliot got it. "Talk about something else, Daphne," he advised gently.

"Oh, okay." Daphne looked at Mallory. "Sorry, Mal."

Mallory shook her head to reassure Daphne, adding a smile. "Don't worry about it. It's okay."

Daphne smiled back and turned her attention to the art.

"But it isn't, is it?" a woman noted from Mallory's other side.

Mallory's eyes widened, and her mouth fell open.

Dr. Alexander stood beside her.

Relief washed through Mallory in such a wave she wanted to cry. She didn't know why she felt relieved. Instead of bawling her eyes out, she gave Dr. Alexander a big smile and hugged her. "Hi, Doctor Alex!" Her relief, however, exchanged with doubt as it seemed Dr. Alexander wouldn't hug her back, but it was only for a moment; Dr. Alex did hug back. With their hug, the urge to sob rose again, and Mallory didn't want to let the doctor go. "What're you doing here, Doctor Alexander?" Mallory smiled and stepped back, not caring if Dr. Alexander noticed the tears in her eyes. The unexpected wave of relief stayed with her.

The doctor gestured toward the combo-expression exhibit. "You like?" She looked chic in her slim-fit slacks and animal print top.

Dr. Alex wasn't a tall woman. Not at all. Mallory didn't realize that until standing next to her just now. She had the doctor by at least three or four inches. After all their sessions, Dr. Alexander somehow seemed taller. Mallory smiled to herself. She guessed Dr. Alex embodied a confident presence that made up for what she didn't have in height, leaving an impression of tallness despite her maybe being only around five feet two or three (probably shorter).

Mallory turned to the art. "Uh-huh. I'm here because of an article about Viv Phillips and Leslie Alex—" She turned back to Dr. Alexander.

The doctor wore a cryptic smile.

"Aw, man! She's your daughter, niece, what?"

"Daughter."

Elliot nudged Mallory from the side. "Um, *hello?*" He reached around her and extended his hand. "Pardon her rudeness. We're friends of Mallory's. I'm Elliot, also known as 'Kelz,' and this is Daphne," he gestured toward Daphne with his other hand, "also known as 'Three-point Play.'"

Daphne sucked her teeth and rolled her eyes before smiling at Dr. Alexander. "I'm Daphne."

Dr. Alex accepted Elliot's hand with an amused expression. "Pleased to meet you both." She extended a hand to Daphne as well.

Mallory nudged Elliot back a little harder than he did her. "*You're* the one being rude. You didn't give me a chance," she snapped. Hearing the edge in her voice, she smiled to play it off (although, for whatever reason, having her friends there now irritated her).

"Twenty-second rule. Took too long," Elliot said playfully. "But you can introduce the doctor to us. How 'bout that?"

Mallory hesitated. She didn't want to tell them how she knew Dr. Alexander. Elliot knew about the therapy and all, but still.

"I'm Todd's doctor."

Elliot and Daphne smiled and bobbed their heads in understanding.

Mallory contained a sigh. Dr. Alex worked well on the fly.

Dr. Alexander turned to her. "Gotta second, Mallory?"

"Uh, sure, Doctor Alex." Mallory conferred with her friends. "Scuse us, okay?"

Kelz went into comical but thankfully low-key histrionics. "Oh, okay, so *that's* how it is. You meet up with your high-powered doctor friends to hobnob with them—and leave *us* hanging. Okay, okay. I see where we stand now, *Miss* Winthrop." He turned on a heel toward Daphne. "C'mon, Three-point." As they walked away, both turned back with more of their friendly snickers.

"Thanks," Mallory said after them. She turned back to the doctor. "What's up?" She tried to sound casual, but her spine tingled with tension. What did Dr. Alex want to talk about?

"Well, finding you here is serendipitous, Mallory. If I could, I'd like a mini-session with you before the real one next week." Dr. Alex's brown eyes registered concern and sparkled with curious amusement simultaneously. Mallory liked her.

Mallory scanned the gallery's art exhibits. There were plenty times she wanted to talk to Dr. Alex alone. Plenty of times. Now though... "Are you supposed to talk to your patients outside official sessions?" She watched other gallery attendees doing their art-critiquing thing.

"'Talk,' as in counsel? Not really, no."

And Mallory had the distinct feeling Dr. Alexander didn't care one iota about that.

"But," Dr. Alexander continued, "we absolutely do not have to if you don't want to. No pressure. That's not how I roll."

Mallory smiled to herself. Dr. Alex was something else. Still, she didn't know if she wanted a mini-session with her, but she was curious about what the doctor wanted to discuss. "Okay."

Dr. Alexander now surveyed the gallery. "We should probably have this discussion in a more private setting, sweetie. Okay?" She put a hand on Mallory's shoulder. "We won't be long, Mallory. I promise."

Reassuring comfort radiated through her touch, and Mallory relaxed. But Mallory also got the impression the gesture, as natural as it seemed, was unconventional for the doctor. "Okay."

Moments later, they stood in the alcove of a neighboring antique shop. Mallory peered at the antique pieces in the window display, knowing what some items were and not recognizing most of the others. She appreciated the history behind the heirlooms.

The lingering warmth of the fading October resurgent summer surrounded her; she didn't realize how cool it was in the air-conditioned gallery. She dropped her sweater from her shoulders but kept her forearms in the sleeves.

Mallory shifted her attention from the antiques to the flow of pedestrian traffic along the block. Even with the exhibit, traffic was light for a Saturday. Cedar and wood oil smells from the shop tickled her nose. Mallory sneezed.

"God bless you."

"Thank you."

Mallory's unease grew with each second of silence stretching out between them.

Dr. Alexander chuckled. "I'm sorry, Mallory. I don't mean to be overly mysterious about this. I just wanted to ask a few questions about Todd..."

"Oh, okay. He's—"

"And Ruth."

Mallory made an expression conveying her view on the subject.

Dr. Alexander chuckled again. "I know. Just bear with me."

Mallory nodded (not wanting to talk about Ruth). "What about 'er?"

Dr. Alexander propped herself with a lean against the glass behind her. "I visited Todd the other day." Because Dr. Alex was a tiny woman, Mallory once expected her voice to be tiny, too. But Dr. Alex's voice was low, somewhat gruff, yet fascinatingly still warm and kind.

"Yeah, he told me. I wasn't surprised." Although she was a little.

"Did he tell you what happened for him to end up in the hospital?"

Mallory hesitated, unsure if Dr. Alex was fishing for info; she didn't want to betray Todd's trust. She didn't think Todd told her all of it, but he didn't have to. "Did he tell you?" she hedged.

Dr. Alexander smiled a knowing smile. Given her close-cut hairstyle, her smile and eyes appeared more prominent in the shadows of the alcove. "That's right; protect your brother. But yeah, he told me." Dr. Alexander's eyes glimmered with anger.

Mallory believed her. "Daddy thinks we need a mother in our lives, Doctor Alex. And maybe we do, I don't know, we're getting older now, but whatever we need—it's not *her*. I don't mean any harm, but..." she trailed off, shaking her head and fighting tears.

"Hold on. We'll get there, Mallory. That part rests with your dad, but, well,...we'll get there." Dr. Alexander's eyes then narrowed a fraction. "I'm curious to know if you believe this to be the first time something like this has gone on between them or know otherwise."

Mallory didn't answer right away. She watched the doctor for several seconds. Dr. Alexander's small stature did nothing to lessen the imposing impact of her presence. Mallory stood straighter. "Know otherwise."

"Uh-huh, okay." Dr. Alexander watched the people on the street. "Do you think your dad knows, has any idea..."

Mallory didn't think she needed to answer that. If he had any idea of what Ruth was doing—Ruth wouldn't be around. But her dad was so messed-up after losing Mommy.

Watching the people, Dr. Alex nodded her understanding.

Mallory wondered if Kelz and Daphne were looking for her. She took out her cellphone and sent Elliot a quick text, so he wouldn't worry and would wait for her. She didn't want to leave her friends hanging, but this was more important. "She hits him sometimes, Doctor Alex. She doesn't give him a break, always ridin' him about something. Little, stupid stuff. Telling him his asthma was nothing but an excuse and a crutch, and how if he wants to see our mother, Todd can look in the mirror." Mallory stopped herself and exhaled shakily. She could go on and on. She wiped a tear from her left eye. "It hasn't come up in session, Doctor Alex, but she's the reason Todd was on the roof that day, the reason...we came back to you."

When Dr. Alexander didn't say anything, Mallory continued: "I don't know why Todd doesn't fight back; he's bigger now." Her posture deflated, and her shoulders slumped. She hung her head. "I... I don't know why I don't, either. At least say something to Daddy, but..." Mallory sniffed with a shrug. She focused on the welcome mat at the entrance.

From the corner of her eye, Mallory noticed Dr. Alexander no longer watched the people but had turned her gaze on her. "...But as brave as you sometimes feel in wanting to do something, you, and your brother, moreover, are very much afraid of the situation."

Mallory looked up.

The doctor's gaze was steady with compassion.

Another wave of relief washed through Mallory. She turned to watch the pedestrians. She sighed internally, happy to hear how she felt from someone else. Sure, she gave attitude occasionally and talked much smack when she talked to Kelz about it, but it was a bravado she didn't truly feel. Dr. Alex had it right: she was afraid.

Mallory bit her bottom lip. She wanted to hug Dr. Alexander but resisted. She knew Dr. Alex would hug her back. But she resisted because she also knew (on some level) the doctor would prefer she didn't.

"...'Hug' understood."

Mallory gaped at her.

The doctor smiled and checked her watch. When her eyes fell on Mallory again, the smile faded. "I believe Todd's asthma attack was stress-induced, Mallory. I take it you haven't witnessed anything, but rather, Todd's told you about incidents?"

Mallory nodded. Ruth was very good at making sure she and Daddy weren't around when she did those things to Todd. But Mallory believed every word Todd told her, sometimes even sensed when Ruth had done something to her brother. And the term explained itself, but she'd look up *stress-induced asthma* later, anyway.

For a split-second, she started to tell Dr. Alex about being able to sense her mother nearby, smell her. It was a mini-session, after all, and she absolutely couldn't talk about it in an actual session. In the real sessions, she had the feeling Daddy was saying he thought Mommy was still around, too, so, like Todd said, maybe she should let Dr. Alexander know. But, within that same thought, Mallory changed her mind. Right now, this was about Todd; this was more important. And there was also this part of her not so sure she wanted help with the experiences; a "help" that would make her stop feeling her mother's presence, would make Mommy...go away again (for good). Although unsettling at first, the experiences weren't scary; they were...comforting. She'd keep mum for now—unless Todd said she was really starting to act like Daddy.

"So, stuff happens when she's alone with Todd. But around others?"

"She's better, but now I'm sensitive enough to know there's still attitude when she interacts with him. It's not all the time, though." Excitement grew in her belly as if she were the sidekick to a skilled detective putting together the final clues to solve the case. And Dr. Alex was a detective, a sleuth, as it were. But it wasn't unlawful crimes she investigated; it was one's mental and emotional stuff she helped solve.

Dr. Alexander watched her for a few seconds. "Mallory, I want you to run as much interference between Ruth and Todd as possible. I know little brothers can be a pain, and I'm not asking you to—"

"It's not a problem, Doctor Alex. I'm on it." Having a role, something concrete to do to help her family, lifted Mallory's spirits. She thought she was already doing something to that effect—as much as she could—anyway. Dr. Alex asking it of her sealed the deal.

"Good. In the meantime, we'll continue with the sessions...and get your family, your dad especially, well again." Dr. Alexander's expression turned grave. "...Even with our efforts, he may stay with her, Mallory."

Mallory acknowledged this realization with a nod, void of any enthusiasm. She then thought about her dad and the man he was—*before* her mom died. She shook her head. "Not with the stuff about Todd, Doctor Alex. Daddy won't stand for that. Trust me. It'll be over."

Dr. Alexander nodded slowly as she gazed around at the antiques, her mind seeming to process that information in some mysterious way Mallory didn't understand. She then suddenly grinned and clapped once. "Okay then. Thanks for the chat, Mallory."

"You can call me 'Mal,' Doctor Alexander."

"Do you not like your name?"

Mallory shook her head. "Oh no, I do. It's not that. It's just that everyone else calls me—"

"I'll stick with 'Mallory' then. Is that okay?"

Mallory smiled. It was just fine.

"Ready to head back?"

"Uh-huh." Mallory turned to exit the alcove, giving a sad, cursory glance at the antiques she likely wouldn't see again (her mom liked antiques and stuff). "Thanks, Doctor Alex." Mallory started raising the body of her sweater back over her shoulders.

"You're welcome, swee—"

Mallory halted, gazing at Dr. Alexander curiously.

Dr. Alexander stared at Mallory's shoulder. Smiling this strange smile, she gestured for Mallory to lower her sweater over her shoulder.

Her insides doing flip-flops as she lowered her sweater, Mallory smiled a tentative smile that grew to stretch too wide across her teeth. A guilty smile if there ever was one.

"Hmm... Still in the protective dressing, so it's new."

Mallory nodded and forced her smile down.

"When'd you get it?" Dr. Alexander kept smiling that strange smile.

"This morning." Mallory refrained from re-covering her shoulder.

Dr. Alex did it for her. "Hurt much?"

"A little." Mallory stared at a blue Toyota across the street, keenly taking in that sorority placard hanging from the rearview mirror.

"*How'd* you get it?"

With a sigh, Mallory traded glances with her doctor. "I know, right?"

Dr. Alex gazed back calmly, that unusual smirk on her face.

Mallory took comfort in that smirk. "My classmate, Jasmine: her older sister's a tattoo artist..." She shrugged. "We worked it out."

"Clearly." Dr. Alexander's smirk turned musing before it deepened. "J-J-M-T," she recited. "Not bad, compared to. It's relatively small, un-complicated... Shouldn't cause too much of a stir."

"Who says they don't already know about it?"

Dr. Alexander's expression answered for her.

Mallory lowered her gaze. "Yeah," she sighed. "But after Todd told me what happened, I had to do *something*." She now watched the doctor.

Dr. Alexander smiled that strange smile again. "And you came up with getting a tattoo with your family's initials?"

"Like you said, it shouldn't cause a stir."

"I said, '*too much* of a stir.' Where's the 'R'? Because that's where the stir is going to come in."

Mallory's tongue wouldn't move at first. Tears, angry ones, welled yet again. "...You know, I don't have a *boyfriend* boyfriend. Even if I did, there's no guarantee it would last or be worthy enough to mar my body over." Mallory shook her head, shifting from one foot to the other. "...But my blood family will *never* change, Doctor Alex. The four of us? Ruth can't touch that. In session, you suggested I do something for *me*, something to help me get through. Well, this was for me."

Dr. Alex tilted her head. "I understand, Mallory. Just be prepared for something popping off when they see it—at least when *she* sees it." She checked her watch. "I've kept you long enough. C'mon, let's get back."

Resurgent summer or not, Mallory was glad she'd brought her sweater as she stepped back into the chilly gallery. She spotted Kelz and Daphne talking with whom she knew to be photographer, Vivian Phillips.

Whoa. The article photo only did her partial justice. She was this gorgeous woman with dark, reddish-brown hair. The article said she was in her 40s, but with her smooth creamy-brown skin and warm smile, she looked much younger. No wonder Elliot was hot for her. She was married, though (of course), with two children.

Mallory snickered inside. Kelz was still under the age of consent; he need not get his hopes up for any cougar-child-rape scenarios just yet and slow his roll with lusting after *Mrs.* Phillips.

"Take care, sweetie." Dr. Alexander started away toward another section of the gallery. "See you in a few."

"Okay." Mallory smiled after her, thinking maybe the doctor's costume could be some weird combo of a *real* Oz wizard and Glinda (the Good Witch)...

Dr. Alex blended into the crowd.

Elliot and Daphne spotted her and waved her over.

Mallory shook her head and waved them over to her instead. Initially, she eagerly anticipated meeting a few featured artists (secretly hoping to meet Ms. Phillips), but that was before.

Mallory smiled the warmest smile she could muster as her friends headed toward her. She'd had a good time at the exhibit (for all it was worth), but now she wanted to go home.

At least, that's what she thought she wanted.

However, after a four-piece nugget and caramel sundae from a visit to McDonald's with Kelz and Daphne (Elliot going on and on about meeting the current love of his life: featured photographer Vivian Phillips; he didn't even finish his burger and fries, he was so enamored), and as she made her way up Wells-Brown Place to her house (wanting to be alone, she caught the subway home instead of having Daphne drop her off), fresh threads of unease squirmed and twisted around inside her belly.

She tried gazing into homes where owners left their window dressings open during this early Saturday evening, but stared more at the fallen leaves from the maple and dogwoods as she plodded along, counting the concrete panels of the sidewalk.

Mallory rubbed her shoulder; the dull ache commanded a dose of Excedrin. She dreaded entering the house, but reflecting on the conversation with Dr. Alex helped her feel a little better.

Maybe I should go in and show it to everybody.

Bold, but she knew how she'd most likely handle it: Todd first, then her dad, and then, well,…Ruth. If something was going to kick off behind her getting the tattoo, she needed to gather her defense and muster courage individually from those most likely to support her.

Mallory spotted her dad's uncovered white Mercedes parked closer to their house; his Audi sat in front of their home on the corner. She scoffed and rolled her eyes at her stepmother's brown Lexus parked behind her father's SUV.

She knew, without doubt, her father and brother were home. Todd was still recuperating somewhat, and her dad, well: where was he always these days? At any rate, she'd hoped Ruth would be out somewhere.

She paused at the bottom of the steps leading to the front porch, noticing that someone had shifted the container holding the dwarf Japanese Maple planted in her mother's honor. The cascading red leaves heralded the arrival of fall. Mallory hoped it was anyone other than Ruth; she didn't want Ruth touching her mother's tree.

I haven't sensed or smelled my mother lately.

She jostled the shopping bag down at her side with a lively grin. The bag held a few Phillips-Alexander prints she purchased at the gallery. She liked Dr. Alexander very much, and having representative art by her daughter was cool, too. It was a symbolic token of connection to Dr. Alex she'd treasure for a long time.

She thought about her talk with the doctor and released a breath weighted with nervousness.

A stir...

Mallory went inside.

To her surprise, her father and brother were in the upstairs family room (across from the formal living room) playing a videogame. Smells of waffles and maple-flavored bacon wafted in from the kitchen. Strains of "Shackles" by Mary Mary came from there as well. Mallory could also make out strains of "So Good, So Right" by Brenda Russell competing from two floors above them.

"Hey." She greeted her family tentatively; the whole homey setting of things threw her. Mentally trying to banish the butterflies flittering in her stomach, she set her bag down against the foyer wall and stood in the entryway to the family room.

"Hi," Todd greeted without taking his eyes off the television. "How was the museum?" He clicked and clacked his controller from the comfort of his videogame chair on the floor.

Mallory playfully kicked at her brother but didn't strike him. "Art exhibit, not museum, and it was fine."

Todd kept focus on the screen. "Whatever."

"Hey, M-Sweet," her father greeted from his position on the couch. He kept his eyes on the screen, too, but turned his head and puckered with a kissing noise in her direction, air-kissing her. Watching him, Mallory recognized her father was only going through the motions of being involved in the game.

He's not "back" yet, but he's trying.

"Is that Mallory?" Ruth inquired from the kitchen.

"Uh-huh," Mallory answered back. She plopped beside her father on the sofa and leaned her head against his shoulder, watching him play Todd in a game of *Dark Souls* on their PlayStation. She warmed with her dad's kiss to her forehead.

Music from the kitchen stopped. Mallory heard Ruth approaching the family room. "How was it?"

"Okay." Mallory lifted her head from her dad's shoulder. "I bought a couple of prints."

Her father turned to her, smiling with appreciation. She was used to how he looked now, but Dr. Alex had a point about a man having facial hair. Even a soul patch wouldn't hurt.

Mallory smiled back, deciding not to mention seeing Dr. Alexander. She'd let Todd know later.

"Oh." Ruth leaned against the frame of the entryway. "Jeff, Doctor Alexander called. She wants to have our next session without the kids."

Mallory eyed her dad, who nodded without taking his attention away from the screen.

I guess she does. She's already had mini-sessions with Todd and me.

"Wanna play?" Todd asked her from the floor.

"Nah, I'll just watch."

Todd threw her a look over his shoulder. "You bum."

"Takes one," Mallory said back. "So, we're having breakfast for dinner?" she asked no one in particular.

"Yeah." Ruth folded her arms. "Just thought I'd fix some of Todd's favorites." She wore a T-shirt, capris, and flip-flops of perfectly coordinated shades of blue (her sorority crest emblazoned on the shirt's left chest). Mallory had to admit the blue brought out that crocodile-green in her eyes. Her ash-brown hair curled around her shoulders rather than in her usual weekend ponytail.

Mallory offered a nod and a smile, doing her best to keep from gagging at the saccharine lilt in Ruth's tone.

Can anyone else hear how fake she sounds?

Todd coughed. But it wasn't his bronchial asthma-like cough. It sounded much more like the cough he or Mallory would give when around friends if they thought a friend was bullshitting in a conversation. Mallory sighed, thankful to hear it. She looked at Ruth.

Ruth swiveled an uneasy glance between her and Todd. "Everything should be ready shortly. We could all watch a movie afterward."

Mallory wasn't hungry, having nuggets and a sundae not yet fully digested in her stomach. And she didn't think she could stomach the family-gathering-in-front-of-the-TV bit, either.

"Sounds good," her father said.

But why did it feel like he thought the idea sounded anything but?

Mallory leaned toward her father. "Daddy, I can still hear music coming from the attic."

Ruth started for the stairs. "Yeah, your father was involved in the game, and I'd been meaning to go up and—"

"Leave it." Jeff Winthrop turned on the lamp, casting the room in golden light. His tone wasn't harsh—but it wasn't pleasant, either.

Ruth froze: a hand on the banister, one foot on the bottom step.

Todd paused his playing and turned back to them.

Ruth sighed, "Ooh-kay," and returned to the family room, shaking her head. She stood in the entryway with her arms folded before turning and heading back into the kitchen. "Dinner in about fifteen," she announced (a little less sugar in her tone).

Mallory watched Ruth leave. Even from the corner of her eye, she never saw her father so much as look in Ruth's direction.

Forty-five minutes later, the four of them sat in varying stations in the family room again, bellies full (and Mallory's overstuffed) with Belgian waffles, scrambled eggs with cheese, maple bacon, and sweet grits; a quiet and uneventful mealtime—trying hard to be something it wasn't.

"We could stream this; watch it downstairs in the movie room." Todd held the DVD for the movie *Life*. Mallory thought it was time for him to get another haircut; his hair grew exceptionally fast. *Life* starring Eddie Murphy and Martin Lawrence was one of her favorites. She wasn't in the mood to watch it, but she was in the living room, going along with the breakfast-and-a-movie plan to keep the peace.

Ruth kicked her blue flip-flops off and folded her legs under her in the leather recliner. "No, Todd. The DVD's fine. The movie room isn't as cozy as here in the family room. Speaking of which..." Ruth turned to Mallory. "You've had your sweater on since you've been home. It's warm outside and warm in here. You can't be cold. Why don't you take that sweater off?"

Mallory's stomach, although stretched to its limits with breakfast food on top of what remained of her McDonald's treats, still had room enough for the butterflies now renewing their dance.

Her dad roamed his eyes over her with fatherly concern. "Aren't you hot, sweetheart?"

Strains of music still trailed from what Mallory knew to be her father's artist studio on the attic level of their home; more Brenda Russell by the sound of it. Right now, "Think It Over" was playing upstairs. Her mom loved Brenda Russell.

Mallory glanced toward the ceiling (referring to the upper levels) and then gazed at her father. She raised her eyebrows, silently asking him if, one, he was aware music continued playing in an empty attic room (apparently so loud, one could hear it two floors down) and, if so, then two, would it be okay to go turn it off. She didn't know if all that came through her raised eyebrows, but those were her unspoken questions.

Her father gazed at her steadily, almost sternly. He shook his head, telling her, no, it would not be okay to turn Brenda Russell off (so obviously, yes, he was aware music played into an empty attic room).

Mallory left it alone. She replied to his original question. "I guess I am a little warm." But she didn't remove her sweater right away.

Todd went back to loading the DVD and setting up the audio.

Her father now raised an eyebrow of suspicion toward her, but Mallory shifted her attention to the television.

Ruth made herself more comfortable in her chair. "Girl, please take that sweater off. You're making *me* hot," she said with an easy lilt. She plucked a magazine from the table and started flipping through it.

As the DVD previews began, Todd backed away from the television. He started to sit in his videogame chair on the floor but changed his mind, sitting in the recliner next to where Mallory sat on the sofa with their dad. He tossed the remote onto the ottoman.

Mallory did her best to focus on the previews, but the vibe from her father's suspicious gaze interfered with her concentration, so she shifted her focus to the other faces in the room.

Ruth's attention bounced between the magazine in her lap and the previews; she stopped doing both to look over at Mallory. A questioning frown shaped her features as she looked from Mallory to her father.

Here goes...

Mallory took in a deep breath and freed it over quiet seconds. She leaned forward just enough to shoulder-roll the sweater partway down her upper arms and leaned back against the sofa cushions.

The tattoo was on the shoulder opposite her dad and Ruth. Her father relaxed against the sofa cushions and turned his attention back to the previews (one for an action flick released years ago). Ruth, too, returned to her DVD previews and magazine-perusal multitasking.

Mallory took a little more time to think.

Todd, however, picked that moment to reach for an accent pillow from the sofa. Mallory clenched her teeth, bracing herself.

"Oh, sweet! You get that today?" Todd's grin and eyes radiated warm appreciation.

He looked so much like their mother; Mallory drew courage from it. "Yeah, Kelz and Daphne got 'em too," she added, hoping there was safety in numbers if she mentioned her friends. She knew better, but she hoped anyway.

An article in the magazine held Ruth's attention. "Got what?"

"Let me see it, Mallory." Her father's voice was low but not angry.

Ruth looked up from her magazine. "What's going on?"

The previews finished; the DVD main menu occupied the screen with its musical movie theme playing in the background. DVD forgotten, everyone's attention focused on Mallory.

So much for the divide-and-conquer approach.

Her butterflies, at first content to enhance her anxiety with intermittent flutters in her stomach, now morphed into the heavy flap of a giant-winged bat. The pressure in her abdomen created mild pain.

"Let me see it, Mallory," her father repeated.

She looked at her brother. His expression reflected what she'd been thinking anyway: get it over with.

She took her sweater off and laid it across the arm of the sofa, then twisted her body around so that her father and Ruth could see the tattoo visible through the protective plastic. She didn't want to see their facial reactions; instead, she peered through the window at the tree branches and portion of sky visible through the partially closed blinds.

"That's not so bad." Her father sounded amused.

Mallory closed her eyes in thankful prayer. *Shouldn't cause too much of a stir... Dr. Alex may have been right.*

He reached over, running his fingers over the lettering using a careful touch, inspecting her shoulder and the artistry. "Hurt?"

"Just a little sore." Mallory craned her neck to see the tattoo again.

Ruth tossed her magazine onto the coffee table and rose from her seat. "I don't believe this!" She moved closer to Jeff, sending a lip-curl of disapproval down at them. "What d'you mean 'not so bad'?"

Her father didn't respond. He stared at the tattoo.

Ruth leaned over Jeff, closer to Mallory's shoulder.

Mallory struggled not to draw back from her.

"J-J-M-T..." Ruth mused. Her eyes darted between Mallory, Todd, and their father before settling on the tattoo. She smiled at it. But the crocodile shading in her irises dissipated with the bright smile emerging from her lips. The false smile was one thing, but Mallory lived with Ruth long enough to know: Ruth's eyes always told the tale—and crocodiles were cold-blooded. "Nice, but you know how we feel about tattoos." She dispatched that cold-blooded combo of eyes and smile to Mallory.

"I know how *you* feel," Mallory responded.

Ruth's smile faded. "How'd you even—? I *certainly* didn't sign any—"

Mallory's stomach clenched.

"I'm okay with it, Ruth." Jeff turned to Mallory. "I would have preferred she talked to me about it first, but Jules and I always encouraged self-expression to some extent." He gently ran a thumb across the plastic covering her tattoo. "This seems mild enough." He sent her an inquiring smile. "But how'd you get it without—?"

Ruth snatched Mallory's tattooed arm, pulling her to stand. "So, what's this supposed to be? Some sort of slap in *my face?!*"

Mallory winced as Todd sounded a choked, whimpering gasp.

Jeff Winthrop stood. "Hold on now, Ruth." He spoke calmly, but Mallory lived with him sixteen years; his tense posture meant suppressed rage. "Just hold a fuckin' minute." He seized Ruth's wrist. "Let her go."

Some of her father's fury must have still come through when he gripped Ruth: she grimaced with both surprise and pain. "Ow, Jeff! What—?" Wisely, Ruth let go, but she stared hard at Mallory.

Her father's focus on Ruth reflected the rage he suppressed otherwise. "You don't touch my children, Ruth. Not with harm in mind. Oh, no." He shook his head, and although he still gripped Ruth's wrist, that headshake appeared more threatening than anything.

Ruth gazed at her father, and Mallory saw surprise and hurt feelings battling against Ruth's own rage; it was all in her eyes, body posture, and alternating facial expressions. "Jeff...?"

It went quiet, everyone breathing harder than normal.

From upstairs, Brenda Russell's "In the Thick of It" traveled down from the studio. Mallory fleetingly wondered if some mysterious deejay was upstairs, selecting thematic song tracks—because they were in the thick of things with this tattoo business. Her mother, maybe?

Mallory's heart raced, and her stomach clenched tighter. Tears welled. She expected debate about her tattoo, but not like this. She let out a long breath, her bottom lip trembling as she rubbed her arm.

A fragrant blend of iris, vanilla, and roses wafted in, solid and robust. Todd stood. "Ma?"

Mallory whipped around to him. The look on her brother's face would have been comical under different circumstances.

I thought he couldn't smell her.

She turned back to her father and Ruth.

Back to her old self, Ruth flexed and shot Todd a sharp look. "What did you just say?"

"I— I thought... I mean,...I don't know. Nothin'." Air from the cushions whooshed when Todd plopped back into the chair.

Mallory kept her eyes on her father.

He released Ruth's wrist and now stood with his eyes closed—a vacant smile on his lips.

Her mother's scent strengthened (*and did the music upstairs stop?*). An extra set of nerves joggled Mallory's insides. "Daddy?"

Ruth turned to him, too. "Jeff?"

When he opened his eyes, Mallory noticed mild irritation before his expression softened. "Yeah?" His eyes held a far-off look.

"What the...?" Ruth turned back to her. "Look, go upstairs, Mallory. You too, Todd. This isn't finished, but I need to speak to your father." She shook her head and huffed. "So much for family time."

Mallory focused on her father.

He stared back weirdly, vacantly blinking as her mother's scent dissipated. Without another word, he headed toward the kitchen.

"You heard me, Mallory. Go on upstairs. After I talk with your father, we'll be up. I'm still a parent in this situation, in the role of mother, regardless of..." Ruth covered her mouth as if stifling a sob. She turned and went back to her seat.

Mallory started away, gesturing for Todd to follow. "C'mon."

"Regardless of what any *tattoo* says," Ruth added from her chair, her anger clear and present...and dangerous?

Four hours later, the house was eerily still (only intermittent footsteps from upstairs), and Mallory realized the likelihood of her father and Ruth coming to her room to talk about the tattoo was close to nil, at least for now. In that time, she'd cleaned out her closet and drawers of unwanted stuff to donate and started on her dreaded math project.

In keeping with Dr. Alex's request, she checked on her brother, alternating between sending texts and going to his room. Todd looked a little irritated with her that last time she poked her head in, but she saw he also appreciated it.

Although not the least hungry, Mallory sat on her bed indulging in a methodical consumption of peanut butter crackers, listening to the Staple Singers' "Respect Yourself" playing on repeat through her earphones. She'd been listening to the song a great deal since Todd mentioned it weeks ago.

The only light in her room came from the SpongeBob SquarePants nightlight she received as part of the Secret Santa exchange in fifth grade. Her window was open. A mild October breeze wafted fragrance from the Aislichs' recently planted autumn collection of sugar maple, roses, hydrangea, and amaryllis: each teasing her nose with interchanging waves of prominence, seemingly enhanced because it was night.

Mallory bobbed her head to the music, sometimes staring at the photo on her chest of drawers: of her and her mother. They're laughing so hard in the picture; their mouths showing all kinds of teeth. It was the day of her menstruation initiation, and her mom had taken her out to lunch to commemorate her womanhood induction (as Nana Sophia had done similarly for her). Nana took that picture as they left the restaurant, laughing at a joke about boys and men. She turned 12 a couple months after that fun day. Her mother would be dead a month before she turned 13. To keep things light, Mallory focused on the russet-brown pin-pattern newsboy cap her mother wore in the picture (cocked to the side in her mother's free-spirited way). Yeah, that was a fun day.

Mallory stopped the music and removed her earbuds. She sat, wondering about her father and Ruth.

Will he cave in to her, whatever she comes up with?

Mallory struggled with similar thoughts before giving up. Finished with her peanut butter crackers, she threw the wrapper in the trash, turned off the nightlight, and left her room. It was almost midnight.

Mallory's room sat at the front of the house. Todd's room and the hall bath occupied the middle of the house. Combining two bedrooms to form it, her father's bedroom took up the rear. She'd tipped within a few feet of her father's bedroom when she noticed voices trailing from the floor above, where, hours ago, Brenda Russell sang into the empty art-music room. She crept up the stairs to the attic level, avoiding the third and fifth steps that always creaked when you landed on them.

Despite the resurgent summer and heat tending to rise, the top floor of their home somehow remained October cool at night. The door to the attic storage room was closed; the door to her father's studio stood ajar. Hues of blue and gray filtered around the doorframe. Eyeing her dad's poster of Sam Cooke on the door, she made out Maysa's "Love So True" playing on low. Her parents loved that song. Mallory edged closer, pressing her back against the wall. Breathing as shallowly as she could, she listened.

"I didn't break 'em, Jeff." Ruth sounded pleading, but Mallory could hear the edge there, too.

"Well, my children don't have any reason to break 'em, so..."

Break what? And how was it Ruth was allowed in the studio? Only Mommy could go in there. Mallory guessed he caved on that, too.

"I have no reason to break your bottles of Michael Kors, either, Jeff."

Silence, then: "Don't worry about it. I didn't wear it anymore, anyway. Not since..."

"Go ahead, Jeff. Say it. Not since *what*? Since Julia died?"

Someone moved inside the room. "Love So True" stopped.

"Dammit, Jeff. The other night was *so* good. The way you please my body, honey. How you touch me, move inside me. When you make love, you really know how to—"

Mallory grimaced and held her breath, trying to pause her hearing, hoping with all her heart Ruth didn't finish that sentence. She'd already heard much more than she ever wanted to—for as long as she lived.

"But one minute it seems like we're making progress, Jeff, and then the next minute it's like…like…when we first got together."

"Turn that back on."

No one spoke for what seemed like minutes. Mallory imagined a staring contest between them: her father's unrelenting cocoa-brown eyes versus Ruth's defiant crocodile-green ones. With the mood her dad was in, it was a contest he wouldn't lose.

"You know, you didn't want to talk about Mallory's tattoo earlier, and it appears you don't want to talk about it now, either. But we'll address it, Jeff. Everyone is going to church in the morning, including you. I'm not dragging your spoiled brats into the House of God alone this time."

Mallory frowned. They were not brats. She clenched her fists.

"My children aren't brats, Ruth. You know that. Spoiled? Maybe a little. Mallory and Todd share in my financial blessings; that's as it should be. But *brats*? Unh-unh."

Thank you, Daddy.

Sweat trickled down her back, causing it to tickle and itch, but she dared not move.

"Fine, Jeff. Okay, they're not brats. Which is why we have to deal with Mallory getting that tattoo without talking to us first and getting permission. She's underage. I thought—"

"Would you have approved the one she got?"

"Huh?"

"You heard me. If Mal had told us of her idea for her tattoo, would you have okayed it?"

"That's not the point—"

"Oh, I think it's a big part of the point."

"Why? Because it insults who I am and what I do for this family?!"

Damn right. Mallory thought about Todd—and unclenched her fists. She took a deep breath and released it as quietly as possible.

"It's not an insult, Ruth. Let it go."

"Oh— Oh, you can be such a punk sometimes!"

Someone moved inside the room again.

Silence.

Mallory didn't know what her father's reaction would be, but she had to admit, ruefully, that Ruth was right on that one—if only as far as standing up to Ruth for them.

Before her mom died, though, her dad was far from weak. He was an assertive man, decisive. She recognized a bit of her dad-of-old when he grabbed Ruth's wrist earlier, telling her not to touch them with harm in mind. The way he shook his head at Ruth... *That* was the Jeffrey A. Winthrop III Mallory knew.

But her mother did die, and now there was a *dad-of-old*.

Mallory heard her father's all-too-familiar sigh. "Money, clothes, nice homes, and cars, Ruth. What more do you want?"

"I... I want *you*, Jeff."

This time, the silence did last a minute or two. Footsteps approached the door. Mallory hurried to the shadows near the stairs.

"I don't know anymore if I can give you that," her father answered. Maysa's "Love So True" restarted.

More light filtered into the hall as the door to the studio widened. Mallory didn't know if Ruth responded or what she said if she did. She was already closing the door to her room when she heard someone on the stairs. It was another five minutes before her heart returned to its normal rhythm. When it did, Mallory said her prayers, put on some pajamas, then snagged her sleeping bag from her closet and a pillow from her bed.

She didn't want to take Dr. Alex's advice to the extreme, but something told her to spend the night in her brother's room (you didn't always have to understand the why).

Mallory opened her bedroom door and listened for any signs of activity. Hearing none, she moved quickly to Todd's room.

Her eyes adjusted to the natural nighttime lighting of the house, but Todd's blackout drapes made navigating his room a minor challenge. The illuminated numbers from his alarm clock and knowing the layout of his room helped some. Mallory allowed the minimal light from the hall to illuminate his room enough to plot out the quickest (and safest) route to the other side of his bed (she didn't want him stepping on her if he got up in the middle of the night).

Todd's mild snoring accompanied the hum of his humidifier.

He hasn't used that thing in a while.

Mallory sidestepped but still almost tripped over Todd's Coppin State duffle bag on the floor. Menthol and eucalyptus overpowered the stench of sweaty clothing combined with what Mallory knew to be the remains of the hoagie from two days ago that he left in his trash instead of taking downstairs to the kitchen trash.

I'm not sleeping in here with that.

Moving as quietly as she could, Mallory set her sleeping stuff down and picked up Todd's trashcan. Holding the offensive culprit away from her, she put it outside in the hall. Movement from the direction of her father's bedroom hurried her steps. She returned to Todd's room (he didn't so much as stir) and closed his door. Sleeping bag and pillow in hand, she settled on the floor beside his bed, farthest from the door.

Tired as she was, sleep didn't come right away. Mallory stared into the dark space above her, trying to make out shadows and forms from the objects in Todd's room—and debating going back to her room for her gum. Her eyes fell on Todd's dresser and the outline of the five-by-seven photograph of Todd and their mother. That picture was from the night of his little band recital in fifth grade. He'd finished his French horn solo without a hitch and came hopping out from backstage, beaming. Their mother had scooped Todd up in a big hug—and their dad snapped the moment up. Mallory grinned into the semi-darkness thinking about it.

I want my mother.

She pressed a hand to her mouth to contain a sob. She listened to her brother's rhythmic breathing, hoping her wish would manifest itself with the scent of Guerlain Shalimar.

Sleepiness finally reared its comforting head with promises of rest and escape in the dreams of slumber when Todd's bedroom door opened and subdued light from the hall filtered in. Instinct told her it was not their father.

Mallory held her breath. Curiosity, courage, and traces of absolute fear commingled and prickled along her arms and torso. She suddenly needed to pee.

"Todd?" Ruth called in a crude undertone. "Todd, wake up."

Todd stirred. "Mmmhhn?"

Ruth left the door ajar, leaving Todd's room in semi-darkness, but she hadn't left. Mallory sensed her (and her anger) through the dark.

"Wake up!" Ruth repeated her harsh whisper, the decibel level doing nothing to disguise the vehemence behind the words.

What the...?

Mallory wanted more than anything to rise, but she stayed her place.

"Huh?" Todd answered, half-asleep. There was movement in the room (Ruth's?), then: "Ow! What? What'd I do now?" In the semi-dark, Todd's near fifteen years sounded much younger.

"Why is your trashcan in the hall?"

"I— I don't..."

"Never mind. Did you break your father's cologne bottles, boy? You trying to set...me...*up?*" Ruth punctuated each of the last three words of her question: Mallory heard three muffled but discernible sounds of a fist or hand striking covered skin. Ruth was hitting him.

Todd grunted with her strikes, ending with this low gulp of pain from her last one. "His what? No, I don't— No. I didn't break any bottles, Ruth." Todd sounded weary—and that wasn't right. He also sounded accustomed to what was happening—and that was worse. He coughed.

"Don't start that shit; you're all right. Your father's upset about the bottles. I didn't do it. Mighta been your sister, but, well, I'll find out, Todd. Please be telling the truth." Her threat echoed off the shadows.

Mallory sat up. "Or what? He said he didn't break anything, Ruth. He has no reason to lie—and I didn't do it, either. Don't hit him anymore." She breathed fast and with force. In that moment, she would have had no problem fighting Ruth.

Even with little light around them, Mallory saw their faces. Todd's wide eyes registered first surprise, then gratitude.

Ruth's wide-eyed shock disappeared into anger mixed with something Mallory could feel as smoothly calculating. "What're you doing in here, Mallory?" Her tone was soft and slithery with disdain.

The child in her wanted to explain and appease (Ruth's tone alarmed her), and the rebellious teen in her held on to some of the fight that rose moments ago. But the young adult in Mallory found its voice instead. "It's not important, Ruth. Let's all settle down, get some sleep, and get ready for church in the morning." She paused. "That would be best."

Mallory reclined without waiting for a response, holding her breath, her heart racing. She didn't know where things would go next, but she wasn't as scared.

Moments later, Todd's bedroom door widened. "Say nothing to your father. He can't handle any additional stress, so I'm all you've got. I have enough to deal with regarding your brother, but the rod won't be spared, Mallory, so you'll get it, too, if it means keeping order around here. The rod rules." The door closed, and darkness surrounded them again.

Her brother plopped back onto his pillow with a sigh.

Mallory let out her breath, too. She'll wait to pee. "You okay, Todd?"

"Yeah, I guess. Pain's subsiding, but it might bruise. I can say it was football. She usually aims for my back..."

His words hurt her: her stomach, her feelings, her...soul.

Todd released another sigh and went quiet. "...Why *are* you in here, Mal?" he whispered into the dark. "Did you know she was coming?"

"No. No, I didn't know. But let's say a little birdie's been whispering in my ear," Mallory offered, thinking of Dr. Alexander.

Todd coughed again. "Doctor Alex?"

Mallory didn't answer that. She settled into her sleeping bag and closed her eyes. Slumber didn't withhold its lull this time. "...Did you move Mommy's tree?"

"Yeah. Shade shift."

So, it was Todd (not Ruth); that was a relief. "Okay, cool."

"She's... You're in her sights now, Mal. Now that you know. Now that you've...witnessed it. Even with what Dad said downstairs..." He spoke with a resigned sadness.

The notion of Ruth coming for her scared her, but she couldn't let Todd know. She couldn't. "We'll cross that bridge..." She sounded more assured than she felt, for her brother's sake.

Their dad was under some serious mental strain, and Mallory didn't want to cause any more. She lost her nerve when she tried to tell him about Todd before. But if Ruth laid a hand on her, she was telling their father. He'd have to deal—just like they were.

"...Thanks, Mal," he whispered.

"Go to sleep." She started to tell her brother she loved him but let the moment pass.

Todd groaned with pain as he changed position.

Mallory shifted her head on her pillow, moving away from the area now wet from her tears.

Chapter 16

Cards on the Table

It was no longer pro bono work, but Naomi still thought she'd bitten off more than she cared to chew with the two souls before her.

During the past ten days, tall, gangly Porter Ralston and his much shorter (and rounder) counterpart, Dawsyn Haynes, showed up at her office at some point, requesting she take them on as patients.

Why these two (Porter mainly, Naomi had the feeling Dawsyn may have only been along for the ride) insisted that one, they had issues requiring therapy, and two, Naomi be the one to treat them, Naomi didn't know. But she relented, and here she was (again) serving as sounding board and being paid a mental maintenance fee. The two didn't need psychiatric counseling. Not really. Not in the sense they thought they did, anyway. Naomi made that clear to them. Porter and Dawsyn didn't care. So here they were.

The patients in her upcoming session, though, were a different story. The Winthrops indeed needed her help.

"It's like you said, Doctor Alexander. Dawsyn doesn't open up to me. She may start trying to share what's going on with her, but if I try to get her to explain or explore further, everything becomes a joke. It frustrates me." Porter's mulberry-and-silver striped tie swung between his thighs as he leaned over his knees.

Dawsyn didn't reply, but her eyes held mild amusement and something close to embarrassment. She adjusted a small diamond-accented butterfly hairpin pinned at the base of her schoolteacher bun atop her head. The yellow-almost-orange butterfly coordinated well with her spiced-cognac-colored hair.

"Maybe you shouldn't probe or ask questions when you think she's opening up," Naomi suggested to Porter. This perhaps rated as one aspect of their relationship that possibly could use some professional exploration. *Possibly.* "Let her come at it her way. And you may learn something from what she says while 'joking.'"

Porter nodded.

Dawsyn nodded.

Naomi stood. Time was up.

Porter and Dawsyn turned to glance at the clock. Although romantically attached to other people, this simultaneous move (as well as some others) clued Naomi to how in tune they were with each other. It was cute (reminding her, fondly, of one particular married couple, almost supernaturally in tune with each other). Porter and Dawsyn each rose to their feet and extended a hand to her.

Naomi accepted each hand, Dawsyn's first. "See you in two."

"We appreciate this, Doctor Alexander." Porter grinned his thanks. His ears didn't seem so big this time.

"So you keep saying." Naomi gave a head tilt. "I know you do."

Porter and Dawsyn said their goodbyes and were gone.

Naomi wasted no time pulling the Winthrop file.

Because she spoke with Todd at the hospital last week and with Mallory over the weekend, those discussions served their purpose as sessions with the younger Winthrops. She had yet to see an aura-flicker from Todd (and may never), but during her brief meet with Mallory at Jamison-Ajai, she saw an aura-flicker from her: a less dull, muddy magenta and more soft violet (good). She'd gleaned some key psych components related to their family dynamics she planned to utilize for her treatment approach—and the coming session.

Real work needed to be done with the adult Winthrops—primarily (if not singularly) Jeff Winthrop.

She also needed to address the Ruth-Todd situation.

Concerning domestic or family abuse, people commonly thought of wife or child battery. But the boundaries were more obscure with isolating and defining abuse and its many forms. The subject included any psychological or emotional abuse or intimidation where one person in a position of power or control afflicts harm on another within a close relationship.

As a doctor, Naomi was duty-bound to report suspicions or evidence of abuse. Still, Naomi realized she could be more effective doing her thing while her report moved through the administrative crawl, thus severely reducing opportunity for any progression of violence (whatever its form) between Ruth and Todd. She'd report her findings, but with her help, the Winthrops would be well on their way to okay by the time the social workers came knocking.

Knee-deep in shades of gray.

Four raps on the door startled Naomi. The jolt to her system solidified her resolve.

"It's open," Naomi called with challenge rather than welcome. She took a deep breath. She had work to do, yes, but she also needed to maintain a degree of neutrality and objectivity (what little there was) to be effective.

Jeff Winthrop opened the door enough to poke his bald head in cautiously.

Naomi smiled and waved him in. She liked Jeff. "Please. Have a seat." She gestured toward her mustard-colored seating group.

Jeff returned a smile of his own and opened the door wider. He backed up to allow Ruth to enter first. "Hi, Doctor Alexander." Ruth smiled, but the lines around her mouth indicated stress and attitude, giving Naomi every reason to believe the whole tattoo episode with Mallory didn't go so well.

"Ruth," Naomi responded with a nod.

Ruth sat on the loveseat. Her solid turquoise BCBG dress and matching bag offered unusual yet pleasing contrast to the yellow furniture and the auburn hue cast into the office from the sun bouncing off the fall foliage outside. The deep-purple pumps with a three-inch heel added a fashionable touch.

Jeff sat on the loveseat as well, but as fully expected, he sat on the end opposite Ruth. The loveseat wasn't an enormous piece of furniture to begin with, but watching the couple, the distance between them had little to do with proximity.

Naomi believed Mallory's tattoo contributed to their current dispositions and figured the metaphorical distance might work to her non-metaphorical advantage.

Jeff Winthrop worked the crease of his right pant leg. The forest-green Canali dress slacks and the chartreuse shirt fit rather loosely over his once large and imposing muscular frame. Naomi guessed those clothes appeared tailored-fit on him at one time. She hoped to have him putting on the pounds again soon.

"How're Mallory and Todd?" Naomi sat in her yellow counsel chair.

Ruth made a sound (something part-grunt, part-scoff) before turning to Jeff.

Jeff smiled but continually worked the crease in his pant leg. "Pretty good, I think." He nodded reassuringly. "Yeah, we had a scare, but Todd's much better, and Mal... Well yeah, Mal's good, too."

Ruth made that same sound again and shook her head.

Jeff cut his eyes in Ruth's direction but didn't turn her way.

"You don't agree, Ruth?"

"If you're asking how Todd and Mallory are doing physically, then yes, they're fine. But as far as progress as a family unit? No." Ruth glanced at Jeff and continued: "Mallory came home with a tattoo on her shoulder, illustrating her sentiments on the matter."

"Oh?" Naomi returned a perplexed look. "What did she have done?"

Jeff groaned an air of exasperation. "All she did, was have the letters 'J-J-M-T' inked on her shoulder." He shrugged. "No big deal."

"It's a big deal *to me*, Jeff." The tension in Ruth's lips suggested anger rather than hurt feelings. Ruth tugged at the hem of her dress. "And as your wife, the fact that you don't think it's a big deal makes my job that much harder."

Jeff focused on his crease.

"Jeff?" Naomi prompted.

He shrugged without looking up.

Ruth raised and dropped both hands in exasperation. She looked away from Jeff (and Naomi) toward the bookshelves along the wall, shaking her head. This time, she appeared hurt, but Naomi couldn't let that interfere with the realization of how Ruth treated Todd. One of the main things she hoped to accomplish at the end of this session was illuminating Jeff accordingly.

"Okay, Black people. Recent events dictate we're short on time here, so I'll dispense with a lot of the therapy via exploratory dialogue and take a more direct approach. How's that?" Nervous, Naomi ran a hand over her hair (she needed to oil her scalp—or have Kev do it).

"Uh, okay, I guess." Jeff sat up straighter, leaving his pant crease alone for the time being. His cocoa-brown eyes held guarded anticipation.

Naomi turned to Ruth (still focused on the library). "Ruth?"

Ruth sighed, "Fine," turning her green eyes to Naomi. "Will this 'direct approach' hurt?" she asked facetiously.

"Maybe. What I intend to do, is lay my cards on the table in terms of my take on what I've deduced from my sessions and other interactions with you all thus f—"

"Yeah, Todd said you visited him at the hospital. That was nice of you, Naomi."

"I'll go the extra mile sometimes when kids are involved, Jeff." Naomi looked pointedly at Ruth.

Ruth gazed back steadily.

"So, I'll lay my cards on the table and encourage the two of you to do the same, if you will." Naomi eyed the couple, her gaze falling on them alternately.

The couple nodded to Naomi in agreement without conferring with each other.

Naomi cleared her throat. "Okay, good. I want to ask a few questions first."

"You don't want Mal and Todd here for this?" Jeff looked hopeful, as if Naomi didn't know her job and had forgotten how necessary his children were to the process.

She realized Jeff's children subconsciously served as a security blanket for him. "No," she stated, wanting her tone to end further debate. "Now," Naomi began, leaning forward in Jeff's direction, "do you love Ruth?"

Jeff frowned. "Of course."

"Okay, a little further, then. In marrying Ruth, did you feel the love for Ruth as you do for Julia?"

He blew a breath of impatience. "Come on, Naomi. We're not here—"

"Yes, we are. I'm not asking you if you loved Ruth more than Julia or vice versa. Love has degrees. We all know that. I'm asking if you felt the same *type* of love that you do for Julia?" Naomi wasn't sure if either of them picked up on her use of present tense regarding Julia—and past tense regarding Ruth.

Jeff glanced sideways at Ruth and shrugged uncomfortably. "I guess, yeah." His demeanor, more than his answer, said everything.

"Your affirmation moves me." Ruth's raw sarcasm echoed.

Jeff threw his head back with a sigh. "If this is your direct approach, Naomi..." He looked at her. "I don't get it."

Naomi offered a reassuring smile. "You will."

Jeff shook his head.

"Close your eyes, Jeff," Naomi directed.

He hesitated, looking at her questioningly.

"Go ahead," she encouraged.

He closed his eyes.

"Now, I want you to answer the question again. But this time, take yourself back to when marriage came up for you and Ruth. When it came up...for you and Julia."

Jeff sighed yet again. "But I answered already." He opened his eyes.

"Then your answer shouldn't change, should it?" Naomi checked Ruth: she didn't look too keen on having Jeff revisit his answer, either. Naomi nodded at Jeff. "Go on. Take your time answering."

Jeff closed his eyes again.

Naomi busied herself with fake note-taking while waiting for Jeff to answer. She made it a point not to look at Ruth.

Two, maybe three minutes later, Jeff opened his eyes. He stared at Ruth for several seconds, then turned to Naomi. His mouth opened, but no words came out. He closed it.

"It's okay. I don't think your answer will surprise anyone here."

Jeff looked over at Ruth again.

Ruth gazed back.

Unable to maintain eye contact with his wife, Jeff turned to Naomi. "Well, I... I guess..." He cleared his throat. "I loved Ruth, love her now. But if you're asking if it's the same love I feel for Julia or that I would need to marry someone for real, then..." Jeff fervently worked both creases now. "Then...no, it's not the same."

"Do you hear yourself, Jeff?" Ruth's question held a blend of anger and disappointment. She shifted her body so that she faced him more. "*Do you?* The love you *'feel'* for Julia? 'Marry someone *for real*? I never had a chance." Ruth looked away, then back to Jeff. "Why'd you marry me?"

Jeff looked up from his creases. "You know why!"

Incredulity shaped Ruth's features as she regarded Jeff. "*That's* the only reason, Jeff? Because you thought I was *pregnant*?!" Ruth glanced at Naomi, self-conscious about her outburst.

Naomi gazed back with plain eyes; she'd concluded that long ago.

Ruth returned her focus to Jeff. "Well?"

"What's wrong with that if I did? But it's the main reason, yeah. And yet I'm still here—sans Jeff Junior."

Ruth's eyes narrowed. "What does *that* mean?"

Jeff stared at Ruth long and hard. Finally, he returned to working his creases, smoothing them to razor-sharp edges. "I don't know. Nothing. It doesn't mean anything."

This wasn't exactly what she had in mind for the session, but it would do. In a roundabout way, they were getting where she wanted to go.

Ruth rose, moving haltingly toward the window.

Naomi and Jeff exchanged curious glances.

Ruth continued facing the window. "You don't believe I was pregnant anymore, do you?"

Jeff stared at Ruth's back for a moment. He lowered his head, going back to his creases. It was answer enough.

Ruth dropped her head.

Naomi shook hers. In her line of work, she didn't put too much past anybody. So, although not surprised, she still couldn't believe her ears. A shotgun wedding? Their ages alone made the ruse outlandish. Ruth was too old to pull it, and Jeff too old to fall for it. But here they were.

"Come sit down, Ruth." Naomi gestured toward the loveseat. "We need to finish this." Even though she didn't like Ruth, none of this was easy. Naomi kept her mind on Todd and Mallory to stay focused on the task at hand. She needed to bring Todd's situation with Ruth to Jeff's attention to begin phases of treating Todd (and Jeff and Mallory) for the mental and emotional repercussions of that ordeal. Reining Ruth in entailed Jeff reclaiming his power of *No*. Jeff deciding to end the marriage would be a bonus.

Ruth didn't sit right away. When she at last approached the seating, Naomi fully expected to see she'd been crying.

She hadn't.

Seeing Ruth's tenacity buoyed Naomi's. She started to ask Ruth if she was okay, but changed her mind, not really caring if she was or not.

Family therapy, indeed.

Naomi cleared her throat. "Okay. Here's my take on your sessions…"

"Cards on the table time?" Jeff smiled wanly.

"Cards on the table," Naomi affirmed. "Now,…" Naomi placed her pad on the coffee table and sat back against the chair cushion. "I want to start with you, Jeff, because you're the key to everything getting better for your family. Fair enough?"

Jeff nodded and leaned forward, leaving his creases alone. Perhaps that wee admission to Ruth about the (didn't happen) pregnancy proved liberating.

"Good. First, Jeff, and this goes without saying, you weren't ready, nor did you want to remarry when you did. Julia was and still is—your all."

Jeff's eyes softened.

Ruth's jaws tightened.

Naomi continued: "Without getting too bogged down in medical psychoanalysis of complicated grief, Jeff, you're more comfortable in a continued fantasy life with Julia via daydreams and constant sleeping." She chose not to mention her suspicions of hallucinations, too. Her exploration of his illusory occurrences required a series of devoted sessions beyond the focus of this one.

Ruth grumbled a humorless laugh.

Jeff opened his mouth and then closed it.

"It's a coping mechanism, but—"

Ruth lifted her eyebrows. "Over three years later?"

"I'm sure he yielded to this form of coping at various times since Julia's death, but now it's affecting his children and his health."

"The weight loss?" Ruth asked.

Naomi nodded. "Now remember, Jeff, this is your second time around with me, so I still have nuggets I held on to from those sessions. Based on what I know about Julia's physical features and those of the two women you dated before Julia, Ruth is against type for you."

Both Ruth and Jeff looked puzzled.

Naomi sat forward and scooted up a bit. "See, in your absolute devotion to Julia, Jeff, I believe your reason for pursuing a relationship with

Ruth was twofold. One, you wanted a mother for your children, and two, you married the exact opposite of Julia because, as no one could replace her, it made it easier to make sure you preserved her memory."

Jeff and Ruth remained silent.

Naomi allowed them a few moments for her words to sink in.

Finally, Jeff spoke. "Okay, Naomi. We've got me sleeping too much and not eating. We can begin to fix those. The whole Ruth-opposite-Julia thing: I don't know. But you mentioned time being short earlier. I know the kids are affected by all this, but 'short on time'?" He frowned. "Why?"

Ruth, too, appeared confused.

"Well, that has a lot to do with Ruth's side of things,...and where the hard part begins, I guess." Naomi focused on Ruth, then Jeff.

Ruth put a hand up. "Wait, I thought you said we had to focus on Jeff becau—"

"And Jeff's getting better involves knowing what's going on with you."

Ruth lowered her hand. The expressive confusion remained, but she also looked defensive. "Going on with me?"

"In a manner of speaking. You...and the kids."

"The kids?" Jeff's confusion seemed to deepen.

"Well, Todd, mostly."

Ruth's eyes narrowed. "I'm a good mother to both of those children."

"'Those children,'" Naomi repeated slightly mockingly. That revealed everything right there—if you were paying attention. Keeping her annoyance at bay, she looked at each of them. "May I finish?"

Jeff nodded, but his brows remained furrowed.

Ruth gestured with her hand for Naomi to continue.

Naomi took a deep breath. "The dynamic here, if you will, is that while Jeff married 'opposite' Julia to honor her, Ruth, conversely, hates Todd because he looks so much like her."

Ruth moved forward in her seat. "I do not hate Todd!"

"'*Hate*' is a pretty strong word," Jeff agreed, but he glanced at his wife.

Naomi bounced a shoulder. "Qualify the word as you see fit. Point's the same."

Jeff extended both hands in the air in front of him with a waving stop motion. "Wait. Just wait a minute here. For you to say she 'hates' my son suggests she's expressed this in some way, and...I don't— I mean..."

He trailed off, studying the floor. When he looked up, his eyes searched Naomi's. "What—? What are you saying, Naomi? What's going on here?"

"I do not hate Todd. Please stop using that word."

Jeff sat forward, rounding on her. "So there's another word to use?!"

"That's not what I'm saying." Ruth eyed Naomi with suspicion and accusation. "Direct approach?"

Naomi ignored her and turned to Jeff. "In realizing your devotion to Julia, Ruth takes her frustrations out on Todd because his looks are a constant reminder. She took advantage of his quiet disposition, plus he was young: eleven or so when things started, and especially vulnerable with his mother dying, so..."

"So, you're accusing Ruth of abusing my son, Naomi?" Jeff shook his head. "Nah, Todd would have said something. I would have seen..."

Ruth fumed. But apparently, words failed her.

"Maybe, maybe not. Jeff, you've been in and out of emotional connection with Todd and Mallory. Right or wrong?"

"Rrright, I guess, but..." He put his head in his hands.

"No buts. It is what it is. What we're doing now is addressing it. Todd hasn't been subjected to gross violence, Jeff. Ruth's physical abuse is 'mild,' although there's no such thing; Todd primarily suffers from Ruth's emotional abuse. And, I believe, it aggravates his asthma." Naomi paused. "I hesitate but want to say she tries to bring on attacks." She had reason to believe Ruth might try to sue her, but caring any less about that wasn't possible.

Jeff lifted his head, eyes angry. "What?!" His glare at Ruth included this momentary scowl of outrage—and protection over his children.

"I do not! That is a lie!" Like magic, the color in Ruth's green irises achromatized. She got up and strutted to the window, shaking her head. "I don't believe this." She turned back to Naomi. "What is *wrong* with you? This— *This* is family therapy? You're 'helping' us like this?"

"I believe it is. I believe I am. At the very least, I'm helping Todd." Naomi paused. "And it's not a lie. I severely limit my fibnation."

Ruth's eyes narrowed on her before she turned back to the window.

Jeff stood. He pivoted between Ruth and Naomi, looking lost. After pacing for quiet seconds, he paused, searching Naomi's face. "The kids told you this?"

Naomi nodded solemnly.

Pain fixed Jeff's features. He turned toward Ruth and held out his hand. "Ruth?"

"'Folly is bound up in the heart of a child, but the rod of discipline drives it far from him.' Proverbs: twenty-two, fifteen," Ruth proclaimed, her back to them.

"Whaaat?" Jeff's extended hand went up to grasp his bald head. Naomi watched the fury move from his shoulders to his hips in an almost-imperceptible tremor.

Ruth turned to face him. She stepped closer. "'Discipline your son, and he will give you rest; he will give delight to your heart.' Proverbs: twenty-nine, seventeen."

Naomi expected as much. She curtailed her urge to smirk.

Jeff stepped back from her, confusion and anger working over his features. "Are you telling me the Bible told you to *hurt my son?*" His hand came down to his side. He peered at Naomi as if to be sure he'd heard Ruth correctly, then returned his attention to Ruth, staring at her. Watching him, watching the outrage ripple through him, if Naomi didn't know any better, she could have sworn, if she wasn't present to bear witness, Jeff was inclined to hurt Ruth—for *real.* Protective parental rage lived in all animals.

"I'm saying," Ruth began, "that Todd had the most difficulty getting over his mother, and he acted out because of it. I did what was necessary to help him transition and bring us together as a family. My faith in The Word encouraged me." She paused. "I don't hate Todd, Jeff. I don't."

Jeff turned to Naomi again, wanting to confirm she heard the same thing he did. He sent his gaze around her office, frowning and shaking his head. "Todd doesn't 'act out.' Never has been a— He's not... He's not an 'acting out' type of kid."

Naomi silently agreed. This was an initial step for Jeff to reclaim his power of *No.*

He sighed, the air pushing through his lips heavy with annoyed hurt. "I— I...don't believe this." He plopped onto the loveseat. Lines of worry and ire moved across his face. "I don't believe this," he repeated with sincerity. Jeff peered up at Ruth, asking *Why?* without speaking.

Ruth knelt beside him, placing her hands on the armrest of the loveseat. "Jeff, listen to me. Doctor Alexander is making this out to be something it's not. Did you hear that psychobabble she came up with?

It's craziness. Listen, we'll see someone else, okay? I love you, Jeff. We can get past this, okay?"

Jeff gazed in Ruth's direction, but Naomi could tell he wasn't seeing her. He was slowly withdrawing from the situation. Naomi couldn't allow that to happen.

"Jeff?" Ruth placed a hand on his thigh and kissed his cheek. When he didn't respond, she glared at Naomi. "Children lie, Doctor Alexander. They do. Whatever I did, it was only to help him get over his mother, the *revered* Julia. That's all."

Naomi offered her a stare devoid of emotion. That woman left the prudencesphere some time ago, with few to no visits since.

"... Ya know..." Jeff sounded as if coming out of a trance. "You keep saying 'get over' her. You said something similar to me weeks ago, and I didn't like it then. I don't like it now." He focused on Ruth, seeing her this time. "Maybe you mean well, but I don't think you do."

"Jeff, don't do this," Ruth pleaded.

Yes, Jeff, do this.

Jeff gazed at Ruth steadily. "I believe Naomi."

Ruth searched his face as if trying to gauge his sincerity. After a moment, she dropped her head, but Naomi doubted tears would come.

Jeff moved her hand from his thigh, placing it back on the armrest. He stared at the top of Ruth's head. Expressions of confusion, worry, sadness, and anger created alternating contortion on his face.

When he turned to Naomi, though, his expression was static. "What do I do now?" He maneuvered around Ruth to stand.

Ruth gazed up at Jeff, defiant disbelief hardening her countenance. She then rose and moved to the window. No tears.

Naomi watched Ruth for a few seconds before looking up at Jeff. "Well, that depends. First, do you want to save your marriage or end it? I apologize if I seem insensitive, but I prefer cutting to the chase whenever possible."

No one spoke.

Jeff trudged over to Naomi's bookcases, inspecting the volumes there.

Ruth remained at the window. Her aura flickered in with this orange-red hue: confident, willful, full of ego. The hunter-green of envy from before was one thing; Ruth still possessed a jealous insecurity regarding Julia Winthrop. But currently, the impasse concerned Todd

Winthrop. Ruth's orange-red aura-flicker moments ago: unflappable confidence over her treatment of Todd.

They were on opposite sides of her office with their backs to one another. After watching them for several minutes, Naomi went to her desk. She'd committed the rest of the day to the Winthrop case, so Jeff could take his time deciding. And while he surely didn't have to decide anything right now, Naomi wanted him to. Why? She didn't know. Ending a marriage wasn't easy, but to her, saving one was much harder. In Jeff's case, though, it wasn't a matter of easy or hard. He didn't want to remarry in the first place. Not at the time, anyway.

Naomi busied herself with reviewing her notes from the Ralston-Haynes case.

The minutes passed.

Ruth faced Jeff. To Naomi's surprise, she had been crying. Ruth looked hopeful. "If it's taking you this long, Jeff, you must want to save what we have." She sniffed and looked at Naomi.

Naomi gestured toward the box of tissues on the end table.

Ruth mouthed, "Thanks," and reached for it. She plucked a few tissues and wiped her eyes and nose.

Jeff turned away from the books, slowly regarding Naomi and Ruth, before settling his gaze on Ruth. "...I love you, Ruth. I guess. But it's not a deep, enduring, life-sustaining kind of love. Not having that kind of love for you, and then with what's happened to Todd..." He shook his head. "No, I'm realizing Julia was it for me. I don't know what the future holds, but I do know, *now* anyway, that I don't have to be married to be a good father to Mal and Todd. I'm a little old-fashioned about some stuff, yeah. But it's clear I will have to be a little more contemporary in my thinking." Jeff lowered his gaze toward the floor. "...It's over, Ruth."

Naomi wished he'd especially looked Ruth in the eye when he said that last.

"Don't tell the floor. Look me in my face, Jeff, and tell me our marriage is over," Ruth commanded. She stepped in his direction.

Naomi thought she looked nice in her dress.

Jeff lifted his head, eyes on Ruth. "What difference does that make?! I mean what I'm saying, whether or not I look you in the eye. But, for your sake, okay..." He held Ruth's gaze. "It's over, Ruth." He maintained eye contact with her for solid seconds, then whipped his focus to

Naomi. "What do I do now?" A tear escaped his right eye. But he also sounded...relieved. Owning one's power of *No* had that effect. There was still work to do, but threats to his children's safety had him moving in the right direction.

"You don't mean this, Jeff," Ruth murmured.

He glanced in Ruth's general direction. "I mean it."

Ruth sat on the loveseat.

Jeff turned back to Naomi. "What do I do?"

Naomi removed her eyeglasses. She laced her fingers and set her hands on her desk. "Well, whatever happens, you, Mallory, and Todd must continue therapy—*you* especially. Okay?"

He nodded halfheartedly.

Naomi maintained a steady gaze at Jeff, wanting positive confirmation he'll continue with the sessions.

Eyes locked on Naomi's, he nodded definitively. "I'll continue."

Naomi returned his definitive nod with one of her own. "Very good. Now, the rest depends on how much you want to hurt Ruth."

Jeff looked back at Ruth (holding her head in her hands). He turned back to Naomi and shook his head: not too much.

Naomi nodded her understanding. She didn't much care for Ruth, but if Ruth's treatment of Todd was an isolated occurrence (which Naomi believed it was), then she didn't want to hurt her too much, either. But there must be some comeuppance, however minor. Regarding leniency, for Naomi, it was TLTB in that department. "I can downplay the instances in my report enough to prompt only an inquiry from child protective services, and you can take it from there, or we can explore charging her with some violation of child endangerment laws, or—"

"Let's go with the 'downplay' approach," he said, cutting her off. "That should be enough." He didn't sound too sure.

"Sounds good," Naomi expressed strongly, hoping to reassure him. She glanced at Ruth before focusing on Jeff. She continued, using a lower tone of confidentiality. "I'd suggest anger management counseling when or if CPS visits." She raised an eyebrow to convey her meaning.

"Okay." He released a long breath, and looked back at Ruth again, then suddenly jerked his head around to Naomi. "Do you smell that?" His eyes widened with either wonder or alarm. Naomi couldn't tell which. Maybe it was both.

She shook her head. "Smell what?" She sniffed tentatively. "I don't smell anything different. Why? What do you smell?"

Jeff's eyes softened. "I thought..." He scanned Naomi's office. "I... Nothing. Never mind." He inhaled deeply, smiling to himself.

Is he hallucinating here, now?

Naomi was glad he agreed to continue with the sessions.

"Are you allowed to do any of this?" Ruth asked the floor. She looked up at Naomi, her eyes questioning.

"Yes..." Naomi shrugged. "...And no. But mostly yes."

Ruth's eyes narrowed. "I'll pray for you, Doctor Alexander." A facsimile of a smile dawned on her face.

"Only for my positive well-being; otherwise, please don't." Naomi resolved to include Ruth's positive well-being on her prayer list.

Jeff peered at Naomi with creased brows, fathoming her meaning.

Naomi put a hand up. *Let it go*, the gesture said.

Jeff checked his watch. "I guess we'd better go. No need to fill up the whole time with this." He rapped on Naomi's desk twice and pointed at her. "I'll be in touch?"

Naomi smiled, then instantly changed expression, looking at Jeff seriously, almost sternly. "I have you down for this coming Friday at nine-fifteen."

"Oh, okay. Gotcha. See you Friday then."

Naomi pointed an index finger his way in affirmation. Sometimes it came with the job, an accepted fact, but being the impetus for breaking up a family never felt good—whether or not the breakup was justified.

Countdown to a glass of Hennessy.

Jeff turned partway from Naomi toward Ruth. "Let's go, Ruth."

Ruth alternated stares at Jeff and Naomi before finally resting her eyes on her husband. "You don't mean this, Jeff," she stated from her seated position. She shook her head and reached for her purse. "You don't."

"I mean it. But this can be amicable, Ruth. It doesn't have to be drama and acrimony." Jeff closed his eyes and inhaled deeply. He smiled softly and then opened his eyes with this far-off, goofy expression that did not line up with the current topic of discussion.

Naomi thought it weird. Friday couldn't get here soon enough.

Without another word, Ruth rose from the loveseat and stormed toward the door. She reached for the doorknob.

"'Fathers, do not provoke your children, lest they become discouraged,'" Naomi said. "Colossians: chapter three, verse twenty-one."

Ruth parted her lips, but then apparently changed her mind. She left.

Jeff's once-expansive shoulders slumped. "I guess that's it then." He turned to Naomi. Tears welled but didn't fall.

"Well, it's really the beginning."

"The beginning..." He turned to the window.

"Go talk to Mallory and Todd, Jeff."

Jeff sniffed and sighed. "Right." But he didn't move.

Naomi gave him some time; she reviewed her Ralston-Haynes notes.

"...I had sex with her when I was missing Julia terribly."

Naomi didn't speak; she wasn't supposed to.

"Jules was dead. I was missing my wife, and Ruth was there, and..." He stared out of the window. "Believe it or not, there are times when a man regrets having sex with a woman. Times when he regrets listening to the little head. Times when he realizes the climax just wasn't worth it. But Ruth was there, Naomi. And my head was so f— *is* so messed up. But Ruth was there, and I just... I just went with it. You know?"

"Explanations aren't necessary, Jeff. Not for this. But, for what it's worth, I figured as much already."

Jeff nodded, his concentration still out of the window. "Do you believe in ghosts, Naomi?"

"I don't know. Why?"

"...Just askin'." He stared out the window a little longer and then headed to the door. "See you Friday. Just me, or with the kids, too...?" He paused at the door and turned back.

"There will be some targeted counseling for Todd soon, but for now, just you. I'll include Mallory and Todd sporad— Oh!" Naomi opened her top right desk drawer: two eight-pack Goldenberg's Peanut Chews candy packages rested inside. One was milk chocolate with blue labeling; the other was dark chocolate with red labeling.

Jeff walked toward her. "What's wrong?"

"Nothing. Here." She held the candy out to him. "These are for Todd and, well, whomever, but Todd mainly."

He chuckled as he accepted the candy from her. "Yeah, I'm partial to the Original Dark myself. He'll probably go for the milk chocolate, though. Thank you." He headed toward the door again.

"Probably. I told him my preference was Original Dark, too, but I wanted him to have the choice, you know." Naomi paused. "Didn't want him feeling he was stuck with just the one choice; that he has options…"

He turned back, his eyes probing with this bend of curiosity to his brow. "…Are we still talking about candy?"

Naomi shrugged.

Jeff Winthrop held her gaze. "'Options,' huh?" With a cursory parting survey of her office, he nodded and was gone.

Dr. Naomi Alexander plucked the remote from her desk and aimed it at her player, sending Brahms' Violin Sonata No. 1 in G major, Op. 78, *Rain* into the room. She then opened the Winthrop file on her laptop and got to work.

Chapter 17

New Beginnings, Old Habits

Jeff Winthrop spent several hours driving around the outer limits of Washington DC before returning to Capitol Hill, so he wasn't surprised to find the house dark when he entered. Only a warm glow from the kitchen and light from Todd's bedroom upstairs illuminated the main foyer. He stood in the foyer, his eyes adjusting to the gloom.

"Where's Ruth?" Mallory's voice trailed from the dining room area.

Jeff frowned in the dark. "Where's Todd?"

"I'm here, Dad." In the dark, Todd sounded much older.

Jeff's frown deepened. "Why're you two sitting in the dark?" He headed in the direction whence their voices came and found his children sitting at opposite ends of the window seat, stationed between the formal living and dining rooms. Their silhouettes faced each other.

The wood blinds were closed, allowing only fine slivers of light from the streetlamp outside to filter through. He paused several feet away from them, looking from one dark silhouette to the other, seeing them but not seeing them. "Again, why're you sitting in the dark like this?"

"Where's Ruth?" Mallory asked again.

"Answer me."

"Answer me," she retorted.

Jeff waited. Whatever he was going through, he was still the parent.

Perhaps his daughter sensed his displeasure across the darkness. "You finished with Doctor Alex hours ago, Daddy. You didn't respond to my calls or my texts, either." Mallory's accusations didn't mask how scared she was or had been. Surely, she didn't think he wouldn't *come home*.

Sixteen and six all mixed in there together.

Jeff walked toward them. Todd swung his feet around so that their father could sit between them. Mallory stayed her place, hugging her legs to her body. She rested her chin on her knees. The position reminded him very much of the way he'd found Todd on the roof. Watching her, Jeff didn't ask why they were sitting in the dark again. The lack of light did nothing to conceal his daughter's distress. She'd been in this spot a long time, waiting.

"Hungry?" Mallory's knees restricted the movements of her chin and face. She looked like a ventriloquist's puppet as she spoke. "I made a chicken casserole."

Jeff shook his head. Food was the least of his concerns.

"C'mon, Dad. It's pretty good. Or I could make you a Dagwood." Todd's words were calm, but Jeff didn't need to see his son's face, either; he could hear the anguish in his voice.

His children needed comfort. Jeff held both arms out, one to each side. "Group hug, guys." He looked to his right at Todd, then to his left, then at Todd again.

Todd frowned. "Huh?" But he was the first to lean under his father's outstretched arm. "Love ya, Dad," he whispered.

"Love you too, son," Jeff whispered back and hugged his son. He couldn't help thinking about what his son had gone through at Ruth's hand. An image of Todd's fearful expression (amid the "PayDay" discussion at the hospital) popped into Jeff's head. Reflecting on it, he realized: he saw it, dismissed it—and for that, he'll be forever sorry. He hugged Todd tighter to tamp down the anger striving to claim him. "*Love you, man.*" He kissed the top of his son's head.

One down, one to go.

Jeff turned to Mallory. His left arm began aching with fatigue, but he kept it outstretched.

"It's been hours."

"I know." Jeff kept eyes on his daughter. "Group hug."

Mallory quickly shifted into the arch of her father's arm.

Jeff hugged his children tight, with a snugness his recent session with Naomi commanded. They huddled together on the window seat, listening to the steady tick of the grandfather clock and each other's breathing. It was some time before anyone spoke.

"Where's Ruth?" Mallory asked yet again.

Todd lifted away from his father and resumed his original position. He eyeballed his sister with a sneering squint. "Why're you so worried about it? She's not here. So?"

Two, three days ago, Jeff would've been on Todd about that attitude.

But it wasn't days ago. It was hours after a very revealing session with Naomi. Jeff said nothing. He looked down at Mallory for her response.

Mallory, too, resumed her position, gazing at her father. Light through the blinds lit her face enough, for her expression told Jeff that she, too, had expected him to admonish Todd. Jeff's eyes adjusted to the low lighting; he could read Mallory's confusion (and suspicion). She ignored her brother. "Where's Ruth, Daddy?"

Todd sucked his teeth and exhaled a harsh breath.

This should have been easier. Todd and Mallory didn't like Ruth very much, so this perhaps ranked as good news for them. The last several hours delivered eye-opening revelation, and whenever Jeff thought about what Ruth did to his son, it incensed him beyond anything he'd known before. It didn't matter, however. Ending a marriage wasn't easy. There were always nasty leftovers.

Jeff didn't know what to say.

"Where is Ruth, Dad?" Todd asked this time. Jeff figured his hesitation in answering alarmed his son.

"Ruth is fine." Jeff swallowed. "She'll be back...to pick up her things."

Jeff watched his children. Their brows furrowed. It took a moment for comprehension to dawn, and then eyes widened. Mallory and Todd shared a look, doing their sibling-communication thing.

Todd spoke first. "Seriously?" His voice carried disbelief, but Jeff heard unmitigated relief, too. And the relief in his son's voice made Jeff want to strangle Ruth for harming his child. Just clamp both hands around her neck and—

Jeff nodded solemnly. "Yeah. We may want to make ourselves scarce over the next few days while she packs up." He glanced at his children.

"...I don't think that's a good idea, Dad. We...We should be here."

Jeff peered at his son through the gloom, the dim lighting doing nothing to camouflage Todd's meaning. His response revealed more about his three years with Ruth as a stepmother, revealed more about a Ruth Jeff didn't know, that Jeff, again, wanted the woman within arm's reach for about ten seconds (truth be told, he wouldn't even need ten seconds). "You got it. I'll make sure I'm here at least."

His son's gaze steadied on him. "That's all the 'we' we need, Dad." The gloom deepened his cryptic yet heartfelt message, but Jeff received it loud and clear. His son sounded much older than his fourteen years, wiser, and Jeff couldn't escape the notion that Ruth's abuse matured him, stole good portions of Todd's childhood. Ruth had been ruthless. Five seconds with her would be more than plenty.

Mallory put a hand on his shoulder. "I'm sorry, Daddy."

Jeff turned to his daughter. "Thank you, M-Sweet." He looked down at his shoes, or rather, at their shadowy outline. Anger, sadness, regret, disappointment, resignation, and relief waged a battle for dominant position within him.

"We'll be okay," Mallory offered.

Jeff observed his daughter. Tears wet her cheeks, but they were the only clue she'd been crying.

Mallory's voice was strong, unwavering as she continued: "We'll be fine. You don't have to be married for us to have maternal influences in our lives." Her eyes pleaded for his understanding. "Okay?"

He shrugged and resumed studying his shoes. It sounded good, but his emotions still jockeyed. In the end, resignation won out. Maybe some relief, too. He slapped his children's thighs, startling them. "You know what? I am hungry, so I'm gonna grab some of that casserole." Jeff stood and headed toward the kitchen. "And you two are gonna have seconds and eat with your father. C'mon." He turned on the dining room light. Light, any light, would do to dissipate (and repel) the gloom. He imagined more silent communication between his children behind him before hearing their footsteps as they followed.

Weeks later, Jeff was standing in front of the Jamison-Ajai Art Gallery with his son and daughter. Aromas of cinnamon and coffee wafted to him from the pastry shop a few doors down. The brief resurgent summer gave way to colder temperatures over the last couple of weeks. The newly grown hair on his head and face (he wasn't balding naturally yet) provided some protection against the chill. Still, Jeff breathed in the piercing late-November air and pulled his newsboy cap further down on his forehead. He was glad Naomi encouraged him to let it grow. It... It turned out to be a healing exercise for him. He had a lot to be thankful for this quiet Thanksgiving.

"When and what made you do this?" He didn't show any enthusiasm with his question, wanting his daughter to think he was upset.

"You don't like it?" Todd asked.

Jeff ignored him, keeping his eyes on Mallory. "I'm listening."

"Uh..." Mallory fiddled with the bill of her newsboy cap. The cap originally belonged to her mother. She averted her eyes to garner some support from her brother. Eyes back on Jeff, she swallowed hard and continued: "I submitted them back in August. I didn't find out they were featuring you until after Todd went into the hospital. That's why I invited you that Saturday. I thought we'd see something then. I— I just wanted to see what would happen," his daughter said in a rush. She glanced at Todd and then looked past Jeff into the gallery.

"You mean, to see if I still had it." He kept his tone stern to throw her off while she wasn't looking at him, but he smiled to let his children know he wasn't serious. Since Julia died, he'd been in rare contact with his agent, Thomas Clude. It seems M-Sweet picked up the torch with those discounted and forgotten paintings from their basement. Jeff winked at his son.

Todd nodded back with an impish grin, then watched Mallory. These days, how much he resembled his mother didn't stir the pain of loss inside Jeff, as it once did. Since finding out about his son's ordeal, Jeff dedicated the last few weeks to getting to know his son better, reconnecting with him. He couldn't get three years back, but he did his best to get most of it back, bonding with Todd the way he used to before Jules died.

They sometimes hung out on the field after Todd's practices, talking late into the evening. Todd even camped out with him in his bedroom for several nights over the last few weeks. It was a bit of private therapy for them both, as he and his son let it all hang out—the good and the bad. It was sobering to learn Todd wasn't a virgin anymore, but Jeff took it in stride (and suppressed his pride) while giving his son honest, no-holds-barred advice on being intimate with a young lady.

Unfortunately, Jeff anticipated little more than five-fingered-shuffles for himself in his foreseeable future.

And although he advised his son to abstain from now on, he knew Todd might not listen. Once you feel it with a girl for the first time, that feeling becomes the chase from that moment on (at least until you gained enough control over your dick to be selective, be monogamous). But his son was also mature for his age, so there was still hope.

Jeff also made extra time to be one-on-one with his daughter more often, allowing them time to reestablish bonds that, although not broken, certainly started to bend while Ruth was in their lives.

"I'm sorry, Da—" Mallory began her apology and then saw her father's face. "Oh, you are so wrong!" She swiped at his arm.

Jeff belted a laugh. Although sincere, it somehow sounded hollow on the near-deserted street. Mallory and Todd soon laughed with him. Their laughter, blended with his, made things better.

When their laughter faded, M-Sweet grinned at him. "Your stuff's *good*, Daddy. People should see it. Mister Clude helped me. I'll show you the letter: the gallery was excited to hear of your return... You were a shoo-in for selection." Her grin shifted into this bright smile of pride. The tilt of her mouth on the right side, said *Jules*.

Jeff didn't know how to respond, other than nodding acceptance of the compliment.

I wish Julia were here for this.

He gazed along the relatively quiet street, at the few pedestrians window-shopping.

Grief crept its somberness through him, hollowing out his chest, a hollowness threatening expansion beyond his chest. Despite embarking on new beginnings, depression wanted to set in. Jeff took shallow breaths to ease the familiar abstract pains, to ease the dull, achy disquiet inside him. Grief, in all its glory, was...excruciating. Words didn't help it; there was no value in staid words—not the way people believed. And time didn't heal; it only eased the coping. He missed his wife. Over three years later. Still. "Well, I guess we'd better head on back in there. Don't want to miss out on any potential offers." Jeff took Mallory's hand and wrapped an arm around Todd's neck. "C'mon..."

The three engaged in a round of hoots and giggles (Jeff believed, born out of a family rising from the "ashes") as they went back inside the gallery together.

Jeff thought he performed the meet-and-greet the artist thing well to have been out of the game for so long. He talked about the inspiration behind two of his sculptures, accepted compliments with a warm smile, and even received two substantial offers for one of his paintings.

Recent sessions with Naomi progressed well (or so he thought, anyway). He didn't get his prescription filled yet, but he'd get around to it. And although he'd had sense enough to get a prenuptial agreement, Ruth still wanted to haggle. She seemed to be coming around, so Jeff didn't think it'd be long before the proceedings moved along without complication.

But because she wanted to haggle over assets, because she *hurt his son*, Jeff went ahead with the child-endangerment charges for whatever it was worth.

There were always nasty leftovers.

"—cise balance of color and composition," a woman finished. Her copper-brown irises sparkled as she offered a teasing yet confident smile. Her dreadlocks were neat and freshly twisted, their honey color pleasing to Jeff's artist-eye.

Jeff smiled back. "Thanks. Thank you very much."

"I didn't see a name. What do you call it?" She raised a thick eyebrow.

"Oh. It's entitled: *In Search of Black Doves*."

She nodded, this expressive twinkle in her eyes. "I guess, the point being since there is no such thing."

"The search is pointless, yes." Still smiling, he now stared while nodding, surprised at her insight. Was she an artist, too? "Two movements influence the piece: Symbolism, but primarily Post-Im—"

"Impressionism. Yes, I see that."

"Oh, okay." This couldn't get any more intriguing.

"...I'm Isolynn, by the way." She extended a small, ginger-brown hand, and her scent's soft, spicy orange flower elements traveled to him.

Looking at her, Jeff tried guessing her age, but with some difficulty. She conducted herself like a woman of a certain age, but visually, she looked all of 30.

He shook her hand (Isolynn's shake was feminine but firm). "How—? How old are you?"

She didn't appear at all upset by the question. "Forty-five. I'll be forty-six in January. And you?"

"Forty-nine in February. Sorry. I know that was extremely personal, but..." He realized he still held her hand (and he couldn't help staring).

"If I didn't want to answer, I wouldn't have," she replied with gentle candor. The honey-colored hair and the ginger complexion complemented with alluring effectiveness. Lips: heart-shaped but not smeared with any unfriendly color—accentuated by some shimmery, deep earth tone. Her copper irises drew him in.

Enthralled and in awe, Jeff couldn't move. It lasted only an instant, but in that instant, he wanted to know if she was married.

"And no, I'm not involved with anyone at the moment." Her voice carried husky notes of promises in the offing. Soft fingers trailed across his palm as she released his hand.

Jeff's heart fluttered. Someone waited behind Isolynn for their turn to greet him, but he didn't want her to go, wanting just a few more moments with her (or maybe more than a few more moments). "Would you mind...? I mean, don't—"

"I'll wait, yes." Her warm, copper-brown eyes held his before she turned away, wearing that smile again.

Absently shaking the next greeter's hand, Jeff watched Isolynn saunter toward the other side of the gallery. She held her coat across her forearm as she strolled and perused the art, her dress outlining her lithe body to full effect: small but round, pert breasts (the nipples pointing with the gallery's chill), a toned, plump rear. She carried 45 well.

Another greeter sang Jeff's artistic praises. Jeff shook and nodded and responded graciously, but he barely made eye contact with them. His gaze followed Isolynn—and she carried 45 so well.

Isolynn paused to speak with two ladies viewing his painting entitled *Dusk Meets No One*. She smiled and talked with the women, pointing out something in the painting obviously pleasing to her as she spoke about it, the other ladies nodding their agreement. Jeff again wondered if she had an art background, when she looked his way, nodding with that intriguing smile again before resuming her conversation. She... She was beautiful.

Jeff watched Isolynn—feeling something for her extending beyond sexual.

His loins stirred for her, yes. His groin twitched in an aroused way it hadn't since Julia—in a way it never did for Ruth. Yes, watching her, he wanted Isolynn naked and spread wide, pushing deep inside her and grinding nastily...(maybe lovingly).

But—and this was the kicker—he also wanted to *know* Isolynn: who she was as a person and where she'd been in life; what made her happy and why oh why didn't he meet her before Ruth; how soft were those heart-shaped lips and when could he see her again...

"Isolynn," Jeff whispered, her name unique and sweet, rolling over his tongue. He imagined saying it during quiet conversation in a secluded corner of a bistro... or moaning it in the heat of passion with her. He had the feeling sex with her would be—

No.

He shook his head, trying to repel the attraction. No. As lovely as she appeared, he insisted the woman did nothing for him. The one woman that did something for him (to him and with him) died three years and five months ago. He didn't know if Naomi could help him with that, didn't know if he wanted her to. He was not fain to begin dating again.

Speaking of Naomi, Jeff caught her eye across the room as she chatted with Mallory and Todd. She waved. Jeff waved back, glad she came.

A whiff of Guerlain Shalimar tickled Jeff's nostrils. He jerked around, checking behind him. Turning back, he scanned the patrons, only to find Naomi watching him in that caring but analyzing way of hers. Julia's scent stayed with him as he smiled at Naomi and excused himself from those closest to him. He needed a moment.

Familiar with the layout of Jamison-Ajai from past appearances, Jeff made his way up the back stairs to the prop closet, locking the door behind him. Traces of iris, vanilla, and roses followed him, overpowering the artist-specific perfume of oils and painting supplies.

"Jules?" He flipped the light switch: easels and tripods littered the space. Several were strewn across an out-of-place leather recliner. Jeff moved them to the side and lowered into the chair. He shoved a stack of boxes away with his foot and pushed back into full recline, falling back into an old habit.

Jeff closed his eyes, taking several deep breaths. When his rhythms returned, he opened his eyes with a sigh. "I can't get over you, Jules." He shook his head and covered his eyes with his hands. "I can't."

Can't or don't want to?

"Is there a difference?" He sat up and reached over to flip the light switch, sending the room back into darkness. He reclined and allowed Julia's scent to shroud him. "I miss you," he whispered. Relaxing into the soft leather, he closed his eyes. Thoughts of Julia overpowered any concerns for the people downstairs.

Memory-dreams beckoned.

Jeff followed.

He gripped the arms of the recliner as he moved deeper into the memory-dream. The arms of the recliner tethered him to the here and now and against the lure of believing absolutely in the world of the dreams that are, but are not, reality (or so it seems).

Iris, vanilla, and rose fragrances give way to the potpourri of smells now invading his nostrils. Scents of pine, wet leaves, forest flowers, and dirt merge in tremendous harmony to establish the setting. It is a fall day four years ago. It is a fall day today. Jeff doesn't need to look around. He knows where he is: Rock Creek Park. Their sixteenth wedding anniversary. Mallory and Todd are with their aunt, Malila. He and Julia have the day to themselves. Jeff leans against the trunk of a hickory tree as he did years ago, waiting for Julia to return. Through the trees, he sees a mini nature-center kiosk several yards away.

The self-explore center didn't exist four years ago.

It is four years ago, but it is now.

Jeff leans back against the tree, hands tingling with anticipating his wife's return, not caring about insects along the trunk or any woodland creature's approach. Waiting, he observes his surroundings, listening to the sounds throughout the wooded area, which coalesce into a piece of music all its own.

He recognizes the churr-churr-churr-brrt sound of a red-bellied woodpecker and looks up, spotting a male bird high in a tree to his left. Its red cap and black and white bar-patterned back stand out in stark contrast in this memory-dream. The bird calls and then drums against the tree trunk in an alternating rhythm, wanting, at the very least, to attract a mate.

Noise from the ground draws his attention. An eastern towhee (female this time) hops in his direction; her red eyes warn to stay away. Although late in the season, perhaps her young were nearby. Jeff smiles: the mother bird had nothing to worry about. The bird hops closer and waits. The raw umber and copper tones of her head and body blaze in the autumn sun. Jeff doesn't move. Satisfied, the she-bird returns to her family.

"Where are you?" Jeff says but doesn't say. The oddity of communication without vocalization in these "dream" states still fascinates him.

"Right here," Julia answers. She rests a hand on his chest. Her touch is feather-light. She is there. Jeff neither saw nor heard her approach, but she is with him. The scent of iris, vanilla, and roses overwhelms him with familiarity and enchantment; she is here! Anticipation of her return shifts into painful desire, and he tastes her tongue before realizing their kiss. Her tongue alternates joyous flavors of cool strawberries and warm cocoa, and he holds on to the tree behind him with both hands to keep from falling to the ground.

Julia leans onto him. He only knows this because of the increased pressure at his front and the pricks from tree bark against his back. He feels his wife's body against his. "I love you," she says in his head before deepening their kiss. She reaches down to massage the swell in his pants. And Jeff remembers this, precisely this, from four years ago.

It is then, but it is now.

Jeff allows Julia her time to be pleasure-giver. His erection strains against her hand; he grips the hickory trunk tighter, trying his best to hold back from the pleasure he wants, no, *needs* to give her.

The red-bellied woodpecker begins his call again.

Jeff moans into Julia's mouth, wishing the bird gets as lucky as he at this moment. Julia teases his senses until, at last, Jeff wants his turn. He lets go of the tree and grabs his wife. Holding her essence close to his body, he switches places with her, bracing her against the tree. As much as he wants to lift her legs and thrust inside her, he...wants to bring her to the brink of ecstasy just as much.

Jeff holds Julia's gaze (or does she hold his?) as he runs his thumbs over her nipples through the thin fabric of her top. There are fewer words now than four years ago, but that is okay. Julia's eyes tell him everything he needs to know. A haunted look in her eyes, however, tempers the desire he sees. Jeff sees it, understands its meaning, and ignores it.

Sadness is not welcome here.

Julia's words build in his head (words of instruction tinged with regret), and he covers her mouth with his to thwart them. Julia's moans soon replace her words, and that is better.

Sadness is not welcome here.

Jeff continues caressing the round yet firm mounds that once fed his babies. Profound love weakens him, but Julia holds him, strengthens him. He lifts her leg, and her skirt falls back along her thigh. He slides his hand up that thigh and around the almost nonexistent barrier of her panties. His mouth never leaves hers. Cool strawberries, warm cocoa.

Jeff's fingers play as his wife tenses and then relaxes with what he is doing to her. She is as moist and pliant as he expects. His focus sharpens with the intensity of their kiss, the subtle movement of her hips.

Julia struggles to release his erection with an urgency only they understand, and he knows she is close. He doesn't remember removing her panties, but his access to her is unencumbered now. Scents of roses, iris, and vanilla intensify with her excitement, and he breathes in the cloying aroma as life's oxygen.

"...finish together," Julia says in his head.

Jeff wastes no time. When he enters her, he hears movement far off to his right as leaves shift under the weight of someone or some...*thing*. Perhaps a slight breeze rustled them. He doesn't care about being seen. There is nothing but the warmth and love of his wife.

It is four years ago. It is now.

Carnal pleasure gravitates from his lower abdomen to the core of his maleness. *Ecstasy* is not the word for this. Julia's walls contract around him as she climaxes, and Jeff's immediate release inside her seems to go on and on... *Ecstasy* is not the word for this, either.

Time shifts and they stand at the nature-center kiosk, poring over the pamphlets and other park information materials. Julia flirts with him around and through the booth windows. The conversation plays only in Jeff's head, but the haunted look in her eyes persists. He remembers fixing their clothes and talking awhile before leaving the park for ice cream and heading to their getaway condo for more anniversary festivity. But that was then. Four years ago. The kiosk didn't exist then, so...

Time and location shift this time. Jeff kisses Julia in front of the Jamison-Ajai Art Gallery.

It is one week before Julia enters the hospital, never to return.

It is now.

Two of Jeff's featured sculptures have been sold for a great deal. Their kiss is only part-celebration. The sun dips below the horizon of office buildings at the end of the street. Clouds catch the last orange-red rays of the sun as it sets, making way for the soft purples of evening.

Their kiss is not long but lasts forever. Jeff remembers how, years ago, they arrived earlier in the day, but the heat of her lips and taste of her tongue (cinnamon-hazelnut this time) obliterates any details. Mallory and Todd are with them, but they are inside. Somehow, that is important, but Jeff chooses not to ponder it.

Their lips part and they hold each other. Julia traces her fingers up and down his spine and then massages his lower back. Jeff smiles into her hair. The woman does not know how much he loves her. No idea. He has never been as happy as on that (this?) day.

"You can love another, Jeff," Julia says but doesn't say.

Jeff pushes Julia back from him and stares into her eyes. Grim acceptance replaces the haunted look in them, and Jeff realizes it is more now than then. Very much so. He doesn't like the look in her eyes, refuses to accept the implication of her words.

Sadness is not welcome here.

Jeff grabs Julia and holds her to him. If he holds on to her like this forever, there will be no goodbyes. And he can do it, too, Jeff asserts, trying to hold fast to his wife so that her body melds into his. Her body doesn't meld, however. Once again, it is like holding the mist of heavy, dense fog: she is there—but not really.

Rocks of sorrow knot his stomach and line his throat. He coughs and sobs with abandon. No. No goodbyes. He won't allow it. Can't do it...

Jeff clenched his eyes tight, desperately trying to hold on to the memory-dream, but it (she) is gone.

"No," he told the darkness. "No." He snatched his pants closed, ignoring the wetness there as he zipped. He opened his eyes and stared into the black, somehow still smelling four-year-old leaves from Rock Creek Park. Tears dampened his face.

"No." Much less conviction this time. He wiped his face with a hand and sniffed as the obscure ache of sorrow traveled through him.

You can love another.

Jeff thought of Isolynn. She was waiting for him. He thought about Isolynn's gentle candor, her teasing, confident smile, and that lithe form,...and a glimmer of something light and comforting traveled through his heart, spreading warm and mellow throughout the rest of him with promise of a new (and enduring) Black love.

Jeff shook his head with the heaviest of sighs.

He loved Julia. That was it. And she was still with him. The memory-dreams would have to be enough. They *were* enough.

Listening to himself, Jeff sat up in the chair. He moved so fast; he knocked what sounded like a can of spray paint over. The metallic clunk and subsequent rattle gave away its new resting place. In the dark, the sound resonated within the closet walls, bouncing off the various parts of wood and metal housed inside.

His wife was dead, but he intended to continue this closed-off existence with what he wanted to believe was a form of her still here.

She'd essentially said *goodbye* to him just now.

Or did she?

He didn't know. But Jeffrey Adair Winthrop III left the closet, intent on seeking Dr. Naomi E. M. Alexander to find out.

Chapter 18

Progress?

A serving of jollof rice or okro stew would have been better. The football weekend special from Popeye's was tasty, but she'd had a taste for Ghanaian food, so those specialties would have been better. She could have gone for Kevin's African chicken stew, even. The dish was rather spicy for her tastes, but still very good. Between the two, Kevin's niece, Faustina, possessed the better of their Ghanaian cooking skills, but Kevin did all right.

Dinner, however, ended half an hour ago.

It was time for dessert—Leslie-style.

Naomi forked her slice of cake and took a bite. She closed her eyes and moaned appreciatively, not the least bit surprised by the wonderful flavors dancing on her tongue, exciting each taste bud. Naomi didn't chew, didn't swallow. She savored. Bananas, brown sugar, and crunchy pecans rested on her tongue before the moist cake melted: Leslie's banana upside-down cake. Leslie was in elementary school when Naomi first showed her how to make it.

Since then, Leslie perfected its creation, so much so, Naomi preferred Leslie make it. Last year, her daughter improved the recipe by adding dashes of rum and cinnamon. The cake was so good; Naomi had Leslie make another on the spot. Even now, Naomi quickly abandoned her craving for Ghanaian food. Swallowing that initial mouthwatering piece, Naomi filled her mouth with another and then another. She closed her eyes again.

When she opened them to take her last bite, she found Leslie and Kevin watching her with amused smirks.

"What?" Naomi asked around a mouthful of cake. It was halftime of the second game of a football doubleheader. Washington was leading the Vikings by a safety: a celebration indeed. More cake. She plucked her empty glass from the coffee table and headed to her kitchen for another piece.

Leslie and Kevin followed.

Naomi pressed her glass against the refrigerator's ice dispenser as they entered the kitchen. While ice filled her glass, she stared at a postcard affixed to the refrigerator door announcing a local end-of-season flea market she had no intention of visiting (the time wasn't right yet). She then pressed the water button and carried her iced water to the island counter to get more cake.

"I told you," Leslie said.

Kevin chuckled. "So, I see."

Naomi lifted the cake container lid. "I repeat: What?"

"Better than sex, Ma? No offense, Doctor Oheneba."

"None taken." Kevin smiled at Leslie conspiratorially. "I'm not too keen on cake, but I guess you've got some skills, young lady."

Naomi thought it cute that Leslie still addressed Kevin formally. Their little tease about the cake, however, wasn't all that cute, because her sex with Kev was very good—but cake and sex were unrelated arenas of joy (although she and Tyson managed to mix the two on their ninth wedding anniversary). She scoffed. "You know what..." She shook her head. "You know what? Don't worry about how good this cake is. You just keep 'em coming as requested. Okay?" Naomi smiled at them with a wink and cut herself another piece.

"Yes, ma'am," Leslie answered, adding a salute.

Something about Leslie's salute bothered Naomi when it shouldn't have. She reflected on the dream (nightmare?) she'd had some months ago: the almost threesome betwixt Tyson, Leslie, and herself. Naomi shook her head again, this time to clear it. She shifted her attention to Kevin to redirect her thoughts.

Kevin stood before her, smiling, looking adorable in Levi's jeans and an Art Monk #81 Redskins jersey from back in the day. The wire frames of his eyeglasses glimmered highlights of burgundy and gold: too much. Naomi smiled at Kevin, thinking, first, she wanted him, and two, maybe, *maybe*, she could love him, too. She did love Kevin, just not the way...

Naomi's smile faltered.

Kevin frowned questioningly in response.

Naomi brought the corners of her mouth back up. "So, new subject: What's up after the game? Scrabble, anyone?"

Kevin shrugged. "Sure."

"Trevor's coming over around eight, so..." Leslie shrugged her uncertainty about how the evening would go from there.

Trevor. For a while, it was Scott. Naomi liked Scott. Trevor was okay: polite, educated, and articulate. But Scott had those qualities, plus a sense of humor, and was a delightful conversationalist. Naomi hoped there was luck yet for a Scott comeback.

"Well, let's see how things play out, shall we?" Kevin looked from Naomi to Leslie for consensus.

Leslie bent her lips in considering agreement. "Fine by me."

Naomi took a bite of cake, resisting the urge to close her eyes and savor. "Well," she started and then finished her bite, "I'm going to finish preparing for a mental-health presentation I have on Wednesday. After that, I'm all yours." She directed her last sentence more to Kevin than to her daughter.

Kevin leaned his lanky form against the refrigerator door. "Now?"

"No. I'll watch a series or two of the third quarter first. Then we'll have to see. I found several key psych components in my analytical review of Friday's newspapers that I can use for the presentation. I also want to review a journal article or two before applying them."

"Ahh... *Sankofa*." He liked using that Akan tribe word from his Ghanaian heritage, on matters related to her profession, believing her a vehicle for enabling one struggling mentally to reach back to the knowledge and essences gained (and lost) in their past and bringing them into the present to make positive progress toward getting well (again).

Naomi issued him a half-grin, her lip cocked to one side. "I guess. It's not a lot to do; I want to get it over with and free my time up."

Leslie snapped her fingers. "That reminds me. Boppa wanted to know when you were coming to see him. ...I told him Wednesday."

Naomi stared at her daughter with disbelief, her irritation instant and full. She did not quite understand Leslie's latest actions or the angles behind them regarding Tyson's father. Whatever Leslie's issues were, Naomi did not intend to have her force anything. "Well, I guess that won't happen now, will it? And you've had plenty of time and opportunity to tell me this, Leslie Diane, I don't—"

"Well, I don't see why—"

Kevin put his hands out, a palm facing each of the women. "Ladies. C'mon now. Can't this keep until later? Huh?"

Leslie's feelings were hurt, indicated as much in the dip of her brow and the quiver of her bottom lip.

Naomi looked from Leslie to Kevin and then nodded. She didn't want to discuss the matter in front of Kevin, anyway.

Kevin turned saddle-brown eyes on Leslie, sending a smile of caring concern her way.

Leslie studied the island counter, giving a minimal nod. "So, how's the man with the dead wife?"

Naomi sipped her water. "Which one?"

Leslie looked up. "Artist, I think. Wife was a nurse, or...?"

"Coming along," Naomi answered. Doctor-patient confidentiality reigned, and Naomi never revealed more than she should. But like anyone else, she sometimes talked about her work. Only to Leslie or Kevin, maybe Viv Phillips, and even then, only in the most basic or generic terms, but she talked about her patients indirectly when discussing her work. Sometimes she did, yeah. And any psychiatrist claiming never to discuss patients with anyone, including colleagues? Naomi didn't believe it; human nature leant no credence.

Jeff Winthrop, however, wasn't coming along. He currently rented sizable acreage in Stage Five: Depression and Sorrow. His aura hadn't yet flickered in for her this counseling go-round, but Naomi imagined it being the same muddy, heavy blue (thick with woe) it was when he and the kids first came to her. He'd come to her at a recent showcase for his art and told her about his wife still being here and how he spent time with her in something he called "memory-dreams." He remains resistant to the idea that he's hallucinating.

In his latest session days ago, he purported Julia said goodbye to him in the memory-dream at the gallery, but he later convinced her to come back. So yeah, Stage Five. Now even more compounded by the loss of his second marriage. Yes, he'd ended it, but it was a loss, nonetheless.

Todd's counseling related to recovery post-Ruth progressed smoothly, but Naomi had plenty work to do with Jeff Winthrop. He was sleeping less and eating more, exercising quality interaction with Mallory and Todd daily, so that was good. Her work wasn't exactly cut out for her.

Mallory also revealed her dad occasionally spoke with a woman named Isolynn, whom he met at the showcase. Mallory seemed to think her father was falling for Isolynn but taking it extremely slow with her. Naomi thought that might be because of his Stage Five residency. It was a start. Hearing Mallory relay these updates, Naomi knew the kids liked Isolynn very much.

What stage of grief are you in, Love?

Naomi pushed the thought aside, thinking how bizarre (or maybe not so bizarre) it was that she'd never seen her own aura flicker.

"Coming along," Naomi repeated to Leslie with a nod.

He was more than emphatic about Julia being real.

Naomi sipped her water. "I have a question. Do either of you believe in ghosts, an afterlife?"

Leslie and Kevin gazed at her for a moment with puzzled expressions that dissolved quickly.

Kevin moved to get cake.

Naomi took another bite of hers.

"Well," Kevin began. He shrugged as he sliced. "I guess I believe there's an after-something; not so sure about the ghost part."

"I believe in 'em." Leslie prepared to cut a slice of cake, too.

Naomi slightly hated them both.

"Those paranormal or specters, or whatever they are, look mighty real on those reality shows," Leslie finished.

"The key word there is *look*," Kevin offered. His slice was entirely too big as far as Naomi was concerned (it looked more like half). Didn't he say he wasn't keen on cake?

Naomi listened to the exchange without comment, but she tended to lean toward Kevin's line of thinking. Although she wanted to ask, she left the heaven-and-hell question alone.

When Leslie was a child, Naomi did her best to encourage Leslie to foster a spiritual relationship with God. She believed she was successful, but Leslie was grown now—Naomi couldn't make assumptions regarding her daughter's religious or spiritual views, her "spiritual compass." It was something, she realized, the two needed to share their thoughts on more, perhaps.

Leslie shrugged and pursed her lips with a look, saying: *Think what you want. I just hope I'm not around when the evil forces come for you.* She took an also-too-large piece of cake with her back to the great room and the football game. "Hey, hey! Come on in here. Washington's up by nine and now just intercepted the ball!"

"'Washington' *who?*" Naomi called back.

Kevin rumbled a mild guffaw.

"Very funny! C'mon, you'll see," Leslie encouraged.

"You go 'head. I'm going to tidy up my presentation now instead. It won't take long. Should catch most of the fourth quarter."

Kevin watched her with a serious expression. Concern lined his face. His saddle-brown eyes probed. "Your patients have you thinking about death and dying lately? You okay?"

"I'm fine. Of course, I think personally about the issues my patients have. Don't think I'd be a good doc if I didn't." She sipped her iced water. "As far as death and dying, I used to be scared to death of it, pardon the pun. Still am sometimes, but it's more a fear of the unknown than anything. We should anticipate death more with wonder than dread, shouldn't we? I mean, we're finally seeing God then. And well, God is good." Naomi took another sip, this time to settle her nerves.

"Feeling religious, are we?"

Naomi swallowed and smiled at him. She set her glass on the counter. "You know better than that. A spiritual journey for me is not necessarily a religious one."

"Ahh...that restful soul. Just checkin'."

"Check yourself," she replied with humor. She resisted getting another slice of cake. She picked up her iced water instead. Naomi gestured toward the family room with the hand holding her glass of water. "Go on in there with her and watch the game. She'll be fussing any min—"

"Y'all comin' or what?" Leslie called (making Naomi's point).

"See?"

"Okay, okay." He chuckled with a shake of his head. "Since your Ravens won their game, you're not pressed, huh, my Sankofa Bird?"

He didn't call her that often, so Naomi allowed it, accepted it in the spirit it was given. She pointed at him with a click of her tongue. "You got it. Now go on, shoo. Shoo, fly, shoo. Maybe I'll make Fuzzy Navels for our Scrabble game later."

"Sounds nice." Kevin smiled and leaned across the island for a kiss.

Naomi couldn't get a handle on her vacillating moods. One minute she wanted to jump his bones. In this minute, it was all she could do to make the kiss seem genuine. His full lips were soft and sweet, however. The kiss ended.

Please don't say, "I love you."

He didn't. He turned from their kiss and went back to Leslie and the game.

Naomi left the kitchen through the alternate entrance.

Classical music always played softly in her home office, whether or not she was in there, and the low-wattage bulb in the lamp on her credenza stayed lit. Well, the light would get turned off, but rarely. It was an unnecessary additional use of energy she let be. Schubert's Rondeau Brillant in B minor, Op. 70, D. 895 (for piano and violin) was on when she entered. She plucked Friday's issues of the *Washington Post* and the *New York Times* newspapers from her chair and settled at her desk to listen to Schubert.

When it ended, Naomi put on "I Would Die 4 U" by Prince. As with Marvin Gaye's "God Is Love," Prince's lyrics spoke to her on as deep a level as any evoked by a traditional gospel song. She bobbed her head and raised her hand in praise as the rhythm moved her. She played the song twice more before giving up the ghost, then let it play once more for the Gipper.

When that ended, she turned the music player off, then sat in her chair by the window, gazing at the Elizabeth Catlett lithograph Tyson gave her. It was, by far, her favorite spot for a bit of soul-searching or psychological analysis of a case or two.

Naomi focused on the lithograph, appreciating the lines and shadings. She reflected on Jeff's emphatic belief he'd seen his wife, that she was still *here*. And although Mallory hadn't intimated as much, Naomi had an inkling Mallory, too, circled related supernatural suppositions.

Naomi shook her head with a wry chuckle. Grief counseling was one thing; being a ghost-whisperer was quite another. She detected signs of improvement with Jeff, so she'd hang in there with him and see it through. Besides, the twist renewed her interest in the psychological sciences—a much-needed plus.

What stage of grief are you in, Precious?

Again, Naomi ignored the thought. Or tried to, deciding any progress she'd made in that arena was all relative. She'd lived with her grief over Jassiel and Tyson, her dad and brother (her mother?) for so long; she'd gone through all the stages and back again, such that the boundaries of transition from one stage to the next were too obscure to delineate.

But if she had to analyze herself (and who doesn't try to analyze themselves?), she'd say she lived and breathed at Stage Two: Pain and Guilt.

If she had to, that's what she'd say.

If she had to.

But she didn't have to (or have anyone else do so, for that matter).

So, all was well.

Chapter 19

Epilogue

Jeff let out a mouthful of laughter. "I am *not* joking!" He dropped the cloth over the painting, re-covering his daughter's graduation gift—*one* of her many gifts. He was a proud papa for sure.

Isolynn pecked his lips with her own light chuckle before turning to put away the brushes in her hand. "Well, you cannot name it that, Mpenzi; Mal would not be amused."

Jeff concentrated on the fit of her sweatpants: loose but not, showing enough curve suggesting the goodness beneath the fabric—and there was plenty of goodness, too. He'd just finished caressing and holding on to all that round goodness while taking her beneath the painting that was Mallory Èkerie Winthrop's gift. He still heard her moans of release in his head as her contractions gripped him deliciously in climax as she straddled him. "Well, what would you name it, then?"

She turned to him, that teasing-yet-confident smile the same turn-on for him as it was the day they met. "I'll have to think on it." She winked and turned back to the cabinet, placing his red and yellow paints just so.

He shook his head, happily in love again. "I still think my title is fine."

His wife tossed her head back with more laughter, her dreadlocks (modest strands of gray now mixed in with all the honey ones) swaying in the afternoon light. She arranged a few containers holding his binders and solvents.

They did laugh a lot, and that was best of all. Well, the sex was pretty topnotch, too. And their conversations. Perhaps it was time spent together in spiritual communion and prayer. Or was it something as simple as the way she organized his art supplies? Maybe.

She looked at him, a hint of smirk bending her upper lip just so. "We're tabling the title right now, but it's a very nice tempera, Jeff. I see the beautiful but hard work put into it." Her continued career as an art director for several media businesses around the DMV created a natural, lifelong affiliation between them.

"Thank you. The glazing can be a bitch, but M-Sweet especially likes my expression of that media, so..."

"I do, too; you offer such subtle artistic surprises." She grinned her adoration.

He grinned his appreciation back.

"...So, did you want me to pick up the flowers for Julia's grave or have Todd pick them up on his way from work? Or Kelz? Walter's got his end of the logistics for the day covered, picking Mallory up on the early side. Once the day starts, you're going to be all over the place..." Her eyes of copper were compassionate and sweetly knowing.

And Jeff realized the laughter and sex and pleasant conversation and spiritual communing with her were all very good. Isolynn's indulgence in his artistry ranked high, too. But it was her loving, willing acceptance of him and all that entailed that was really, truly, best of all. Black love, man. You couldn't get any better than that.

He couldn't remember any long, hard laughs with Ruth. Maybe in the beginning...or not. Some mistakes weren't worth a serious ponder.

Jeff glanced at Jules's portrait on the far wall.

He'd taken it down while married to Ruth (at her insecure insistence)—and it was Isolynn who put it up again, in no way jealous or intimidated by Julia's memory (a stance which only turned him on more). "Let's *both* pick them up and go early. You're right: I'm going to be all over the place."

His wife nodded as she finished her lemonade and set her glass down. "So, we'll pick up the flowers and visit her gravesite at the beginning of the day...before 'all over the place' starts." Isolynn grinned at him, making the artist studio even brighter.

His first marriage constituted the beauty of beginner's luck, and his third marriage was indubitably the charm. "...I love you, Solly."

He loved Julia, too. But that love was different now. Jules was dead, many years now, and he'd found love again. *Good* love again. With Naomi's help (the woman was a godsend), memory-dreams were a thing of the past. And it was okay. He knew Jules wasn't mad at him. Not like she was when he'd married Ruth—but he understood all that now.

He was mad at himself sometimes when he reflected on it.

Ruth ended up serving six months for what she did to Todd, but he didn't know where Ruth was now or what she was up to. Restraining orders impeded keeping in touch.

That, too, was okay.

Isolynn ambled her lithe form toward him, hardened nipples pressing through the thin fabric of her fave Angela Davis T-shirt (her bra still draped an easel). When she reached him, she cupped his cheek and kissed him, her lemony-sweet tongue soft and communicative in his mouth as he breathed in her wonderfully marked scent of spicy oranges and flowers—still his favorite on her. She pulled back and pecked his lips. "I love you, too." Her sincerity touched him, made him happy, but Jeff also saw her other nickname for him about to spill from her lips just as her smiling-smirk burst through. "...JAWS!"

Jeff laughed with Isolynn, not the least fazed at believing he heard, somewhere high and above, the faint, echoey chortle of his first wife as she joined them.

Author's Postscript

Child abuse can take many forms, often carried out insidiously. If you suspect child abuse or have questions, please contact The Childhelp National Child Abuse Hotline: 1-800-4-A-CHILD (1- 800-422-4453).

So, here we are again, Bodacious Bibliophile. Did you enjoy the story?
- Did I illustrate Jeff's grief, well? How about Mallory and Todd's sibling bond?

- Did you like Naomi's approach to the case?

Reviews Help Authors Telling Good Stories!
Word-of-mouth makes a huge difference for authors trying to attract readers. If you enjoyed the story, let others know with a review on your preferred retailer platform, Goodreads, or even on social media. If you enjoyed *Obscure Boundaries*, please leave a review.

As always, I appreciate your support.

Find more book-series fun on sfpowell.com and connect via social platforms online: author.sfpowell and/or S.F. Powell.

Up next: book 3, *Broken Benevolence*, in which Naomi provides trauma counseling. Cecily Brooks is getting treatment...but perhaps her husband should be.

About the Author

A native of the Washington DC Metropolitan area, S.F. Powell writes fiction focusing on life, relationships, and love in all its many forms.

Despite her full-time gig in accounting, she pursues writing, preferring rooms featuring pens, composition books, and hot herbal tea, over rooms with spreadsheets and calculators.

Her stories touch on the elements of several genres because life is sometimes a suspenseful mystery carrying moments of romance and humor; maybe with enough drama, it seems right out of science fiction.

Her submission for *Like Sweet Buttermilk* (featuring fictional psychiatrist Dr. Naomi Alexander) won first place in the Black Expressions Fiction Writing Contest.

When she isn't absorbed with the written word, she likes game nights, generous goofy moments with her family, watching a documentary, or working on a puzzle.

Powell continues writing works featuring Dr. Naomi Alexander, along with developing other planned series.

Find more book-series fun on sfpowell.com and connect with her via social platforms online: author.sfpowell and/or S.F. Powell.

www.ingramcontent.com/pod-product-compliance
Lightning Source LLC
Chambersburg PA
CBHW050245110726
47898CB00007B/2288